I rushed to Mother. It all happened in an instant—she whirled to face me and I saw the knife plunge down in a flash. An indescribable pain erupted in my shoulder, between my collarbone and the base of my neck, like nothing I had ever felt. I heard screaming and knew it was my mother's. I knew also that as quickly as the knife had sunk into my flesh it had been pulled clear again. The world tilted. I felt myself falling—saw blood flowing across my shoulder and chest—and I collapsed onto the floor. The pain immediately became something more akin to a numbness, as if I were disconnecting from my body and looking down upon it as a separate being. I felt that I was part of another world even as I was there, on the floor, with my eyes open, watching as the men rushed at my mother. There was the sound of glass shattering as she hurled the doctor away and his back crashed into a kitchen window. Sheriff Wyre reached for the knife in her hand, but was a moment too late. She plunged it into her own heart—deeply, I saw—more deeply than I would have imagined possible, so deeply that nothing but the knife handle could be seen, the knife handle in her hand now covered in a copious, flowing river of blood. There was a terrible silence as Sheriff Wyre backed away in shock and all expression died out of my mother's eyes and she fell forward, the knife being plunged ever more deeply her body as she collapsed onto the floor directly beside me, her empty and now lifeless eyes only inches from my own. I heard screaming then, but whose it was I did not know...

Annabel Lee

The Story of a Woman, Written by Herself

by Christopher Conlon

Annabel Lee

It was many and many a year ago,
In a kingdom by the sea,
That a maiden there lived whom you may know
By the name of Annabel Lee;
And this maiden she lived with no other thought
Than to love and be loved by me.

I was a child and she was a child,
In this kingdom by the sea,
But we loved with a love that was more than love—
I and my Annabel Lee—
With a love that the wingèd seraphs of Heaven
Coveted her and me.

And this was the reason that, long ago,
In this kingdom by the sea,
A wind blew out of a cloud, chilling
My beautiful Annabel Lee;
So that her highborn kinsmen came
And bore her away from me,

To shut her up in a sepulchre
In this kingdom by the sea.
The angels, not half so happy in Heaven,
Went envying her and me—
Yes!—that was the reason (as all men know,
In this kingdom by the sea)

That the wind came out of the cloud by night,
Chilling and killing my Annabel Lee.
But our love it was stronger by far than the love
Of those who were older than we—
Of many far wiser than we—
And neither the angels in Heaven above

Nor the demons down under the sea
Can ever dissever my soul from the soul
Of the beautiful Annabel Lee;
For the moon never beams, without bringing me dreams
Of the beautiful Annabel Lee;
And the stars never rise, but I feel the bright eyes

Of the beautiful Annabel Lee;
And so, all the night-tide, I lie down by the side
Of my darling—my darling—my life and my bride,
In her sepulchre there by the sea—
In her tomb by the sounding sea.

—*The Works of the Late Edgar Allan Poe: With Notices of His Life and Genius, Volume II, Poems and Miscellanies.* N.P. Willis, J.R. Lowell, R.W. Griswold, eds. New York: J.S. Redfield, 1850.

To the Reader

My surname is not Lee, nor my Christian name Annabel; yet it will serve my purposes to so refer to myself in these pages. It is by these fetchingly melodic syllables, after all, that I have attained a certain queer, impersonal sort of notoriety in the famous poem by the late Mr. Poe. That bit of verse, romanticized beyond any recognition, is in truth based, however remotely, on certain events in my own life. How ironic that schoolchildren made to memorize and recite the lines might walk straight past me on the street without suspecting for a moment that it is my story—my story as filtered through the imagination and verse of Poe—that they have so assiduously studied in their classes.

That the poetical narrative "Annabel Lee" is highly fictionalized is attested to most obviously by the fact that I am here to write these reminiscences at all, rather than silently moldering forevermore in my "tomb by the sounding sea"—though there was a tomb of sorts that was not very distant from the sea, as will be made clear in due course. But Mr. Poe took what was a pathetic and even squalid episode in my life and transformed it into something everlastingly beautiful. He did this by altering almost every aspect of the true facts, bending them to his artistic will. Most profound were the changes he wrought upon the narrator. The reader will recall that the poem is told to us by one of Poe's sensitives, a man of melancholy but loving temperament who pursues a doomed quest to be always with his "life and bride." The truth was quite different, as the reader shall soon see. I imply no criticism of the poet, who used his God-given genius to build from my life's humble clay something immortal and timeless. Poe was known to me personally, and I have never had anything but great sympathy for him—his tragedies, his addictions, the sorrows of his star-crossed days. But Poe is a minor player in this drama—the drama, that is, of my own woeful life. Others have roles far vaster and more great, or more terrible.

This reminiscence, then, is to be a work of recovery—of excavation—of finding what is lost if I can and making sense of it to myself. I do not know if I can do this; I know only that I must try.

It is my hope that in the process of penning this chronicle I can recover what I seem to have misplaced over my long years on this Earth—that being the dynamic and ever-changing colors and textures of my life as I actually lived it. Indeed, even as I sit writing these words on sheets of foolscap paper I have obtained for the purpose, small things seem to come back to me: a friend's laughing voice, the bright red cover of a favorite book. Faces that have lain dormant in my mind for many years seem now to become reanimated, and with them all the memories I associate with the people—my parents, Selwin and Maud; poor little Mary Mahoney; my dear darling Jim Gamble; the monstrous Doctor Hudson Blackthorn, author of so many of the ills of my life; and of course Mr. Poe, whose gentle soul was perhaps a bit too sensitive to survive in this merciless world. I have a particular reason—a vital reason—for writing this memoir just now, at this particular moment in time. But it is a reason, alas, that can make no sense to an individual not yet acquainted with the myriad facts of my life. Therefore I will reveal the reason only at the end of this narrative, by which point the reader will be able to comprehend and perhaps to sympathize with the choices I have made—including, I pray, the latest and profoundest of them all.

Other than Poe, who surely belongs now to all of mankind, the persons who appear in the following pages do so, like myself, under pseudonyms. Some of these persons were wonderful; some were horrible; but all are long dead now, and I am unworthy to pass public judgment on them here. Their judgment has already been rendered in a Cosmic Court of which we know nothing here on Earth, and that is enough.

But be forewarned. The tale I shall impart in these pages is one so *gruesome, morbid, and fantastic that it may well beggar belief. I have been through much. I have heard, seen, and done things that no human being should have to experience or, having experienced, remember. I can but write it all as I recollect it, hoping the patient reader may listen with open mind and forgiving heart. That same reader may, upon paging through to the conclusion of this macabre history, choose to pray for its unhappy author. For any such prayers that author would feel only humble gratitude.*

– "A. L."

BOOK ONE

It Was Many and Many a Year Ago…

1

In my memories of childhood it is always raining. I am sitting in the little nook off our kitchen, a snug recessed space just sizable enough for a plain armchair and small side table on which rests in its saucer a cup of steaming, aromatic tea. Three windows in a semicircular arrangement around me look out on the garden, the fields beyond it, and the blue hills in the distance: the very landscape, it may be said, of my early youth. In my lap rests the book I am currently reading, usually a novel from Father's library—Walter Scott perhaps, or Fanny Burney, or else the natural philosophers Mother worries are somehow inappropriate for my delicate feminine mind. Father, it should be said, emphatically does not believe his daughter to be so limited, and among his hundreds of handsome leather-bound volumes I am encouraged to graze at will.

I have looked up from my reading to watch the rain slide down the windowpanes, listening as it taps the rooftop and spatters the glass. I sip at my tea, a familiar, not unpleasant melancholy settling over my soul. The quiet seems eternal. The world, gray and glistening, seems timeless.

Chair, teacup, book—my brain's private image of a period in my life which then gave the impression of stretching forever, but which in reality was no more than nine or ten years. As with all memory, the image is somehow both perfectly true and oddly misleading. Reduced from reality, oversimplified, this still life of myself in the little alcove off the kitchen is less an actual remembrance than a kind of representational one, a moment perhaps never really lived as I think I recall it but rather a fusion of different moments crystalized into a figurative whole.

Mayhap this is the reason it is always raining in these visions I have of times long ago, the falling showers a metaphor for a certain mood I believe, rightly or wrongly, permeated my childhood. For in truth the state of Maryland, in the eastern portion of which I was born and spent the first twelve years of my life, receives, according to my *Farmer's Almanac*, only some forty inches of rain per annum—hardly the Noah-like deluge my mind seems to suggest. I know, intellectually, that there were many days that were cloudless and sun-blooming, and when I try, I can just picture the fields around our house on the outskirts of Grimsleytown as they would have been in spring— the Indian grass and bee balm, the bright daffodils and black-eyed Susans. And yet I am unsure if such memories are any more true than the picture of myself in the armchair looking at the raindrops trickling down the glass. They seem to have no staying power in my mind, no lasting reality. Are such remembrances truer, then, or less true than the others? All these years later, is there any way to tell—to be sure?

The one common point between these, so to say, competing memories is the fact that in all of them I am quite alone. I picture myself strolling in the garden, the umbrella in my hands protecting me from the wet; no one is with me—and yet I know that I walked in the garden hundreds of times with Father in all sorts of weather. Now there I am in town, looking in shop windows, umbrella again keeping me dry, and again I am alone, even as I know that this could not have been so. The downtown area was a forty-minute carriage ride from our house, a venturing-out I certainly would never have undertaken by myself; Father or Mother would invariably have accompanied me. And yet there they are, my memories: rain-drenched, solemn, and solitary.

And, at times, terrifying—for if I let my reverie continue, reliving my early girlhood or some approximated simulacrum of it, I invariably find that as I sit there in the alcove with my tea-cup and book the rain becomes stronger, steadier. The sky darkens until it is nearly like night. Thunder explodes. Lightning slashes the sky. The downpour batters the glass so strongly that I begin to fear the panes may burst. But that is not all. What were pleasant rain-moistened fields only a moment ago now seem, in the strange dim light, like something else altogether. The shapes of the trees and flowers and wild grasses seem to *move* in the darkness—not simply swaying with the wind but moving entirely on their own, as if they have somehow uprooted themselves and are sliding grotesquely, impossibly toward my little alcove. My breath comes fast as the trees and flowers and grasses enlarge, inflate, grow gigantically until they are toweringly tall in the lashing rain. Unconsciously I have placed my tea things on the table. My book has fallen from my lap onto the floor. I stand as the nightmare world slithers toward me, yards away from the glass, now feet, now inches. I try to turn but cannot. I try to scream but my throat is tight. I can only watch as the fantastic wild world looms up before me and I hear a sound now, an unnatural, unearthly *moaning* somehow emanating from the outside, from the terrible invaders themselves. They press against the glass—there is a scraping sound like knives on bone—the glass bends inward—

Of course, the reader must think, this is but a little girl's fancy. And indeed I agree. Obviously nothing like this ever occurred, or could have. Yet there is something to it, something that, as I have written, perhaps did not happen in a literal sense, but which nonetheless reflects something quite true, quite real, about my life—the sense of a melancholy peace suddenly turned to appalling, inexplicable horror. That is a process with which I am, alas, all too familiar.

One aspect of this youthful vista which I have not yet described is a house that stood in dark majesty several miles away, at the top of the highest of the many hills in the area. I could see it, just, when the weather was clear and fine—a tall, brooding structure it was, known thereabouts as "Blackthorn House" after its owner, Doctor Hudson Blackthorn. He it was who had built the local hospital and who indeed, according to my parents, had delivered my own infant self unto the world. I knew the doctor; he paid our family members house calls from time to time; yet in all he was a figure of some mystery to the people of Grimsleytown. He had had Blackthorn House built himself many years before, obviously at great expense;

Father and I sometimes rode together in that direction on fine mornings and beheld, at least from the bottom of the hill, the strangely forbidding aspect of the place. It is tempting to call it a castle, but it was not one; it was merely the imposing nature of the structure's appearance that left such an impression. Rather it was a mansion in the Gothic Revival style, dark-stoned, with countless pinnacles and parapets, battlements and steep gables and much decorative tracery around the whole. But much of the lower portion of the building was hidden by the grounds dotted with weeping willows, and Father never made any serious inspection of the property; Doctor Blackthorn was understood to value his seclusion, and the sole narrow road leading to and from the house was considered private. Doctor Blackthorn himself, despite a manner of geniality, made me uncomfortable, though in my early years I would have been unable to say why. Thinking back in later years, however, I would come to realize that there was always something a bit strange in the tone of his interactions with me. He was a large and corpulent man with long white hair and a sparse white beard that had odd empty patches, like a field of crops planted in infertile or poisoned soil. The loose flesh around his face joggled disturbingly as he walked. His dress was appropriately professional for a man in his position. It was, I think, his eyes that discomfited me. They were big and gray and would follow my every movement when I was in his presence; the *pince-nez* he balanced upon his nose only seemed to add to a somewhat sinister effect. I did not like how he looked at me, always with his wide smile showing his big block-like teeth. There were times too that, in touching me for a medical examination—my forehead or cheek or forearm— I felt that he was thinking about something else—something strange—which I could not possibly discern, and did not wish to. I much preferred when I instead saw his assistant, Doctor Bailey, a handsome younger man with a brisk and friendly style who could make me laugh comfortingly.

Doctor Blackthorn, as everyone around there knew, was also an inventor. A young child at the time, I was not particularly interested in the stories I heard of his creating improved farming implements or better parts for steam engines; but his genius was unquestioned. When I was very young I remember him bringing along a little toy for me, a clever thing I had never seen the likes of: roughly the size of my palm and made of wood, it held at its center a glass lens that, when I put my eye to it and held the device to the light, disclosed marvelous images, shapes of people and animals that, as I turned a little knob on the side of the machine, seemed to actually move. It was quite wondrous, and fascinated even Father and Mother. The doctor merely smiled and dismissively called the mechanism one of his "lesser experiments."

I do not wish to leave the impression that I thought overmuch about Doctor Blackthorn or his grandiose home in my youth. Though both he and Blackthorn House would later play a profound role in my life, at the time they were just, so to say, background to my childish thoughts and fancies, and no more important than any number of other people in and around Grimsleytown.

It sometimes seems to me that I was a frightened and melancholy child, but much of this impression is, I think, a later distortive gloss of my actual experiences. I was not in truth very different from other girls. Those early years, bleak and cheerless as they seem to me now, were much like any child's of my place, time, and class. We were not rich. The house in which we lived was not grand or ostentatious. We employed no servants and yet we were, I suppose, modestly comfortable. Selwin, my father, had a head for numbers, and he performed jobs of accountancy for various prominent townspeople, for which he received a sufficient salary to sustain our little household. At least this is what I was led to believe.

I loved my father very much. He was kind and gently witty, and he took me seriously. To his everlasting credit, he never made me feel that he might have preferred me to be a boy; he talked to me as he might have to any son, soliciting my thoughts and opinions on all sorts of matters—even ones which my mother occasionally protested were "indelicate," such as, say, the question of legal rights for females. (Mrs. Wollstonecraft's *A Vindication of the Rights of Woman* was a well-thumbed volume on Father's bookshelves, and represented one of the first fully adult books I recall reading.) Shocking works of fiction such as *Mathilda* and *The Mysteries of Udolpho* were comfortably familiar to me, as were the sensual poems of Keats and the terrifying verses of Coleridge. These were obviously unusual choices for a girl of eleven; although I doubt my comprehension of some of these works could really have been very high, they nonetheless excited and moved me. Father thought me perhaps preternaturally gifted in the art of reading; be that as it may, I know that I was enchanted by the rhythmic sway and transcendent visions of Milton, Donne, and Shakespeare. American poetry seemed to speak to me more directly yet—Bryant was a favorite, and Rebecca Hammond Lard. Freneau's "The Indian Burying Ground" I committed to memory, while the marvelously dark "House of Night" Father and I frequently read aloud together, alternating the verses between ourselves, the terrifying lines invariably giving my spine a wondrous chill ("Trembling I write my dream, and recollect / A fearful vision at the midnight hour; / So late, Death o'er me spread his sable wings, / Painted with fancies of malignant power!").

It must be clear by now that when I was young my mind leaned toward the Gothic and romantic, and there was another such volume in Father's library which exerted a strange hold over my imagination as well. A slender, cheaply printed booklet titled *Tamerlane and Other Poems*, its author was listed simply as "A Bostonian," but by the time of my own girlhood this anonymous scribe was well known as having been Mr. Edgar Allan Poe, whose critical writings often appeared in the newspapers attacking the works of various poets and writers in surprisingly intemperate terms—someone, I recall reading, dubbed him "the Comanche of Literature" as a result of these pieces. But I was too young then for literary criticism, and I much preferred Mr. Poe's creative works. His stories occasionally appeared in magazines and newspapers that Father brought in to the house— suspense-packed adventures such as "MS. Found in a Bottle" in the *Baltimore Saturday Visiter* and, even better, such tales of shocking horror such as "Berenice" and "Morella," which I recall from the *Southern Literary Messenger*. A little later I discovered Poe's fascinating tales of ratiocination, "Murders in the

Rue Morgue" and its sequel, "The Mystery of Marie Rogêt," both of which featured his brilliant amateur investigator, *Le Chevalier* C. Auguste Dupin—and I confess that I went through a childish phase in my youth dreaming that I might become Dupin's female equivalent, calmly sifting through evidence of some terrible crime and deducing through my wits and application of logical principles its perpetrator. Since there were no terrible crimes to be investigated in or around our little house, however, I was mostly reduced to discovering where I had left my favorite doll or where Father had hid the sugar bowl.

It was Mr. Poe's poetry, however, that spoke most deeply to me. Like Freneau's, it had a rhythmical, dreamy quality which my girlish imagination found irresistible, and *Tamerlane* was a volume that I constantly pulled from the shelves, eventually memorizing a goodly portion of its contents, including the somber "Dreams" and "Visit of the Dead" as well as the coldly beautiful "Evening Star." One poem that particularly spoke to me was "The Lake"—the poet's delicious description of how a simple body of water, lovely in daylight, becomes a "terror" and yet also a "tremulous delight" by night—"a feeling undefin'd, / Springing from a darken'd mind." Such imagery and ideas played in my own mind both by day and in darkness; yet I little knew how prominently "undefin'd" feelings would eventually come into play in my own life.

But to return to Father. We would talk for hours in his study, a small room decorated exclusively with row upon row of books. I remember intense conversations we had when I was only seven or eight years of age, Father explaining something to me in his soft, whispery voice—he was a slender, asthmatic man, never physically strong; his watery blue eyes would fix on me as he spoke, his silver mustache moving with his lips. And yet he listened just as intently: nodding at my little-girl fancies, smiling at my childish ideas, but never mocking or patronizing my youth or naivety. We would enjoy tea together, just the two of us, Father finishing off with his pipe while I chewed on some little cake or other.

Sometimes we talked about God. Father was an unbeliever, though a handsome old Bible was among the many volumes on his shelves, and he was never dogmatic about his lack of feelings toward the Almighty. (Mother, a Catholic by birth but not an observant one, left theological matters alone altogether.) Father knew the Bible quite well, and along with our steady diet of poetry we often read stories from it—Adam and Eve, Jonah and the Whale, Samson and Delilah. These were vivid and thrilling to my young imagination, even if, as with Father, the religious aspect of the texts never quite managed to center itself in my soul.

When I was with my father I felt important.

Would that I could say the same of my mother! Already in this narrative I have hinted darkly that all was not well between us, and while that is certainly true, I wish in these pages to be neither unfair nor unkind. Mother was possessed of a nervous disposition. Several years older than her husband, she had thought his sudden appearance in her life to be something of a miracle. Hers was a poor New York-based family; her own mother worked as a washerwoman in a third-rate hotel in the city there, and she never knew her father. There were six or seven siblings with, it seems likely, six or seven fathers, none of whom played any role in the upbringing of their offspring. They were a family of Irish slum-dwellers, all sharing one room in the notorious "Hell's Kitchen" district of New York—"a miserable hovel on a miserable street in a miserable neighborhood," as Mother later described it to me. There was very little money, and as a girl she sometimes took to those miserable streets along with her brothers and sisters to beg for pennies from passersby. As she grew older it became apparent that some of those passersby took a more than, shall I say, passing interest in her, and she soon found she was able to collect more pennies by separating herself from her siblings and standing on some street corner or another by herself.

I must be careful how I express this. I do not know with certainty what all transpired in young Maud Kelly's unfortunate youth—Maud Kelly being my mother's original name—but by piecing together some clues she would leave in her ramblings when in her cups, and by applying these clues to what I know to be true of men generally, I have come to the conclusion that by the age of nine or ten she was performing in back alleys favors of the most abominable and unnatural sort for such degenerate men as would pay for these services. I imply no judgment—no judgment, that is, of my *mother*; the men I judge most harshly, and utterly without forgiveness. But not Mother. A starving child with a starving family does what she must, surely. But I believe that those horrid early experiences in many ways formed my mother's character. When her own mother died—I know not the cause—she was fifteen, and immediately took over the job of washerwoman at the hotel. To the best of my knowledge, her life from then on was morally beyond reproach. She kept the job for years, rising to become head of housekeeping there. One by one over time the siblings drifted off to their own lives, and at the age of twenty-five my mother was a respectable working-class woman, but quite alone in life—and with no realistic prospect of marriage other than to some man even poorer than she.

This was when the miracle of my father occurred. Like a figure from a storybook, he arrived in New York as a guest at the hotel and took a fancy to this rather faded but still attractive female. And my mother *was* attractive, even in her last years. She was naturally tall, very slender, and quite pale; her features were dark and her face dominated by her extraordinarily large, liquid eyes, stormcloud-colored eyes which seemed to possess endless depths (which only later became disquieting, as she slid off into madness). Her hair was long and jet-black, her lips naturally a deep and lustrous red not unlike the color of poppies. I have no images of my mother to consult today, but my own memory combined with the long-ago remembered comments of those who knew both of us indicate that I look very much as she did—not quite so tall perhaps, but otherwise quite similar. This explains a good deal about why men have responded to me as they have throughout my life. I am unable to recognize any beauty in myself, whether due to modesty or a poor sense of self-worth, but my mother's beauty was obvious to anyone—any resemblance I might have to her could only be to my advantage.

But I have wandered from my point. Selwin had come to New York seeking employment, and possessed little money of his own. His looks, he acknowledged, were never much worth discussing. (To his proud daughter of course he was the handsomest man on Earth, even as I knew that objective reality disagreed with my perception.) His clothes were threadbare; he owned but a single cravat. But to my mother, who knew well a gentleman's manners and ways of speaking, he was nonetheless a ticket of sorts—a ticket out of a life that, whatever her success in service, yet hardly rose above the squalid. He *did* take an interest in her; she *did* reciprocate; and soon enough he was headed back to Baltimore, still without a job but with a new bride.

How much did Father ever know of Mother's past? All of it, I suspect. Mother was not one to hold confidences, even those concerning herself, especially when she was drunk. I learned as a young girl never to tell her my secrets. But between my father and mother there were probably no secrets at all. She discovered quite early in the marriage that, whatever his admirable personal qualities, Father was a gentleman in name only. Any dreams she may have harbored of a glittering, carefree life with her new husband, attending operas and plays and hobnobbing with the celebrated persons of the time, would have been quickly dashed. Father was in fact nearly penniless. But a penniless gentleman is quite unlike a penniless poor man; the gentleman still has his family name, his social connections, and his breeding to use to his advantage. Moreover, Father had what I understand his family termed "the little cottage"—the house in which I spent my early years—which he inherited as a kind of unwanted castoff of the main branch of the family.

This inheritance saved Father from ruin. It allowed him to marry and to raise a child respectably—a poor relation of the main line, it is true, but a relation nonetheless. Of course it was his poverty and his resultant lack of intimacy with the rest of the family which allowed him to marry a cleaning woman without a word of protest from anyone.

I went to school at Mrs. Hubbard's Improving Academy for Children, which, despite its somewhat exalted name, was a plain country school down the road from our cottage. I can hardly remember Mrs. Hubbard—elderly she was, frail and stooped, with her *pince-nez* ever perched upon her nose and a knuckle-swatting yardstick generally in her hands. Whether she was a good teacher or no I cannot say. I mostly recall feeling very lonely there, painfully friendless through the rainy schooldays—yet even here I know that this is not entirely correct, for I *had* a friend, a girl named Gracie Winston. She was a year younger than myself, short and petite, quiet and calm of demeanor. She and I played jacks and skip-rope and Scotch-hoppers together; I think I can hear in my mind's ear the tinkling sound of her little laugh, but what my brain has recorded could well be another girl, another time, another laugh. I know we spent much time together for a while, but the rest is lost to me.

Such was my life, and doubtless the patient reader by now is wondering, "Wherein is the tragedy that makes this author reflect on her youth with such melancholy?" The years of which I have thus far spoken were not in themselves particularly sorrow-laden. I had troubles with Mother, troubles which included her drinking, but these were not yet extraordinarily onerous. Father was a jewel. I seem to recall that for the most part I enjoyed school. In all, it was a girlhood not unlike thousands of others.

But today all my memories of this period are colored—clouded—darkened—by my knowledge of what was about to happen. Unbeknownst to any of us, a series of catastrophes was looming on our familial horizon which would change everything, for all of us, forevermore.

2

The decline of our family began, in retrospect, with an event which should have brought us only unbridled joy. One summer's day when I was eleven years old my mother announced that she was with child.

The excitement of that day! I had longed for a sibling, a girl I might fondle and kiss and play with, dress up in the day and tuck into bed at night. My parents were happier in the months following the announcement than I had ever seen them, or would see them again; after a long period of quiet distance between the pair, they were suddenly like newlyweds again, laughing, touching each other, gazing into one another's eyes. The new child would be a new chapter in our family's life, surely.

But it was not to be. Late one rain-swept night in October—and it *was* rain-swept; this is clear in my mind—my mother went into screaming convulsions, staggering between rooms in the dark house crying repeatedly that something was wrong. My father ordered me to my room while he in his nightclothes followed his wife anxiously with an oil lamp in his hand, begging her to go back to bed. I did not return to my room; the night held not only rain but bellowing thunder and flashing lightning. My terror kept me from walking back into that darkness on my own. And so, at a distance, I followed my father as he followed my mother, weeping now myself, listening as Father said he would ride for the doctor, though looking out the window at the downpour it was obvious that the roads would be mud-choked and likely impassable. "Please, Maud!" he cried. "Please go to bed and I shall fetch the doctor somehow!"

But upon reaching the kitchen, huge flickering shadows

from Father's lamp looming malevolently on the walls, Mother emitted an appalling cry and collapsed, blood soaking the lower region of her gown and flowing like a purple curtain across the floor. Something—my little sibling, I understood with horror—flopped out from between my mother's legs and lay unmoving, tangled in what for a moment I took to be rope or cord. My mother fell to unconsciousness. Father knelt helplessly over her, shouting "Maud! Maud!" and pulled helplessly at his hair, moaning even as his eyes passed to the dark, still lump between her legs.

It was then that I, all without thought, stepped forward in my bare feet into the sticky puddle, knelt quickly and took the silent, slick, unmoving little thing, a girl, into my arms, held her to my chest, aware that she was much too small to be a baby, much too small to be any kind of living human, and as I felt blood and bits of gore sliding through my fingers and over my hands I held the child for a long time, trying to will her to live, whispering the terrible untruth, "She is not dead, Father. She is not dead. She is not dead."

My memory darkens as to the rest of that night. I know not how Doctor Bailey came, but eventually he was there in the room. Father *must* have gone for him; but surely he did not leave me in the kitchen with a dead fetus in my arms and my mother hemorrhaging on the floor. Did he run for a neighbor? Did *I*? I literally cannot recall, yet sometimes I have dreams of running through a night rain in hastily donned galoshes, lightning turning everything a bright ghastly blue, thunder making me shriek and fall again and again into the mud. But all this may be nothing more than a recurrent nightmare with no basis in reality. Perhaps Father locked me in my room and went out himself. Which would be more terrible—the awful tempest screaming down upon my eleven-year-old head, or sitting alone in my room in the darkness, covered in blood, knowing that the scene of horror was but a few feet away, my sister dead, my mother dying, and I alone and helpless?

Whatever way it happened, young Doctor Bailey reached us somehow in the hours before dawn. He and Father carried my mother to my parents' bedroom and the door was shut. No sound at all came from the room. After a while the rain began to abate. Then it ceased altogether.

Around sunrise I recall the man coming out of the room, hair awry, blood on his hands, and my rushing to him, seizing him by his shirt cuffs and demanding to know, "Does she live? Does my mother live?" and the doctor looking down at me, smiling a little through his obvious fatigue, and saying quietly, "She lives, Annabel. She is very ill. But she lives, and shall go on living."

My mother was months recuperating. I saw little of her; she stayed in bed almost all the time, and Father took to sleeping on the sofa in the sitting room. When I asked him on the day following that night of horror what had happened to the body of my sister, said he sadly, "Doctor Bailey took it with him."

This was another blow. I felt that my sister should have been given a name and been buried somewhere in our fields and provided a proper memorial stone.

"Her," said I.

He looked at me, puzzled.

"Her," I insisted. "Not 'it.'"

He looked at the floor. "Of course. I'm sorry."

I was so distressed by the idea that there would be no memorial to her that when Father was out one day I took an old cloth, dampened it, and ran it over the floor where her body had lain upon leaving Mother's, praying that the cloth might absorb some trace amount of my sister's skin or blood somehow missed by Father in cleaning the room, an amount too small to see but nonetheless there—a small bit of her—an essence. When I was done I walked out into the fields and among the fall leaves I dug a small hole with my hands as deeply as I could and placed the cloth into it and covered it with the soil again. I marked the spot with several stones in a circular arrangement and brushed leaves and bits of grass over it all—I knew that neither of my parents were likely to approve of my makeshift shrine, or rather were unlikely to approve of my visiting it daily, which in fact I did. On the pretext of playing with my dolls I went to the spot every day except in the very worst of weather, talking quietly to what I hoped was the spirit of my sister, telling her the things that had happened that day, wishing her well in her afterlife. As I have written, ours was not a religious family, but I found myself *wanting* to believe that my sister still existed somewhere, somehow, if only in some incorporeal, unknowable form. I had no idea if any of my thoughts communicated themselves to her, or indeed if there was anything anywhere in any world with which to communicate, but the process brought me some kind of solace.

But my life was to change once again, even more dramatically—and in a fairly short time.

3

Mother recovered physically, but something in her changed after the awful night when the baby was lost. She rarely left the house. Her manner, even after Doctor Bailey confirmed that there was no longer anything bodily wrong with her, was listless and morose. She appeared to take little interest in what happened around her. She took to drinking alcohol, something she had done in moderation before (my father was abstemious), but which she now did with much greater frequency. As time passed I watched what had been left of her beauty fade—her wonderful dark eyes took on an unfocused, lusterless quality—her lips turned pale. One night, despite Father's and my pleas, she used a kitchen knife to cut off much of her beautiful hair, claiming that it had become too difficult to maintain properly. What was left afterward she generally did not care for at all, rarely so much as running a brush through it. Thus the unevenly chopped remainders stuck out from her head at odd angles, and her general appearance was strange and disquieting.

With time she became slovenly, no longer taking care of the house or even dressing properly for the day, instead remaining in her nightclothes—that is, unless she knew that the doctor was coming. Then she would make an effort to appear normal again, correctly cleaned up and properly attired and at least slightly more animated than before. Hers was an act which fooled Doctor Bailey, even as I warned him outside as he was getting into his carriage one afternoon that the woman he had just interviewed was not the one we knew on a daily basis.

"Well, these things take time, you know," said the doctor

blithely, stroking his bare chin. "Try not to worry, young lady. Your mother will be fine."

"I do not believe that is true," said I.

"Well, if you like, I will consult with Doctor Blackthorn. Perhaps he would wish to see her."

"Yes," I replied eagerly. "Yes, do."

He patted me patronizingly on the head, smiled, and went on his way.

With Mother hardly functioning, Father and I shared the household duties. I cleaned the rooms and we often cooked together, a practice which might have been quite enjoyable except for the funereal air that had settled over the place. Our conversations became awkward, even when Mother was not in the room. Father seemed helpless in the face of his wife's new crisis. He would forget to lay fires or to light them. He would neglect to fill the lamps. As a result I would do these things, along with tending to the horses and to the garden. Several times I tried to interest him in resuming our nightly readings of Shakespeare and Freneau and Poe, but he was distracted and listless. Once when I passed the library I saw him behind a partly closed door sitting with his face in his hands, weeping.

Mother took to wandering the house at night, a kind of living ghost in her white nightgown that shushed quietly along the floor. Her butchered hair would be wildly askew. The look in her eyes, when I happened to see it in lamplight, was vacant, as if she knew not where she was or even that she existed at all. Father would follow her at such times to be sure she did not somehow injure herself, but he did not try to speak to her. These spells were all-consuming and left her unable to communicate with us. Again and again after watching her like this I would collapse into bed, shedding into my pillow many grief-heavy tears. School provided me some hours of relief each day, but after a time I was too heartsick to continue attending. No one said a word about it.

Several months later, another blow struck—and from this one there could be no recovery. My father was killed.

To this day, I know few details about how it happened. He was driving the carriage home after dark when a sudden downburst—yes, rain again—began to flood the roadway and caused his wagon to become stuck in the mud. As I understand it, Father, who was by himself, got out of the vehicle and was examining the problem when a tremendous crash of thunder spooked one of the horses, which kicked him directly in the back, felling him instantly. He was found, so I would hear later from the local constable, collapsed face-down in the road, the carriage and horses still as they had been. I would learn later that his body was carried to the hospital in town; the authorities knew that my mother was in no condition to learn of such a disaster, and the carrying-in of her husband's body might well completely derange her.

It was morning when the imposing Doctor Blackthorn—not Doctor Bailey—came to the house. I had not seen him in some time, though his house loomed always over our own, distantly atop the blue hill. I knew he only visited the homes of the most serious cases, leaving Doctor Bailey to handle the rest, so I felt a terrible foreboding in his presence. He gave Mother an examination and then quietly asked me to accompany him to his carriage.

His manner was grave. He looked down at me in his black overcoat—it was winter, and cold, though the skies were clear—and said, "Annabel, I have horrible news. I see no way to avoid telling you, but it is extremely important that you keep calm. Do you understand? You mustn't scream or carry on. This is very important for your mother's health."

"It's about Father," said I, "isn't it?" He of course had never come home the previous night.

"It is, I am sorry to say."

I seemed to see it all. "He is dead, isn't he?"

He looked down at the ground. "Yes, my child. He is."

I remember feeling nothing in particular, merely a gray numbness. I asked how it had happened. The doctor told me.

"I understand," said I at last, my voice very quiet.

"By rights I should talk to your mother, but I don't believe she could stand it. I believe it is most important that she not know of this—at least right now."

"I understand."

"I will find a woman for you," said he. "Someone to help

with the daily chores. But I fear what will happen when your mother suddenly finds herself faced with a stranger who has come to live with you. I fear she will suspect."

"It isn't necessary," said I. "I can take care of Mother."

"Annabel, you are eleven years old."

"I am twelve. My birthday was last month."

"Still...much too young." He looked at me with that odd expression which had often disquieted me in the past. I could not have named or described it. There simply seemed to be something unusual—even peculiar—in how his eyes, invariably foregrounded by his *pince-nez*, fell on me.

"I can cook," said I. "Father taught me. I can clean. And Mother is not really much trouble. Mostly she just sleeps."

"I cannot leave you here like this. It would be inhuman."

"No, it would not," I insisted. "It would be for the best."

"I can have a woman visit each day. And I will do so myself, as well."

"All right. But I am really quite capable."

"But, child..." Now he crouched down before me in that way adults have when they are trying to show a child how much they care. "You yourself—to lose your—your father, and so suddenly, so without any—any rhyme or reason. It's monstrous. You need someone to help *you*."

"I need no help, thank you."

He studied me for a long time, then stood straight again. "This is—it's a terrible thing."

"Yes, terrible."

"Perhaps..."

"I can take care of my mother," said I again. "I can take care of us both."

"Well...for a short while, perhaps. Until I can make arrangements for you, which I will do as your family physician."

We stood in the icy blue morning.

"The funeral...we have to keep all knowledge of it from your mother for the time being."

"Yes."

"You must come, of course," said he, scowling in thought. "I will take you."

"No. I will stay with Mother."

"Yes." He nodded. "Yes, perhaps that is the best thing all around."

"Can he be buried here?"

"On this property? No. It will have to be in one of the cemeteries nearby."

"Oh. All right." I nodded.

"I will sell the horses, of course," said he.

"As you wish."

"Annabel," said he, a curious look in his eyes, "you are taking this extraordinarily well. Not like a little girl. Better than many grown women."

"Carrying on won't help, I think."

"No, I suppose not." His face was deeply pained. "Annabel, I will go into town and begin arrangements. Please don't worry about a thing. I shall return this evening before dusk to check on you both."

"All right, Doctor Blackthorn."

All these years later I realize that this was the very time that a certain emotional reserve, even coldness, began to creep into my soul. I was shocked, of course, by Father's sudden vanishing from my life, but I did not scream or wail. I knew immediately that if I did so, Mother might well not survive. She was still deep in mourning for my lost sister, and this new burden would be more than her feeble frame could carry. She had to be protected from the truth, and I was the one who must needs protect her.

If this seems remarkably mature for a girl of twelve, I can only speculate that I was already drained of sorrow because of the loss of my sister. Perhaps this allowed me to look at the new situation regarding Father with nothing but cool clarity. I was not in mental denial; I believed what the doctor had said, and accepted it. But part of my brain, the part prone to hysterical emotions, I kept walled off. I would care for Mother. That was what mattered. Even when I went into the house later and entered his library with those many hundreds of books— Shakespeare on the table open to *The Tempest*, where he and I had left off reading some time before—I thought of Father without emotion. It was not as if he were in the next room and might enter at any moment, as some say who have just lost a loved one; no, I recognized that what had happened was quite permanent.

That night, after putting Mother to bed (I said that Doctor Blackthorn had told me Father had been detained in town and would not return for several days), I lay in the dark of my own bedroom and wondered at my own lack of emotional response. Was I uncaring? Indifferent? I knew these things were not true, just as I knew that a twelve-year-old girl who loses her father but sheds no tears is not normal. I was a twelve-year-old girl with no father and a mad mother. Perhaps the enormity of the thing simply made me incapable of thinking about it in any but practical terms.

We stayed that way for some days, Mother and myself. I cooked the meals and kept the house tidy. She continued her somnambulistic wanderings at night. She slept during the day, waking only to drink from our store of kitchen sherry and then slip back into slumber. She ate nearly nothing.

Every now and then she would suddenly say to me, "Annabel, where is your father?"

I would answer, "He is away for a few days, Mother. You remember. I told you."

"Oh. Yes. Of course." She would nod pensively and fall silent.

She did not remember, you see. This was a symptom of her malady: her memory had splintered into shards and she remembered little from one day to the next. It was easy to satisfy her with simple answers regarding Father's whereabouts: always gone, always coming back soon.

Doctor Blackthorn visited each morning, always on the pretext of seeing Mother, but really to speak with me. Despite my subtle discomfort with him, he truly seemed most considerate and concerned. He told me about the funeral and explained where Father had been buried—a nondenominational cemetery a few miles from the house—offering to take me there whenever I might like. A woman from town appeared once, telling me that Doctor Blackthorn had sent her to do whatever work needing doing, but I sent her away.

One afternoon the doctor sat down with me in the kitchen.

"Annabel," said he, "some decisions must be made."

"Decisions?"

"About you. And your mother."

"Mother and I can get along quite well here."

"Yes, but—child—" His countenance was grim. "As you know, I interview your mother each morning. I fear that she is not improving. If anything, she is declining."

"Yes. I know. She has no memory."

"That's true." He looked at me pensively. "She is mad, Annabel."

I swallowed. "I suspected as much, yes."

"You can see—" He grimaced. "You can see that this situation cannot go on here. She needs medical attention. And you need—a home. A proper home."

"I do not wish to be placed in an orphanage, Doctor Blackthorn."

"Child—" He sighed. "The situation here—untenable. It cannot continue. Your mother may become—dangerous. Anything may happen."

"She is not dangerous."

"But a woman like her—disconnected from reality—she cannot just stay here under a twelve-year-old's care."

"You may hire a nurse."

He sighed again. "It is impossible, child."

"What does that mean?"

"It means…she must leave here. And so must you. At least for a while. If in time she improves, and as you become a bit older, well…I will see to a caretaker for this house, of course, and for the land. Everything will revert to your mother when she regains her health, or else to you when you reach your majority. It—it can't be helped, child."

"What is to become of my mother?"

"She will be placed," said he gently, "in a fine institution, the best in the state, for as long as it takes her to—to become herself again."

"And I?"

He stared at the ground. "There is a very nice…a very nice facility only a hundred miles or so from here. I have been there myself. It is known as Sadmore Place. It is for—for Orphaned Girls."

"I am not an orphan."

"Legally, child, I fear that you are. Your mother has been ruled incom—"

"*I am not an orphan!*"

The violence with which I shrieked these words shocked Doctor Blackthorn, and surprised even me. "Child," he pleaded, "try to understand...."

"What right have you to determine my fate?" I cried.

"The court, child—given that you have no relatives who can be traced—the court chose me—asked me..."

"*Go away!*" I screamed, shoving him as hard as I could with my hands and then turning and running to the house. I rushed in, slammed the door and locked it. I pressed my back against the door as if to keep the doctor and the rest of the world out— out forever.

After a time I heard the clop-clop of his horses taking his carriage away, yet I felt no relief. I knew he would be back.

"What has happened, Annabel?"

My mother stood in the doorway, her eyes strangely unfocused, as they always were now. Her nightdress was wrinkled and soiled.

"It's nothing, Mother," said I, trying to sound confident.

"But the doctor—"

"Everything is fine. If you will sit in the kitchen I will see what we might have for lunch."

"Oh. Yes, lunch. That would be very nice." She stepped out of the room.

The day proceeded normally, at least to all outward appearances. My mother and I had lunch—she had only a little bread with butter, along with her sherry—and for a few minutes we played a simple card game she liked. Then she went to lie down again. I journeyed outside to the place of my sister's grave and sat there for a long time, feeling very alone. Fat gray clouds gathered and sprinkled a few drops of rain on me.

They were coming. I knew that they were coming, even if I knew not who *they* would be. I pictured them in my mind as giant Vikings, Visigoths, man-eating monsters from the Moon. Their huge angry visages would blot out the sun, their weapons flay our skin, their fangs rip our bodies to shreds. My breath came fast as I sat there looking up at the sky, the raindrops splashing on my face. I thought of fantastic plans to defend my mother and myself, imagined weapons I might use—we had a long kitchen knife that would surely be effective. My father had an old rifle but I had never been taught how to shoot it...Still, it might prove useful, if only as a club...Could I set fire to their carriages? No, that would only hold them here, that wasn't what I wanted....

They came in the late afternoon, as the sun blurred down behind the hills in a cloudy sky.

There were three of them. One was Doctor Blackthorn. The second was Sheriff Wyre, whom I knew from town—a normally friendly, gregarious man who this day looked grim and determined. The third was a weed-thin, sour-faced woman in a plain brown dress who was unfamiliar to me. I watched from the front window as the carriage arrived and the sheriff saw to the horses. I watched as the doctor helped the woman step down. And I watched as they marched, heads down, to our door and one of them knocked.

I stood motionless, breathing fast, willing them to vanish— to disappear—to explode.

"Annabel?" came the doctor's voice, with more knocking. "Annabel, let us in, child."

"Go away!" I shouted, then cursed myself. I hadn't meant to say anything at all.

"Come, little girl." It was the sheriff's voice now. "Open the door, if you please."

I stood trembling.

Again came more knocking. Doctor Blackthorn called, "Annabel?"

I could not seem to catch my breath. Small high-pitched sounds emanated involuntarily from my throat.

After a moment the woman spoke. Her manner seemed gentle but her voice was harsh and hard. "Annabel? This is Mrs.

Krasnoff. We have never met, but I would very much like to speak with you. Would that be all right, Annabel? Could you open the door for us?"

There was more knocking, and then Mother was in the doorway.

"Who is it?" she asked.

"It's—it's no one," said I in a whisper. "It's no one, Mother."

"Nonsense," said she. "They're knocking."

"They're—they're robbers. We mustn't open the door, Mother, not for anything, no matter what they say."

She cocked her head at me, puzzled. "What in the world are you talking about?" She stepped to the front window and looked out. "Why, it's only the doctor. And Sheriff Wyre is with him, I see. I wonder what they want?" She moved to the door.

"*No, Mother!*"

But she pulled the door open. I backed away, my breath jumping in erratic hiccups. Trembling, I pushed myself into the far corner of the room. I tried to push myself out of the room— out of the house—out of the world.

"Good afternoon, Mrs. Lee," said the doctor with false joviality. "May we come in? Oh, excuse me. This is Mrs. Krasnoff, a friend of mine."

"How do you do," the sour-faced woman said with a forced smile.

They entered. Mother, socially appropriate as she always was when the doctor came by, offered to make them tea. They declined. Everyone stood around awkwardly for a long moment.

"Mrs. Lee, we have come to help you," Doctor Blackthorn said at last. "You and your daughter."

"Help us? How?"

"Madam," he continued in his best professional manner, "things have been difficult for your family of late, haven't they?"

"I do not know what you mean, Doctor Blackthorn."

"But I see you are not dressed."

"I have been ill."

"Yes, of course. It is just that which we are here to talk to you about."

Mother's eyes grew suspicious. "What do you mean?"

"Mrs. Lee, we feel that you are in need of assistance."

"A maid, you mean? A housekeeper? We haven't the money."

"No, not exactly that," the doctor said. "Not—we feel that another environment might aid in your healing."

"What environment? What are you talking about?" She turned away, holding her arms close to her chest. "You will have to see my husband about it when he returns. There is nothing I can tell you about environments. Thank you for calling, but please go."

"Mrs. Lee," the sheriff interpolated, "listen a moment, please."

"My mother told you to go!" I shouted suddenly from the corner.

"But we cannot," said he, sighing. "It is impossible. Mrs. Lee, we have come to tell you about some necessary changes that will be occurring here, in your life, with your family."

"I wish no changes," said she, her voice rising, her eyes opening wide. "I forbid any changes. You will leave my house now."

"Mrs. Lee—"

"Please leave! You may return when my husband is home."

"Your husband..." the sheriff hesitated.

"What? What about my husband?"

"Mrs. Lee," said the doctor, "please sit down."

"Why?" Her eyes were wide now, rapidly growing frantic.

"We need to talk to you about...about..."

Mother's eyes, momentarily focused now, fell upon me. "What do they want, Annabel?" she cried, her voice breaking. "What do they want here?"

But I could not speak.

"Mrs. Lee, there is calamitous news, and you must know it," said the sheriff. He glanced at the other two. "I know we were to stay silent, but..."

"Silent about what?"

"Mrs. Lee, it's about Mr. Lee—about your future here, in this house..."

She gasped. Her mouth opened wide and she covered it with her palm.

"She can't withstand it, Sheriff," warned the doctor. "She mustn't be told."

"Told what?" she whispered shakily, hands at her sides now. "Told what? Annabel, what are they talking about?"

I felt light-headed. I hardly breathed. But I sensed we would all be here forever—for all eternity—unless someone said something. "Mother," said I, forcing the words out, "Father is not coming home. Father is dead."

There was a terrible silence in the house. Wind blew through the trees outside.

"It's a horrible thing, Mrs. Lee," said the sheriff. "If you will sit down we will try to explain…"

"It is not true," my mother said, her voice taking on an odd cadence I had never before heard.

"Mrs. Lee," said the doctor, moving toward her, "please…"

"Stay away." Her voice was very low and tense. "Stay away from me." She looked around the room at all of us, but what she saw I knew not. "All of you. Away. Stay away." She ran her fingers through her short, wild hair and turned herself in slow circles.

"Mother…" I began.

She moved suddenly, wordlessly, to the kitchen. I was the closest to the doorway and followed her there. Her back was to me but I saw instantly that she had picked up the large kitchen knife and was holding it suspended in the air.

I heard Mrs. Krasnoff cry out. One of the men shouted. I rushed to Mother. It all happened in an instant—she whirled to face me and I saw the knife plunge down in a flash. An indescribable pain erupted in my shoulder, between my collarbone and the base of my neck, like nothing I had ever felt. I heard screaming and knew it was my mother's. I knew also that as quickly as the knife had sunk into my flesh it had been pulled clear again. The world tilted. I felt myself falling—saw blood flowing across my shoulder and chest—and I collapsed onto the floor. The pain immediately became something more akin to a numbness, a strange lack of feeling, as if I were disconnecting from my body and looking down upon it as a separate being. I felt that I was part of another world even as I was there, on the floor, with my eyes open, watching as the men rushed at my mother. There was the sound of glass shattering as she hurled the doctor away and his back crashed into a kitchen window. Sheriff Wyre reached for the knife in her hand, but was a moment too late. She plunged it into her own heart—deeply, I saw—more deeply than I would have imagined possible, so deeply that nothing but the knife handle could be seen, the knife handle in her hand now covered in a copious, flowing river of blood. There was a terrible silence as Sheriff Wyre backed away in shock and all expression died out of my mother's eyes and she fell forward, the knife being plunged ever more deeply her body as she collapsed onto the floor directly beside me, her empty and now lifeless eyes only inches from my own. I heard screaming then, but whose it was I did not know. The sound seemed to fade away and I heard it as from far off, down a long empty canyon. The world darkened as I heard hurried shufflings around me, felt hands touching and pressing around my neck. I could not move. I stared helplessly into my mother's dead eyes and the world turned white—then gray—then black.

I believe that at that moment I died. The sounds around me were remote and I felt myself suddenly dematerialize—become lighter than air—float free—and somehow was witnessing the scene from above: Mrs. Krasnoff rushing to us with towels in her hands, the doctor frantically applying the towels to me and trying to stanch the flow of blood, the sheriff asking, "Do I take it out? Do I?" and the doctor saying, "Yes, yes," and the sheriff wrenching the knife from my mother's heart, blood burbling forth then as from a cauldron, soaking her nightgown, his hands, the floor, my dress and hair. Then higher—as if I were suspended in the sky now, past the ceiling and roof, looking down at the top of the house which was now somehow transparent, and seeing them working desperately to save us, or rather to save me—I saw the sheriff give up on Mother and turn his attention to the doctor and his young emergency patient. They worked and worked and somehow, though I was far above in the sky, I felt them maneuvering my body this way and that, felt the hard press of the towel against my neck, heard the doctor say, "Annabel, are you there? Can you hear me, child? Try to respond. Can you speak? Can you squeeze my hand?" And just then I realized that my left hand was within the doctor's big palm and I slowly forced movement through my fingers, enough that he said, "She is alive. Keep the pressure on the wound, Sheriff. Hold it as tightly as you can. Mrs. Krasnoff, more towels, please, or cloth, whatever you can find. And water." After a moment, more quietly, "I think her artery is all right. If that is so, she may live. She may just live."

The sounds faded then, and yet I felt myself descending from the clouds—slowly—gently. In a way I was sad to leave them, to leave my weightless existence in the sky. I did not want to go. But drop I did, softly, growing nearer and nearer the group and the blood-drenched scene, until I was directly above them and then among them again, in my own body, and the world faded again but this time into unconsciousness, not death—into sleep—into myself once more.

4

I awoke in a bed, not my own. The room was quiet and cool and the walls were plain white with a seascape or two hanging on them. Next to me was a simple chair and table on which were scattered a few medical instruments. I was dressed in a simple white shift. There were, I realized, bandages wrapped around my neck and upper torso. I felt no pain until I tried to move my head, when a searing jolt shot through me—centered around my neck but spreading in a cold rush throughout my body. I did not try to move again.

My mind was hazily trying to reconstruct what had happened to me when Doctor Blackthorn stepped into the room.

"Child," said he.

"Hello, Doctor Blackthorn," said I, or tried to say. My voice was a dry croak.

"Don't speak," he advised. "You've suffered a terrible shock. You must rest." I began to speak again and, sitting, he pushed his finger gently to my lips. "Please, Annabel. Let me explain. I can answer most of your questions without your asking them at all. First, you are in the hospital. You were terribly injured. Do you remember? Just nod very slightly, or shake your head."

I nodded, almost imperceptibly.

"We almost lost you, young lady," said he, smiling and touching my cheek softly. "But you are all right now. You need rest and recuperation."

"And Mother?" I whispered.

He looked down and said, "No. She did not survive, child. I am sorry. It will be best not to think on it much. Your mother was very ill. You know that." He paused, then said, "Everything is taken care of. You are to worry about nothing. You will rest here for whatever time is necessary."

"Home?" I croaked.

"Your home will be kept for you, child. I shall see to it myself. The house will be taken care of, and the grounds. The court has appointed me in this task."

"It is an orphanage for me, then?"

"Yes, child. It is."

"I understand," I whispered. "No one wants me."

Doctor Blackthorn's eyes behind the *pince-nez* showed traces of pity and even a tender sorrow. "Life can be a terrible thing, Annabel. It can be cruel and very unfair. It has certainly been so for you. I can only believe that you have suffered a lifetime's worth of troubles in just a few years and that the rest of your life will be filled with joy. You must believe this."

I had no response. I watched his eyes—his strange eyes—as they gazed upon me as if I were someone else, or else he was.

"Sadmore Place is really a fine institution," said he. "The matrons are gentle and caring and you will meet other girls— girls like yourself."

"There are no girls like myself."

"No, you're wrong, Annabel, very wrong. Many children have felt grief, many have even gone through scenes of horror, as you have done. It is a tragedy but nonetheless true."

I felt nothing about what the doctor was saying to me. I was beyond feeling, I thought. I would never again feel anything whatsoever about anything.

I touched my neck bandage gently. "Will there be a scar?" I whispered.

"There may be a small one. But it will fade over time. All scars do."

"All of them, Doctor?"

He looked at me. "Perhaps not all," he admitted. "But the ones that can be seen, yes. Those fade."

And then, to my surprise, tears began to fall from Doctor Blackthorn's eyes. He took a handkerchief from his pocket and, removing his *pince-nez*, wiped them. Without the lenses before them his eyes looked raw and naked. He reached out his hand then and touched my arm—grasped it tightly—while studying my face as closely, I imagined, as a man might study a mirage. After a moment I turned my head away, acutely uncomfortable, and in a moment I heard him stand and shuffle out of the room.

And so it was that one obscenely bright and crisp dawn I found myself in a wagon being driven by a Mr. Carp, a wrinkled, smiling old gentleman who told me he had worked at Sadmore for thirty years and knew it to be "top notch, my dear, absolutely top notch. You'll have no worries there, none at all."

When we stopped for a rest I asked if I might be allowed to ride next to him rather than in the wagon itself.

"I don't see why not," said he. "It's against the rules, actually, but I can see that you're a fine young lady who will give me no trouble. You won't, will you? Give me any trouble?"

"I shall give you no trouble at all, Mr. Carp."

And indeed I did not. I simply sat beside the man, wrapping myself in a blanket and feeling the cold air on my face while I watched the stark landscape passing by. The horses moved quietly and methodically. It was a beautiful winter's morning, yet on the horizon I saw clouds that seemed to threaten a significant change in the weather that would surely arrive soon.

Though in terms of the calendar it still had some time to run, I date the end of my childhood from this wagon ride, a long day's voyage to a place of which I knew nothing. He talked to me of many things, this kind gentleman. He knew the flora and fauna of the area, and all the birds. He talked to me of his own wife— and his children, who, said he, were grown now, and "scattered to the four corners."

At times I listened to him, at times not. My mind seemed frozen. My mother—my father—my sister: all gone, all dead, and not one to be seen again except perhaps in a Heaven in which I did not truly believe. I would know them no more on this Earth. I had not so much as visited either of my parents' graves; it was as if they had simply vanished from the world. I had been removed from Grimsleytown, the only home I had ever known—the only sky—the only land. I was alone in the universe, without a friend. I had nothing but what was on my back and in a small case inside the wagon which contained clothes and a few toilet items, nothing more. I had wandered in Father's library before leaving, wondering if I should take a volume or two with me—our Bible, perhaps, from which we had derived so many hours of fond enjoyment, or our Shakespeare, or *Tamerlane*—but I found myself unable to generate any feelings of sentimentality about any of it. I seemed not to care. I believed that I should be crying, but somehow could not. This was my life but none of it, just then, seemed to hold any reality for me. It seemed an impossible life—an impossible fate. After all, I did not believe myself a bad person. What had I done to deserve what had happened to me? What had my mother done, my father, my stillborn sister? What, indeed?

The wind began to rise. I wrapped my blanket more tightly around my shoulders, trying not to shiver as the afternoon chilled and finally grew damp and even raw. The skies were darkening toward night when, after some hours, Mr. Carp suddenly said, "There she is," and, as we entered a deep valley, pointed toward what looked to me in the rapidly failing twilight like a huge, dread castle out of a nightmare, a place of hard stone and tall windows that somehow made me think of eyes, huge eyes watching me—judging me—condemning me. The oak trees and wildflowers and grasses all around the property waved in the wind as we approached them and became larger and larger in my range of vision, as if they were somehow sliding toward the carriage under their own power, looming now over me, reaching threateningly to me. A moaning sound caused by the wind in the valley seemed to instead be the cries of the abandoned, the lonely, the lost—my sister, my father, my mother, myself. I wanted to scream, to run away. I wanted, O God, I wanted passionately, in that moment, simply to die.

"Welcome to Sadmore Place," said he, smiling.

Rain spattered my cheeks like winter's tears.

BOOK TWO

All the Night-Tide

1

What I recall of that first night at Sadmore Place consists of no specific memories, only vague impressions. An obese woman in black at the front door staring down at me with a face that looked as if it had been hacked out of her skin with a hatchet, wearing an odd-looking black towel on her head and a strange white cloth around her face which made me wonder if she suffered from a toothache—the sound of this weird woman's boots echoing hollowly from the polished stone floor as she led me down a long, dark hall—stepping in my nightgown into a hard, narrow plank bed with a too-thin mattress and sheets that smelled pungently of lye—the sounds of the other girls in the large room, twenty or thirty of them—sighs, grunts, snores, bodies shifting about—a door snapping shut somewhere with sharp finality—and then silence, or what passed for silence in a place like Sadmore Place, for many dark hours.

It was only with the dawn that anything like reality seemed to regain some foothold in my perceptions. On hearing a key shifting in the door I realized for the first time that we had been locked in for the night—a fact I would have found disturbing if I had had any time to consider it. But immediately the door opened and a woman, this one slender and gentler of mien than the woman I had encountered the night before, entered, adorned in the same kind of peculiar black clothes. The reader may be allowed a smile at the uncomprehending way I have described what must obviously be a nun's habit; but the truth is, I had never seen such a thing. I might mention here what would become clear to me only later: that Sadmore Place was in fact a Catholic orphanage, but this faith was something with which I was completely unfamiliar. My placement (again, as I would learn at another time) was the simple result of my mother's Irish roots and her ostensible Catholic background. She was registered as a worshipper at a Baltimore Catholic Church, a fact which would quite surprise me when I realized it, as I never knew her to observe any religion at all. But it was enough for Doctor Blackthorn and the court to place me in an orphanage of this faith.

The moment the nun stepped into the room she began clapping her hands briskly and calling out—not unkindly—"Time to rise, girls! Time to rise! The Lord has no use for lazybones!" Pink light was only just beginning to glow through the tall windows. The woman moved up and down the rows of beds, calling to individual children: "Come, Charlotte! Virginia, get moving! Celie, let's have no complaints from you now!"

When she reached me she stopped and offered a small smile. "I am Sister Rose, young lady. You are Annabel Lee?"

I sat up blearily. I had not slept. "Yes, ma'am," said I.

"Ah, good. Welcome, Annabel. It is time for morning ablutions. Have you soap and washcloth?"

"No, ma'am."

"I will issue them to you. And Annabel, the correct way to address me is as 'Sister Rose' or simply as 'Sister.'"

"Yes, ma'am. Sister. Rose."

She smiled again. "Just follow the other girls. Do as they do."

First I saw them making their beds, so I did the same as best I could. (Later I would be taught the "correct" technique.) Then the sister led us to a room where we were to wash, using small basins and pitchers of water. As promised, Sister Rose gave me a washcloth and a sliver of strong-smelling soap. I was too self-conscious in this room of twenty and more unfamiliar girls to do more than to wash my face and hands—I was a shy girl, and a rather large hourglass-shaped mole on my belly embarrassed me—but I did that and it made me feel somewhat refreshed. We were then led back to our dormitory bedroom.

"Into your uniforms, girls!"

I had no idea what "uniform" she referred to, but then I saw that a simple black dress, a kind of house dress with a long plain skirt, had been placed atop my bed. Hard-looking black shoes with plain buckles were on the floor before it. The dress proved not particularly comfortable, as it was made of some cheap itchy material, but the shoes fit surprisingly well. Looking down at myself (there were no mirrors anywhere) I felt that I had become another person, a different sort of person, living in some other reality. Only twenty-four hours before I had been in the only home I'd ever known, living the only life I'd ever lived. Now I was here. It seemed impossible. Was my home still there? The fields, the flowers, my own sister's makeshift grave? Did any of it still exist?

We went to another room for our breakfast, which consisted of a bland porridge and weak tea parceled out by two large, silent women in white. I quickly noticed that there was no talking at all, and assumed—correctly—that this was the rule. We ate quickly, Sister Rose and several other nuns carefully watching us, and stood up when instructed, moving to place our used bowls and spoons and cups in big tubs for washing at the corner of the room.

Then it was time for our lessons. Sister Rose led us to yet another room. Here the world felt a little more familiar: to my eyes the teacher, again Sister Rose, was dressed oddly, but other than that this felt like the kind of schoolroom I knew. There was a blackboard at the front on which the sister wrote problems of arithmetic (rather rudimentary ones, I thought); we were to copy and solve them on slates which were given to us. For a time things felt almost normal.

But that feeling would not last. I quickly realized that all aspects of life at the Sadmore Place for Orphaned Girls was highly regimented, virtually to a military standard of precision. We went the same places at the same times every day. No talking was allowed except during our mid-morning break, when we were allowed outside in good weather, and in a brief period after we had finished our lunch, which normally consisted of potatoes and boiled meat of some kind. In the afternoon we were put to work sewing. My skills at this task were limited, but not distractingly so; I was able to keep up well enough with the making of the pillowcases and tablecloths we were required to create. But the constant imposed silence caused a gloomy atmosphere to pervade all.

Then it was time for Prayers. For these we entered the chapel, a big room with old wooden pews and a big, rather ghastly image of a bleeding Jesus Christ in the window glass. The woman I had met the night before led these services. Her name, I learned, was Sackett—Mother Sackett, as she was called. I understood little of what she said that first day, with the sound of her voice echoing throughout the big hall. I merely attended, sitting when told, placing myself on my knees when told, praying when told—though in truth I was not really praying, my inability to believe stifling any thoughts I might have sent heavenward. Prayers were always combined with some sort of religious lesson, often lengthy, generally taught by Mother Sackett. Her readings from the Bible seemed so mechanical and joyless that it was almost impossible for me to connect them with the book my father and I had read together with such verve and interest.

Dinner then—more boiled meat and potatoes, sometimes with a small piece of fruit—and bed.

That was life at Sadmore Place. I stepped through everything that first day as some wooden automaton; I thought no thoughts, felt no feelings. Somehow I knew that if I allowed myself to do so I would begin crying or screaming. And once begun, I might not ever stop.

During those first days, in the brief times we were allowed to speak, I met some of the other girls. I was reserved with them and said little of my background; some of them, however, were more forthcoming. They ranged in age from six to fifteen, and certain age groups naturally banded together in friendships. At twelve, I was known colloquially as a "middle girl," neither a youngster nor a near-adult. The children who spent time with me were all my age, more or less—say, eleven to thirteen. They were, I quickly learned, mostly a sad lot. Many were not actually orphans, I was surprised to discover; their stories, though, were just as dire. One girl, Helena, told me casually that her father and mother were consumptive, and their children had been parceled out to various orphanages and agencies to keep them from becoming infected while their parents—why dissemble about it?—went through their processes of dying. One motherless child, Edwina, had been taken from her violent father after he had broken several of her bones, including her left arm, which, though long since healed, was yet much weaker than her right. Still another, a small girl called Tabitha, had been abandoned one fine morning by her father and mother, who simply took the family wagon and rode away. Mother had prepared a breakfast for her daughter and left it on the table, telling the girl to eat it, then walked out the front door to join her husband at the wagon. Tabitha had watched them go, ignorant of the fact that they had no intention of returning.

Some girls were more obviously damaged than others. One, Rowena, had a habit of turning her head slowly back and forth, over and over again, for hours at a time, and never spoke a word to anyone. Whether the cause of her distress was a physical malady or a mental one I never knew. Another, Georgia, never stopped whispering apologies—"I'm sorry, Mother Sackett, I'm sorry, Sister Rose," even, eventually, "I'm sorry, Annabel"—though in most cases she had done nothing whatsoever in the wrong. Still another child, Susannah—she truly *was* an orphan, I believe—was a habitual practicer of self-abuse, and could sometimes be heard at her ritual during the night; as a result she often had her hands tied to the bedposts for her protection.

Some of these girls, those who were clearly mad, frightened me. Others, however, were very much like myself: just adrift, lost, without family or friend. I felt pity for them without completely acknowledging to myself that my situation was just as unfortunate as theirs. Some part of me felt aloof from these girls—distanced, superior—for I could not yet quite accept what had happened to me. Soon, I felt, Doctor Blackthorn would come get me, or Doctor Bailey, or something else would happen to remove me from this strange, echoing, shadow-haunted world. This queer, laughterless life amongst the world's helpless and miserable could not possibly last. This was not where I belonged. I would be removed soon, taken somewhere—anywhere.

But I lived at the Sadmore Place for Orphaned Girls for nearly a year.

2

In a life filled with events many would consider intolerable I have learned that the human mind is endlessly malleable. It can find ways of functioning even within situations that are heartrending, terrifying, or profoundly degrading. For my first months at the orphanage I survived by behaving, doing what I was told, and speaking very little. In my silence I witnessed punishments of girls that struck me as needlessly punitive and violent, though at first I was rarely their victim. Other girls, however, were subjected to beatings over the knuckles with a special black rubber strap which was housed in Mother Sackett's office exclusively for this purpose. Such a punishment was never doled out at the time of the infringement but only at the end of the day—the sister would say to an unfortunate miscreant caught, say, talking out of turn, or with some chore undone: "Elizabeth, you must go for three today," which meant that after dinner and before bed Elizabeth would be required to report to Mother Sackett's office. Here, she would be made to place her palm on one particular spot on the woman's desk as the woman brought down the rubber device from where it hung behind her, just below a large portrait of Jesus on the cross. She would consult her written record and say something to the effect of "You are here for three, I believe." The wise child would simply mutter, "Yes, Mother," and accept her fate. A brief speech from the mother would ensue, always on the themes of obedience, discipline, and piety, and the punishment would commence.

The more reckless among the girls might try to bargain down the number or claim that the record was incorrect; but that way lay disaster. The records, at least to Mother Sackett, were infallible, and her sisters unquestionable; those who attempted to defy either were likely in for an extra set of strikes. Down would come the strap, once! twice! thrice! Many a time we would hear from our places at chapel or in our dormitory room the sound, like a sharp slap, carried all the way from Mother Sackett's office—and behind her closed door—to us at the other end of the building. It would be followed instantly by the high-pitched scream of the punished. But it was never more than a single scream, however many layings-on might follow. One strike was enough to numb the hand; the remainder went mostly unfelt, at least at the time. Later, however, one realized that the pain of a hand which had been struck three times took far longer to fade away than one that had been struck but once.

And yet, I say, life at Sadmore Place was not so much terrifying as it was joyless, glum, and, ironically, spiritually empty. It was there that, in the middle of the night, I would wake suddenly from a dream, something gray and terrible—I recall dreaming a great deal about being with my father in the library of our home, reading the Bible and Shakespeare together as we always did, yet with the dreadful knowledge that Father was *dead*, that the gentle and caring man beside me was nothing but an animated corpse that would presently collapse back into its grave—and feel that the darkness surrounding me was eternal and hopeless, that I had been abandoned by man and God—if God existed.

I would berate myself then, silently: "There are many worse off than you, unfortunates without food, without water, without shelter. Be grateful for what you have, spoiled girl!" This was, after all, very much the message constantly imparted to all of us by the nuns. And yet, though I understood and appreciated it intellectually, emotionally it was of no help whatsoever. Many a night I wanted to cry. But I was no more able to do this than I was able to speak to the Lord during Prayers. I was a closed vessel.

One night, however, and much to my surprise, a voice next to me whispered, "Annabel?"

The whisper belonged to Mary Mahoney, the girl who

occupied the bed to my left. She was a quiet child, like myself, polite and reserved, with the familiar red hair, freckles, and green eyes of the pure Irish. She did, however, have an unlucky physical problem. Her eyes, which were otherwise quite pretty, did not track together. They seemed perpetually to be looking in slightly different directions, which gave an unsettling effect to her appearance; when I first noticed it I had assumed this to be a symptom of insanity, but watching and listening to her convinced me that her mind was not affected by her condition. Mary was one of the few true orphans at Sadmore Place, her parents being a pair of immigrants from Ireland who had died in, as Mary told it, violent circumstances. All this was commonly known by the girls in our ward; yet despite the fact that we slept only a few feet from each other every night, I knew her but little.

"Yes?" I whispered in return. Talking during sleep time was strictly forbidden, and could result in a fearful visit to Mother Sackett's office. There was no one to observe us, however. The door was closed and locked for the night.

"You were making sounds," Mary whispered. "Are you all right?"

"Sounds?"

"Little whimpers, like."

"I was?"

"Were you having a nightmare?"

"I don't think so. Perhaps I was." I was not inclined to tell Mary about the dream I had so often: my father, the library, the ghastly knowledge that he was dead.

"You do that a lot. Those little sounds."

"I'm sorry. Have I kept you awake?"

"No. I don't sleep much anyway. I get bad dreams too."

We lay silently in our beds for some minutes.

"What do you have bad dreams about?" I whispered finally.

"Sometimes my parents," said she. "Sometimes fire. Like I'm burning in Hell."

"That's awful."

"I'm sure I will."

"What?"

"Burn in Hell. I'm sure I'll burn in Hell."

"Oh, Mary, don't say that. That's nonsense. Have the sisters made you feel that way?"

"No, I will. I know." There was a pause. "I'm rotten."

"You don't seem rotten to me."

"Do I not?"

"Anyway, what's the use—" I grew even quieter in my whispering—"what's the use of a God who punishes little children for not being perfect every minute of their lives?"

"That's what I wonder sometimes," Mary whispered in return. "It don't seem fair to me."

"Can God really be worried about whether we remember our every chore every day?"

"That's what I mean. He seems—small-minded to me. Like a little boy. And not a very nice one."

I smiled in the dark. "Better not let Mother Sackett hear us."

I heard Mary let out a quick breath or two—as if she were giggling silently. "Sacrilege! We'd be going for three for sure. And then maybe isolation."

Isolation was another, far graver punishment for the truly recalcitrant. I had heard of it, but none of the girls in our ward seemed to have ever actually experienced this unhappy fate. It happened in the basement of the building, according to legend, where none of us had ever been. There was a small dark room with nothing whatsoever in it—no bed, no chair, no table, nothing. No light reached this room, and no candles were allowed. One was simply put in it to stay for days, utterly alone. One slept on the hard floor. No one was sure if there was any provision made for eating or the elimination of waste; all we knew— if indeed we knew it—was that it was darkness—darkness all the time—and silence—absolute nothingness. Stories were passed around that some girls who had been taken there never returned at all; they went completely mad and were transferred to an asylum for insane persons. Or they died and were buried in anonymous graves somewhere behind the property.

"Do you think isolation is real?" I asked Mary.

"Oh, I'm sure it is. That awful Mother Sackett would enjoy it. I suspect the corpses ain't buried out back at all. She probably *eats* them."

I gasped, then shook with suppressed giggles. "That's shocking, Mary!" Then: "But you're most likely right."

Wind touched the windows, rattling them softly in their frames. I lay there looking at the dark ceiling.

"Annabel?"

"Yes?"

After a moment she asked: "Do you have any friends here?"

"I?" A sadness lodged itself in my throat. "No."

"I don't either. I don't like the girls here."

"Some of them are all right."

"I suppose. But they don't like me. They think they're better."

"They're not better."

"It's my eye," said she, with a frankness that startled me.

"What do you mean?"

"You don't have to pretend," Mary said. "You know what I mean."

"Mary, I..."

"Everybody thinks I'm crazy because of it."

"Oh, Mary. That's terrible."

"It don't stay where it ought. I've tried to make it. I've tried so hard. But it's just wrong. I don't see out of it very good, either."

"Does it cause you pain? I mean—physically?"

"No, I don't even notice it myself. But other people always do. That's one good thing about this place. There are no looking-glasses."

"Don't say that, Mary. You're a lovely girl. Truly."

"Maybe I should wear an eye patch. Like a pirate."

I stifled another giggle. "According to the storybooks I've read, you would need a hook for a hand."

I heard her breathing fast, amused. "Now that would be something, wouldn't it?"

We were silent for a time.

"Do you," she whispered finally, "have any physical defects?"

"I—no." I thought. "No, I do not." Strangely, this embarrassed me. I suddenly wanted to be able to reveal to this girl that I had physical issues of my own. Perhaps she would feel less lonely.

"I thought not. You're too pretty to have any."

I knew not how to respond to her, so I said nothing. But after a few minutes I found myself silently reaching out my hand toward the girl across the space of darkness between us. I left my arm suspended there for some moments, my white limb floating in a sea of black, before I felt her slim fingers tentatively graze my own. Presently we clasped hands.

"Will you be my friend?" she asked in a suddenly urgent whisper.

My heart swelled. For the first time in I knew not how long I felt something like happiness flow into my soul. I had been concerned for this poor girl's loneliness, but suddenly realized that my own was perhaps just as acute and painful, just as in need of assuaging.

"Of course I will be, Mary," I whispered in return. "Of course I will be your friend."

Thus it was that Mary Mahoney became not just my friend, but my inseparable companion. This new relationship completely transformed my experience of Sadmore Place. While we had little time to actually talk, we took advantage of what time we did. And yet much of our mutual bonding occurred quite outside the purview of words. This kind of friendship, I believe, can occur only between girls, and indeed only between girls of a certain age. Much that is communicated in such a relationship happens wordlessly, through looks, smiles, giggles, and little touches. For a time a sense of the absurd becomes prominent, and suddenly things that were never funny before seem hilarious to both of you. The other girl becomes like an extension of oneself—a better, brighter spiritual twin. For a time—invariably short—there is another girl in the world who perfectly understands you, sympathizes with you, lives in you and for you. It is a romantic relationship in the purest sense. Such a relationship Mary Mahoney and I suddenly had.

At first we tried to keep our friendship a secret. This is another quality of being a particular age—the fervent desire to have something entirely one's own, free from the prying eyes of others. But soon enough the other girls were aware that Mary and I seemed to share something intimate, and whispered comments sometimes made their way to my ears—sarcastic words regarding my devotion to an "imbecile," a "moron," a "mad girl." Though there were times I wanted to slap one of those silly children in the face, for the most part I was able to ignore them. Mary and I would smile at each other in the mornings, bathe next to one another, have breakfast, and take morning classes all almost entirely wordlessly. And yet even without words I sensed that we were very intensely together, in a way I had never felt with someone my own age. Perhaps my feelings for Father (Father, lost now in the mists of time, never to return) were the closest I had ever come to this strange, indefinable sense of closeness I felt for Mary Mahoney.

It was after lunch that we were able to enjoy some brief conversation, wandering around the paths outside Sadmore Place together. Often we would walk to a certain gnarled old oak tree not far away and sit under it, sharing our thoughts with each other. Sometimes we wandered in the rear garden, all purple loosestrife and golden asters and spotted touch-me-nots. Mary appreciated the beauty of nature but knew none of the names of anything, and I took joy in being able to teach her. She was an eager and able student.

When I think of Mary and me together at this stage of our knowing each other, I picture us like this—leaning close together on a cloudless afternoon, smiling at one another as we study leaves and stems and petals. I remember that we would even put flowers in each other's hair when no other girls were nearby. Naturally they could remain there only a few minutes, as upon returning to Sadmore Place any such adornment would certainly have earned each of us a session with Mother Sackett and her black strap, but for a short while it would be as if we were in our own world, quite outside the judgment of cold, imposing women in black or even an indifferent, uncomprehending God.

Of course as we spent time together our discussions became increasingly free. I found myself telling her about the catastrophes of my family—my sister, my father, my mother—and she responded in kind.

"My parents were very good people," said she thoughtfully one day, as we sat under the oak tree in warm sunshine. "We lived on a farm near Westminster. They worked hard, but there was never any money. I never had shoes. I went to school barefoot. But it didn't matter to those children," she admitted, suddenly glum. "Only my eyes mattered."

"You mustn't let yourself be so preoccupied with that." My heart always sank a little when she talked about her eye.

"That's easy enough for you to say," she replied, looking at me with a sad smile. "Your eyes are beautiful. Dark and beautiful."

"Mary," said I, "I don't care about your eyes. I care about *you*."

She looked down and picked at some grass. I realized that she was blushing, and the realization made me blush myself.

"Mary," I ventured finally, "what happened to your parents?"

She cleared her throat. "There was a fire," said she. "Some papers were left too close to the stove in the kitchen. I ran out, but both of them…they were trying to put out the blaze…" She fell silent.

"I'm sorry, Mary."

"Neighbors came and took me in for a few days, but eventually they put me here."

"What about your farm?"

"I don't know. It seems as if it was taken away. It doesn't seem to be mine. I heard something about Father owing a great deal of money to the bank."

We were quiet for a time.

"Sometimes I wonder," said she, looking away into the vague distance, "what will happen to me."

"I wonder that myself, Mary. About myself, I mean. I'm sure all of us do."

"It's just that I get so sad sometimes. Especially at night. Do you get sad at night?"

I looked at her. "Yes. I do. Every night."

"I call it the night-tide," said she. "Like an ocean tide. Just darkness, closing in on me. But not a darkness from the outside, a darkness from the inside. From inside me. Just dark, dark, and nothing but. Overcoming me. As if I'm drowning in it."

I touched Mary's hand with my own. I understood—I understood completely. She had just given voice to something I myself had experienced night after night since my mother died and my life had changed so utterly.

"'The night-tide,'" I repeated back to her. "What a perfect phrase, Mary."

"You know it? The night-tide?"

I nodded. "I know it well. Thank you for giving it such a perfect name. I will never forget it."

3

There followed some months of quiet at Sadmore Place. We lived out our routines, Mary and I, very much together though we spoke but little. She helped my spirits immensely with her humor, her attention, and her caring. After that first conversation we rarely spoke at night—it was too risky, as sometimes a sister would come in for a spot check, to be sure we were all in our beds and sleeping, or at least pretending to. There was also the risk that one of the other girls would turn tattletale and inform on us. Jealousy is quite real in such an institution, and if it sounds horrible that girls would tell on each other in this way I can only remind the reader of something I often had to bring to mind myself: that all these children were in different ways damaged, abused, and heartbroken. Looking back on it all these years later, I can recall certain girls whom I disliked intensely at the time and feel genuine sympathy for them now. It is not easy being in an orphanage, feeling rejected by one's people and one's world. Hence my memories of short-sheeted beds, deliberately soiled dresses, and squirming insects in the toe of one's shoe fade in importance now, pale in the glare of my knowledge of such girls' personal issues of pain and abandonment and their resulting hostility toward others, especially those who showed any measure of happiness themselves. It is true that Mary was already a target of the more abusive girls, but I was not particularly disliked by them until the friendship developed. Then they turned their anger on me as well—and such girls *are* angry, even if they don't understand it themselves. Inside these otherwise mild-mannered, nicely dressed children often lay a fearsome rage. I could record their names here, along with their more heinous deeds, but in the end they were sad souls, not villainous ones. I shall in these pages leave them their anonymity.

Mary, however, soon proved to have other problems than just the girls around her. Happy enough in the day, she routinely shrieked in the night, waking from some terrible dream or other. I would reach out my hand, of course, and she would reach out hers; touching thus, I would silently commiserate with her in the darkness. But there were other issues as well. Once during dinner I noticed that she had begun crying, big tears flowing down her cheeks and splashing onto her plate.

"Mary, shhh," I whispered. "Try not to cry."

"I—can't help it," she whispered in return, her eyes tightly shut, her mouth contorted.

"What is it? What's wrong?"

"The night-tide," said she. "Sometimes it comes—comes in the day."

Just then Sister Rose came up behind us, frowning. "Mary?" said she, looming over her from behind. "What is this? Why are you crying?"

"I—I don't know, Sister Rose," said she, keeping her head low.

"You don't know? That's absurd. How can you not know?"

"I—don't know."

"Are you ill?"

"No, Sister."

"Have you received upsetting news of some sort?"

"No, Sister."

"Then you will stop crying this instant. You will *stop*, Mary."

"I-I'm—trying..."

I attempted to intervene. "Sister Rose—"

She turned quickly to me. "I have not spoken to you, Annabel."

"I am sorry, Sister, but..."

"Are you in the habit of addressing your elders as you might your little friends?"

"No, Sister. I'm sorry, Sister. It's just that—"

"D-don't, Annabel," Mary choked out.

"What is this?" I saw Sister Rose look from one to the other of us. "A private conversation?"

We remained wordless. Mary cried quietly.

"Mary, you will stop that or I will send you to Mother Sackett. We cannot have such foolishness here. Children are trying to eat their dinner. Such a display is disgusting."

This made Mary cry all the more.

"Get up, Mary," said Sister Rose, grabbing at Mary's arm. "Get up and go to the washroom and compose yourself. After Prayers you will go to Mother Sackett. You will go for three."

With that, Mary cried out piteously and ran from the room.

"And you?" said Sister Rose, turning to me. "What of you, Annabel? What do you know about this?"

"Nothing, Sister Rose. I was just sitting here. She started crying. I don't know why."

"She's your friend, isn't she?"

"I—Yes, Sister Rose."

"Perhaps this is not a healthy friendship," said the sister, as if to herself. "I have wondered about this for some time. So much whispering together, so much giggling. It is not right." She looked at me again. "Perhaps you should be separated."

My heart seemed to drop out of my chest then, down somewhere into the pit of my stomach. I wanted to leap up—scream—slap her face! But in that moment some instinct saved me—saved *us*, Mary and me.

"As you wish, Sister," said I in an unconcerned voice, taking a bite of boiled potato.

"Hm. I shall consider."

And with that she walked off up the row of girls. I knew from the tone of her voice, however, that I had triumphed. A show of emotion would certainly have doomed us; a display of indifference decided her that the record-keeping involved in making such a change was not worth the trouble. She would forget about it—for now.

Mary and I said nothing to each other for the rest of the evening. But after Prayers were finished she marched grimly off to Mother Sackett, and as I was putting on my night things I heard the first strike followed by the inevitable scream. Knowing that the victim was Mary caused my breath to come short. My body began to tremble. The second strike came, and the third. I jumped quickly into bed, covering myself completely over so as not to let the other girls see my anguish.

"Have you ever thought of running away?"

We were seated at the foot of our usual oak tree, the sun shining down on us on a beautiful summer afternoon. Lunch, just finished, had included an unexpected pleasure—one ripe red apple for each of us. Thus I was in a state of quietude, of relative equanimity when Mary leaned forward conspiratorially and asked me this question.

And yet I was not shocked by her words. Mary had suffered a great deal in recent weeks. Her night-tides arrived ever more often in the daytime, with predictable consequences. The other girls had become even more hostile toward her; in part because of her perceived weakness but partly, I think, because any child who, as it were, "rocked the boat" in Sadmore Place created a potential hazard for everyone. There was never any telling who else might be swept up in a disciplinary action initiated by Sister Rose or Mother Sackett. I myself had been made to visit Mother's Sackett office twice for punishment when I had been doing no more than trying to comfort Mary in her tears. But, far more dangerously, this had also happened to others. A girl called Beulah, for instance, who sat on the other side of Mary from me at meals, had once hissed, "Be quiet, Mary!" and found herself assigned two strikes that evening. Sister Rose overheard another, Emily, call Mary a "cry-baby" during morning ablutions, and she was given two strikes as well. Though such incidents were hardly Mary's fault, they only served to harden the other girls against her.

It might be thought that I would naturally recoil from Mary's words—that shock or disbelief might be my response. But in the months I had been in residence at Sadmore Place I had grown evermore alienated from everyone there—everyone but Mary. Once an indifferently thought-of girl, I was now aligned all too clearly with the main object of these girls' hatred, and so was excommunicated along with her. Too, life at Sadmore Place seemed to stretch interminably before me, a tunnel of dark without any promise of soul-filling light at any time; I wrote several times to DoctorBlackthorn, asking him to have me removed from this place (we were allowed one letter per week), but received no response. I was utterly adrift, a reed floating precariously in stormy seas, and had no one who cared a whit about me—no one, that is, except Mary Mahoney—Mary my friend, my confidante, my only source of happiness in that miserable prison.

"Yes," said I, without hesitation. "I have thought of it."

"I think about it," said she, pulling absently at some spears of grass, "all the time."

"But where would you go, Mary?"

"I don't know. I would find my way somehow."

"You are twelve years old."

"There are lots of children on their own in the cities," said she, suddenly looking at me with her misaligned eyes. "I saw them when my family rode in sometimes. They are just out in the streets, playing stickball, begging passersby for coins."

"Where do they go at night?"

"I'm not sure. Probably they sleep in doorways or abandoned buildings or something like that."

"But Mary, what kind of life is that? It sounds dirty and horrid."

"Better than this place."

"I…" I had, of course, had similar thoughts—I am sure that most girls at Sadmore Place did. But the problems were enormous. I did not wish to live in the streets and sleep in doorways, but neither did I wish to lose Mary, my only tether to a world in which there was any love, any caring whatsoever. "Are you sure it would be, Mary? Here at least we have food, safety, a bed to sleep in at night."

"I hate it here."

I looked away from her, toward the great imposing building that was Sadmore Place. "I do too," I finally admitted.

We were silent for a time.

"Annabel?" She touched my arm, which caused me to look at her again. "Would you come with me?"

"Oh, Mary…"

"It would be better with two of us, wouldn't it?" she asked, her voice suddenly eager. "We could…you know, pool our resources, like. And keep company for each other. Help each other. We wouldn't be alone that way."

"That's true."

"Everything would be easier if we had each other. A friend to lean on for support. It would be hard. I know it would be hard. But together…"

I looked carefully at my dear friend. It occurred to me that, however difficult such a life would be for me, it would be vastly more difficult for her. Wherever she went, because of her eye she would invariably face the cruel assumption that she must be mad, or else an imbecile. I could see all too clearly in my imagination the tauntings she would receive, the braying and laughter of street children that would rain down on her. She envisioned befriending these children, but I knew that would never happen. The girls at Sadmore Place were testament enough to this conclusion. My visions of her future quickly grew nightmarish—not just teasing and mocking from girls, but assaults, beatings, and who knew what other violations administered by boys and even grown men—after all, other than her wandering eye Mary was rather pretty. Any girl in this situation would be helpless, but Mary would be doubly so, an obvious and inevitable target.

We said no more of it that day. Yet she had planted a seed in my mind—in both our minds—that, over time, would eventually sprout. But the tree that thus grew proved unpredictable in its size and shape, and would ultimately provide fruit of a most poisonous kind.

In the end it was isolation that decided us—that mysterious ultimate punishment.

In the weeks following the conversation I have just related, Mary seemed to decline further in her mental well-being. Weeping in the night became customary, and I found myself getting out of bed to embrace her and comfort her no matter the potential consequences. Whispering, she would say, "It was the night-tide, Annabel, I was drowning," or "I was being pressed into a terrible black fire, I could smell my hair burning," or "Someone was on my chest, their hands were like iron around my throat, I couldn't catch my breath." Nightmare after nightmare, night after night. But the days were little better. Once while we were at Prayers she suddenly shrieked, jumping up and batting at her arms, crying, "Take them off me! Please take them off me!" Another time while we were sewing I watched aghast as Mary pricked her finger with her needle—accidentally, I thought, until I saw her do it again and then again, quickly turning her finger into a bloody mess and then pushing the needle deeply and repeatedly into her palm. I stood to rush to her aid, but Sister Rose barked at me to sit down while she marched over to Mary and issued the hardest slap across the face I had ever seen any human being receive. It whipped poor Mary's head to the side as surely as if she had been punched, sending her reeling back against the stone wall as her chair tipped over.

"Wicked girl!" Sister Rose shouted, standing threateningly over the stupefied child. "Wicked, wicked girl! You will *stop* all this nonsense! I demand it!"

Mary rolled onto her side, groaning a little. Two girls near me, Rebecca and Jane, snickered. Without conscious thought or plan I found myself on my feet again.

"Sister Rose, you must not abuse Mary in this way!" I shouted.

The sister looked at me closely. I felt all the girls' eyes on me.

"You will go for three to Mother Sackett's office, Annabel," the sister said.

"I will do no such thing. I have done nothing wrong. You have abused this girl. I will report you. To Mother Sackett at first, to Father Thomas if necessary." We rarely saw Father Thomas, but understood vaguely that his was the final, unquestionable authority, above even that of Mother Sackett.

There seemed to be—or was it my imagination?—a general intake of breath on the part of all the girls, and perhaps Sister Rose as well. Eyes wide, she stepped closer to me.

"I am stronger than Mary," I warned her. "I may be stronger

than you. I am prepared to find out."

She stopped in her tracks. Her jaw literally dropped, her mouth hanging open stupidly. She looked around the room; all the girls suddenly busied themselves with their mittens and pillowcases once more.

To my astonishment, Sister Rose proceeded to stalk out of the room without a word.

I went to Mary, kneeling and cradling her head in my lap.

"Are you all right?" I whispered.

"Annabel," she moaned, "you shouldn't have done that."

"I had to. She hurt you."

"I am afraid of what will happen now."

I looked up. All the girls' eyes were on us again. No one made a sound.

"I too," said I finally.

The result was not long in coming. Mary was eventually able to right herself and resume her place, though she accomplished no further work. Her hand, which must have been in terrible pain, was streaked with rivulets of bright red blood. I returned to my seat, sewing for a time, badly, since my own hands were shaking. I felt on the verge of an explosion. If any of the girls just then had seen fit to make a cutting remark I would have attacked her on the instant, pummeling and possibly killing her. They seemed to sense this, and maintained their silence even without any adult immediately present in the room.
 Finally I heard footsteps coming down the hall—several sets of them, making hard echoing sounds. Then Mother Sackett stood in the doorway, flanked by Sister Rose on one side and Sister Victoria on the other.

"Annabel Lee," said she, her voice cold.

Mary and I exchanged a glance and I stood. Mother Sackett moved toward me. "Sister Rose has told me that you threatened her with physical violence a few minutes ago. I don't suppose you are willing to admit it."

"It would be futile to deny it," said I, my voice surprising me with a strength and confidence I did not feel. "Every girl here heard what I said."

"You admit that you threatened Sister Rose."

"I do not admit it," said I. "I proclaim it. With great pride."
I thought of saying what she had done to Mary, but I did not
want to bring my friend to Mother Sackett's attention. Later, I
thought, in her office, I would reveal all in making my case; but
that was not to be.

Mother Sackett's watery eyes opened wide. She looked me
up and down slowly.

"It is isolation for you, then," said she. She gestured to the
two sisters, who moved quickly to me. I backed up a step.

"There is no need to restrain me," said I defiantly. "I am
perfectly willing to go wherever you wish me to."

I have no notion from whence my bravado came. My mind
had not even begun to process the dreaded word *isolation* as
the truculent, even mutinous words escaped my lips. I had
astonished everyone in the room, but none so much as myself.
And yet I could not regret the words. Looking at Mary I could
plainly see her cheek, burning red from the blow Sister Rose
had delivered, as well as the thick trickles of blood on her hand
to which no one had attended. What Mary needed was comfort,
sympathy, and understanding; what she received was vicious
mistreatment at the hands of a sadistic and brutal woman. No, I
could not regret my words.

Despite my calm demeanor, the sisters moved beside me
and each took me by an arm.

"You will repent what you have said," Mother Sackett said.
"You will soften your heart of this hatred you feel. You will
learn respect."

I met her gaze head-on. "We shall see what we shall see," I
replied.

I was marched out of the sewing room.

My memory is uncertain and wavering here, as if I were somehow looking at events through a pool of water. It seems to
me that it was a long walk down many stone steps and then
through a big wooden door which Mother Sackett unlocked
grimly. I was so shocked at the sudden turn of events, and my
own unprecedented behavior—though I did not regret it a bit—
that I was as meek as a lamb as I was led down a short, very

dark hall. The only illumination came from a torch Sister Rose had lit. I could not make out what was further down the hall, if anything; all I could see was the small door to my right as Sister Victoria unlocked and opened it.

"Step in," Mother Sackett said, without emotion.

I did so.

"Turn and face me."

I did so. She was lit from behind in the glow of Sister Rose's torch. I could make out no facial features, only the strangely glowing outline of Mother Sackett's clothing and that of the two sisters behind her.

"You will receive three meals a day," said she. "You will be allowed out once a day to empty your slop bucket. Any misbehavior will be punished severely."

"How long am I to be here?" I asked in a strong voice.

"Until you repent, of course," said she.

"What am I to do here?"

"Pray."

The door closed with a thud. I heard the key being turned in the lock.

I turned and looked at my new home, immediately realizing that it was not completely dark. There was a small window, far out of reach, above me in the wall. Through this window shone a feeble gray glow. The room measured about ten feet by twelve. There was a narrow plank bed with one brown blanket atop it and a tiny flat pillow. There was also a small wooden counter with a dented metal pitcher; the pitcher was half-full with water. A metal cup rested beside it. A plain wooden chair was at the opposite corner.

Nothing else was in the room.

I stood unmoving for a long time, listening. For a while I thought I could not hear a thing; but the longer I remained there the more a variety of quite distant sounds came to my ears. Water, dripping slowly somewhere—an echo of footsteps—possibly even the sound of a voice. But far away, all of them far away, as if I had been placed in a room on the Moon.

I remained still. Even then I was surprised at my lack of emotional response. Surely previous girls who had been brought here must have kicked, screamed, wailed, begged to be let free. But I had no desire to do any of these things. I thought of nothing. After a time I moved to the pitcher and poured an inch or two of water into the cup. I placed the cup to my lips and sipped. It was cool but tasted metallic. I placed the cup down again. Finally I sat in the chair, which was old and loose-jointed. I watched the light in the high window turn a darker shade of gray, then slip entirely to black. No one came. I was alone. I sat there all night, staring without thought into the darkness.

At dawn I heard footsteps approach. I thought to rise respectfully but then decided not to, exactly because the gesture would have been seen as a respectful one. The door rattled open; Sister Rose stepped in first, followed by Sister Helen, who carried a breakfast tray. Without a word she crossed to the counter and placed the tray there.

"You will pray," Sister Rose said. "Then you will eat."

I realized that my room must face the east, since as the sun rose a perfect rectangle of light spilled across the middle of the floor.

"Kneel," Sister Rose said.

I did so. I considered refusing; I considered hurling verbal epithets at them both; but in the end I knew that would not shorten my time here. Mary's fate had begun to weigh heavily on my mind and I feared what was being done to her up above. I needed to be allowed out from this place, to be able to resume protecting my friend.

"Pray," Sister Rose said.

I pressed my palms together in the accepted manner, lowered my head and closed my eyes. I did in fact pray; but what I prayed for was not in the accepted line of prayer topics at Sadmore Place. First, I prayed that Mary would be all right. Then I prayed that Mother Sackett, Sister Rose, Sister Helen and all the rest of them in this grotesque parody of a house of God would die—die lingering, horrific deaths involving enormous pain. I prayed that their brains would be eaten away by cancer lesions. I prayed that wild dogs would rip them to shreds. I prayed that highwaymen would come and violate their precious pristine bodies ever and again until these sour, malevolent women ran mad.

When I was finished I opened my eyes slowly and stared at the wall opposite me.

"Perhaps there is hope for you," Sister Rose said in a gentler tone. "I watched as you prayed. I could see the passion on your face. You felt the prayer deeply, didn't you, Annabel?"

"Yes, Sister Rose," said I. "I felt the prayer very deeply indeed."

She allowed herself a small smile. "Eat your breakfast. If you continue with such impressive piety, perhaps your stay here need not be long."

"Thank you, Sister Rose."

In fact, my stay in isolation lasted three unchanging days. The only variation came at dinnertime on that first full day, when in addition to my boiled meat and potatoes there was on my tray a small Bible.

"Read," said Sister Rose. "Find your way to God, Annabel."

"I will try my best, Sister."

The book at least helped me fill the hours; I read a great deal of it over the next two days of my confinement. Remembering some of the stories that Father and I had read together, he with his wonderfully animated voice and mannerisms, I was tempted to cry; but I steeled myself. Tears would do no good at all—quite the opposite. I knew I must be strong; that I must not succumb to weak girlish emotions.

Reading through the Bible convinced me of something I had never really grasped about it before: that it is a fundamentally self-contradictory, incoherent document. The Old Testament and the New presented largely opposite worlds—one of vengeance and pestilence and fiery death, the other of love, caring, and forgiveness. The closer I studied the text the more I realized that religious people such as Father Thomas and Mother Sackett chose their sermon and lesson quotes carefully, picking as one might cherries from a tree the sweet, ripe lessons they wished to convey to us while tossing aside anything they decided was misshapen or unflavorful. It began to seem unsavory, this manipulating of impressions to what was, after all, a captive audience of children. I soon suspected, when I would find portions of the

Bible which I had heard the Father or Mother quote, and which I now knew were completely contradicted by certain other portions of the book, that this religion, or interpretation of religion, was, in fact, a kind of grim game designed to manipulate and control the impressionable minds of the girls at Sadmore Place. I did not see how any intelligent person could edit the words of the book as they so clearly did without realizing that they were distorting and misrepresenting the full text. Should we not have been studying and reflecting upon the *complete* book, analyzing it in all its beauty (for I could see considerable beauty in it) and contradiction? Yet I fancied that if I were to bring such an idea to any of the holy ones in charge of Sadmore Place I would likely end up with even graver punishments than I had thus far experienced. And so I said nothing.

At the dawn of the third day, the sisters opened the door as usual, but neither carried a breakfast tray. Sister Rose addressed me.

"Annabel, do you feel ready now to resume your life among the other girls?"

"Yes, Sister."

"Do you understand that what you said was wrong, a threat not only to Mother Sackett and the sisters but to Sadmore Place itself, and thus to God?"

"Yes, Sister."

"Are you sorry for what you said, Annabel?"

"I am most grievously sorry, Sister," said I, adding mentally: I am sorry I did not threaten to murder you in your bed and disembowel your corpse.

"Very well. Your punishment is officially concluded. Bring your things upstairs and join the rest of the girls at breakfast."

"Sister?"

"Yes, Annabel?"

I lifted the little Bible in my hands and pressed it to my heart. "May I keep this Bible, Sister? It is special to me now."

She smiled the biggest smile I had ever seen on her. Her face almost seemed to crack, being so unfamiliar with the stretching of the skin that this smile required of it.

"I prayed you would ask that," said she. "Of course you

may, Annabel. It is my gift to you."

"I shall treasure it always, Sister."

We went upstairs. Although Sadmore Place was fundamentally a dark place, with little direct light in any of the rooms, it seemed intensely bright to my isolation-dimmed eyes. Sister Helen accompanied me to the dining hall, where I sat in my usual place. Mary was there, and my heart soared; but as I sat next to her I saw that her face and hands were covered with blue, black, and yellow bruises. Her arms appeared to have been done further injury: bandages covered parts of both forearms. Our eyes met momentarily; my face must have registered my shock, since she quickly if almost imperceptibly shook her head. I knew she was warning me not to speak.

I looked down at my porridge, utterly without appetite. But I resolved to eat every morsel in the bowl, and drink all the bland lukewarm tea in the cup before me, lest I again call attention to myself. In this dank, depraved place I would seem, from now on, polite and gracious, gentle and pious. No one would hear another rebellious word from me, no matter what goading I might receive. I would appear, from this moment forth, the ideal child at the Sadmore Place for Orphaned Girls. If anyone asked me of my experience in isolation (anyone besides Mary, that is), I would tell them only that I had used the time and the wonderful guidance of Sister Rose to read the Bible and bring myself closer to the Holy Spirit; that I now looked back on my earlier behavior with shame and embarrassment, and could only hope that everyone could find it in their hearts to forgive the wayward sinner I had been.

But my heart was filed with loathing and rage.

For some days, while Mary and I were still allowed to sit together at meals and still slept side by side at night, I was clearly on a kind of unspoken probation. The sisters patrolled our sleeping quarters much more than before, and on no apparent set schedule. Mary was given extra lessons at lunch, in a clear effort to keep the two of us separated during what little time we would otherwise have had to be alone together outside. We did not speak at meals; we did not whisper to each other in bed. I was anxious to learn what had happened to her during my days in isolation but knew that the best strategy for both of us was to wait—to wait until the sisters were convinced of my repentance and allowed their eagle-like gazes to shift elsewhere. I communicated this to Mary in individual words, whispered as we walked to meals or as we made our beds or performed morning ablutions.

"Soon," I would whisper, or "Patience."

Her whisper would come in return, "Yes."

I missed her horribly during those days, even as she was standing next to me, even as I could hear her breathing, for we dared not even look at each other besides a darting glance such as one might offer any person.

In time, it worked. It was perhaps two weeks after I returned from my subterranean punishment that, one cold afternoon, I was delighted to see Mary out in the garden after lunch. I wandered over to her, careful to betray no enthusiasm that might be noted by any of the sisters.

"This one is called bloodroot," said I in a quiet, casual voice, gesturing gently to a wildflower before us.

"What a strange name," said she, carefully studying the flower.

"Yes, well, I understand that the root exudes a red juice that people use for potions and such. I believe that's where the name comes from."

Staring at the flower, Mary whispered, "I've missed you so much."

"I've missed you too, darling Mary. What did they do to you?"

She smiled ironically. "Brought me closer to God."

"Oh, Mary." Then, in a louder voice: "It's not in bloom now, but when it is, it shows the most lovely white flowers."

"Yes, I think I remember them from a few months ago." Whispered: "And what did they do to you in isolation?"

I smiled a little, touching the plant. "Brought me closer to God."

"I was worried that you—that you had actually changed."

"No. I hate them, Mary."

But we could talk no more. I saw Sister Helen off down the hill, her head turned toward us. Slowly, leisurely, Mary and I went our separate ways.

It would be weeks before we began to interact more casually, always cautious not to betray any particular emotion toward each other. I was careful to spend time with other girls, talking with them, kneeling with them at Prayers. But in truth all I thought about was Mary.

Finally there came a bright autumn afternoon when I found her under our old oak tree. It had been nearly two months since I had been in isolation and my record had been beyond reproach since then. Mary too had remained as unobtrusive as possible and had been sent to Mother Sackett's office for discipline only once or twice in that period, for minor infractions. I sat next to her, not too close, and enjoyed the cool November breeze on my face.

"We should only talk for a moment," said I. It felt good to be able to *talk* at all, as opposed to monosyllabic whispers.

"Yes."

"How are you, Mary darling?"

She shrugged.

"You look sad," said I.

"I am sad. I'm lonely, Annabel."

"As am I."

She looked at me, her unmatched eyes glinting in the sun. "I don't think I can stay here anymore."

"No?"

"D'you know what these are?" She showed me her arms, covered now with light white scars.

"They are scars. What happened to you, Mary? Who did it to you?"

"I did it to myself."

I swallowed. "Oh, Mary."

"When you were in isolation. The second night. I couldn't..." A tear trickled down her cheek. "I couldn't last any longer. I used a fork I stole from the dining hall."

"Mary, oh Mary, no."

"It might have worked, but a girl saw me. Jane. She got up

to use her commode and she saw me there, in bed. The blood. She called for Sister Helen. They took me to the infirmary." She looked down at the ground. "They said the wounds were superficial. Apparently I did a bad job."

I swallowed. I tried to breathe slowly. "And the bruises?"

"Sister Rose. The next day. In the alcove off the kitchen. She hit me. She said was a wicked girl for trying such a thing."

We sat silently.

"I must leave here," said she. "I must run. Or else die."

After a time I said, "We will go back to my home. No one is there anymore but it is being held in trust for me by a family friend, Doctor Blackthorn. We will live there."

Her face brightened. "Really, Annabel?"

"We will escape," said I. "I just don't know yet quite how."

4

But as the days passed—days, then weeks—the impossibility of it became crushingly clear to me. I wrote more unanswered letters to Doctor Blackthorn, appealing for his help. I thought of a thousand schemes: we would tie up Sister Rose, gag her, take her keys and run away; we would use lamp oil to start a fire in the building and, in the ensuing panic, make our way out; we would steal away in one of the wagons which came from town to deliver supplies to Sadmore Place, hiding ourselves under blankets or in crates. But none of these notions, or others like them, stood up to the glare of clear analysis. We were not strong enough to overcome the nuns. We had no weapons and no access to any beyond forks and spoons. There was no possibility that we could go unobserved long enough to hide in a visiting merchant's wagon—and if we did, we would inevitably be quickly discovered. Even if, I supposed, we somehow made our extremely unlikely escape in some such a melodramatic way, where would we go? It was many hours' journey to my family home and I was not at all sure of the route, which had involved numerous unmarked, unnamed paths and roads. How could two girls, assuming we managed to get to the nearest town from Sadmore Place, then travel any further? Without adults to protect us, it would be obvious we were escapees from the local orphanage—our standardized dresses would tell everyone that as soon as they saw us. And exactly how long could we be gone from Sadmore before the ever-vigilant nuns discovered our absence and sounded a general alarm? Fifteen minutes? Thirty? I could see no scenario in which we could possibly be gone for more than an hour without it being known. Nor could we rely on the discretion of the other girls; some of them would be more than delighted to inform on any escape attempt we might effect. And in the entire time I had been in the orphanage—some six months now—I had never heard of a child escaping, or trying to. Grimly I began to realize why this was so.

I was careful, however, in what I said about it to Mary, whose sallow skin and nervous manner convinced me ever more that the poor girl desperately needed help of a sort I did not know how to offer. When we would meet outside she would quickly whisper, "Annabel, when shall we go? When? We must go," and I would respond with evasions, evincing an enthusiasm I no longer felt for any such plan but giving her the impression I was still very much focused upon it. She herself came up with many wild schemes, none of them reflecting in a real way the profound challenges that any escape plan presented.

"We could get the other girls involved," she whispered one day, as we looked at the wildflowers in the garden. "We could get them all to agree to be part of it. We could overwhelm them with sheer numbers."

"And then?"

"And then we would take over! We would run Sadmore Place ourselves! You and I would be in charge—two queens running the castle! We would make Sister Rose and Sister Helen and Mother Sackett and all the rest do our bidding. We would make them scrub the floors while we stood over them and laughed. We would beat them when they talked out of turn. We would…"

She went on like this for a time; my mind drifted hopelessly to a story I remembered of Poe's, "The System of Doctor Tarr and Professor Fether." When she was finished talking I said quietly, "That is a very interesting plan, Mary. I am not sure it is entirely workable. But let me think on it."

I looked at her in the bright sun. I noticed that there were numerous pock marks on her cheeks, as if she had been plucking at them with her fingernails. Her hair was untidy. And suddenly I had a terrible flash of memory: Mother, in her final decline, sinking into madness.

"Mary," I whispered desperately, heedlessly throwing my

arms around the girl and pressing her to me. "Mary, sweet
Mary!"

What remains to tell of this part of my woeful life must be written in very few words, as the memories are still, after so many
years, too painful to fully dramatize here.

We never put into action any escape plan. We talked about
it for weeks, Mary's ideas growing more and more fantastical
(building a balloon that would lift us away was discussed), until
I believe she began to sense I was only humoring her, at which
point she stopped sharing such ideas at all. We grew apart. My
dear friend shut down like a machine in need of repair, which
in many ways she truly was. She grew pensive and stubborn.
She began to earn more and more rebukes from the nuns, more
and more punishments. Finally, after an hysterical outburst in
the dining room in which she threw her bowl of porridge at me
and accused Sister Rose of trying to murder her, she was put in
isolation. I can still hear her screaming as they carried the twisting, writhing girl from the room.

I knew well what isolation entailed and was not sure Mary
could survive it. But she came back three days later, her manner listless and confused, her face gray. Her unfocused eyes
were dull and expressionless; she hardly looked at me when
I greeted her. At breakfast she sat before her porridge as if she
were entirely unaware of it. Grief, guilt, and sorrow all overwhelmed my soul then. I sat staring straight ahead, mechani-
cally spooning the porridge into my mouth without appetite
but in the knowledge that unhappy consequences would ensue
if I refused to eat the food.

"Mary, eat," I whispered. "Eat."

She offered no response.

When breakfast was finished we went to classes, as usual,
and then to lunch. After lunch I wandered alone in the bright
fields, passing by our old oak tree but not stopping to sit under
it. I did not see Mary at all and had no idea where she was. It
was only when I returned to the building and stepped into the
dormitory room that I saw her hanging motionlessly in the air
in front of her bed. She had used a bedsheet and wrapped it

over a metal pipe that ran perpendicularly along the wall above us. Her eyes, the cause of such torment to her in life, were closed now—closed forever. I stared at her. If I breathed, I was unaware of it. I may have blacked out, somehow, and yet I did not collapse; I simply stood there until others came. Then there was much screaming and crying which I hardly heard at all. It was if I were underwater and everyone was moving in that way, in some sort of slowed motion. I backed numbly out of the room as girls and nuns frantically rushed in. The hallway was entirely empty as I moved like a somnambulist toward the front door and then through it. I walked unhurriedly down the front path, entirely unobserved. Finally I left the path and made my way into the woods. It was a cool, cloudless day in early autumn. I walked and kept on walking. I walked for a very long time. I never looked back, and never saw Sadmore Place again.

5

Early in this chronicle I fretted that the reader might wonder, "Wherein is the tragedy that makes this author reflect on her youth with such melancholy?" Perhaps the answer to this question is somewhat clearer now. I was but a child and had already lost my father, my mother, my unborn sister, and my closest friend—each of them suddenly and horribly; two by the ghastliest of all devices, suicide. I had been forcibly removed from the one home I had known and subjected to harshness and abuse in a strange, shadowy institution whose trustees knew neither caring nor pity. Now I wandered the back roads of eastern Maryland, bereft and alone.

Was my unhappy fate the result of a vengeful Old Testament God enraged at my defiant unbelief? Or was my life an illustration merely of the indifference of the cosmos—the play of random chance, abstruse and meaningless to everyone but myself? I pondered this bitterly as I made my way through beautiful but hardly noticed groves of magnolias and redbuds and sourwoods in the late afternoon light. Tall wild grasses made swishing sounds against my skirt as I moved. I paid little attention to where I was or what direction I was going, though given the position of the sun low in the sky I realized I was walking roughly northwest. But toward what, I could not imagine.

Did Mary know that by ending her own life in the way she did she offered me perhaps the sole possibility of a child ever escaping Sadmore Place? I would like to think so—to imagine that hers was a gesture of love, sacrificing herself to allow me a chance to go free—but I am not enough of an egotist to actually believe such a thing. I am sure that I was far from Mary's thoughts in her tragic final minutes; no doubt she was drowning in her dark and unspeakable "night-tides." And yet, most probably entirely unplanned by her, a chance is what her death offered me—a chance which I took, though entirely unconsciously in those first hours. I had left Sadmore Place with no plan—without even an awareness that I had begun my escape. I simply could not be there anymore. And so, having packed nothing, I walked. I wore only the dress and shoes I had on. I had no food with me, no money. As I have indicated, this was not an *escape* in any conscious or conventional sense. But that is what it became.

I do not know what happened in Sadmore Place in the time after my departure, but it is easy enough to imagine the chaos that must have continued for hours after the discovery of Mary's body—the panicked nuns—the screaming, weeping girls—the confusion—the frantic prayers—the disorder. The entire place must have been up in arms. And though I had been Mary's friend, we had been careful to conceal this ever since my own time in isolation, and in the last days we were entirely separate. Thus I suspect that young Annabel Lee was far from anyone's thoughts in those first chaotic hours; most likely my absence was not noted for quite some time.

But I did not concern myself with such matters at the start of my journey. I did not even think of it as a journey. If some adult authority had come racing up to me on a horse and demanded my return to Sadmore Place, I most likely would have uncomplainingly complied. I was in a state of numbed shock, hardly aware of my surroundings. Logic might have dictated that I move as quickly as possible, stopping for nothing—after all, in the first hour I could have ventured no more than a mile or two from the institution. One would think that the secret to a successful escape would lie in constant, hurried motion and careful concealment. But I wandered; doubled back on myself; stopped to look at wildflowers or to splash water on my face from a little creek I discovered. Such would obviously seem to be the recipe for quick recapture, yet it did not come.

But the darkness seemed to drop down upon me with great suddenness, and with it came an abrupt realization of my predicament. I can remember stopping and looking around, grasping in a terrible moment of insight how I was cut off from everything now, everything and everyone—lost in a world of cold, encroaching night—the direst of night-tides, indeed. It seems to me that I panicked then, my breath short, my heart smashing, and ran pell-mell through those newly strange, hostile, shadow-haunted woods; it even seems to me that I may have made an abortive attempt to return to Sadmore Place, but with the arrival of the dark I had grown so discomposed as to have no idea in what direction I ran. Navigation by the stars was a skill of which I had read in books, but its principles were quite beyond my youthful inexperience. As a result I became completely disorientated. I stumbled again and again in the lightless gloom. Little whimpering sounds came from my throat, like the sounds of a small, helpless animal in a trap. Finally in my wild haste I twisted my ankle painfully against a log or stump and cried out, collapsing to the ground.

Breathlessly I looked around myself. Black tree trunks surrounded me, crowned with black limbs and branches with their black leaves whispering in the night breeze. I might have screamed, but could not. I sat there, kneading my ankle, trembling with fear and exhaustion, waiting for what I was sure would be the end of all.

In that moment I did something quite impulsive and quite without thought or preparation: I began to pray. I did not attempt to pull myself into the proper kneeling position, nor did I press my palms together in the familiar gesture used for standard supplications to the Lord; instead I merely sat there motionlessly and closed my eyes. "Dear Lord," went my thoughts, "I have never believed in You and do not believe in You now. I tell you this frankly. I feel that You might want to know this about one of Your children, if truly You are there. This child, myself, is in peril. I am alone and friendless. Everyone I have loved in this world is dead. I feel that the burdens which have been put upon me are more than anyone might be reasonably asked to bear. Job himself was an adult man with children when he underwent his trials; I am but a thirteen-year-old girl. If You are there, Lord, I humbly ask for a sign. Let me know that I am not alone, that You are with me."

After a time I opened my eyes. If I had been hoping for a vision of a burning bush or the form of Christ Himself hovering benevolently before me, I was disappointed. Nothing had changed. No voice spoke from the sky. I felt no sense of any comforting presence in my soul. I was still alone and adrift in the darkness, my ankle paining me, and now a sensation of hunger beginning to gnaw at my innards. The prayer, I felt, had accomplished nothing. I had prayed to nothing and in return had received nothing.

And yet I noticed that the simple act of prayer itself seemed to have had some beneficent effect. I no longer trembled. My breathing had returned to something close to normal. Moreover, as I looked at the forest around me the terrifying phantasms that had preoccupied my imagination seemed to have abated; it took me a moment to realize that the moon had risen, and with it came some illumination of the scene before me. With my anxieties somewhat quieted, I was able to realize that the forest at night was not different from the forest in daylight. The rustlings I heard were only the breeze, or else some small creature no doubt more frightened of me than I could ever be of it. My soul calmed. Adjusting myself so as to lessen the discomfort to my ankle, my hand brushed across something low to the ground—something, or rather many things, very small and soft. I had discovered a bramble bush, and on it many dark berries which, strangely out of season, proved under-ripe but edible. I ate my fill.

With dawn came calmer reflection, and a different sort of anxiety. I had slept but haltingly, being uncomfortably cold, and my body was sore from the night spent on the hard ground. Yet my ankle, while still tender, seemed not too burdensome, and I found that I was able to walk well enough if I was mindful of the slight injury. The sun now allowed me my direction, and I resolved to progress toward home—that is, what had been my home some eight months before. The fact that I might be viewed as a fugitive upon arrival did not overmuch concern me; the family home was mine, I had been given to understand, and Doctor Blackthorn held monies that seemingly belonged to me as well. At least the man might be counted on to take an interest in my welfare, as he had done before—though his silence to my many letters to him raised some concern in my mind. Still, I had nowhere else to go. In the clear, cool morning it did not even occur to me to turn back toward Sadmore Place.

I made my way down the hill to the little creek and drank the delicious water there. The sun was rising rapidly and I knew I must move on. Wherever I was, I could not possibly be far from Sadmore Place, and the dawn light seemed to tell me that I had to continue traveling. To be caught now, to be taken back, to be thrown bodily into isolation once more—the thought was intolerable. I would die first. Gathering up some berries and placing them in my skirt pocket, I resolved to continue on.

As I walked, carefully staying far from the road where I might be all too easily seen, thoughts crowded in on my brain. I saw Mary hanging lifelessly, eyes shut against a world which had never loved her. The vision momentarily overwhelmed me, and I had to stop to try to breathe slowly and settle my stomach. Thinking of Mary's fate made me want to cry, to scream, to vomit, but I did none of these things. I thought also of the strange experiences of the previous night. My prayers that had been answered—or had they? It was true that in prayer I had found some level of peace which allowed me to reflect upon my situation more coolly and rationally. But that effect might just as well have been caused by the simple act of staying still for a time, breathing calmly, and focusing my thoughts. It was also true that just after completing the prayer—and realizing my hunger—I had suddenly found the bramble bush with its very unexpected berries. But here again, my logical mind told me that this was nothing—that I would have found the bush anyway as soon as I leaned back in the way I had. In the end I came to no conclusion. If God existed, I wondered, why did He speak in riddles that could so easily be explained away? Surely a feeling of peace and a handful of under-ripe blackberries hardly constituted evidence of the Almighty's intervention.

As I walked that morning I passed several houses—simple farms, with plain cottages and a few cows and pigs about. Twice I espied people—once a sole woman in a man's hat standing at her door, once two children tossing pebbles at their family's chickens. In both cases I moved on as stealthily as I could, drawing no attention to myself. It was vital that I somehow leave this general area unobserved.

It was also vital, however, that I somehow obtain more substantial food, along with warmer clothing. My muscles still ached from the cold of the night before, and my stomach demanded more satisfaction than a few berries could give it. I was determined to not reveal myself, and yet my physical needs were pressing. Here again the reality of my situation came upon me and oppressed my spirit. I possessed nothing but my orphanage dress and my shoes. I had not a single penny of money with which I might secure any necessary supplies. It disturbed me that I might be reduced to outright thievery as a means of resolving my problems, but even here, I had no conception of how I might do this—*what* I might steal, or *from whom*.

Late in the morning I saw through the trees two official-looking men riding at high speed up the road in the general direction of Sadmore Place. Was it possible that word of my disappearance had only just now made it to the authorities? If so, this could only be to my advantage. But it also meant that I was being hunted. It was a remote area; I had no idea how many lawmen might be raised in order to locate a single unimportant orphan girl. But I was sure that they had techniques of tracking of which I knew nothing. No doubt I had left shoeprints in the damp soil, and other evidences of my presence along the way. As I walked I became convinced that it was but a matter of minutes before I would be discovered—that the hard sound of hooves clopping on earth would rise ominously in my ears— that the harsh bark of some man would sound my name and demand that I stop. I imagined the two men I had glimpsed rushing up to me then, pushing me rudely to the ground, tying my arms and legs, throwing me over the back of one of their horses and conveying me at high speed back to Sadmore Place.

But then again (and I kept on moving as I had these thoughts, my ankle slowing me only slightly) of how much interest could my obscure and friendless self really be to such men? Perhaps their search would be no more than cursory, under the assumption that a thirteen-year-old girl who had run off would quickly find the surrounding country inhospitable and thus would soon return? And—I was surprised at how long it took me to realize this—it could be that the men were only riding out because they had received their first reports of Mary's passing. Certainly the women of Sadmore Place knew of my absence by now, but mayhap it was considered of little importance next to Mary's catastrophe. It could easily be that I was no more than an afterthought to any of them, and worthy of no more than a formal note sent to my guardian Doctor Blackthorn: "Dear Doctor Blackthorn," I imagined, "We regret to inform you that your young charge Annabel Lee voluntarily escaped from Sadmore Place last night. We have called in the local law officers, and every effort is being made to recover her. We have much hope of quick success in this endeavor. We shall of course immediately inform you of any developments in this matter. Yours Sincerely, &tc."

I had no way of knowing, and there was nothing I could do but continue to move. I ascended a low, well-forested hill from which I could look down on the road at some distance without being seen. Over the ensuing hours I observed several men on horses charging at high speed either toward or away from the direction of Sadmore Place. Once a breeze seemed to bring to my awareness, very far away, hardly audible at all, a man's voice calling my name over and over. But this might very well have been my imagination.

Presently the sun was high overhead and I stopped to rest, chewing on what few unsatisfying berries I still had and massaging my ankle, which had begun to throb. I did not know how much further I could travel. I had wild fantasies of stealing a horse somewhere and riding off, though of course this plan, even if I had been able to effect it, would certainly have proved disastrous—the first official to pass me on the road would surely have guessed my identity at once. I had to stay away from roads and keep myself as unobtrusive as possible. But my need for food had become acute. My stomach gurgled with dissatisfaction and I found myself feeling faint. I finished the last of the berries and allowed myself to lie down on a blanket of leaves for a few minutes of much-needed rest....

When I opened my eyes again it was twilight. I looked around myself, astonished both at the passage of time and at the fact that I had remained unfound, even as I had been here for hours, inert and defenseless. Perhaps I was indeed of no importance at all to those who might seek my discovery. I stood. The sleep had improved the condition of my ankle, but done nothing for my ever-increasing hunger. Wearily I continued on, aware that with darkness approaching I would again find progress slow if not impossible. My situation had to change.

After an hour's additional walk in the deepening night I came across a small farm nestled at the base of the hill which I had been traversing most of the day. The simple wood frame house reminded me somewhat of the one in which I had lived with Father and Mother, though this one was in much poorer repair. There was at least one person in the house; through one of its front windows I saw an oil lamp bloom into light. I wondered what would happen if I walked up and knocked on the door, but immediately rejected the idea as a likely path to my re-imprisonment at Sadmore Place. Instead I studied the property as closely as I could in the near-dark. It had a decrepit look, as if whatever farming was once done there was done no longer. I did, however, see a small barn some distance behind the house. It too looked in need of repair, with its sagging roof and missing slats, but at the very least I could, I reasoned, pass the night there if I could enter it very quietly. Happily the family appeared to have no dog which could reveal my presence through its barking.

Moving toward the barn, keeping as much distance between myself and the house as I could, I came upon a well with a half-bucket of water beside it. I drank my fill and then moved to the barn. To my relief I saw that among the other repair issues here was the fact that the door was not flush with the frame: a missing slat in the wall created a narrow opening through which I was able to slide, scraping my dress against the rude wood.

Within the barn were two horses, neither of which appeared healthy; fortunately they evinced no interest in me. There was an abundance of hay, and a loft in which I might pass a few relatively comfortable hours—but there was nothing else in the barn; surely nothing I could find that could tolerably be considered food. Standing there, I found myself suddenly unutterably weary. A night-tide of hopelessness engulfed my soul. I felt that I had reached the end and must either die or be returned to the orphanage. Listlessly, I ascended the rickety ladder and lay down in the hayloft. I fell asleep instantly.

A loud sound broke my slumber with shocking abruptness. My head shot up, my eyes alert; the first feeble hints of daylight were beginning to glow through the slats of the barn. What had wakened me was the sound of the door suddenly being pulled open. I sensed that whoever had come in was standing and listening; I may have gasped or rolled over audibly when the door opened. If not, this person would certainly have simply moved straight to the horses and begun morning routines with them. But there was no sound of boot steps, no rustling around in the barn. There was only silence. I was, I knew, doomed.

"I know you're up there," came the voice at last. "Might as well show yourself."

The voice was male, but that of a boy, not a man. This gave me some strange, desperate sense of hope.

"Come on," said he. "Who are you?"

He sounded more curious than threatening, and I knew I had no choice. Slowly I raised my head and looked down. In the dim light I could see that he was indeed a boy, wearing much-patched overalls and a colorless old floppy hat. He had overlong black hair and dark freckles. I estimated his age at twelve or thirteen. There was a rusty pitchfork in his hands.

"Hey," said he. "Are you a girl?"

I cleared my throat. "I am."

He was clearly surprised. "Sometimes we get a vagabond up there," said he. "Never no girl before."

"I am sorry," said I. "I had nowhere else to go."

"Well, come on down."

I did. My limbs were sore. When I reached the bottom of the ladder I stepped onto the barn floor, brushing straw from my clothes, and turned to face the boy. Looking at him, I changed my estimate of his age: he was younger than I had thought, no

more than eleven. He was thin as a whip and had very prominent front teeth which were yellow and crooked. He was quite
ugly, in fact, but that concern was far from my mind at the
moment. He leaned on the pitchfork.

"Who are you?" he asked.

I told him my name.

"Hey," said he, eyes brightening, "there was a man out here
yesterday."

"Yes," I acknowledged. There was no point in lying. "I imagine there was."

"You ran away, huh? From the orphanage?"

"I ran away from the orphanage, yes."

"Well, hell." He seemed to think. "Why'd you come here?"

"As I said, I had no other place to go. May I ask *your* name?"

"My name's Theodore," said he. "Theodore Jones."

I tried to smile. "It is good to meet you, Theodore."

He studied me, his head tilting one way and then another.
"Beats all to have a girl in here," said he.

"Again, I apologize. Theodore…" My voice instinctively
grew more quiet. "I'm sorry to have invaded your barn. I will
just take my leave now, if I may."

I took a single step toward the door. He made no effort to
stop me, but said: "You want something to eat?"

I could have cried out in joy, but remained cautious. I had
no idea who lived with him in that house across the way—his
father might be the sheriff himself, for all I knew.

"I—I had best just keep moving, Theodore, but thank you."

"My mama ain't up. She's sick."

"I'm sorry to hear that, Theodore. I hope it's nothing serious."

"She's dyin'."

"Oh." I looked down. "I am—I am very sorry, Theodore.
What about your father?"

"I ain't seen him in a long time."

"Is he away?"

"I ain't seen him since I was five."

I knew not what to say. But the state of disrepair in which I
had found the whole property was suddenly, terribly explained.

"Just you and your mother live here, Theodore?"

"Yeah."

"Do you—do you go to school?"

"I usta. But then I had to stay here and work the farm."

"Of course. I see."

"Look, you want some food or don't you?"

"I—yes, I…But I'm not sure I should come into the house. Your mother…"

"I'll bring it to you," said he. He looked at me for a long moment with an odd expression on his face. Then he turned and walked back to the house, leaning the pitchfork against the wall outside the barn.

I nearly ran. I had no way of knowing if the boy would reveal me to his mother, or indeed if he was even telling the truth about his father. I imagined a huge, hulking man in suspenders with a shotgun in his hands suddenly shoving open the back door, shouting my name, demanding that I stop and subject myself to arrest. But as I stood there, hunger caused me nearly to collapse. I simply had to eat something. I had to take this chance.

In a few minutes, the boy returned; I was relieved to see that he was by himself. He had a small cloth sack in his hands. "Some bread in here," said he, looking into the sack. "Carrots. Couple of taters. Old jar of preserves."

My heart soared. "Thank you, Theodore. Thank you very, very much."

He shrugged. "I ran away before. Mama sent the law out."

"I—I'm sorry."

"I hate the law. That's why I'm helpin' you."

"Yes, I—I understand."

He closed the sack again. "You got anything to carry this stuff in?"

"No, I—I have nothing."

"Aw, you can take the sack. It don't matter, I guess." He held onto it still, however, looking at me strangely. "But…"

"Yes, Theodore?"

"I figure…" He hesitated. "I figure you should pay for this."

My heart dropped again. "Pay?"

"How much you think it's worth?"

"Theodore, it is worth a great deal indeed, but I have no money. Not a cent. I am sorry, but I cannot possibly pay you." I patted my skirt pockets. "You see, they are empty." I stared at the ground for a moment, then sighed. I could not really blame this impoverished boy. "I shall just take my leave," said I, making a step toward the door.

"Wait." He looked at me. "Maybe you could pay another way."

"Do you mean with work?"

"Naw," said he, kicking his boot into the dirt. "I don't meant that."

"What, then?"

"Well…" He grinned a grin I found decidedly unamiable. "Maybe you could—do something else."

I stared at him. This boy could not be older than eleven. "What?"

"Maybe—maybe you could take your clothes off."

I flushed to the tips of my toes. "Theodore, that is an outrageous suggestion."

"Why? Only take a second."

"It is obscene."

"You're hungry, ain't you?"

"Yes. I confess it. I am hungry. But I am also respectable."

He snorted. "Ain't nothin' respectable about starvin'."

"Theodore, please. This is monstrous. Surely you are a nicer boy than this."

He narrowed his eyes, staring at me. "I reckon I'm not."

"Theodore…"

"I ain't never seen a naked girl before."

And somehow, his saying these words eased the terrible burden. Suddenly the situation seemed more a result of small-child innocence than unwholesome lasciviousness. I was still deeply uncomfortable and horribly embarrassed. But I could smell the bread in the bag he held in his hands.

I said, "Only for a moment, correct?"

"Sure, just a second, that's all."

"You won't try to touch me?"

"Naw."

"And you promise you will give me the bag?"

"Here." He placed it on the floor between us. "Hell, you're bigger'n me. You could just take it and run now if you wanted."

He might have been right; I was several inches taller than he. Too, I remembered the pitchfork outside the barn door and suspected that I could get to it first. But I was groggy with hunger. It was all I could do to hold myself from leaping on the bag like a wild animal and devouring everything in it. I took a step back and realized I had walked onto an old blanket on the floor. I glanced down at it. The blanket was dirty and filled with holes, but it was made of wool.

"May I have this blanket too?" I asked.

He shrugged. "Sure. Don't need it. Okay."

With that we had struck our bargain. But as I reached for my dress I hesitated.

"Theodore, please look away."

"Naw," said he, grinning in that ugly way. "I wanna see."

I sighed. I felt myself trembling, but whether from hunger or humiliation I knew not. With a deep breath I pulled the dress over my head and stood there in the dawn light wearing nothing but, absurdly, my shoes. He came no closer, instead simply studying me in the way, I imagined, a painter might study his undraped model. I felt raw and exposed—not merely physically, but in some deeper, more visceral way. I felt like sinking into the earth forever. I felt disgusted with myself, hopeless. I could not imagine anyone receiving anything but revulsion from looking at my filthy face, my disheveled hair, my half-starved bare body, the hourglass-shaped mole on my belly. Yet he seemed fascinated.

"Move your hands away," said he.

I moved them.

"Turn around."

I did so.

Finally I turned to look at him again but was unable to raise my eyes for shame.

"I have satisfied my end of the bargain," said I quietly, trying to hold my voice steady.

He studied me a moment longer, then, seeming to lose interest, shrugged and said, "Okay."

I hastily pulled my dress on again, his eyes never leaving me. Watching him carefully, I picked up the sack.

"Get out of here now," said he, his tone abruptly turning hard and angry. "Get out of here and don't come back or I'll tell my mother. I'll tell my mother that a *whore* was in here."

With that he ran out of the barn and back to the house.

How I exited that property and left that terrible boy behind I do not completely recall. I believe that I ran, ran for my life, keeping always away from the road—ran until I could no longer see that house or barn or anything of that property behind me. I felt dirty. I felt that I had committed an unpardonable sin. I felt I was a monstrous creature, a grotesque parody of a girl—of a human being. I remember that I stopped to retch, my stomach heaving violently, but there was nothing inside me; sour spittle was all that came from my lips.

But I had the sack. In it was everything the boy had described: a fist-sized lump of dark bread, two small carrots, a pair of wrinkled old potatoes, and a dusty jar of some sort of preserves. Over my shoulders was the filthy blanket which had also been part of the bargain. My brain told me that I had negotiated wisely even as my soul kept chanting the word *whore* inside my head.

Secreting myself on my blanket in a thick grove of white oak trees, I sat and, involuntary whimpers of joy rising from my throat, chewed ravenously on the hard bread. It was quite stale, but I have always possessed very strong teeth and at that moment the bread compared favorably with the most soft, fresh loaves Mother had ever baked. I twisted open the jar and poured some of the preserves onto the bread; they were blackberry, and the result of the combination of bread and preserves created something close to what I imagined Heaven to be. I quickly devoured both my carrots as well, hardly tasting them. But finally I stopped, realizing that I must parcel out what remained so that it would last me for a time. I licked my fingers savagely so as not to waste a precious morsel of bread or blackberry.

I allowed myself a few minutes' rest after my sumptuous repast, and then placed what was left of the bread and preserves along with the two little potatoes back into the sack. It took me a few minutes to calculate how I might carry my new-found belongings. In the end I widened three of the holes in the blanket, making from it a kind of cape or shroud—my head fit through a hole in the center, my arms through holes on either side. No doubt it looked odd, but in the cool autumn morning I found it comfortably warm and entirely satisfactory. As for the cloth sack, not wishing to have to carry it in my hands, I took a roughly straight fallen branch some three feet in length, cleaned it of any leaves or other protuberances, and tied the top of the sack to one end. Placing the branch over my shoulder, something in the manner of a soldier and his rifle, I found that I could carry the burden, which was after all not heavy, with considerable ease. Thus equipped, I set out again with my spirits refreshed and buoyant.

6

In ten days I reached home. My adventures on the way were many, but few are pleasant to recall. Food was a constant preoccupation, and for want of it I finally turned thief. More than once in the darkness I would approach a house in the hope of finding fruit trees or a vegetable garden, and I sometimes did; often I pawed through piles of trash to locate ends of bread or, best of all, the half-eaten remains of a chicken. I confess that on more than one occasion I investigated hogs' troughs, though to my recollection I never actually removed anything from them.

Dogs became my bitterest enemies, their barking raising the alarm in a house and forcing me to run away. Several times I saw men in their nightshirts burst out of their doors, demanding to know who intruded on their property. Some of these men had rifles in their hands which they appeared all too eager to fire. At times I had to remain stock-still as some farmer lurked about the property, searching for me; once such a man passed so close to where I crouched hidden behind his wood pile that I could literally have reached out and grasped his leg. If such events strike the reader as picaresque and exciting now, rest assured that they were nothing but terrifying and desperate then.

Sleeping was another problem. After the incident with Theodore Jones I resolved to no longer attempt making unauthorized entry into others' barns. That meant sleeping outside every night, which could be frightening in its own ways. I found myself unafraid of the wildlife—red foxes and white-tailed deer held no terror for me—but distinctly concerned about other wayfarers I would occasionally espy traveling the back roads during the day. I was very much aware (again, the incident with Theodore Jones had made me so) that I was a girl—a girl alone—and as a result might quickly find myself in a situation of utter helplessness. Not all whom I encountered were likely to be young boys, and coming upon a grown man or group of men at the wrong time, in the wrong place, could, I knew, lead to my ruination. I was innocent of the ways of men but I was not stupid. I possessed good common sense, and knew that I had to make a wide berth around any men I might find, or who might find me. There was, of course, not only the possibility of my being attacked, but there was also the question of legal authorities who could be on the hunt for me. In either scenario, my capture would prove my undoing.

As a result I slept but little in those weeks, taking short naps in the day when I was somewhere that I could see clearly all around me for some distance and determine that I was safely alone. I was fortunate in that there was but little rain during this period. Although I frequently found myself near pleasant streams and brooks, I did not bathe beyond splashing water on my face and hands; it was too cold to get my dress soaking wet, and the idea of standing naked and helpless in the untamed outdoors was intolerable. Perhaps the single point in my favor in terms of safety lay in my appearance, which day after day became wilder and more disturbing. My clothing was dirty. I had no way of composing my long hair, which sprouted every which way. Poor nutrition caused me to grow skinny and pale. The reflection I would see in the river water told me that I looked like a mad girl, and such apparent madness, I reasoned, might keep interlopers away. I remember thinking of how Father and I had read *King Lear* together, and how it had moved me; not only Lear's plight but Gloucester's too, and perhaps most of all, young Edgar's—I pictured him out on the stormy heath in his disguise as a crazed wanderer, crying, *"Poor Tom's a-cold!"* Perhaps, I imagined, I might put on the face of madness myself, and so frighten away those who would interfere with me.

Fortunately things did not come to that pass. One fine day in November I crested an otherwise undistinguished hill to realize, suddenly and with tremendous joy, that I recognized the country before me. I knew the road down below, and some of the buildings off in the distance. I had reached my destination. I had come home again.

An hour's walking brought me to my old house—my parents' house—or rather it *should* have done; but it was not there. Instead of the familiar bungalow I beheld a partly built new home, all raw lumber in skeletal shapes, with numerous men and horse-drawn wagons all around it. The fields immediately around the house had mostly been trampled into the dirt. I stood some distance away, aghast; for some time I looked this way and that, trying to convince myself that I had somehow come to the wrong place, that this was not the land of my parents' home at all. And yet no matter how I reviewed the landmarks I came to the same conclusion: this was the correct spot, the location of the home where I had grown up, and it was gone!

After some time I approached the site. Men were busily sawing and hammering and at first did not notice me at all. I stared up at the wood beams—this house was destined to be much larger than the one I knew—and felt I was in a dream. I could not be seeing what I was seeing. My eyes moved around the largely destroyed fields. I stepped over to where I thought my sister's grave should have been, but all was in disarray and I could not locate it.

At last a voice came behind me: "Hello, there!"

I turned. One of the men, a spindly creature in denim who sported a long black beard, had stopped working and was looking at me. He did not seem hostile or contemptuous of what must, to his eyes, have appeared to be a very downtrodden and helpless waif. In fact, he smiled at me.

"Are you lost, miss?" he asked. His voice was deep and manly.

"I am not sure," I confessed, self-consciously aware of my disheveled appearance. My hand passed ineffectually through the tangles of my unkempt hair. "I thought that this place was my home."

"Your home?" He looked at me.

"Yes, I—I used to live here. Or I think I did. My name is Lee. Annabel Lee."

I saw a dark flicker of recognition in his eyes. "You're of the family that lived here before, are you?"

"Yes, I—but...where is my house?" The words sounded stupid, I realized, but the question was sincere.

He seemed to take pity on me, his expression softening. "It was demolished, Miss Annabel. I am surprised the doctor didn't tell you."

"The doctor? Doctor Blackthorn?"

"Yes, miss. Ordered the house torn down and this replacement built." He looked up at the partially constructed structure. "It's going to be a beauty, miss."

"But—I did not authorize this!"

He looked down. "I don't know anything about that, miss. We're doing what Doctor Blackthorn hired us to do."

"He had no authority to do so!"

"He had all the necessary papers, I believe. I think you'd best talk to Doctor Blackthorn about it."

"Indeed I shall. Do you know where he can be found?"

"You just missed him; he was here only two hours ago. I believe he is at the hospital this afternoon."

"I..." I looked bewilderedly this way and that—at this man, at the wooden pillars of the house, at the ruined fields. I thought of my sister—lost now—lost forever.

"Young lady," said he gently, "would you like something to eat?"

"I—I must talk to Doctor Blackthorn immediately."

"Yes." He nodded. "But, begging your pardon, you look a bit the worse for wear, miss. I have some bread here, and fruit. Let me suggest that you have a bite to eat first, and then I'll see if I can ride you into town myself."

I looked at him gratefully. "You would do that?"

"I will be happy to. But please eat something, miss."

"I have nothing to pay you," I admitted.

"When the time comes that I charge money for food to a hungry child, miss, that's the day I sign my ticket to Hell. Pardon my language, miss."

I did not know how to respond. "I—I can only thank you, sir. May I ask your name?"

"Robert Simpson, that's me. I am in charge of this site."

"Mr. Simpson, I can only express my deepest gratitude to you."

Another man found a bench for me and placed it a safe distance from the ongoing work. My sympathetic friend brought the promised lunch, which included a big tin cup of cool water along with half a loaf of fresh bread and two apples. He excused himself, going back to the work project, while I looked around hopelessly. I had no idea what had occurred or how, but Doctor Blackthorn had not kept his promise.

When I was finished Mr. Simpson invited me onto the back of his horse and we rode at a good pace down into Grimsleytown. In less than twenty minutes we had arrived at the little hamlet of my youth, which appeared unchanged from the last time I had seen it a year before. Mr. Simpson deposited me in front of the little house known as the hospital and tipped his hat to me.

"I hope things work out well for you, Miss Annabel," said he. "Please never hesitate to come to me for anything you need."

"Thank you, sir. I wish you well."

With that he rode off, leaving me standing in front of the hospital house. I stood there for a long time, nerves jumping in my skin. I found myself anxious and angry.

At last I stepped into the house and a young man behind a small desk greeted me with an odd expression on his face. I realized that I must look a fright: hair wildly askew, dirty blanket-shroud over my shoulders.

"Is Doctor Blackthorn here?" I demanded.

"Why, yes," the young man said. "Are you a patient?"

"I am Annabel Lee. The doctor knows me."

This man too registered a flicker of recognition in his eyes. "Of course. If you will just sit—" he gestured to a plain wooden chair—"I will see if the doctor is available."

He disappeared for several minutes, then returned.

"The doctor will see you," said he, and led me back to a consulting room. There, behind an ornate oak desk piled with papers, sat Doctor Blackthorn.

I have said that I had been gone from Grimsleytown for approximately one year. In that time I had certainly undergone many changes; my appearance, I knew, must have been all but unrecognizable to anyone there. And yet my alterations could hardly have been more dramatic than those which Doctor Blackthorn had undergone himself. When he looked up at me I saw that his hair and beard were white and unkempt; his eyes, watery and oddly unfocused, were deeply sunk into his face and undergirded with heavy gray bags. His hands, in which he grasped several papers, were thickly spider-veined and quivered slightly. In the year since I had seen him he seemed to have aged a decade.

"My God," said he, dropping the papers on the desk and standing. His suit hung loosely on his frame; like me, he had lost considerable weight. He came around the desk and put his hands on my shoulders. "I would not have known you, child." I realized that on his breath was the odor of alcohol. I stepped back and his hands fell to his sides. "I received a note," said he, turning toward his desk as if to look for it, but then immediately facing me again. "It said you ran away from the orphanage."

"That is true."

"My God, child, it must be nearly a hundred miles. How did you come here?"

"I walked."

"I..." He looked at me carefully. "All that distance—incredible."

"I asked you for help," said I in a cold voice. "I wrote you again and again."

"Did you? I...Child, sit down. Please sit down." He gestured toward a chair. He moved back behind the desk and sat facing me again. I was tempted to be proud and refuse the offer, but in truth I was very tired. I sat in the chair. "Yes, of course you did," he muttered, as if to himself. "Yes, I received letters from you, I believe."

"You *believe*? Doctor Blackthorn, I wrote to you in the most extreme distress!"

"I—yes, I...I believe I remember. You were unhappy at the orphanage, I think."

"It is a horrible place. They are uncaring and abusive there."

"Yes, well..." He rubbed his jaw with his hand. "Orphanages, you know—they are not luxury hotels, Annabel...."

"Doctor Blackthorn, my best friend *hanged* herself there!"

"Hanged…? My God, that's terrible, yes."

"And you did not help me! You did not even answer my letters!"

"Annabel, I—things have been very difficult here."

"Not more difficult for you than for me, I think."

"I have had some financial setbacks…"

"I regret to hear it."

He looked at me with his rheumy eyes. "So you see it was not that I did not care, Annabel. It was just…many things have gone wrong…"

A thought occurred to me. "You say you have had setbacks, Doctor Blackthorn, yet I have just now come from the building site where you have demolished my home and begun constructing another."

"Yes. I plan to rent or sell it in order to generate more income."

"Why could you have not rented the house as it stood?"

"It was too small and too old, Annabel. A larger house will fetch a far better price."

"Still, you told me that it was *my* house, Doctor Blackthorn. How could you have destroyed my house without so much as consulting me?"

"Well, your house—yes—but all in *trust*, you see, until you reach your majority. Until then I am to make all decisions regarding your monies and property."

"Would not any rental monies from the house—whether the new house or the old—belong to me?"

"Well, of course—upon your majority—"

"Doctor Blackthorn, I think that you are robbing me."

"Child—"

"If it is my property, with all funds to be held in trust until I am an adult, then why is it a concern of yours whether the property gets a good rental price or a poor one? It is not your money, in any event."

"It is my job," said he, eyes darting this way and that, "to do a *responsible* job, to see to it that a maximum yield is attained…"

"Yet building an entirely new house seems extremely

ambitious for a man in such a sorry state as you claim to be."

"Annabel…"

"Doctor Blackthorn, where exactly is my money? How much do I have?"

"Well," said he, "it would require time for me to gather the relevant papers…"

"How much time?"

"Well, perhaps—perhaps a week…"

"A *week*?" I stood. "Doctor Blackthorn, I demand a clear and honest accounting of any and all of my holdings with you right now, at this instant!"

He seemed to shake his head slightly, as if to clear it, and when he spoke again it was with a new resolve. "Child," said he, "it is obvious that you are in a bad way. You have my deepest apologies for not acknowledging your problems at the orphanage. If you dislike it so, you need not return there."

"Return? I would have to be hog-tied and kidnapped to return there!"

"Yes, yes, I—I see." He seemed to consider. "You must understand that there is very little money just now. It is tied up with the new house at the moment."

"I demand what is mine."

"Yes." He looked at me. "It is not exactly yours, as I say, not for some years. But—allow me to help you." He reached into a desk drawer and brought out a small stack of bills. Standing and coming around the desk again, he extended it to me. But as I took it, his other hand reached out and covered mine.

"Annabel," said he, his voice suddenly quieter, "allow me to suggest something."

I slipped the bills into my skirt pocket and tried to pull back, but his hand firmly held my own.

"What is it?" said I.

"Yes, well…I have a thought that might prove satisfactory to both of us."

It distressed me that he would not let go of my hand. I stepped back but he stepped toward me. As he spoke we did a strange sort of forced dance around his office; I moved backward again and again as he moved forward.

"Annabel," said he, his voice stronger now, "a man needs a woman."

"That is not my concern," said I, pulling.

"I have known you since the moment of your birth, remember," said he, excitement distorting his voice to huskiness. "The very moment. I delivered you to this world. What could be—more satisfactory, more *natural*, than you and I forming a—a union?"

I froze. A sensation of horror sliced through me. "What sort of union?"

"Annabel, think of it—if you were to become my wife…"

"Your *wife*?"

"I need a wife, someone to take care of me. You need a home. If we were to form a bond…"

"Doctor Blackthorn, I am thirteen years old!"

"And I am fifty-seven. What of it? There are many such marriages."

"I know of none!"

"You would be surprised, child."

"It—it surely would not be legal!"

"Yes, there is that. But I can easily make adjustments to the relevant documents. We shall make you eighteen and all will be well."

"All will *not* be well!" At last I tore my hand from his. "Doctor Blackthorn, this is grotesque! You are reprehensible!"

"No." He looked down, and to my surprise a small smile played on his withered lips. "I have always had a—a special feeling about you, child. Surely you know that."

And in truth, although I had not realized it until that moment, I *did* know. The little looks he had always given me—the many touches—how his hands would linger on my shoulders or back when giving me a physical examination—the sentimental expression on his face when we talked—I knew all these things, and wondered about them. But I had not understood.

"It is why I sent you away to the orphanage!" he cried suddenly. "With you—with you here—and your parents gone—I could not *trust* myself, do you understand? My love for you—it was too great. But now—it is as if Fate has decreed—"

He looked at me again, an entirely new emotion radiating from his eyes—an emotion which sickened, horrified, and disgusted me. I had on my dress and shoes and blanket-cape yet I felt as naked as I had with that young boy in the barn. I wrapped my arms protectively around my shoulders.

"Child, it grieves me to see you like this," said he, motioning generally at me. "To think of you having gone through such deprivation. You have had a fearful existence of late, and I must be held accountable for part of the blame. But think! With marriage you could move into my house—a roof over your head, a position as my wife, my helpmeet and soulmate with her husband who has always adored, *will* always adore you."

"You are insane," said I, moving slowly to the door.

"My madness is called love," said he, gesturing plaintively. "I have always loved you and always will. Nothing can change that. Whether you love me or no, child, I will be with you always. There is no escape from my love. Marry me, Annabel."

Choking back my revulsion, I ran from the room—from the house—from Grimsleytown.

Later—how much later I know not—I found myself back at the construction site where Doctor Blackthorn's new house, the profits of which I now strongly suspected I would never receive, sat like a vast skeleton in the twilight. The workmen were gone for the day. I walked into the structure, thinking to myself that I was now walking where our family sitting room had been, now our kitchen, now my own bedroom. And here, I thought, here was the very place of Father's library, our countless long talks, our many hours of reading together, our laughter and tenderness. I wondered what had happened to all Father's books. Sold, no doubt, like everything else. I painfully regretted my failure to take some volume or other when I had left the house for the orphanage—how I would treasure our copy of the Bible, or Shakespeare, or Poe's *Tamerlane and Other Poems*! But my feeling was abstracted, because where I was standing might have been anywhere on Earth. Nothing was as it had been; nothing was recognizable. I wandered again to the approximate place where I believed I had constructed the little shrine for my unborn sister, but again I could find no trace of it.

As darkness began to descend, what poor Mary had called "the night-tide" consumed my own soul. I thought myself worthless, or worse—I recalled how the little boy Theodore Jones had called me a whore for undressing before him, despite the fact that it was he himself who made the demand and would have refused me food had I not acquiesced to it; and yet I did now in fact *feel* like a whore after my ghastly interaction with Doctor Blackthorn. His alcohol-besotted eyes hovered before me in the dark, along with his declaration of what he called love. I wrapped my arms around myself again, feeling soiled and unclothed. I found myself wondering if he would physically pursue me. His countenance had been such that I could place no limit on the possibility of what he might do. It would be easy enough, after all. A girl alone, on foot—I would not be difficult to find, surely. And I had come to the very place where he might anticipate that I would come.

Wandering about the building site I found, partly concealed behind some lumber, a small metal storage bin. It was latched shut but not actually locked, and upon my opening it, the bin proved to contain a number of small hand tools along with a torn gray work shirt. Moreover, in a trash can nearby were buried under dirty papers and broken bits of wood the ripped and paint-spattered remains of an old pair of work trousers.

I looked the things over carefully, thinking. I had money now; though I had no doubt that Doctor Blackthorn had kept the greater amount of it for himself, I had sufficient bills in my skirt pockets to feel positively wealthy. This money would allow me to continue for some weeks, certainly, perhaps even months; but where would I go? What would I do? Every possibility seemed closed to me, a young girl alone in the world. I thought about the leering look I had received from Doctor Blackthorn. It was a look I now recognized I had often received from men, but the import of which I had been too innocent to comprehend. I had often been praised as beautiful, and had accepted the compliment with pleasure. But now I found myself oppressed with a different feeling toward the males who said such things: I now began to understand a new motive in these men and their behavior toward me. It seemed to me only a matter of time until some man or other, or group of them, spotted the solitary girl on the road or among the trees—a matter of time until I would be despoiled and made a whore in fact rather than just feeling.

But something seemed to whisper to me as I looked at poor goods before me. The work trousers, in particular, were surely at the end of their useful life, and I imagined a man would wear them only when his wife had taken his better ones for washing; these in my hands held numerous holes, tears, and old patchings. They were quite soiled, and the shirt was hardly better.

My curiosity aroused, I then sifted through the tools, one of which suddenly intrigued me: an old knife with a serrated blade. What its use was on such a site I knew not, but it was there in the bin, its blade slightly bent and quite rusty. I picked the knife and tested it. It was sharp, sharp enough to pierce my heart or throat had I but the courage to drive it home and end myself as Mary had done, and my mother. I stood for a long time in the ripening darkness with the pointed blade of the knife first on the hollow of my throat, then pressed lightly against my chest. I experimented with pressing it harder and harder, finally raising a small bloom of blood that left a tiny, nearly invisible stain on my dark dress. Just a *little* more, I thought—only press a *bit* harder—

I would like to report that a voice came from a cloud, counseling me to avoid self-murder lest I lose my immortal soul; but no such voice came. Nothing did. I simply stood there for a time, reflecting upon my life. Of a sudden, a thought occurred to me—a solution to my various crises that involved something less than my own death. I felt the edge of the blade with my thumb and wondered if I could really do such a thing. By day the thought would have seemed ridiculous, I am sure, but our thoughts are different at night. I stood there in the darkness, considering.

A young girl had walked into Grimsleytown the day before, but out of it the next morning walked a young boy.

What I had done should be fairly obvious to the reader. The workman's clothes ill fit my slender frame, but I managed well enough. It was a strange, constricted feeling, having trouser legs wrapped around my own; looking down at myself, at my well-defined limbs, I felt oddly bare. The shirt was better, though it was made of some scratchy material and smelled heavily of male body odor. Still, as I had as yet no bosom worthy of the name, the illusion here seemed quite satisfactory. As for the knife, suffice it to say that by the time I had finished with it the most obvious evidence of my femininity was strewn over the worksite like corn silk after a mass husking—and, like corn silk, a few light breezes caused it all to quickly tumble away and disappear. I could complete the task but crudely, yet in the end my head was as close-cropped as any boy's. Grim thoughts of my mother's self-cropped locks faded as I felt the night breeze on my scalp and neck, a sensation that was most extraordinary—even sensual in some strange way—shocking but not at all unpleasant.

While I of course had never before worn male garments, I was not unfamiliar in theory with the concept of a girl passing as a member of the other sex. Here was Shakespeare my guide; I remembered Viola in *Twelfth Night*, Rosalind in *As You Like It*, and Portia in *The Merchant of Venice*—comedies all, yet so vivid and well-wrought that it seemed to my youthful imagination such imposture might indeed be capable of being put into practice. For how long I might maintain such a fictional identity, I knew not; but I feared Doctor Blackthorn's rediscovery of me, to say nothing of any agents of Sadmore Place who might still be making their invisible pursuit. I knew that I had to start afresh if I were to survive. I had to become a new person, a *different* person. The "beautiful" Annabel Lee must needs disappear from the face of the Earth, at least for a time, and these were the only means at my disposal. I had no idea if my new persona would prove at all convincing—I was terrified that the first person who saw me would immediately laugh in derision at my attempt. But I had to try.

The costume itself, misfitting though it was, seemed adequate as a start. Poor boys, after all, often wore the hand-me-downs of their elder siblings, and such garments rarely fit properly. My shoes, worn now to the point they were almost falling apart, were identifiably a girl's, but there was nothing I could do about that except to fold the ends of my trousers low to cover them as much as possible until I could procure another pair. I also needed a hat, but could think of no solution to this problem. I did not think that I could cut a convincing one from my old blanket, though I nearly tried. I would just have to find my way to a village—not Grimsleytown—and purchase one as soon as I could.

And so, with great trepidation, I began walking. I made a wide swath through dew-damp meadows—morning approached—keeping myself as far from Grimsleytown as I was able. After I had made my way a considerable distance, I deposited my dress and old blanket as best I could under a large rock, where I felt certain they would not be found; I was far from any established footpaths. I then recommenced my journey, watching as Grimsleytown slowly woke in the dawn and people began dotting its streets, going about their early-morning business. At one point I saw a man on a horse riding up in the direction of the incomplete house I had just recently departed; I could not be completely sure, but from a distance I could make out that he possessed a long white hair and a beard, and I felt sure the rider must be Doctor Blackthorn, determined to locate me. I hastened my steps away from that place, and that man.

Preoccupied as my mind was by the specter of the doctor, it was easy enough to forget my fantastic attire altogether; it was not uncomfortable, really, and no one was near to make me self-conscious. I wondered about my style of walking; was it identifiably that of a girl? It seemed to me that boys used a somewhat more aggressive form of locomotion, pitching their bodies forward in a way unfamiliar to the gentler sex. I had also observed how often boys kept their hands in their pockets. Walking along, I experimented with what seemed to me a manlier way of moving my body. I also tried leaving my hands in my pockets for a time, which created a very strange sensation indeed.

As the sun rose I found myself approaching a wagon trail some distance from town, and there espied a man and woman

with an empty cart drawn by a pair. They were making leisurely progress, and saw me descend from the hill.

"Hello there!" called the man in a friendly tone.

I swallowed, all the anxiety I had not yet felt suddenly rushing over my spirit. Could I really do it? Could I impersonate a
boy—and fool anyone?

There was nothing for it but to wave my hand and answer,
"Good morning." Instinctively I did not attempt to lower the
timbre of my voice; boys who looked my age sometimes had not
yet undergone their adolescent voice-change. "Might I have a
ride in your wagon?"

The man brought the pair to a stop, looking down at me.
He was perhaps forty and had a corncob pipe in his mouth.
His wife was plain and silent. "Where are you headed, young
man?"

Oddly, I had not considered my answer to this question
beforehand, and was left to stammer, "Just—just the next town."
As I stood before them I carefully placed my hands in my pockets again.

"Burl?"

"Yes, do you—do you know how far it is?"

"Sure I do. Seven miles. Wife and I are going there ourselves, for supplies. And to see our daughter. She lives there
with her husband."

"I—I see."

"Jump on, if you've a mind to," the man said, and in a
moment started the horses moving again.

I leapt onto the back of the wagon and pulled myself up. For
a moment I wondered if this friendly man would try to continue our conversation, but to my delighted relief he turned to
his wife and began speaking to her instead. I could not make
out his words, and did not wish to. Settling myself in the far
corner of the wagon, I was suddenly overcome with an exhila-
ration I had never before felt. I wanted to cry out in happiness.
I had succeeded; the old couple in front of me had suspected
nothing; my impersonation had convinced them! I was, to their
certain knowledge, a boy—a boy! And it had been simple—
shockingly simple. It made me wonder, really, what truly was

the difference between boys and girls, other than the obvious anatomical ones. I wondered too if there might not be others like me, girls who for whatever reason donned male costume in order to live a different sort of life with different, wider possibilities. The idea was as outrageous as it was appealing.

But I was getting ahead of myself. Deceiving one harmless old farmer couple was no harbinger of future success; I would have to be careful, on my guard always. I knew that I should speak as little as possible, and meet others' eyes but rarely. And then—the idea suddenly occurred to me—perhaps it was important to not claim any sex for myself at all. Let others look at me, I thought, and form what conclusions they would. If some were unconvinced by my male disguise, what did it matter? The important thing was that no one would easily recognize Annabel Lee, late of Grimsleytown and the Sadmore Place Orphanage for Girls.

My ruminations were interrupted by our arrival at the village of Burl. As we slowed to make our way down the main street, I called my thanks to the farmer couple and leapt off the back of the wagon, quickly putting distance between myself and them; I saw the man wave, and they disappeared down the long street.

In truth, Burl was hardly a village at all; it was really just a handful of buildings including a saloon, a blacksmith's, some sort of government office, and a high-ceilinged general store which no doubt was the main point of commerce in the town. Keeping my head low and trying not to look at anyone, I made my way through the open doorway of the general store and looked first for boys' hats. A smiling, heavyset women behind the counter approached and efficiently helped me, handing over several cheap hats for my inspection; I chose a light gray wool number, more of a cap than a proper hat, but much like what I had seen other boys wearing. I asked about trousers then, and shirts, and shoes. The friendly woman hesitated only once, stopping to ask, "Are you sure you have the money to pay for all this, young man?"

"I have the money," I answered quietly, and brought out a few bills from my pocket to prove it.

From then she was but sweetness and light, asking no further questions. She let me feel certain rough shirts and hold trousers up to myself to see about the fit. When it came to shoes, I told her I was looking for a pair of sturdy boots but did not know what size I might wear. She was patient with me, allowing me to experiment with several pairs until I found what seemed right—I did my best to hide the girl's shoes I was wearing, and fortunately the lady was distracted by other customers while I shopped. At long last I was finished with making my selections, and handed over the money for them. At that point I asked if she might have a room in which I could change into my new clothing and she happily showed me a small chamber nestled away at the back of the store.

One of the notable aspects of this chamber was a looking-glass that virtually covered one entire wall. I pulled away my stolen clothes quickly and pulled on the new things. Trousers were not so strange to me now, and these fit quite well, as did the shirt and cap. The boots were heavy but sturdy and comfortable, and when I finished lacing them I looked up and beheld, for the first time, my new self.

The sight caused me to inhale sharply. I had done well—*very* well; indeed, I could hardly recognize the image that stared back at me. The illusion was sufficiently convincing, I saw, that few if any would ever ask questions. Most strange! The eyes I knew, and the cheekbones and chin; but all had been re-visioned, as it were, like a picture whose whole character seems to change when placed in a different frame. The sight was deeply peculiar and in a way comical, though I was in no manner inclined to laugh. For a single hysterical moment I wanted to tear everything off, forget this masquerade and become my natural female self again; but I instantly realized that I had no way to do this, since the only other things I might wear were those male garments taken from the building site. The idea of returning to the friendly lady at the front of the store and asking for a new collection of clothes which I might try, this time a girl's, was obviously impossible.

And so I would be a boy. I transferred my money to the pockets of my new trousers and, with a sense of resolve, gathered up my old things in my arms and exited the store; as I walked out the woman thanked me for my business, and I told her that she was most welcome for it. Out in the street, which was sparsely populated, I looked for an ash can or other receptacle where I might discard my now-useless first costume. Around a corner I located a black barrel half-filled with rubbish which was ideal for the purpose; I pushed my things down carefully under the rest of the trash, reasoning that, while it was unlikely anyone would ever come looking for them, it was just as well to make them disappear as completely as possible.

With that, I stepped onto the main street again and wandered up and down the thoroughfare for a time, growing accustomed to the clothes and feeling satisfaction that no one seemed to take any notice of me. I kept my hands in my pockets and tried for a time to look masculine, but it quickly became apparent that such playacting was not really necessary. In truth, we none of us really *look* at other people in the street; they pass by as blurs only. I was soon aware that I was no one worth noting here—just a young boy like many others.

After a time I felt sufficiently confident to return to the smiling lady at the general store, this time to purchase an apple and a small loaf of bread. Then I sat on a street corner eating while I contemplated what I would do next. From time to time I looked up and down the street, fearful of Doctor Blackthorn's arrival in the town; but I wondered if he would have any hope of recognizing me—and even if he did, perhaps my radical alteration would prove repugnant to his unholy desires. I had, however, no intention of finding out. I knew that I must move on, and quickly.

But where must I go? It is a strange sensation to have, for the first time in one's life, literally complete freedom. *Annabel Lee* no longer existed; in her place was a new-hatched boy arrived as if by magic, but one without family or friends, with no commitments to any school or job of work or anything else in the world. And, because I had money in my pockets, I had the ability to move freely about. But it was as if I had walked into a restaurant with a limitless repertoire of meals: how was one to even begin to choose?

While reflecting on these matters, it also occurred to me that I would need a name. I initially thought through the entire list of masculine names familiar to me, but soon realized that I had no desire to become a Silas or Horace or Peter. I momently considered Cesaro, Ganymede, or Balthazar, but these Shakespearean antipodes to Viola, Rosalind, and Portia seemed too clever by half. I felt that choosing a name somewhat more in line with my own would be preferable, and quickly arrived at "Andrew" as the nearest analogue to "Annabel." My surname would remain, I decided; it was common enough not to be any strong identifier. "Andrew Lee," then—a good, strong boy's name. I sounded it to myself several times, fitting the sounds, both familiar and unfamiliar, to my mouth. It would do.

Lunch finished, I stood and looked up and down the street. I had to decide on a direction and a plan. I was unencumbered by any responsibilities. I had the world before me—but could I grasp it?

BOOK THREE

To Love and Be Loved

1

I decided that my best course would be to lose myself in crowds. Certainly continuing to wander the rural back roads of Maryland was dangerous, even in my male guise; I knew full well that Doctor Blackthorn sought me, and had no reason to believe that Sadmore Place's agents would have abandoned their search—after all, though it was difficult to believe, I had been gone from that hellish place of misery for less than two weeks. I could easily envisage Doctor Blackthorn raising a ruckus with the orphanage, outraged at the disappearance of his precious young charge—a ruse, of course, to demand that the institution redouble its efforts to find me. Thus it was that I found my way back into the store I had already patronized twice that morning, to ask the friendly lady how one might travel to Baltimore.

She suggested that I stand at the corner of the two main roads in Burl, where carriages sometimes arrived to take on passengers for a fee. This I did, standing for nearly two hours under a clear sky, when a carriage actually did arrive, and I discovered that for a few pennies I might ride it all the way into the city—some twenty miles. Again I was exhilarated, as the mild-mannered old driver never looked twice at me; he simply took my money and allowed me to step into the carriage, which as it happened was otherwise unoccupied. What luxury! For the first ten miles I had the vehicle entirely to myself, opening the window and breathing the lovely fresh air, delighted at the fast progress we made. Eventually we did stop to pick up two others, a young man and young woman, and for a moment this caused me anxiety; but it quickly became apparent that they were newly married, and had no interest whatsoever in the young boy sitting across from them except insofar as his presence forced them to behave with a certain decorum.

I had never been to Baltimore. Indeed, I had never been in any true city, and thus had little idea of what to expect. Books I had read generally presented the urban metropolis as a place of tall buildings, glittering facades and elegant, sophisticated people. I pictured myself alighting on the busiest street of the city, confidently striding into the most beautiful hotel, demanding and receiving the finest suite in the establishment. And yet I remembered too the stories I had heard from Mother: of life in the slums of Hell's Kitchen with its filthy people, trash in the streets, and her "miserable hovel on a miserable street in a miserable neighborhood." Still, I reasoned, I had money, and that would surely indemnify me against the worst of the city's poverty until I might find suitable employment. Employment at what, however? I had no skills anyone might be likely to want to pay for. When I considered these things, my view of my future in the city of Baltimore darkened considerably.

But the carriage eventually stopped and the young couple stepped out, moving quickly down the street and disappearing around a corner—clearly they knew where they were going. I sat there for a moment, unsure whether I should ask to be deposited somewhere else in the city, but in truth I had no idea where I should ask to go. Finally I just stepped from the carriage and it pulled away, leaving me standing there on a wooden plank walkway.

I looked around. It was mid-afternoon; the scene was a busy and heavily populated one. I had, in fact, never seen so many people packed together in such a small space. Men, women and children all rushed to and fro as if certain of their destinations, while I stood stupidly bewildered. It seemed to me that the neighborhood I was in was quite squalid, with dirty brick buildings looming over me on all sides whose bricks were cracked and crumbling and whose windows were often so dirty as to be completely opaque. Carriages careened heedlessly by in both directions. Confusion seemed everywhere. The *volume* was extraordinary—so much talking, so much shouting, so much coarse vulgarity—words I had never heard spoken aloud bellowed proudly from the mouths of men, and even children!—and the *stench* literally breathtaking. My nostrils had never before encountered such a vile, nauseating combination of rotten food, festering animal deposits, and I-knew-not-what other execrable odors; it made my stomach turn dangerously, and for a moment I thought I would suffer the humiliation of vomiting in the street. Passersby ignored me, pushing me rudely this way and that, as if I were no more than a sack of vegetables in their path. I was surrounded by people—loud, vulgar, ill-mannered people—but had never—not after Father's death or Mother's, nor when I beheld my sister's bloody body on our kitchen floor, nor while in isolation at Sadmore Place, nor even when I beheld poor Mary Mahoney lifeless and dangling in mid-air, *never* had I felt so alone, so melancholy, so hopeless, as I did at that moment. My life seemed, so to say, *over*; I had somehow paid for my transit directly to Hell.

I had to make some sort of move, so I chose a direction at random and began walking slowly, staying to the dirty plank walkway so as to avoid the traffic as well as the enormous amount of horse dung everywhere in the street. I noticed that the farther I walked, the more I began to see commercial businesses of a sort—a busy blacksmith's, a dark and mostly empty tailor's shop, a fruit and vegetable establishment selling soft, gray produce vile and inedible in appearance. I spent hours wandering a few city blocks, walking roughly in circles so as not to lose my bearings—though what difference that made I knew not, since I had no real idea where I was and one place was much like another as a result. Still, it gave me some small peace of mind to be able to identify the corner where I had been dropped off each time as I passed it by. The world had some sort of balance then, some sort of orientating structure.

I knew that I had to decide what to do. The idea of renting a room in a grand hotel now seemed naïve; if there were grand hotels in the city of Baltimore they were certainly nowhere near the district in which I found myself, and I was too afraid of everyone around me to consider asking. Occasionally on a side street I would see a sign outside a residence indicating a room to let; but these places were, all of them, so dismal of aspect, so

squalid and depressing to behold, that I could not bring myself
to even approach any of them, let alone imagine what their
interior rooms must be like. Everywhere were people, poor people wearing little more than rags, their faces covered at times
with horrible rashes or boils or other evidence of sickness. All
of them, women and idle men, appeared malnourished; but it
was the children who struck closest to my heart, little stick-fig-
ure girls and boys running barefoot in the disgustingly filthy
streets desperately in need of bathing, proper clothing, decent
food; some of the youngest ones were entirely naked, frolicking
in the dirt, covered with it and even putting it in their mouths.
I remembered the lovely, graceful meadows of my own early
childhood—my looking out from my chair in the little alcove,
book in hand, hot tea on the table beside me—and was overcome with a sensation of horror.

As if to complete my memory of that childhood scene and
its profound contrast with the city vision before me now, it
began suddenly to rain. I had been so preoccupied that I had
failed to notice the gathering clouds. Uncertain what to do, I
watched as others ducked under awnings or into doorways, and
resolved to do the same. Stepping quickly away, I soon found
myself at the entrance to an alley which was partly protected
from the downpour by the overhanging roof of the building
several floors above. Pressing myself against the grimy brick
wall, I looked around and saw only trash cans, some overflow-
ing, along with some broken lumber and shattered glass on
the ground. The sky had grown very dark and, while I could
not be sure, I believed that I saw movement in the can directly
opposite me. Such movement, I suspected, could only be caused
by rats, and again I recoiled, aghast. Perhaps I would return,
I thought—find a carriage and return, if not to Grimsleytown,
then at least Burl—safe in my disguise, it was possible that I
would never be recognized; I could obtain employment somewhere, I could spend time with the nice lady I had met at the
general store where I had bought my things, I could live a real
life, a *human* life, not the kind of nightmare existence trapping
me now like a terrible spider's web. I had no choice; a few hours
of this urban Gehenna were all I could withstand. I determined

that when the rain cleared I would buck up my courage and ask some shopkeeper how I could travel back whence I came.

"Well, *hello.*"

I gasped. Lost in my reflections, I had failed to notice a black shape moving toward me in the darkness of the alley. I froze in terror at the voice. It was that of a boy, and something in the tone warned me immediately that I was in danger. And yet, for just a moment, I relaxed slightly; the boy, wet from the rain, moved toward me, and I saw that I was in fact taller than he. Yet that comfort was short-lived as I saw in the dimness his grubby street clothes and insolent expression. He had a small, mocking smile on his greasy and pockmarked face. His hands were casually in his pockets, but I sensed that there was nothing casual about him.

"I said hello," he repeated, more insistently this time.

I had to swallow twice before I was able to respond quietly, "Hello."

He looked me up and down. "Ain't seen you 'round here."

I could not speak.

"I said, *ain't seen you 'round here.*"

"No, I—I arrived—I arrived today."

"Yeah? From where?"

"I—from…" I did not want to tell him, but could think of nothing else to say. "From Grimsleytown."

He scowled. "Where's that?"

"It's—not far." Though it was, in truth, a world so different from this as to be on another planet entirely.

"What's your name?"

"It's—Andrew."

"Well, Andrew, it's right nice to know you. Sure it is. We love strangers around here, Andrew. We like to welcome 'em in a—in a *special* way."

He reached out then, impertinently touching my shirt. I had to remind myself that I was a boy now, not a girl. To reveal my true sex seemed to invite catastrophe. At least if he thought I was a boy, he might think twice before interfering with me.

But suddenly his hand moved up and he pulled my cap violently down on my head, covering my eyes, and I was pushed against the garbage can next to me, nearly falling. It took me a moment to right my cap and in that moment my distress increased a thousandfold, for I heard laughter—not just this ruffian's, but the laughter of several boys. By the time I had regained my balance two additional villains had appeared behind my original tormentor. Both were approximately his size, though I could see neither clearly in the darkness.

"What'd you bring with you from that—what'd you call it? Grimsleytown?" demanded the first boy.

"Bring with me? What do you mean?"

"Come on, Charlie," said one of the boys in back. "Let's get to it."

"What I mean is," said he with elaborate mock courtesy, "did you bring any nice foodstuffs or anything like that? What you got under them nice clothes?"

Even in this moment of extreme crisis I managed to note that Charlie would be surprised indeed to discover what I had under my nice clothes. But I managed to say, "Nothing. I don't have anything."

"Nothin'? You mean to tell me an' my pals here that you came all the way from good ol' Grimsleytown without nothin' at all for Charlie an' the boys? Now, do you call that neighborly? You mean to tell us you ain't got so much as a penny on you? See, me an' the boys—we like pennies. Lots of 'em."

I felt as if I were drowning in this darkness—this rain—this terror. "I—I have nothing."

Charlie shook his head. "We don't like liars, do we, boys?"

"Nope, not a bit," said one of them in back.

Charlie leaned close to me. I could smell his foul breath. "Know what we do to liars, Mr. Andrew from Grimsleytown?"

At that moment I knew nothing could save me from disaster, so I screamed, "*Help! Help!*" and tried to run up the alley to the street. They caught me almost immediately, pulling me down into the mud. I kept screaming until someone struck me directly in the stomach and an excruciating agony suffused my entire body even as all my breath left me in a dreadful rush. My cheek was hit then, and my chest, whilst at the same time I felt hands rummaging all over my person, rifling my pockets.

I tried to cover the pocket which held my money but my hand was swatted away as easily as one would swat a fly. I felt fingers roughly pulling the bills out and one of them, I believe it was Charlie, cried, "Jesus, would you look at this! Boys, we hit a gold mine!" Suddenly they seemed to all but forget about the collapsed figure in the mud—the figure that was myself—as they leapt up, whooping and dancing in the rain. "See, Andrew from Grimsleytown," laughed Charlie, "I knew you weren't so bad as all that! I knew you'd brung somethin' for us! Thanks a lot, pal!" And with that, I saw him aim his grimy shoe, his foot sailing toward my head. In a moment I was lost not just in the city darkness, but in my own.

"You awake, young fellow?"

The voice came to me from a far distance. There was a blinding pain in my stomach, another in my head. My chest hurt as well, making it difficult to breathe.

"Yes," I whispered. My throat was in pain. "I think so."

I opened my eyes slowly. I was still in the alley, but the rain had passed and I could see a strip of cloudy blue sky far above me. Crouched over me was a man with a large walrus mustache wearing a dark uniform and narrow-brimmed hat of some sort.

"Can you sit up? Take it easy now."

The man gently helped me to attain a sitting position.

"I'm Constable Barry," said he. "Looks like you've been roughed up, young man."

"Yes," I whispered.

"What happened to you?"

I offered him a brief summary of recent events.

He shook his head. "This area is no place for a newcomer, especially one dressed so well as you." He looked at me carefully. "You're lucky they didn't take your clothes. They do, these hooligans. I've seen men left in alleys naked as jaybirds."

"I am lucky," I agreed, not without some irony. I stood slowly, my balance uncertain.

"Did they take anything of value from you?"

Again I considered. If I told him how much money the boys had robbed me of, this constable might be inclined to pursue the matter. "No…just a few pennies. It's of no importance."

"Do you want to file a report? Not that it would do much good, I'm afraid. This is a lawless place…" He hesitated. "What is your name?"

My brain was sufficiently muddled that I nearly offered the true answer, but I caught myself in time. "Andrew," said I. "Andrew Lee."

"Well, Andrew, would you like to file a report on this?"

I considered. Spending time in a police station seemed a very bad idea to me. "No. No report is necessary. I am fine."

"Well, it's as you wish. As I say, you're lucky you're not naked."

"Very lucky. Thank you, constable."

"Yes, well." He leaned down suddenly, picked up something. "Look," said he, smiling slightly. "They even left your hat, and it's only a little dirty." He brushed it with his palm and handed it to me.

"Wonderful. Thank you," said I, taking it and replacing it upon my head.

"You're sure you're all right? No report, you say? What about the hospital?"

"I am all right, Constable Barry."

"Can you make it home? Do you live nearby?"

"Yes, just around the corner there," said I, gesturing vaguely. "A block or two."

He shook his head. "Terrible place, this."

"Yes, terrible."

"Well, good day to you." After writing something quickly in a small book, the constable turned and walked away.

I was at that moment in too much pain to feel fear. I walked in a daze out of the alley and up the street. It occurred to me to check my pockets, but I knew all too well what I would find there—nothing. Charlie and his friends had left me completely penniless.

I must have looked like a staggering drunk in the ensuing hours. I noticed passersby giving me a wide berth as I made my way directionlessly along the street. At one point I passed some sort of shop with a plate glass window in which I could see a reflection of myself: I was scuffed and bruised, and there was a nasty gash on my forehead, but on the whole I looked far better than I felt. I sat on a street corner for a time, people moving hither and thither everywhere around me. I held my head in my hands, blotting out the scene, and wishing I could somehow undo the past day—magically reverse my decision to have ever come to this horrible city. In my mind I asked God to take me away, back to Burl or Grimsleytown or even Sadmore Place—anywhere. But when I opened my eyes I was still on the same feculent street corner, still utterly without hope.

The following days are dim in my memory, if not entirely black. My body's wounds healed for the most part across the span of the next day or two, but the wounds to my spirit proved more profound and of longer duration. I wandered restlessly and endlessly, having no place I might rest. My wanderings took me briefly to the handsomer sections of the city which, while not quite as beautifully breathtaking as I had imagined, were nonetheless stately and handsome—on North Calvert Street (I quickly began to recognize street names) I remember standing in front of Barnum's Hotel, imagining how different my fate in the city might have been had the carriage which brought me here deposited me before this tall, majestic establishment surrounded by respectable businesses and well-dressed, civilized people. I spent time wandering in the large, lovely park at Franklin Square too, and studying the many handsome stones at the Western Burying Grounds. These reminded me that I had never yet beheld the gravestones of either of my parents—but there was nothing I could do about that now.

But the majority of my time during the day was spent, alas, in attempting to obtain food. Without money, I was reduced to begging; yet I was too shy to be especially effective at this. Sometimes I might meet the eye of a particularly gentle-looking lady and ask, "Please, ma'am, a penny, ma'am?" and occasionally such a woman would deign to hand me a coin that would allow me to eat for the day. But constables in the more affluent sections of the city were fierce toward panhandlers, even those as young as myself, and I was quickly chased away from the more desirable locations. The only places one could really ply the trade, I discovered, were the very ones that held no persons with any substantial money—the same slum neighborhoods I had first encountered.

It became apparent that the best way of securing food, far more efficient than begging, was stealing. I watched other street urchins—keeping my distance from them—and studied their techniques. The easiest thing was to loiter not far from a fruit vendor or greengrocer. At times their wares fell naturally out of the sidewalk display baskets and bins containing them, and it was an easy matter to happen by and pick up a stray apple or radish—at times the vendor himself would not even have noticed that the item had dropped out of the container, and so the incident was completely trouble-free and hardly theft at all. These vendors were on the whole quite vigilant, however, and sometimes a pair of boys might work in concert—one distracting the man while the other pocketed, with lightning speed, several pieces of fruit. The two would then dash of in opposite directions, no doubt to meet up again at some prearranged location to divide their spoils.

I would like to say a word here about these children. While many adults, secure in their homes and enjoying comfortable incomes, viewed them as mere criminals—some even claim for them a kind of moral degeneracy—what I witnessed at that time, and in which I in fact participated, had little to do with morals, ethics, or indeed the law itself. It was a matter, simply put, of hunger. These children had no homes, or, if they did, they were certain to be dismal places of poverty and pain; rather than judging the children, as society is wont to do, it seemed to me that respectable, law-abiding citizens should pity them and organize programs to help them. I saw little such help, however, in my days on the streets of the city of Baltimore.

What I have described thus far are my days, as far as I recall them. Nights were something quite different, and far more frightful. The child without a home is at the mercy not only of the elements, but of everything and everyone around him. Sleep is rarely effectuated successfully; like a stray dog or cat, such children must always be keenly aware of their surroundings

and any potential threats. As a result, the street child is perpetually exhausted and dull of thought. As best I remember,
I hardly slept at all in my weeks in the city. Terrified of the
utter, obliterating darkness of the streets, I would find myself
some narrow crevice or doorway somewhere and hide in it,
the hours passing with terrible slowness, my senses always on
alert. Stray cats, it seems to me, must live in much the same
way.

This situation of endless roaming and searching for food
by day while hiding somewhere at night might have continued
unabated had not a man espied me late on just such a night,
huddling in a doorway just off a narrow alleyway. The man
was by himself, walking slowly and seemingly not too certain
in his step—I wondered if he was tispy. He wore a worker's
plain cap along with a flannel shirt and denim trousers, looking every inch what I suspect that he was, a manual laborer.
The weather was warm; he had no coat. Where I was hiding
was not a well-traveled end of the street, and so few people
walked by at such an hour—it must have been past midnight.
The only light was provided by a half-moon in the clear sky
over us.

Upon noticing my figure in the doorway, he stopped. This
immediately caused fear to suffuse my soul; this man was
notably larger than I, and if he chose to attack me, there would
be little I could do about it. And yet I did not get the sense of
aggression from him. He looked at me from a distance of several feet, his expression curious. He had large dark eyes, a big
flat nose, and a short beard which was somewhat unkempt. I
judged his age to be about thirty.

"Good evening," said he, his voice quiet and gentle.

I desperately wanted to melt into the brick wall behind me.
Terrible memories of the boys who had robbed me flashed in
my brain. "Good—good evening," said I at last.

The man looked up at the sky, then down at me again. "It's
a pleasant night."

"It is, yes."

He leaned toward me. I could smell beer on his breath. "Do
you live near here?" said he.

"Yes, I—No."

He smiled. I realized that his eyes were bleary and unfocused. "Is it yes or is it no?"

"I do not live near here, sir."

"'Sir.'" He chuckled. "What are you doing out here?"

"I am doing nothing."

"Why don't you go home, then?"

I could not see how the truth would be any worse for me than a lie, so I said: "I have no home."

He cocked his head, studying me in the darkness.

"Sir," I managed to say, "I have no money. I have nothing at all. Please don't hurt me."

"Hurt you?" He chuckled again. "I ain't going to hurt anybody."

We stood there in the dark. His eyes made me uncomfortable.

"I have another idea," said he, smiling again.

"What idea?"

"Well," said he, "we could step into the alley here. Just the two of us."

"Sir?"

"I'll pay you." And with that he brought two coins from his pocket. They gleamed in the moonlight.

"Sir, I am not sure I understand."

"Oh, come on. Surely you do. Only take a few minutes."

I understood then. My memory flashed on the stories of my mother, of a certain vile method of obtaining money. And yet I found myself confused.

"Sir," I said, stepping forward enough so that the light shone on my face, "I am a boy."

At that he actually laughed. "I'm well aware of that!"

Utterly perplexed, and yet in dire need of the coins he had shown me, I asked, "You wish to do with me as...as a man would do with a girl?"

"I knew you understood." He nodded.

"Are you—are you sure?" I could not fit my mind around the concept. And yet I felt a desperate hunger for the coins I had been shown.

"Very sure."

"I—" My heart was crashing. "I...sir, I...I will not remove my clothes."

"Well, who asked you to? We'll keep it simple."

"And you will pay me?"

"Here." He reached into his pocket and placed a coin in my palm. "That's to show my good will. There's another like it if you'll join me in the alleyway for only a few minutes." His voice, I noticed, had grown husky, his eyes soft.

"V-very well," said I, my voice trembling with uncertainty.

With that, the bargain was made.

Decency forbids me from describing further what occurred between this man and myself. Suffice it to say that I was not called upon to remove my clothes, and that he lived up to his word regarding the second coin. As for the act itself, it was— what other way is there to put it?—sloppy and disgusting.

The reader might wonder at this point whether I felt, as a result of this sordid encounter, as if I had become the proverbial "fallen woman." Did I feel evil enter into my heart? Did I discover myself to be an insatiable sexual vampire, from then on ever hunting for deeper and more depraved carnal pleasures? Did my soul pass over to some murky and malevolent dark side populated by supernatural creatures of detestable loathsomeness? The answer to all these questions is an emphatic "No!" Such encounters are the least likely way imaginable toward a road of nymphomaniacal passions; in fact they are sad and pathetic, and for a time after the workingman with the coins disappeared down the street I found myself feeling little but pity for him. It is true, however, that once a step has been taken down this particular path—the path of earning one's income through such encounters—it is difficult to turn back; the encounters themselves are the furthest thing to be imagined from enjoyable—indeed they are revolting—but they are short-lived and pay, for the time involved, admirably well. They represent nearly the only services a young person in an unknown city without family or friends or recognizable job skills can perform for money at all. That a lost, homeless child in a city of strangers will eventually enter into the life is almost inevitable, and I acknowledge without shame, or at any rate with very little, that I succumbed to it as well. I became, in fact, a whore, just as young Theodore Jones had called me in his father's barn after I disrobed at his insistence.

I lived this way for many months. Growing surer of myself in terms of streets and neighborhoods, I also learned to read both my fellow street children and my prospective customers quite accurately. I would not say that I gained any friends among my young peers, but I was able to encounter several boys and even a girl or two without the threat of danger. At times we actually helped each other, advising one another of likely places to find food or even a vacant room in some tumbledown building where we might sleep, three or four of us together on the floor, for a day or two, until the landlord discovered us and ran us off. Experienced children of this *milieu* are largely nocturnal creatures, plying our trades of bodily favors or theft (I rarely engaged in this, and never in anything so crude as street robbery) under blanket of darkness. The food we took from vendors was taken generally in the early morning or late evening. During the day we slept, or tried to, wherever we could.

As for the men, it is difficult to find a single category to fit them. There were young ones and old, poor ones and rich. Some wanted to talk while others wanted only the exchange itself to occur, and as quickly as possible. All were furtive and nervous, though some went to great pains to hide the fact; and after all, though enforcement seemed extremely lax in those days, the encounters were in fact illegal, and a man arrested for such activities risked his employment and perhaps his marriage. Certainly he would suffer embarrassment and humiliation. Yet, just as it is tempting for some to dismiss all street children who solicit for customers as morally depraved, others consider the men who hire them to be little more than degenerates. I am inclined to a broader view. I did indeed suffer several unhappy encounters with men who, once they had me alone in a hidden-away place, became violent and attempted certain unspeakable acts, but, unsavory as such meetings were, they represented only a small minority of cases. Most men, as I say, were uncertain of themselves and uncomfortable in the situation, and so tended to ask for little and then overpay for what they had received, in part as a method of trying to ensure my silence about the event afterward. And in all the months I worked the streets, no one ever recognized my true sex. Once or twice there were customers who seemed to look at me queerly, and I remember one who called me a "pretty young thing" in a tone that made me wonder if he suspected, but I was never unmasked.

During this period my fourteenth birthday passed and I found myself distant indeed from all that had happened before. I could hardly visualize the little house outside Grimsleytown, my father and I in his library reading Scripture or Shakespeare or *Tamerlane*, the meadows outside, our long walks—it was nearly as if this had all occurred to a different person entirely. As for my mother's death and my sister's, they were like dark dreams in my mind, and the orphanage like a place out of a frightening storybook. Yet I knew that these people and places were quite real. I knew even that I still faced potential danger from both the agents of Sadmore Place and Doctor Blackthorn, though how anyone would find me now was difficult to imagine. I was completely unrecognizable from the girl who had been Annabel Lee—not only because of my hair and clothes, but because of the marks that months of life on the streets had branded onto me. Studying myself in the glass of a store window, I saw how my eyes were different—harder, more knowing, their innocence lost—and how my lips were thinner and took a harder cast than before. My skin was rougher now, and my entire manner of carrying myself quite unlike that of the gentle, naïve girl who had once sipped tea and read books on rainy afternoons in the alcove of her pleasant home in the countryside. Yet nightmares bothered me at times—nightmares of huge male hands suddenly descending on me, taking me by the shoulder or forearm, and a hard deep voice announcing, "We have found you at last, Annabel Lee!" At times in such dreams I would look up and see, titanically larger than life, the white hair, patchy beard, and liquid eyes of Doctor Blackthorn looming over me, his hands roaming roughly over my body, his voice heavy with morbid passion as he told me what he wanted us to do together, and I would be unable to extricate myself from his vile caresses. From such dreams I would wake with a start, shrieking.

But an end came to my life on the streets. It happened in the following manner.

One night a heavyset man approached me where I stood in the recess of an old stone building, the darkness hiding me to all but those who would specifically seek one such as myself. I have said that the man was heavyset, but this hardly describes his physique—in fact he was enormously fat, his face like a blown-up balloon, the features all but lost therein, and his suit—it a very light powder-blue color which was far brighter than what most men would wear—bulging grotesquely in odd places. He walked slowly and before he even drew very near I could hear his breath wheezing from his mouth. It might be thought that such a person would be too repellant to even consider as a customer, but what I saw was less his physical self and more his semi-formal attire and the money that had surely been spent to acquire it. The man did not look rich, but neither was he poor, and he certainly looked as if he could afford to be generous in arranging for the satisfaction of his desires with me. In this I was not disappointed. He approached me as someone who had entered into such discussions before, calling me "a fine-looking young gentleman" in a surprisingly high-pitched voice, and we quickly agreed on terms. (I was making more money now as a result of my willingness to perform certain additional services, though still nothing involving the removal of my clothing.) Stepping into an alley that was roughly halfway up the street, I leaned against the brick wall while he disarranged his trousers so as to ready himself. Moving to him then, I began my usual performance, my mind drifting as it inevitably did to other places and times far away, when I was suddenly aware that the corpulent man had begun shaking and gasping, but not in the usual manner of such encounters. Pulling quickly away, I looked at him. His face had turned frighteningly dark—what color it was I could not tell in the night, but it was surely very different than it had been moments before—and he began clutching at his collar, ripping at the buttons in an apparent effort to loosen its grip around his neck. I stood frozen, wide-eyed; and

I confess that I did nothing to help him. He shook violently for perhaps half a minute, then collapsed in a monumental heap next to an ash can.

I was immediately aware that all the sounds he had been making had ceased. Leaning toward him, but not too close, I looked at his mottled face. The eyes were open but glassy and unblinking. The mouth gaped; saliva trickled from it. I stared at his chest and shoulders for a time, but could detect no movement whatever. The man was dead.

I acted then without thinking. Knowing that it was in my best interest to get far away from this man—this *corpse*—as quickly as possible, I nonetheless recognized that it would take only a moment to rifle his pockets. This I did, pulling from them a variety of bills, a few coins, and a watch which, after it gave me a moment's trouble, I rudely ripped from its chain.

Then I ran off into the darkness.

As the dawn broke on a bracingly cool and clear autumn morning, I walked restlessly from one street to another. I had no direction in mind; no goal; I merely feared the sudden specter of Death I had seen—perhaps my services had even hastened its arrival for the man?—as well as the monies in my pockets. I had seen dead persons before, as the reader well knows, but I had never robbed one, and the feeling was somehow both exhilarating and terrifying: exhilarating because it was a robbery utterly without witnesses, a situation dropped suddenly into my lap from which I could hardly but benefit, yet terrifying also—if I were caught, would they know I had stolen from a corpse? Would the police accuse me of murdering the man? And what— I wondered this too—what would God say of a girl who would rifle the pockets of a dead man and run off with her ghoulish ill-gotten gains?

I was careful in those hours not to bring any of the money out of my own pockets lest I be noticed carrying such a huge and unlikely sum—I did not know how much it was, but I knew it was a fistful of bills, and even if they all proved to be of the smallest denomination the amount would still be very considerable. There were coins, too—I believed I had seen in my rushed thievery that at least two of them were gold—and the watch, the potential value of which I could not even imagine. In one magnificent stroke of luck I had surely gained back all that had been stolen from me when I had first arrived in Baltimore, and possibly much more. It concerned me that my luck had been dependent on another's catastrophe, but after all, I reasoned, in this slum neighborhood the man's body would no doubt have been quickly found anyway, and someone else—some cutthroat robber or half-starved child—would have done exactly as I had. I remembered what the constable had told me after I had been victimized myself, and wondered if the corpse of the fat man had by now been stripped of its fine clothes and left naked in the darkness of the alley.

I was not long in my wondering. Turning up an unfamiliar street, I saw an establishment which, with its outer decoration of three golden spheres suspended over a golden bar, I knew to be a pawnshop. I had never visited such a business, but understood that their owners would purchase items of value for resale. As I stood across the street, looking at the various wares in the shopkeeper's window, I was astonished to see a young man in an inexpensive suit and bowler hat walk into the place carrying in his arms what I immediately recognized as the huge powder-blue suitcoat and trousers of the dead man!

Fascinated, I loitered about on the street, hoping to be able to view the transaction unfolding inside. Alas, I could see nothing past the big painted words "FINKELSTEIN PAWN BROKERS. BUY AND SELL." and the many musical instruments, tools, and gewgaws suspended in the display window; however, after only a few minutes the man in the bowler hat emerged again, a distinctly satisfied smile on his face, *sans* the dead man's suit. He had obviously sold it to the pawnbroker, though I wondered how that businessman might resell such an enormous item of clothing—perhaps, I reasoned, he purchased it for the fine material merely.

In any event, it was clear to me that I could transform the man's watch, which was far too opulent for a street child to risk carrying on her person, into cash. Feeling confident— had I not just witnessed the successful completion of such a transaction?—I crossed the street and stepped through the door into the shop. The Jewish man behind the counter (he had the long beard and Hasidic clothing of one of that faith), who was just putting away the suit on a shelf behind him, looked at me with, I thought, some suspicion in his eyes. No doubt it was obvious I was a street child, and he believed that I had entered to steal something. He greeted me politely enough, however, and, bringing the watch from my pocket, I was encouraged to approach the counter.

"Would you purchase this watch, sir?" I asked.

He looked at me for a long moment, distrust filling his narrowed eyes. He took the watch in his hands and studied it carefully.

"Vere did you get dis?" asked he, in an accent suggesting that the man's roots had been pulled up from some soil very far away indeed.

I stared at him. Stupidly, I had not considered that a pawn-broker might ask any questions regarding an item's provenance; I thought only that he would offer me money for the watch. As the he revolved the device in his hand, I saw that it was fancy indeed—its shell appeared to be gold, with intricate shapes of fauns carved delicately into it. It was not a watch that such as I could have obtained through any legitimate means, certainly. I saw all this as I stood there, a sinking sensation in my stomach.

The pawnbroker held up the watch chain, which I had ripped off in my rush to get away from the dead man. He studied the broken end. Glancing at me, he said simply, "Interesting."

"Sir," said I, desperate to escape, "I have decided not to sell the watch. If you will just hand it back to me—"

"And look here," said he, holding the watch close to his eyes. "It appears dat dere is an inscription. Your name, no doubt? Let us see." He brought a pair of *pince-nez* from his coat pocket and placed them on the bridge of his nose. "'Edvard Filbert Stockton,'" he read. He looked at me again. "Dat is you?"

"Yes—yes, sir. Please..."

Suddenly he scowled, dropping the watch into his own pocket. "You leetle thief!" he shouted. "I vill have the police on you! *Help!*" he shouted as I turned and ran, careening through the door and out into the street as the man's voice followed accusingly, *"Help! Police! Thief! Stop dat boy! Stop him, I say!"* The world blurred: I hurtled pell-mell through the streets, past pedestrians, in front of carriages, blindly, breathlessly. A glance back told me that the pawnbroker in his dark garb was running after me at an absurd speed, as if he were an athlete of some sort. There was some shouting and a constable joined the chase. I knew I must fly! I redoubled my efforts, straining my muscles to their limit, and felt strangely as if the entire world were pursuing me—not just the pawnbroker and the constable but Doctor Blackthorn and the agents of Sadmore Place and the less savory men I had entertained in alleyways, all of them converging on one young girl in her urgent effort to survive.

Rounding a corner, slipping and nearly falling, I headed toward a scene which for a moment I did not comprehend. In an alley there stood a horse, a large brown mare, being held by a boy with the reins in his hand. A man in a black suit was standing before the horse and the boy—no, there was another boy there as well, perhaps two more—and the man appeared to be counting out money in his hand. Surely this alley was a strange location for such a transaction! And yet in an instant it was clear to me—I had seen such things before—the horse had almost certainly been stolen, no doubt by these boys, and the man was making an illegal, so-called black-market purchase. The actors in this particular drama looked up as one as I hurtled into the alley, closely pursued by the constable and shouting pawnbroker. At the sight of the law officer all of them scattered like insects, buyer and sellers both, leaving the horse where she stood.

Desperate chance! I had not ridden in some time, but I rushed to the horse and mounted her—mounted not sidesaddle but astride, a decision I made instantaneously given the saddle perched on the beast but which was also, of course, perfectly appropriate for the boy I allegedly was. One of the thieves attempted momentarily to halt my progress, and glaring down at him I realized with shock, yet also a certain mad hilarity, that the sneering, pockmarked boy was *Charlie*, the one who had led the assault on me in another alley all those many months before! I gifted my nemesis with a boot delivered solidly to his forehead which caused his cap to tumble from his head and land on the ground as he cried out, *"Blast it!"* In the confusion the horse reared up and neighed in startled complaint, nearly spilling me to the ground; yet my equestrian experience told. Pulling the beast's reins savagely, I turned her around and, kicking her with all my might, drove her forward in the direction of my pursuers, who jumped away to either side of the alley. I hardly saw them as I flew out into the road, passersby recoiling in shock as I aimed the beast up Aisquith Street and we soared like some wild runaway carriage away from that neighborhood, away from that terrible city, away, away!

2

I did not realize it in those last frantic minutes, but my life was about to undergo yet another dramatic change. There was no chance of my returning to Baltimore City; I was a wanted criminal now, what with the theft and attempted pawning of the watch—no doubt the authorities would eventually connect said watch, with its owner's inscription, to the corpulent body in the alley, and I would become a suspect not only in the robbery (of which I was admittedly guilty) but in his death, a death *I* knew to have been quite natural, but how would I convince anyone else? They might argue that I had lured him into that alley and proceeded to beat him—I had little doubt his body had suffered some bruises in its heavy final fall, bruises that might conceivably be blamed on an assailant. Then there was the issue of the horse—a mild and quite calm beast, well-trained, surely a prized possession of someone. How would I convince anyone that, while it was true that I did steal the animal, I stole it only from *other thieves*—that I was not, so to say, the originator of the crime? And would that make any difference? Obviously if Charlie and his henchman were ever apprehended they would deny all. I could prove nothing. Thus it was that, in the eyes of the law, I was a horse thief, a stealer of watches, and a corpse-looter (or even murderer). If I were to be caught, surely my life as a streetwalker would be exposed as well. I pictured myself thrown bodily into Baltimore's City Jail, a repugnant brick structure whose fetid cells and violent inmates had been described to me in the most vivid terms by some of my young street cohorts who at various times had been held there. Mixing children with hardened adult criminals seemed exceptionally ill-advised in itself, but—the idea struck me with the force of a hammer blow—what would happen when those criminals discovered my true sex? I would have to reveal the truth earlier, surely; but the notion of being unmasked brought back to my mind the dark agents of Sadmore Place and the abhorred attentions of Doctor Blackthorn. There seemed no good options for me.

And so I rode. Once I had exited the city proper I slowed the beast to a good trot and, staying well away from main roads, followed the line of the Chesapeake Bay north. I had no destination in mind; I had no goal at all other than to put distance between myself and my various pursuers back in the city. After a few hours I found myself in a lovely area, with the blue water on my right and blazing autumn foliage all around me. I knew not where I was, as it was unfamiliar country to me; later I was able to reconstruct that I had entered Hartford County, and in fact passed at some distance the town of Bel Air, which I had read was the home of the famous actor Junius Brutus Booth, said to be the greatest interpreter of Shakespeare in the country. How I would have thrilled to approach his home—to see where such a truly great artist lived! But I knew nothing as I rode past the town, which was handsome and tranquil in the autumn afternoon, and would certainly not have made such a detour even if I had. I knew I had to keep moving.

I also knew that I would have to leave the horse behind. This grieved me, as the beast was so easy to ride and I made such good progress with her, but obviously to be caught with her would spell my doom. When I had made my way some distance past the town of Bel Air, then, and found my way into a serene and quiet valley sparsely dotted with houses, I dismounted near a grove where I saw other horses grazing happily. Removing her saddle, I tossed it into a nearby grove of apple trees. Then, stroking my mare's nose for a moment and offering her my thanks, I left her. Turning once as I walked away, I saw the horse contentedly munching grass.

Progress was slower now, but at least I no longer had a stolen animal under me. In fact, as I made my way along a narrow path not far from the beautiful bay—I was close enough to be able to breathe in odors of water and beach—it seemed to me that my prospects were unusually good. Some time earlier I had stopped to count the money I took from my late alley customer and found it to be, incredibly, nearly fifty dollars—a fortune! With that, I reasoned—always assuming that I could avoid being robbed—I might quit this peripatetic criminal life entirely; I could find lodgings, I thought, and even some form of employment. I would live as a self-sufficient, law-abiding adult and leave my childish criminal past behind me.

There followed several days of pleasant walking through gorgeous autumn vistas. The weather held clear and not too cold, and my energies were high. To eat, I stopped at greengrocers' shops when I saw them and even indulged occasionally in a meal at an inn. More commonly I would purchase food from the seafood peddlers who operated horse-drawn carts in all but the smallest towns along the route: simple but mouth-watering preparations of blue crab, clams, oysters, and of course all sorts of fish—striped bass, sea trout, sturgeon. The abundance of such fare was breathtaking, as was its low price. Salted fish of various types which I purchased and stored paper-wrapped in my pockets kept me satisfied in the times I was far from any town.

It was, in all, a bucolic period—quite the most agreeable I had enjoyed since running away from the orphanage all those many months before. The Eastern Shore was a charming place filled with attractive villages and, in a surprise to my now city-hardened sensibilities, kind and gentle people. I slept where I could, ate when I wanted, and at no time felt myself in danger from anyone or anything. During this period I began, as it were, "auditioning" various towns as possibilities for my settling. I did not wish to choose too quickly; many of these quiet hamlets struck me as perfectly feasible, but I knew I could always double back to them if I wanted. I was enjoying my walking tour of this region I had heretofore never visited. Though not extremely distant geographically, it truly felt like a different world from Baltimore or even Grimsleytown.

But in the end I had to choose a place to stay, at least for a time. I had begun to crave some consistency in my life—a roof over my head and regular, home-cooked meals. I knew also that securing regular employment was important; it was all too easy to keep spending the cash I had on my person (which for safety I had secreted in different places—some in one pocket, some in another, some in the lining of my cap, some in my boots), but, as large as the supply seemed, I was all too aware that it was still very much finite.

At the northern tip of the Chesapeake Bay, in what I would eventually know as Cecil County, I discovered an enchanting stretch of beach, many miles in length and sparsely populated. Walking along I could see the occasional fisherman in his sailboat or skiff out on the water. There were houses here, most of them recessed some distance from the bay, along with a variety of small wooden huts or shacks dotting the beach at irregular intervals. Evening drew on as I wandered, and I began to feel the cold of early winter penetrating my shirt; I stopped at a small cluster of buildings which appeared to be a tiny business district, and there found a shop whose proprietor was happy to sell to me an inexpensive coat more in keeping with the season. Upon my inquiry this gentleman informed me that there were several houses along the way that rented rooms for both short- and long-term use, and gathering the addresses of several, I set off in search of lodgings.

I was quickly satisfied. The very first house I approached was a simple gray cottage with large picture windows and a slightly overgrown little yard; the owner, a pleasant white-haired woman of advanced age named Mrs. Prouty, informed me that she had two rooms available; I soon enough decided on the smaller, less pricey choice, which had limited space but which did possess a closet, shelf, plain chair, fireplace, and a surprisingly comfortable and commodious bed. Mrs. Prouty was somewhat hesitant to learn that I had as yet no employment, but my payment to her of a full week in advance relieved her worries quickly enough as did my claim, when she asked, that I was seventeen years old. I had arrived in time for supper, she further informed me, and I enjoyed a fine hot meal of fish, clams, and boiled potatoes along with her two other resident boarders, Mr. Broad and Mr. David, both rather brawny men in their twenties who worked for the local fishermen. A pleasant conversation ensued which climaxed with statements from the two of them that on the morrow they would attempt to "get me on" somewhere as a fish cleaner or trash hauler.

"You're a bit small," said Mr. David appraisingly. "They won't want you on the boats, I think."

"That's quite all right," said I. "I have no experience on boats. But I can certainly haul trash."

That night I enjoyed the loveliest sleep I had had in months.

Quite to my delight, I was hired on as a trash hauler the very next day. A fishery that occupied a sort of branch office up the beach gave me the job of carrying the remains of the day's catch to a location some distance from the beach, where I was to either bury or burn my load, depending on its exact contents. The loads themselves I carted in big barrows made of metal. It was considered an "easy job," and in terms of mental effort it certainly was, but physically it was very nearly backbreaking. The loads were extremely heavy, and pushing the wheeled barrows over the rough dirt paths was not easy at all. Within a few hours my shoulders and forearms were all but crying out in pain. And yet at some point my body reached a sort of plateau, and it seemed to me that while the pain continued unabated, it was no longer growing worse—thus I was able to continue. The job stank terribly—much of what I hauled were the heads, bones, and tails of dead fish—and I knew I would need to purchase new clothes after this day. Yet after nine hours of these labors I was still ambulatory, and moreover the "boss," a genial older man named Mr. Cotton, smiled and placed several pennies in my palm—pennies which, while they represented far less than I would have made in a similar period of time in Baltimore's alleyways, were the very first money I had ever earned in any properly legal profession. The feeling of receiving these coins in my hand was delightful, and Mr. Cotton's invitation for me to return the next day for more of the same work if I so desired was very welcome.

With that, I had my start in life—a *new kind* of life. I soon found myself well known up and down the miles of beach. "Andy" they called me; I was well-regarded by all, and quickly had more work offers than I could possibly fulfill. Many of the fishermen were willing to part with a penny or two for assisting with dragging in the catch from their boats, helping carry equipment, or even running up to the general store to fetch them brandy or tobacco. These nautical folk were tough, certainly, but invariably gentle with me. They asked no questions, but I sensed that no one believed me to be the age I claimed, and no doubt they understood that I must have some reason for being out on my own while still in such tender years. No one, however, suspected the more important truth—or if they did, they never said a word to indicate it. I was "one of the boys"—a smaller and slighter one, to be sure, but I performed my jobs well, especially after I had been there a few weeks and my body grew stronger and more resilient.

The winter was mild that year, but I was still very glad to have a room with a good fire and hot food available to me. Our little household got along, as it were, famously, and began to feel after a time like a bit of a family. Yet as March arrived and the weather turned more temperate, I found myself beginning to wander farther and farther up and down the beach whenever I was not working. I had discovered that there were little impromptu—what to call them? "Villages" is wrong, as they were hardly organized enough for that appellation, nor were they recognized by anyone as such; but small conglomerations, if you will, of simple low huts built for one or two persons only. These huts were occupied by men who did not work for the fisheries, or did so only occasionally. Instead they lived on their own, far outside the normal lives of men in society. They were not part of society. They had their own little skiffs, or else they fished from land; they ate what they caught, building little fires in front of their beach huts. These men—I would eventually realize that there were also a few women—dressed, talked, and did as they pleased. They had friendly relations with each other but for the most part did not interact a great deal. They were truly outsiders, and I was to learn that they lived in quiet opposition to the kind of structured life experienced by most men. In time I would learn to call this lifestyle "bohemian."

The notion of living out beyond the margins of society

was most appealing to me, since I had the idea I was in a sense already there. Despite their crusty exteriors, the men were generally quite pleasant to me, and more than once I found myself joining a delicious fire-roasted sea-caught dinner on the beach with one or two of them. I was quite content at such times, eating fine natural food, laughing at their crude jokes (even if some caused my cheeks to flame in embarrassment), and occasionally even sampling their alcoholic beverages—though spirits proved too strong for me, wine drunk straight from the bottle I found very enjoyable. Most importantly, beyond an exchange of names, no one interrogated anyone else—if you wanted to share your background and history, you were welcome to; if not, you would not be pressed. I myself shared little other than having lived in Baltimore for a time.

Now I must needs introduce the reader to the most extraordinary individual I happened upon during this extraordinary period of my life—an individual who would prove to have the profoundest effect on my being and beliefs, though our time together would prove all too brief in this period—and would end in tragedy.

One comfortable evening in May or June I found myself walking along the beach in this "bohemian" area when I espied a gentleman crouching before a small fire cooking his fish a few yards down from what I knew to be his hut. I approached him with no idea in mind but to idle away a few minutes with him in conversation before returning to my room at Mrs. Prouty's for the night; I had gotten into the habit of making such social calls with these men, many of whom I quite liked.

"Hello, Mr. Gamble!" I called, for that was the man's name.

He looked up and smiled. Mr. Gamble was a remarkable-looking fellow. He was not handsome, but his aspect was nonetheless pleasing; his big blue eyes were clear and warm, his nose shapely, his lips full and red. But what one noticed about him above all was his hair, which was the longest I had ever beheld on any male human being. A kind of dark blond, it fell straight back across his head in naturally graceful waves all the way to his wide shoulders. A similarly blond beard, rather unkempt, sprouted as far as an inch off his face. His clothing consisted of a pair of short denim pants, crudely cut off at the knees, and a curious variety of denim vest, quite faded and completely open at the front, which appeared to me to perhaps have been adapted with scissors and thread from some fuller garment. He was barefoot. In any other milieu he would have been dismissed as little more than a half-naked savage, yet beyond his appearance there was nothing savage about him. He was easy and open of nature, smiled a great deal (he had beautiful teeth), and held within himself, as I would learn, a sweet and gentle nature.

"Andy!" he called. "Come and have supper with me!"

I crossed the sand and dropped down next to him at his fire. "I have eaten, thank you. Please go ahead," said I, gesturing to his roasting fish.

"I will, thanks."

We talked of everyday things for a time. The sun was setting on the water and a pleasant breeze touched my face. Of late I had begun visiting Mr. Gamble more often than the others on the beach; I found him to be a stimulating conversationalist, and surprisingly well-read. He enjoyed it when I recited the poetry I still remembered from my childhood, even if much of it was only half-recalled. He was, without letters or credentials of any kind, a strangely literary man. He even had a few books in his hut, which he liked to show me. He possessed a small red-covered volume of the English poets—he knew the works of John Keats and Percy Shelley quite well—along with a few other works of verse. On this particular evening when he finished his supper he asked if I would like us to read together, and I eagerly said yes. He stepped into his hut and re-emerged with a small book, not poetry but rather an essay, titled simply *Nature*.

He read various sections of it to me in his quiet yet sonorous voice—paragraphs about how society destroys a person's wholeness, whereas nature revives it. "The wind sows the seed," he read, "the sun evaporates the sea; the wind blows the vapor into the field; the ice, on the other side of the planet, condenses rain on this; the rain feeds the plant; the plant feeds the animal; and thus the endless circulations of the divine charity nourish man." He smiled approvingly as he read. I did not understand everything in this writing, but I gathered enough to see that Mr. Gamble thought of it as a bit of a manifesto for himself and perhaps others like him. The essay championed the primacy of the natural world, and condemned the encroachment of man into it; it had made an impression when published a few years before, and I knew the name of Ralph Waldo Emerson was one that was spoken of by the educated classes.

"Is that why you live as you do?" I asked him.

"It expresses it better than anything else I have read."

"I feel that way too," said I. "About society. It is not for me. I don't belong in it."

He looked at me. "You're young," said he. "You may come to be more comfortable in it in time."

"Perhaps." I looked out at the dying light and felt the coolness of the breeze on my cheeks. "But I prefer it here."

"I'm glad," said he.

After the night of Emerson I came back again and again to spend time with Mr. Gamble. We read; we laughed; we discussed ideas of poetry and philosophy in a way I had never done with anyone since the death of Father. During the day, while hauling trash or loading big bags of fish into wooden crates, I found myself thinking of Mr. Gamble more often than of anyone or anything else. He seemed to me the most sensitive, the most *human* man I had met since Father, surely. Night after night I found myself abandoning the perfectly pleasant world of Mrs. Prouty and her lodgers to instead make my way along the beach to where I knew Mr. Gamble would be, cooking his supper, smoking his pipe, reading by his firelight, or simply gazing out at the water silently. This last he could do for long periods of time, and soon I did it too, the two of us sitting not far from each other in perfect, companionable silence.

The reader may by now have thought to characterize my feeling about Mr. Gamble at this time as something along the lines of a schoolgirl crush. I do not deny that there was that in it. The more time we spent together, the more I seemed to be attracted to all aspects of him—not only his intellect but also his physical person, which grew more and more familiar and pleasing to me over some weeks. The way his eyes danced when he was amused, the flowing way his hair fell over his shoulders—I confess that I began to find these things thrilling.

It happened too that our conversations grew more personal and revealing. Across the course of several evenings he told me the history of his family—he had none, his parents having perished many years before in his home state of Florida; his sole sibling, an older brother named Terrence, he said was killed in the Seminole War. "I had no future there in the wilds of Florida," he told me, drawing reflectively on his pipe, "and so I lit out. Had nothing with me but a knapsack with some clothes and a couple of books. Worked my way up the coast, doing all sorts of jobs." He shook his head slowly. "It's no kind of life, that."

"No," I agreed softly.

"I decided to settle someplace, someplace good and simple, where I could stretch my bones and be left by myself." He smiled a little. "I found this place."

One night it began suddenly to rain, and Mr. Gamble invited me to wait it out in his hut. My heart raced as I stepped into his little home, which contained little but a table, a chair, a trunk on the floor, and a cot with a few blankets on it that were none too clean. We watched the rain fall on the water through the open door for a long time, but it did not diminish.

"Maybe you'd best stay here," said he. "The cot can fit two."

I flushed to the tips of my toes. "I thank you, Mr. Gamble, but I can make it home all right." I moved to the door.

"What are you talking about? Look. There's lightning flashing. Feel free to have yourself a rest here. I don't mind at all. I certainly can't send you out into the storm."

"I..." My breath came short. "I—I can rest in your chair there."

He looked at me. "Suit yourself," said he at last. He closed the door and climbed onto the cot by himself. I sat in his chair, frightened of I knew not what, yet exhilarated as well. The room was lit occasionally by lightning. Thunder rumbled. I slept not a single wink, but somehow that did not concern me. I stared at Mr. Gamble's sleeping form for a very long time, at last leaving the hut when the weather cleared a few hours later.

That night spent under the same roof seemed to warm our relationship still further. Mr. Gamble began to insist that I call him "Jim," which marked the first time I ever referred to a grown man by his Christian name; there was something shockingly intimate about the sound of that single syllable whenever it escaped my lips. At times I wondered what he thought about me, or indeed if he thought anything at all. At times his easy, open friendliness caused me to wonder if, in an irony to defeat all ironies, he might not be the sort of man I had met in Baltimore's alleyways—men who preferred the sexual company of others of their own kind. What in the world would happen if he were to make an advance on "Andy"?

It began to feel like lying, this male masquerade of mine, and after all, it truly was. The fact that I could not be as open and honest with him as he had been with me began to cause me grief and make me feel like the rankest hypocrite. Jim Gamble was my friend—perhaps my closest friend ever, certainly my closest male friend—and I lied to him every time I sat with him, talked with him, ate his food, listened to him read or recited poetry to him.

And yet—could I risk exposing myself? I had never let anyone in on my secret and I had no idea how he would react. He might denounce or ridicule me and I would have to flee. But this world—this sea-centered life without rules or boundaries—was the pleasantest and most fulfilling I had experienced since my early childhood. I had no desire to leave it.

Jim Gamble and I had been friends for some three months, I believe, when I at last resolved to take the risk.

It was an August night, I recall, warm and humid, and while I sweated in my usual garb he was wearing only his pair of short cut-off denim trousers, nothing else. His muscular chest and shoulders gleamed in the firelight. He poured me a cup of cool fresh water from a big bottle he kept and handed it to me. Leaning back again, I watched him filling his pipe with tobacco.

"Jim?" said I in a small voice.

"Yes?"

"Jim, I—I have something to tell you."

"What is that?"

"It's...it's something about myself."

"And what might that be?"

"I...Can I trust you, Jim?"

He stopped what he was doing and looked at me. "Trust me how?"

"With—some information."

He went back to filling the pipe. "I suppose I'm as trustworthy as any man." He lit a sulfur match with the remains of our cooking fire and worked on lighting the pipe.

But for a long moment I could say nothing. I stared at my feet.

"Andy?" he asked at last.

Words simply would not come out of my mouth. To my embarrassment, I realized that a tear had commenced to trickle down my cheek.

"I—I don't think I can tell you," said I in a strangled voice. "Never mind me. I'm sorry, Jim."

"Andy," said he after a long time of silence in the darkness, "this isn't about your being a girl, is it?"

I inhaled sharply and looked at him, my jaw agape.

"How did you know?" For some reason I was whispering.

"Well, I didn't exactly *know* until a few days ago, but I'd suspected. I wouldn't be much of a man if I didn't realize that night after night I was being favored with the company of a beautiful girl, no matter her hair or clothes."

"Does—does anyone else know?"

He shrugged. "I haven't the slightest idea. If they do, I don't guess they care much. People are just people around here, Andy. They don't get into each other's business."

My heart threatened to smash its way out of my chest. My face was flushed and hot. I felt giddy with emotions I could not possibly describe.

"How did you—Jim, you said something about a few days ago...?"

"Oh, that." He cleared his throat. "For that I owe you an apology, Andy. I didn't mean to do what I did. I was over there—" he gestured—"early in the morning, and you were behind a tree and—well—I didn't know you were there. It was just a glimpse, an accident—"

"I understand," I whispered, my face inflamed with embarrassment.

"I'm truly sorry," he said.

I shook my head. "It was an accident."

"Yes." He nodded. "Anyway, that's when I...I knew."

"And yet you didn't say anything."

"What was there to say? It's not my business."

"I think it is." I studied him in the dying firelight. "Jim, how old are you?"

"I'm nineteen, Andy."

"Nineteen! I'd taken you for much older."

"It's the sun. It weathers the skin. No, I'm but nineteen. And you?"

"I am fifteen, Jim," said I. This was true. My birthday had passed a week before.

We sat in silence. There was nothing to say, and everything.

"I have not lived a clean life," said I at last.

"Oh, nonsense. Who has? Do I look perfect to you?"

"Well..." I found myself laughing. "Actually, yes!"

He grinned and looked away. "What is your name, my friend? Surely it isn't Andy."

"It's Annabel." I felt so free saying this, as if I was breaking through shackles of steel that had bound me for far too long.

"Annabel." He smiled. "A lovely name."

"Thank you."

Suddenly the air between us seemed electric, and when he reached out to touch my hand it was literally as if some magic spark burst into being between us—a spark that had been there from the beginning but which my masquerade forced us to ignore.

Here again I have reached a point in my narrative where the bounds of good taste demand that I draw a curtain, as it were, over the activities which ensued over the next hours between Jim Gamble and myself. And yet another part of me cries out in protest: How can I tell the story of my life while erasing the happiest, most joyous moments of it? Why is it socially acceptable for me to write in detail about my sister's premature, bloody death, my father's fatal accident, my mother's ghastly suicide, and dear Mary Mahoney's lifeless corpse dangling from a bed-sheet in the dormitory of Sadmore Place—yet not about the sweet, transcendent hours spent in the arms of one of the fin-est men ever to walk God's Earth? Why are grief and painful death fit subjects for depiction while pleasure and delight must hide in the shadows? Moralists will no doubt cry, "You were too young!" and "You were unmarried!" But age is in some ways relative, and it was by the calendar only that I was fifteen—in terms of life experience I was far older than that. As for our status of being outside the bounds of wedlock, what occurred between Jim Gamble and me married us in every way that could be meaningful to any God in Whom I might ever choose to believe—because we were wed not in rules or in social con-ventions but in Love.

We spent all night in his hut. A light rain passed over us for a few minutes at one point, increasing the intimacy and roman-tic feeling between us. Otherwise the night was quiet, and we were quiet, pleasuring each other, comforting each other, loving each other. I had never known such an experience, or indeed that such an experience was even possible between two people. My heart soared even as my breath came short again and again; and for a while that night I am convinced that we somehow were not two separate people but only one. We hardly spoke for hours. Jim was careful to ensure that no pregnancy would result from our intimate adventuring. From time to time we drifted off into light sleep, holding each other, caressing each other. Then we would come to consciousness again and continue—continue—continue!

The reader might wonder how I could give myself over so freely to such passionate embraces given my squalid expe-riences in Baltimore's darker alleyways. Did such events not forever tarnish my feelings about men and the activities that men naturally engage in with women? Not at all, for the fur-tive things that happened in those alleyways had nothing to do with what occurred between Jim Gamble and me in his hut, any more than a weed has anything to do with a rose. My humiliating experience of having to stand naked before the vile boy Theodore Jones had no relation whatsoever to my standing proudly and thrillingly naked before Jim Gamble. My skinni-ness—the hourglass mole on my belly—I never thought of these things at all. Shelley wrote somewhere that "familiar acts are beautiful through love"; many of our acts that night were quite unfamiliar to me, but of those that I knew, they were utterly dif-ferent now from what I had earlier experienced—filled as they were now with Love.

As hints of dawn light commenced to glow inside the room I surprised myself by beginning, quite without any expecta-tion of it, to weep. I did so nearly without sound, for I wished not to wake my companion and lover; and yet I did weep. At first I thought it was because I grieved the slow vanishing of the darkness, a darkness I wanted to go on forever; and that indeed constituted part of my emotion; but images were start-ing to play in my mind too, images of all the horrible things that had happened to me and to the people whom I had loved, the miserable life I had led, the miserable deaths they had suffered. To think of my lost loved ones never having the opportunity to experience what I had in the night, to be nothing but wander-ing ghosts in empty cold space forever—for, though I wished I could, I believed not in a Christian Heaven—this caused me a heartache beyond reckoning. Sorrow took root in my soul, but it was a sorrow strangely mixed with memories of the ecstasy I had experienced over the previous hours and which I was still experiencing now with Jim beside me, a wild overflow of extreme feelings that roiled up in wave after wave of tears not of sadness or joy but simply of *emotion*, more than my mind or heart could contain.

Jim awoke after a while and for a few minutes stroked my bare shoulders with his warm, powerful hands; then he turned me to him and wrapped me up in an embrace that told me that everything was all right, that I was cared about, that I was loved. This made me weep all the more, and yet my Jim never said a word, stroking my hair, enveloping me in his arms. It was then I realized that even in weeping and anguish one could have and hold Paradise. My tears cleansed me—cleansed my spirit—in a way I had never allowed myself to do before, and it was the love, the love of this night, that had opened the door for me, allowed me to feel, to feel *fully*, as a woman—no longer a girl—and as a human being. When I finished at last we lay silently together. Eventually we laughed. We laughed a great deal, and for a long time.

There are periods in life which are considered happy only in memory. One looks back over a gulf of years and, remembering a particular place or person or experience, thinks, "Then I was happy," although at the time one was not particularly conscious of it. Lost in the minutiae of everyday life, the little daily struggles and squabbles we all of us experience, we never stopped to consider our happiness at that time, or else were unable to see it for what it was. I think many people's childhoods reflect this. We have all known persons who say that they only truly realized how pleasant and bucolic were their early days after they had left those days behind and faced the more complex challenges of adulthood. It is possible that my own early girlhood—those years in the little cottage outside Grimsleytown, so many hours of them spent sitting in the little alcove off the kitchen with my book and tea looking out at the fields where in memory it was always raining—is an example of this phenomenon. Given the many dramatic events which occurred later in my life, it is easy for me to lose how agreeable those first years were to me, and it is difficult to recapture the feeling now.

Not so my time with Jim Gamble. Even today I know not what to call our relationship in this period—"affair" is far too shallow and sordid, disreputable even—but "marriage" is admittedly misleading, unless perhaps it might be called a "marriage of the spirit." For that it is what it really was, and I did not need to wait years to realize it and know it in the deep core of my being. With astonishing suddenness the stormy trials and travails of my life smoothed out to evenness and placidity. It was as if my soul were a pond into which a seemingly endless supply of stones had for years been rudely thrown, constantly exploding into me, causing violent waves to crash outward in all directions, only for the stones to abruptly cease landing and my naturally serene waters to return. It is my belief that this is the truest experience of Love. People talk of fire rockets exploding and of life suddenly taking on a cast of enormous, unpredictable excitement, but I have found the opposite to be the case. With Jim Gamble I realized that I was *home*, and one does not set off fire rockets in one's home. There was excitement, yes, surely—but a quiet excitement, the excitement of a genuine meeting and meshing of minds, bodies, and souls.

Perhaps it would be simplest to say that when I was with Jim Gamble I wished to be nowhere else in the world.

We spent all our time together. I gave up my room at Mrs. Prouty's and moved my meager belongings to Jim Gamble's hut. We had no secrets; I told him all regarding my life in Baltimore, and earlier, about Mother and Father and my late sister, about the peculiar and disquieting Mr. Blackthorn, about Mary Mahoney and the terrors of Sadmore Place. I showed him my money quite fearlessly, completely confident that it would never enter this good man's mind to turn thief—and of course he did not. In fact, he helped me secret the money in different places within the hut in the theory that if someone entered intent on robbery, the malefactor would be unlikely to find anything near the entire amount—instead he would fine a single pile and, assuming it represented everything, take it and flee. This never happened, however. In my months among the "bohemians" I never knew any crime to take place at all.

Our new relationship was of course remarked upon by the various residents of that unusual beach community, but I never faced a single awkward question about it from anyone. Everyone continued to call me "Andy" (including Jim), and if they wondered about my sex, they were not so rude as to inquire. I let my hair grow out somewhat, and my behavior toward my lover must at times have suggested my femininity—and so perhaps they all knew. On the other hand, intimate relationships between males were not unknown on that wild beach, and so perhaps they did *not* know; possibly they assumed we were simply two boys enjoying each other as men and women did, and it was of no concern to them. These were people, after all, who lived as they lived in order to escape the censorial laws and customs of mainstream society. The last thing they would do to any man or woman of goodwill was judge them.

What I describe here is no doubt shocking to some read-
ers—a world whose only established rules were to not harm one
another and let each go about his business as he pleased? Where
few had any proper regular employment? Where unmarried
persons lived as if they were married without censure of any
sort? Many would consider this nightmarish, and would never
adjust to such a community. But I did, and quickly; and I soon
came to the conclusion that on this little northern corner of the
Chesapeake Bay I had found something not too distant from
Heaven on Earth.

Jim and I spent the hot summer days fishing, as did most
others around us. My lover had built a handsome boat, something between a skiff and a raft and big enough for two, in
which we paddled out in the mornings with our simple gear
and made our daily catch, which was rarely difficult. We caught
only what we would eat unless it seemed advisable that we
obtain a bit of money, in which case we gathered enough to be
worth hiking up to the fishery office and selling for cash. If the
weather was rough we might go clamming in the surf instead,
but my memories are mostly of being out in the bright sunshine
on Jim Gamble's wooden craft. At times it was difficult not to
think of us as Adam and Eve and our ocean paradise as our
own personal Garden of Eden. It is testament to our feelings—
and youth!—that we took to venturing farther up the coast than
others, our strategy being to isolate ourselves sufficiently that
we might leave off the fishing for a time and have, so to speak,
intimate relations as we rocked on the gently undulating water.
This we accomplished with, I might say, vigorous regularity.

When the weather began to turn cooler in late September
we spent less time on the water and dressed more warmly when
we did, but the shore was beautiful for all that. October brought
lovely communal campfires at night, eight or ten beach residents gathered around, my head resting against Jim's chest, my
shoulders wrapped in his arms, our hands intertwined, all of us
laughing and singing into the late hours. Occasional rainstorms
relegated us to our hut, but those times were merely romantic in
yet another manner. We read to each other for hours, Keats and
Shelley and Browning, and I heard many of those poems in an

entirely new way when they were spoken quietly by my ardent lover, the sound his gentle voice sensuous over the sound of the rain, the two of us sleepily sharing a book and a bottle of wine in bed in the middle of the afternoon. "My boy-girl," he called me privately, an endearment that delighted me. Everything was new—Love made it so—and I discovered the exquisite comfort and tenderness of a man's body, the heady odor of his skin, the feeling of eternity that sets in as two become, for a time, one.

3

It was November when a serpent reared its head in Paradise.

As we had known rapture in our bayside Garden, so followed with a terrible inevitability the Fall—though at first I did not recognize it for what it was, or what it would become.

The initial sign of something wrong seemed only mildly troubling—perhaps not even that. I had walked up the beach one early evening to obtain some vegetables at the little shop there; I had left Jim behind to build our nightly fire. Wrapped in my coat and a pair of denims, I was comfortable as I made my way along the edge of the beach, calling "hello" to friends, wondering if the shop might have carrots today or perhaps turnips, imagining with a flush that warmed my cheeks and a tingling that ran hotly down my thighs the activities that Jim and I would no doubt engage in later, after dinner was done. I found myself smiling as I approached the shop, smiling for no other reason but that I was happy.

It was then that I noticed for the first time a man in a long black coat and bowler hat standing near the entrance to the shop. He had dark eyes and a heavy brown mustache and, I noticed, he turned away abruptly as I approached him. I thought little of it as I did my buying in the store—carrots *and* turnips, I was delighted to find—and by the time I walked out again, the man was gone.

I just wrote that this was the first time I noticed the man, but that is not entirely correct. I had been somehow aware of him—of some dark figure at the corner of my vision—for the past several days. His presence had been sufficiently invisible that I made no note of him, not even being aware of him in any conscious way; what occurred in front of the store was that I suddenly realized for the first time that this was a man I had seen before, his presence having registered in my brain like some vague itch. I had seen him, so to say, and yet not seen him. Preoccupied with our days, with making breakfast and gathering our clam-digging gear (the weather had been a bit unsettled for fishing), wandering up and down the beach together in the low tide finding clams and mussels and dropping them in our wicker basket, visiting with our friends along the shore, enjoying the bread and wine we packed for lunch, I had noticed on some subterranean level of my brain a man not dressed for such activities, a man in proper city attire, far off down the beach. Once I believed that I saw the man holding a spyglass to his eye, and for just an instant it had seemed that it was aimed at us, but there was considerable distance between Jim and me and this man and in truth I did not know whether it was the same man at all.

I have made it sound as if it should have been obvious I was being followed, but whether due to distraction or a stubborn refusal to believe, I thought little about it until the evening I saw the man before the shop. I was not acquainted with him; his countenance was entirely unknown to me; but at that moment, and when I noted his abrupt disappearance afterward, I began to be concerned about this man.

I returned to Jim. We worked on our fine supper—clams with roasted carrots and turnips—but, with his exquisite sensitivity, he saw that I was somehow preoccupied. As we ate before the fire, he asked me what was wrong.

"Wrong?" said I, feigning innocence as one usually does when faced with that question. "Why, nothing is wrong, Jim."

"Don't you like the dinner? I think the vegetables are excellent."

I tried to smile. "The dinner is delicious."

"What, then?"

I sighed, not wanting to open this matter to conversation—for once opened, I knew, it would be difficult to close again. I had no idea how correct I would ultimately be proved to be about this.

"Jim," said I, "I have noticed a man who seems to be follow-ing us. Or rather following *me*, I suspect." I described him, and the times I had seen him.

"I've not noticed anyone," said Jim, looking around the beach with a scowl.

"That's just it. He stays far away. Tonight was the closest I've come to him. I'm sure he is watching me."

"It could be me he's after. I've left a few debts in my wake over the years," he smiled.

"Jim, you know what I've told you about my past."

"Yes." He frowned. "Do you think he is from your orphanage?"

"He could be. But how long has it been? I can hardly imag-ine they are so dogged as to send agents all over the state for an entire year searching for one runaway orphan."

"It doesn't seem likely, Andy," he agreed, "but I'm not informed about such things."

I nestled close to him in the deepening dark. "Do you think he could take me away?"

He wrapped his arm firmly around me. "Let him try, my boy-girl."

"I'm serious, Jim."

"I'm serious too."

"We don't want to fight him, surely. What if there are others with him?"

"It would be difficult," said he, "to spirit you away. After all, I am always with you. Everyone here along the beach is your friend. He would have to contend with the entire population here."

"If he brought a constable..."

"How would the man even identify you? You've told me you look nothing like you did before."

"No, that's true. But..."

"So your name is Andy and you know nothing at all about anyone named Annabel Lee who used to live in Grimsleytown, Maryland. He would have no proof. I'm sure Mr. Cotton at the fishery would vouch for your being employed there—it's almost true, after all—and for your good character. You are a law-abiding citizen minding his own business and any stranger who tries to say otherwise can go hang…don't you think?"

I buried my nose in his beard. "I hope you're right, Jim."

"Of course I'm right. We have nothing to fear from silly men in bowler hats who carry spyglasses."

And over the succeeding few days it appeared that Jim had been correct. The man in the bowler hat vanished; as much as I looked around for him each day, I saw no one. Aware that he might have taken on a disguise, I tried as best I could to remember his facial features and attempted to find that face in everyone around me, but never did. After some days things seemed to return to normal, both in the world and within myself. I calmed again. And then Catastrophe came.

It came in the darkness, and it came silently.

The night was windy but warm, surprisingly so for December; Jim and I had decided to take a walk far up the beach, as we often did. The moon covered everything before us in a striking blue sheen that made the waters before us and the rocky shore seem unearthly, strange and exotic. But there was no sense of fear; I was in my proud lover's arms, and no harm, so I believed, could befall me. And yet I found myself growing uneasy, as if I had heard something, something that warned of danger. But the wind made it difficult to hear anything at all; it was very strong at our backs.

"Jim," said I forcefully, "let us go back home. Please."

"All right." He smiled with those beautiful teeth of his and we turned to face the wind.

It was then that we both saw the dark figure that had been following behind us. It was a man in a dark overcoat. His hands were in his pockets. He wore no hat—the wind would surely have carried it away—but because the moon was behind him I could make out none of his facial features at all. I immediately feared that it was the same man I had seen before with the bowler hat and spyglass. He stopped and stood unmoving in our path.

"Please let us pass, sir," called Jim over the wind.

The man did not respond, nor did he move.

His arm tightly around me, Jim moved to pass him. The man moved to block us.

"Sir, what is your business?" asked Jim.

The voice said quietly, "The girl." The wind tossed his muted words to us.

Jim studied the dark figure. "You will allow us to pass, please."

But as Jim again tried to move, the dark shape blocked us.

"Sir!" said Jim. "This is intolerable. Please remove yourself from our path or I will remove you myself."

"The girl," said the figure again. He gestured toward me.

"Andy, stand back." Jim pushed me behind him. "I am not to be fooled with, whoever you are."

In a quick motion the figure brought something from his pocket—a small black pistol of some sort. He pointed it at my Jim.

"The girl, I said."

"You will let us pass."

At once a shot exploded in the darkness, the flash all but blinding me, the sound like a whip-crack in the night! To my horror Jim staggered backward, falling against me and knocking the both of us onto the beach. There was a ghastly hole near the middle of his chest, a hole that pumped out horrible red blood onto his shirt. In an instant our eyes met and as his head fell back he gurgled a single word, "Run." I screamed then—screamed in mortal panic. The dark figure, huge now before me, grabbed at my arm—I shook the hand away and, stumbling and shrieking, ran into the wind, my instinct taking me toward the people and community I knew, but Jim and I had walked a long way. I screamed again and again but could nearly hear the screams being swallowed by the wind. Glancing back, I saw the figure looming near me, his hand just short of reaching my shoulder. I could hear his hard breathing, and my own. I was crying now as all hope seemed to fade; my friends were too far away, the wind too strong for my feeble voice, the dark figure too fleet of foot, and the image of Jim, Jim with his chest disgorging terrible red flowers, Jim...

At last I came to an old, disused pier, much rotted, which

had never been used in my time in this place. I know not why I ran out upon it; I can only imagine that I knew I would lose the foot race in which the man and I were engaged, and perhaps hoped to swim down the shore instead. The soft wood gave way in places as I ran across it, my foot pushing through again and again.

At last I arrived at the far edge of the old pier, and turned. The figure was stumbling too through the rotted wood but had lost hardly a step. I was about to leap into the water as he took one step closer—and in an instant I knew the identity of my pursuer. It was not the man in the bowler hat. It was Doctor Blackthorn!

The realization froze me to the spot. I could neither move nor speak as he made his repugnant way toward me.

"Child," said he at last, his breath quick. "Stop this now. I have found you. You are mine again."

I could sense that my mouth was open, yet no sound emerged. I could neither speak nor scream.

"I have searched for you for a long time," said he, moving closer. "At last one of my agents found a girl—he thought it was a girl, but wasn't entirely sure—living on the beach here with a man. He thought it might be the young lady I had hired him to locate. His description was detailed enough for me to travel here and see for myself." He smiled. "And it is you, child. You at last." He said these words with great satisfaction.

I swallowed and pushed a word from my lips. "Why?"

"I have told you," said he. Doctor Blackthorn was close now, close enough to reach out and touch me. His eyes in the moonlight were familiar, heavily veined, yet had a wild expression in them I did not recognize. "I have told you that you are mine. That I will always be with you."

"Jim…" I gestured back where he lay, lost now in the dark.

"Him? He is nothing. He is better dead."

"No!"

"It is time, child, to come with me. I have plans for you, for you and me both. Beautiful plans."

"I will not go back to Sadmore Place."

He smiled. "You needn't. My plans are far better than that."

"I will not accompany you."

He showed me the pistol again. "Child, you have no choice."

And suddenly the hopelessness of everything came crashing down into my soul. All I had hoped, all I had dreamed, all I had loved for these many months was as nothing. In my mind I saw Jim's body prone on the beach—Mary's hanging in the Sadmore dormitory—my mother and father and sister, all dead, dead—and knew that my fate was meant to be tragic and terrible. I knew not why. Perhaps God hated me for not believing in Him. But there was no hope; no hope at all.

"All right," said I, and moved as if to accompany him.

The instant he turned, however, I reversed my course, ran to the edge of the dock and threw myself into the freezing water!

I was determined now to end it all. If it turned out that the Bible was correct and that I would burn now in Hell forever as a suicide, so be it. But I would not continue. Life had become too intolerably painful and I had to leave it. I swam as fast and as hard as I could away from the pier—my clothes quickly grew waterlogged and clumsy—I choked as water splashed into my nose and mouth. Somewhere behind me I heard Doctor Blackthorn's panicked voice crying, *"Annabel! Annabel Lee!"* But nothing would halt my progress except Death. I kept my arms and legs chopping wildly through the water, on and on—more water poured into my throat—I choked and retched—my body grew heavy—my lungs felt as if they were exploding—my limbs weakened—my head sank under the water once, twice—I paddled and paddled, my arms and legs in excruciating pain—my head dipped down again and yet again—a strange warm feeling overcame me, suffused me in a glow that was strange but not unpleasant—I sensed the waters closing over my head but no longer fought, no longer cared to fight—I felt my body sinking, saw a few shards of broken light above me as everything began to fade to night, blissful, eternal night—

I died.

BOOK FOUR

A Wind Out of a Cloud

1

I was the *Angel of Death*—on black wings I soared through the darkness, air cold on my cheeks, night sky alive with every perverse creature of Hell's bestiary, weird things with giant hungry eyes and enormous slimy snouts and blood-dripping fangs many times the length of scythes. Their forms were as nothing in Man's universe, covered as they were with bizarre hard hides of sick, unnatural colors, fantastic writhing lesions moving atop them, and grotesque, impossible limbs that stuck out at disturbing angles from their trunks and faces. They swooped and darted all around me, grunting and chortling and shrieking, their bodies jerking and tumbling spastically along the currents of wind, abnormal and ugly, the dark itself filled with boiling whispers of thousands of damned, lost souls. The uncanny creatures floated this way and that, one or another of them grabbing suddenly into the texture of the darkness itself and sometimes—often—pulling forth the ghostly figure of a terrified man or woman or child and stuffing it into its repulsive maw, chewing at it with horrible liquid slurping sounds, the hapless victim screaming even as it disappeared under the nightmarish teeth of the beast. The screaming continued, only more subdued and muffled, after the victim had been fully devoured, and his body, what remained of it, bulged the monster's belly like a huge rat inside a boa constrictor. It was bedlam—madness—Satan's underworld itself!—and yet I felt no terror, no anxiety. For this was *my* world, a world for which I was entirely fitted—a world in which I belonged—the world of the *Angel of Death*.

I floated for an endless time in the susurrating blackness,

finally becoming hungry and reaching my own winged arms into the night itself and pulling forth my own damned souls. The first I took was that of my sister, tiny and fragile, her soul in this lightless afterworld transparently shining, and I stuffed her small form into my ravenous jaws, feeling nothing at the sounds of her desperate and helpless squeals. Then I found my father, who in my merciless grasp came to me with his head caved in, his expression bewildered and disorientated. I ripped his head from his neck and chewed it up with no more thought than a child enjoying a sweet. My mother, then—she was particularly succulent, with blood running all over her shadowy spirit, over her face, her lips, her shoulders. All these I tore into shreds with my omnipotent clawed paws, grinning at the sight of their bodies rent asunder, laughing at their piteous cries. Mary Mahoney I dangled from her rope, twirling her by her neck in the air like a rag doll before ramming her frail, wailing remains into my huge and insatiable mouth. Jim I located next—Jim, his long hair wild in the wind, his strong arms useless now against my all-encompassing power—Jim who alone among my pathetic victims would neither scream nor weep but fought with all the courage and manliness he possessed, resigning himself in stoic silence to his fate only at the last moment when all hope was lost, when I had taken it away without sympathy—without caring—for I was indeed the Angel of Death, and all who came before me must fall—fall forever!

I woke in a small, dimly lit room.

The walls, what I could see of them, appeared to be a pleasant pastel color—peach, I thought. They were plain, unadorned by any wallpaper or pictures whatsoever. On one side there seemed to be a window—at least there was a curtain, long and purple, which appeared to cover one. Next to me was a rectangular end table on which sat a plain oil lamp which emitted a soft glow by which I could observe some of my surroundings.

I was in a bed. The cover was, again, peach color, and the sheets were white. The pillow under my head was deep and soft. It was very quiet; for some time the only sounds I could make out at all were the ones I myself generated by moving a bit here and there in the bed. I possessed but little strength—it was all I could do to lift my hands to my eyes. When I did so I found that my hands were pale and shockingly thin, even emaciated in appearance. At my wrists I saw that there were white sleeves; I became aware that I had on a kind of loose-fitting shift, seemingly a nightgown of some sort.

Listening, I tried to ascertain some idea of where I was. After a while I thought I heard water dripping—later still it seemed to me that I could just hear the faraway sound of footsteps, echoing footsteps like those created by hard-soled shoes on a stone floor. With a sinking heart I wondered for a moment if I were back at Sadmore Place again, but this was nothing like the dormitory there, nor like the isolation cell; it was only the sound of footsteps that had made me think of it. And this place did not smell at all like the orphanage—the odor here was pleasant, in fact, the smell mostly of clean bedsheets, not at all moldy or fetid.

I wondered if I had somehow been delivered to a hospital. Where I lay did not have the appearance of any hospital room I had seen, but perhaps it was a special hospital, a private sanatorium of some sort. But who had placed me here? Where was I? What had happened?

I attempted to call out, but discovered that I possessed virtually no voice—I could make no sound at all above a whisper. My throat was painful, dry and raw, and the effort to speak was excruciating. My jaws hurt as well. So too, I discovered upon taking a kind of internal inventory, was much of my body in pain. I did not seem to have any bandages or casts on any part of me, but all the same my head throbbed, and my shoulders, my back, my forearms, my legs. Even my feet were sore, as if I had walked barefoot for many miles. I could move, at least to some degree, but only slowly and carefully, and only a few inches this way or that. The effort of so doing quickly exhausted me and I lay back, helpless.

Surely someone would arrive, I thought—a doctor, a nurse. Someone had placed me here and someone was obviously caring for me. Someone obviously must come. But before anyone did I felt myself falling backward into sleep again—sleep, or unconsciousness—the world went dark, and I vanished.

There came a sound. My eyes were closed and it seemed too much effort to try to open them, but I heard a curious humming, quite soft and faint, that might have come from a great distance but which I somehow sensed was rather near me, even perhaps next to me by the bed. I struggled to open my eyes and to turn my head, but was able to accomplish neither. The sound faded as I did, and again there was nothing.

My heart felt strange. In my darkness it seemed to be beating absurdly fast, grotesquely powerfully, as if the organ itself had grown huge and were about to smash its way straight out of my chest. And yet at other times the beating weakened and slowed to the point that an eternity seemed to pass between the sounds and I wondered if my heartrate had fallen to once a minute, once an hour, once a day. I knew that was impossible, of course, and yet time—time felt as if it were passing somehow—and myself both within time and without it, all dark everywhere, not painful but not pleasant—really just nothing, but somehow I was in the nothing, and part of it....

I was aware of myself in time and space but I did not exist. Somehow I knew this. I saw nothing—heard nothing—felt nothing—yet I existed, without existing. I was in a somewhere that was also nowhere. I was and was not. There was no Annabel Lee. Annabel Lee's self and feelings and memories had dissolved, sunk away and vanished. They were no more. And yet I was there, in the nowhere place, without light or darkness, joy or pain, time or not-time—the place of nothing at all.

After what might have been a day or a thousand years my eyes opened again, very slightly, to weak slits through which I saw that I was still—again?—in the room with peach walls. Had I been here all the time, or had my soul gone on some inexplicable journey and now returned? Was this the afterlife? Would the Lord God Himself, in Whom I had never quite manage to fully believe, suddenly appear before my eyes in all his blinding Christian splendor, His robes and His great flowing white beard, in order to pronounce me eternally damned—or perhaps eternally saved?

I had the sense that my brain was somewhat more engaged now in the world around it—that I was somehow more fully a part of this place now, this room, this bed. My eyelids managed to lift completely and I saw the white ceiling, the purple curtain that seemed to cover a window, the rectangular table beside the bed, the oil lamp atop it. All was as it had been before, though I noticed that the white shift I was wearing now had some slightly frilly cuffs at the wrists which I did not recall. Time had passed, then. I was wearing something different now.

My body, too—the multitudinous pains I had experienced earlier seemed largely gone. What I felt was mostly the usual stiffness and soreness experienced by anyone who has lain abed for a long period of time. Had I recovered, then? Would I be able to leave this place soon—today perhaps, or tomorrow? For a moment I longed to return to my former life, but then the events of my final days before this peculiar convalescence returned to me and the memories struck at me with a savage sharpness. Whatever lay ahead, I thought, it was to be a future without Jim Gamble, without the only man—the only man other than my father—whom I had ever truly loved. As I thought of him images and sounds suddenly began flooding my mind—images and sounds of him, of our life together on the beach, of sunrises and sunsets together, of fishing and clamming and loving one another as surely no two people had ever loved before—and my brain reeled. Tears trickled down either side of my face. My breath came short. Whatever life there was left, it was a life without the only person in it who had made that life worth living. Jim!—Jim!

At length I became aware of a very specific sound—the sound of a doorknob being turned. I lifted my head—my neck strained with the effort—to look at the door on the other side of the room. The knob was indeed turning, and the door pushing silently inward. I watched with both anticipation and fear to see what would pass through that door.

What entered was perhaps the most peculiar-looking individual I had ever seen. In the starched white uniform of a nurse, this person approached my bed all but silently. The nurse—a woman, I thought, if only because of the black hair on her shoulders—was very small, surely less than five feet in height, and slight of limb. But this was not what one primarily noticed. What was unavoidably obvious when looking at this person was the fact that she was wearing a mask. My sense of vision was still blurred and unsteady, but there was no question—what covered her face was a mask that appeared to be made, bizarrely, of plain wood. There were dark eyeholes—it was too dim to actually see her eyes—as well as two holes for the nose and one short slit for the mouth. A dwarf nurse with a wooden mask for a face! The idea was so fantastic that I might have laughed had I possessed any energy at all. As it was, I simply stared at her as she took my wrist in her hand—her hands were covered with blue cloth gloves, I noticed—and, I imagined, assessed my pulse. I thought I detected a humming sound then, of uncertain origin; but I could not be sure.

"Where am I?" I asked in the husky whisper that was the only voice I had.

But the nurse made no indication that she had heard me. Instead she dropped my wrist after a long moment and covered my forehead with her palm, no doubt checking for fever.

"Have I been ill?" I whispered.

Again there was no response. The wood-masked woman turned away finally and walked out the door again, returning in a moment with a tray in her hands. On the tray was a water pitcher, a glass, a bowl with something in it I could not see, and a spoon. The nurse placed the tray on the end table and began fluffing my pillow, dislodging my head slightly and angling it upward. I found myself in a position in which I might conceivably be able to swallow.

Slowly, the nurse poured a small bit of water into the glass and then gently held it to my lips. I allowed some of the water to coat the interior of my mouth, which created a most welcome cooling sensation. When she offered more, I swallowed a tiny amount; it made me cough for a moment, which caused my head to throb with pain, but the sensation passed and I had another try. This time I was able to drink the water without difficulty. It was refreshing and revivifying—quite possibly, I thought, the most delicious water I had ever tasted. I felt suddenly as if I could drink gallons, but after a few swallows the nurse took the glass away, placing it on the tray and lifting the bowl and spoon toward me. The bowl contained some variety of gruel, brown and warm and surprisingly flavorful. I managed several good spoonsful of the substance before I felt myself tiring again; the nurse seemed to sense this, and she put down the food things and readjusted my pillow. In what seemed only a moment I was adrift once more on the gentle seas of slumber.

Thus began a routine. The wood-masked nurse visited me when I was awake, and offered me silent but quite gentle and effective care. I received food and water, sometimes a mild tea. My bodily needs were dealt with efficiently. From time to time—I still had no idea how much time had passed, was passing—she changed the bedsheets, in that expert way that a truly competent nurse has, without requiring that the patient leave the bed. She also changed my shift, which was a shocking experience; not because of my being unclothed before her—she was a nurse after all—but because I received brief glimpses of my own body, or perhaps I should say what remained of my body. I was frightfully thin, my ribs showing through my skin. I sported scars I had never before seen—scars, I imagined with horror, resulting from surgery, or even multiple surgeries. The most frightening of these was located across the region of my heart, a raw pink line running vertically from the top of the heart to the bottom. I gazed appalled at this evidence of the violence that had been done to me in the cause of medicine. It grieved me to think that such a scar as this—and others that crossed under my breasts, over my belly, and down into regions unmentionable—would be a part of me for the remainder of my life; they were obviously much too profound to ever fade and vanish.

But *what* had been done to me? Again and again I asked the nurse, in a voice that slowly grew beyond a whisper into a rough, unmelodious murmur, but never once did she answer me. She did not, in fact, ever speak a single word. My location, my condition—even information as simple as her name—all this information was denied me. But in truth, my seeking it was a sporadic process at best. For the most part I slept—and it *was* sleep now, I realized, not unconsciousness. In my waking times I enjoyed my nurse's gentle ministrations, even if she was totally uncommunicative. There was, at least, one thing that I knew, one thing that I was certain of now. I was alive.

This seemed all but impossible, given my fragmented but comprehensible memories of my last moments on the old crumbling pier and in the cold bay water. I could remember the sensation of the liquid washing over my head, being drawn into my lungs, the world above the water fading into darkness. That had been my process of dying, I knew—I was sure. I had never expected to see or sense anything else, except if the afterworld proved to be a real thing and I came to consciousness either floating in the sky with Jesus or, more likely, roasting down below with Beelzebub. And yet here I was, miraculously restored, in a strange room with a silent and mysteriously masked little nurse.

Though I hardly thought of my convalescence as enjoyable, there was a certain peace to it—a simple predictable routine of care and sleep, sleep and care, that was not uncongenial. Of course from time to time my thoughts drifted to dark themes, with my myriad remembered dead rising in my memory and imagination, and I would feel stricken for a time at the loss—O heavy burden!—of so many from my life. And yet these sensations would not last long, as the bliss of sleep was never far from me, a comfortable and familiar friend in whose bosom I could sink virtually at will. My feverish fantasies of being the Angel of Death did not return; my slumber was without visions or dreams of any kind.

Of course this odd twilight life could not continue forever, and over time I became aware of additional footsteps clicking gently in the hallway beyond my room. Once I had a sensation of motion just beyond the partly open doorway through which my nurse had passed as she came in, and I heard soft footfalls moving away. But, though I asked my silent caregiver about this, she, as always, offered no reply. Another time I was far off in deep sleep when I sensed a presence next to me, a presence I somehow knew was *not* the nurse—I know not how to describe it, but something about the very air around me was different. I struggled to open my eyes but by the time I did, the figure was gone.

But at last came a time—I have the idea that it was morning, though I had no way of determining day from night—when I noticed that for the first time the nurse, having finished helping me with my meal and glided quietly out, for some reason left the door open. Always before it had been firmly closed, and I would invariably hear the click of a lock. Now, however, it gaped invitingly. I yearned to go to that door, to look out, to make my way up or down the hallways to whatever it was that awaited me there. But, though I was now capable of rising up off my back by use of my elbows, I was still quite unable to get out of bed by myself, much less stand and walk to the doorway—a distance which seemed to my exhausted eyes something like a thousand miles.

For some time nothing happened. I believe that I passed in and out of a light sleep for a while. Finally, however, there came the sound of footsteps nearing—a sharp clicking that grew steadily more clear and definite as I listened, taut with anticipation. Would I have my questions answered at last? Would I learn where I was, and why, and how long it would be until I could leave? Could I discover at last what had happened, how I got here—and what had been done to me?

When the generator of the footfalls stepped out of the hall shadows into the soft light of the room I knew immediately that I would have my answers if I wanted them. But I knew with a sickening horror that I was nonetheless doomed.

The person who walked into the room was Doctor Hudson Blackthorn!

2

"**M**y child," he said ingratiatingly.

He smiled down at me, big teeth square and yellow. His eyes were watery-gray and his skin so loose around his jaws that it seemed to be in the slow process of melting down his face. His hair and spotty beard were unkempt. I could hear his heavy breathing and detected, to my disgust, his odor—part whiskey, part—so I thought—formaldehyde. He had on a white doctor's coat which was splotched with varicolored stains and appeared to weave slightly as he stood there rubbing his hands before me.

I could say nothing, my mind frozen in fogbound horror. Was *this* the man who had saved me—who had taken me from the dark waters and restored my soul? This monstrous murderer, my personal redeemer? The idea was grotesque and obscene, and yet there it was—there *he* was.

"I have surprised you," said he. "Alas, I was aware that this would happen, and so I delayed my introduction for some time. It was better for you to regain some of your strength before you discovered that it is I who am your savior."

Savior! The very notion made me wish to emit a long, loud, frantic scream from the depths of my soul, but my throat was not ready. I heard myself making only little mewling sounds, like those of an unhappy kitten.

"There, there," said he, and I felt revulsion as he reached out his palm and patted me gently on the cheek. "It is all right now, Annabel. Everything will be quite all right. You will see."

"You—" I began to say, in a whisper that tore at my throat, "you—may go to the devil!"

He chuckled. "You misjudge me, my child. I have never been interested in anything but your welfare. I care about you. I care about you very much."

I wished to spit out the most vulgar oath imaginable at him, but as I could not deliver such a curse with any vocal power, I tried another approach. I actually spit. My energetic discharge spattered his face at dead center and I knew some small, momentary satisfaction.

But he only chuckled again, bringing forth a handkerchief from his pocket. "This is a good sign," said he, wiping away the results of my assault. "A very good sign. You are gaining strength."

"I hate you," I whispered.

"Of course you do," said he. "That is understandable. But in time it will change."

"It will not change."

"Well, we shall see." He smiled. "Would you like to learn some details about your current confinement?"

Of course I was eager, but I would not give him the satisfaction of hearing me say so. I simply glared at him and offered no response whatever.

"You were in a very serious situation, Annabel. You came very close to death itself. Indeed, I thought you had crossed that particular threshold—over time I thought more than once you had crossed it."

At last I whispered, "How much time?"

"You have been here just short of—six months, I believe." He seemed to think about it. "Yes, six months."

Half a year! It seemed incredible, and yet in another way I would not have been any more surprised if he had said six years, or six hundred.

"Where?" I whispered.

He looked surprised. "Oh, I thought that must have been obvious, my child. You are in my home. What people call Blackthorn House."

His house—that dreamlike mansion he occupied at the top of the hills, hidden by the grove of weeping willows. The house my father and I had passed by more than once in my youth, the

strange, turreted brick structure—in my child's mind, a veritable castle—of which we had known nothing but that the distinguished inventor and medical man Doctor Hudson Blackthorn
lived there. The house that played such a role in my early fancies when I would read the Gothic fantasies of Freneau and Poe.
And yet the room around me looked so very ordinary.

"Yes, I brought you here once you were past your initial crisis," said he. "It seemed the best thing." Looking at him, I saw
that he almost seemed to anticipate thanks coming forth from
my lips. If this was the case, he was doomed to disappointment.
I felt nothing but loathing for this repellant old creature.

"You have received only the finest care," he continued after
a moment. "No expense has been spared. Your needs have
stretched me to the very limits of medical knowledge, and
beyond. And yet..." He smiled again; I wished I could slap the
smile from his face. "And yet here you are."

I gestured at some of the scars on my shoulders.

"Yes, I performed surgeries upon you," he acknowledged.
"There was no choice. Otherwise we would certainly have
lost you. They were not simple procedures. These scars..." He
reached out as if to touch one, but my shrinking back caused
him to abandon the effort. "These scars are prominent now,
but they will fade over time. I can promise you that. But have
no worries, my dear. You are every bit as beautiful as you ever
were...to *my* eyes." He smiled.

I struggled to whisper a word. "Hospital...?"

"Alas, the hospital in Grimsleytown is no more," he sighed.
"As I mentioned to you some time before, financial setbacks
made matters difficult, and so I was forced to close the hospital permanently. And I am old. I wish only to stay here in my
home now, reflecting upon my life and amusing myself with
my...experiments."

Experiments...at that I began to slip from the scene again,
my mind tumbling back, darkness closing over the room and
his flabby face above me. I felt myself falling into sleep again,
blessed sleep, the only refuge I had now from a waking life of
disgust and dread.

As my consciousness rose and fell, darkened and then brightened again, I found in my more lucid moments that I was thinking of escape. Not then, of course; I was far from being able to flee Doctor Blackthorn's clutches in my current condition. But when I became somewhat stronger, I imagined—then it might be done. Further, it occurred to me that I might be able to enlist the assistance of the little nurse with the mask. We were both women, after all—surely she felt some of the gentler emotions toward one of her own sex who was in such dire straits as I. As I strengthened over the coming days I observed her carefully; she was always efficient—never a wasted motion ever—and always silent. What, I wondered, was the function of the mask? Was she disfigured? Was it something the doctor himself had done to her, perhaps in some sort of failed operation? Who was she? Did she have a family? Was there anyone on Earth who cared about her?

One morning during my breakfast I whispered to her, "Nurse, what is your name?"

There was no response.

"May I ask," said I, "why you wear that mask?"

She continued with her duties, spoon-feeding me warm porridge.

"Nurse, please talk to me," I said, introducing a note of pleading to my voice. "I need help. I wonder if you do too."

It could be, I thought, that she was deaf—that would explain it. Yet, though I tapped her on the shoulder to get her attention and attempted to enunciate my words slowly in order for her to read my lips, there was no change. She remained completely unresponsive.

"Nurse," I begged in a murmur, "you must help me. I must get away from this place. I do not understand your relationship to Doctor Blackthorn, but I can assure you that he means me no good at all. The man intends to destroy me—I know not how. But I believe that I am imprisoned here, and will be for some time. He is obsessed with me. He has been since I was a child. Nurse—oh, nurse, can't you understand? Can't you show pity for a fellow woman in distress and help me?"

Came a voice from behind the nurse: "She cannot help you."

I had not seen him coming; she was blocking my view of the doorway. I was struck dumb with fear and said nothing. Surely he had some sadistic punishment ready for my temerity in seeking assistance for my escape.

"Worry not, my child," he said, smiling as he always did. The nurse moved away as he approached. "I am not surprised that you tried this—I know what you feel about me. But this one—" he gestured vaguely to the masked woman—"this one can do nothing for you."

"Why?" I asked. I heard my voice growing a bit stronger. "Are you keeping her prisoner too? Do you have her under some sort of spell?"

"A spell!" He laughed. "There are no spells, my child. Don't be foolish."

"But she is your prisoner? You are holding her against her will?"

"I am not holding her against her will. Not at all."

"Why does she not speak? Why is her face hidden behind that mask?"

The nurse stood motionlessly beside us as if unaware of the conversation.

"She does not speak," said he, "because she is mute. As for the other, what you see there is not a mask. It is the face itself."

I looked from him to the nurse and back again. "That is absurd," said I.

"Though I refer to her as feminine," said he, "the nurse is not a woman, nor even a human being. The nurse is one of my little inventions. She is an automaton."

"A what?" I puzzled over the word.

"An automaton. An artificial creature. A machine."

I stared at him. "You're mad."

He chuckled. "That is possible. But the creature you see here beside me is not a living thing. She does not see or hear in anything like the way you and I do. Everything she does is arranged inside her in such a way that, given certain stimuli, she can respond in no other manner."

"There is no such machine."

"There *was* no such machine." He looked at the nurse

with obvious satisfaction. "One of my most successful little experiments."

"I do not believe you," said I, quietly but firmly.

"Truly? Do you not?" He turned and suddenly pushed her violently on the shoulder. Her body wavered and then returned to its earlier position. She offered no other response.

"She is terrified of you," I insisted. "She knows better than to react. Or else you have her mesmerized."

"My dear child, I can assure you that I have told you only the truth."

"You have told me insane things."

He looked at me for a long moment. Then he shrugged and moved to the nurse, standing behind her.

"Watch carefully, please," said he. He made indistinct motions with his hands for a moment. I heard an odd popping sound. Then he reached his hands to the nurse's head—and pulled it from her neck!

I mean this literally. He lifted the head away from her body with no more difficulty than an expert sommelier uncorking a bottle of Bordeaux. The headless nurse continued to stand there, apparently unaffected. Doctor Blackthorn held the head cradled in his arm and looked at me.

"You see?" he said at last.

I heard an odd, hoarse shrieking sound coming from somewhere near. I had only an instant to realize that it had come from myself before I passed into another dark oblivion.

I remember fragments of nightmares then—horribly lucid images of Doctor Blackthorn floating in blackness, swimming through the dark with his hands outstretched toward me, toward my head, reaching and grasping it and twisting my head from my body as I helplessly tried to scream, to no avail. Blood sprayed everywhere. His corpulent face loomed over me, pale and gigantic, like a malignant moon in the sky. His chuckle grew louder and louder until it threatened to deafen me. His palms touched my cheek again and again. I felt that I was in restraints, pulling against them with all my might, screaming until my lungs bled.

Then all was quiet, and I came to blear consciousness again.

The little nurse, her head fully intact, was caring for me as usual. At the moment she was changing the case on one of my pillows.

"Are you really a machine?" I asked her. My throat was not aflame, I noted; the screaming had been in my imagination only. Nor was I restrained in the bed.

But there was no response. The nurse went about her duties, though now I was repelled by the idea that the form before me was not a human one. Listening carefully, I realized that the soft hum of which I had been aware for some time came from her.

"She is powered with coal," said the doctor as he entered the room. This time I was not surprised to see him; somehow I knew he had been lurking nearby. "Her mechanism is extremely efficient. I only need to replenish her supply once a day. It takes only a few minutes." The smile came. "Perhaps you would like to watch the process."

"I would not," said I.

"As you wish," said he. "Did you know how she transmits your readings to me—your pulse and temperature? Here." He reached to the nurse and pulled up one of her sleeves slightly. Embedded in her wrist were several small dials like those one might see in a laboratory. "She is accurate to an extraordinary degree."

"What do you plan to do with me?" I asked.

"Do?" said he. "What makes you believe I plan to 'do' anything with you? I wish merely to see you well again."

"You wish more. I am sure of it."

He removed his *pince-nez* and cleaned them with a handkerchief. "My child, you simply have no faith in me. Yet it is I to whom you owe your life, you know. Without me you would most certainly have died in the surf of that horrible beach."

"I wish I had done so."

"Tsk, tsk. That is no way to talk. Life is a gift, my child. A gift to be cherished. A gift from God."

"There is no God."

"Ah. An atheist, I see. Was it your bohemian friends who put that idea in your head?"

"*You* did. Very effectively."

"Oh, Annabel." He sat on the side of the bed and I moved as far from him as I could. He reached out and, through the bedcovers, touched my thigh. "I must teach you to love life again."

"That can never happen. I will never love life again. I hate life. I hate living."

"Mm." He nodded, seemingly reflective. "That is sad, my child. But I tell you, it will change. You will know joy again."

I glared at him bitterly. "What happened to Jim?"

He blinked. "Jim?"

"Gamble. My fiancé. What did you do with his"—how I hated to say it!—"body?"

"I did nothing with it. I never looked at him again."

For a moment I felt hope. "You did not actually see that he was dead, then?"

"He was quite dead, my dear."

"But his body? Did you see his body in death?"

"I left the beach with your unconscious form in my arms. I never looked at him again after leaving him there and going to pursue you."

"Then there is a chance?" I asked piteously. "There is a chance he is not dead?"

He shook his head. "There is no such chance. You had best forget about your Jim Gamble, Annabel."

"Why? If you don't *know*…"

"But I do." Looking carefully at me, he reached into his coat pocket and brought forth a folded piece of paper. "This confirms the matter wholly. I suspected you would ask about it, so I brought this along. Do you feel that your eyes can read it well enough, or shall I read it to you?"

It is true that I had read nothing in a very long time. My eyesight was weak. But I said, "Give it to me."

He did so. As I unfolded the thing I saw that it appeared to have been clipped from a newspaper somewhere. The clipping was of a column perhaps four inches long, no more.

DEAD MAN FOUND ON BEACH

Residents of the community of Dorset were shocked on the night of Monday, December 12, to discover a corpse at the edge of the surf at Bay Beach. Interviews by the authorities with the local persons determined the identity of the corpse to be one James Gamble, 20 years of age, whose life had been brutally ended by a single bullet to the heart. Witnesses said that Mr. Gamble had been consorting in recent months with a young person—oddly, these witnesses disagree as to whether the person was male or female—who has inexplicably gone missing. An energetic search has been mounted up and down the beach, with the police fearful that this person's body may too be shortly discovered. It is also possible, of course, that this mysterious person may be Mr. Gamble's killer, and fled after the act. A search therefore is also ongoing in the local towns.

I stared at the clipping for a long time. After a while I turned it over and looked blankly at the advertisement for young ladies' dresses which was printed on the other side.

"You murdered him," I said quietly.

He smiled. "It was necessary."

I looked at him. "Why was it necessary?"

"Because you belong to me, Annabel," he murmured, stroking my thigh again. "You know it as well as I do myself."

"I know no such thing. You are disgusting."

"I brought you into the world," said he. "I have known you since the moment you made your debut in it. I know you as no one else ever can."

"You do not know me at all. You are foolish to think so."

"And you are foolish to deny it."

A heavy silence descended between us. I felt the dreadful paper in my hands, rubbed it gently with my fingers.

"When you are a bit stronger," he said brightly, standing, "I will be delighted to offer you a tour of your new home. I have many fascinating things to show you."

"My home?"

"Yes. This. Your home."

"This is not my home."

"What other have you, my dear?"

"That is not your business. I wish to leave this place. Now."

"You are far too weak to travel."

"Let me worry about that. Please call for a carriage with a strong driver who can carry me out of this terrible place."

He chuckled again. "That is not a practical suggestion."

"Then let me see Doctor Bailey," said I. "Bring him here. I wish to consult with him about my condition."

"Bailey left when the hospital closed," said the doctor. "I believe he has taken up practice in Philadelphia."

"Nonetheless I demand to be allowed to leave here."

He shook his head. "As your doctor, young lady, I must forbid it."

"You have no right to forbid it. You have no control over me."

"And yet you find yourself here."

"That," said I, "is a temporary situation."

"Believe as you wish," said Doctor Blackthorn. He turned and left the room.

In the next few days I did in fact grow stronger, to the point that I was able to get out of bed by myself and walk the length of the room, with the nurse's somewhat disturbing assistance. Eventually I left the room with her (the nurse was really "it," not "her," yet I thought of her as a woman) and walked slowly up and down a very dark hallway with numerous closed doors on either side. Once I impulsively reached to one of the knobs; but the door was locked.

Yet I did feel better—at least physically. Excellent solid food— small portions of steak, chops—began to appear occasionally on my plates. I ate by myself, under the mechanical nurse's steady stare—if "stare" it was—but without any assistance. The silverware was elegant but, I noticed, I was not supplied with any kind of knife except a shiny but very dull butter knife.

My walks grew longer, with the nurse leading me down a bewildering maze of corridors when I had the strength to navigate them. I had no idea where I was in the house or what direction I might be moving at any given moment. Still, I calculated that now was not the time to attempt any sort of rebellious action. I was a prisoner, but a well-kept one, and it would have been rash indeed to try to throw over Doctor Blackthorn's insidious confinement of me before I was strong enough to overcome him and the obstacles he would surely have in place for me. I would let him feed me and care for me, I thought, for the time being—but only with an eye to the main chance. Of course Doctor Blackthorn would realize this, and that was deeply concerning—but it was a matter for another time. What I had to do now was grow stronger and steadier.

I did attempt to pry information out of him, but my attempts yielded little. In particular, I wanted to know what surgical procedures had been committed to my person, but he would say only that they were "life-saving measures, my dear, using techniques known only to myself and perhaps two or three other practitioners in the world. You have no idea how advanced were your treatments. I shall show you all, in good time." As for his future plans for me all he said was that "they are not plans for you, Annabel; they are plans for *us.*"

One night—I had a glimpse of a window and could see the darkness outside—the nurse appeared with a burden in her arms. She unfolded it before me and I saw that it was a gown—a very handsome sleeveless gown of some lightweight material unknown to me. It was a soft pink in color. There were shoes as well, quite exquisitely made, and appropriate underthings. The nurse held them out to me.

"I am to wear them?" I asked.

The nurse stood motionless, obviously offering me the items.

I considered refusing, but here again, this did not seem the time to launch a rebellion. And, truth to tell, I was curious about what would happen once I was in the clothing he desired me to wear. I put it on—all of it. Everything fit perfectly, as somehow I knew that it would. When I beheld myself in the looking-glass I could not deny that the effect was an attractive one, though I myself still was sallow and very nearly cadaverous of aspect.

The nurse moved to the doorway and beckoned with her hand. I followed. She led me up and down various corridors, all dark, all silent, until at least we arrived before a particularly ornate door in the French style, quite tall and with intricate carvings in the wood. She opened this door and I found myself looking in on a most refined and gracious dining room—a beautiful room that under other circumstances would have been a pleasure to enter. Numerous candelabra provided the soft light. There was a long dining table with a beautiful white cover and golden bowls of fruit and bread along with elegant place settings. The plates were the finest white china, the silverware golden. The chairs—just two of them, I noticed, at opposite ends of the table—were high-backed and lovely, of a rather olden type. Around the walls were many paintings, none of which I recognized, but the styles of some seemed familiar.

As I looked at the impressive room the door sounded shut behind me, and I realized that I was alone. This caused a strange feeling within me; always in this house I was accompanied either by the nurse or the doctor himself. I would like to say that I attempted an escape right then, but I did not. The idea did not occur to me. I knew this was not the time, and no doubt the ever-present nurse was just outside the door—the only door, that is, except for a single one at the other end, some distance away. I suspected that I knew who would come through that door in a moment, and thus I was not surprised when Doctor Blackthorn made his appearance.

"My child," said he. His clothing was formal and fit his gross form admirably.

I said nothing. He approached the table and glanced over it, seemingly satisfied with what he saw. He then proceeded toward me. I backed toward the wall, but he stopped at my chair—I somehow immediately understood that it was to be mine—and pulled it out politely. He gestured toward me to sit.

The reader may wonder why I did not refuse his invitation. The truth is I was hungry, and at this particular moment I saw no hope of changing my situation. This was the oddity of my imprisonment—at no point did I feel physically threatened by the man, despite his arrest of my person. I also had come to believe that the doctor was quite mad. Thus it seemed a better idea to humor him than to openly rebel.

I allowed him to help me be seated.

Then he moved to his own side of the table and sat. He lifted a small bell I had not noticed before and shook it; in a moment the nurse entered, dressed now more like a server in a fine restaurant—or perhaps it was not the same machine at all. She held a tray with a wine bottle and two glasses. She showed the bottle to him; he nodded and she poured a sample into his glass. He tasted it, pronounced it satisfactory, and the nurse proceeded to fill both our glasses.

"Our meal will be along momentarily," he said smoothly. "Roasted pheasant."

The scene appeared unreal to me somehow. Was I really sitting here, with this man, a prisoner in his house, being served in this elegant room by a wood-faced automaton? When the meal came and I discovered how perfectly the pheasant and potatoes had been prepared, I am ashamed to admit that I ate heartily. I was aware that I was hardly behaving like a distressed prisoner, but he had clearly gone to some lengths to ensure that the meal would be virtually irresistible.

"Who prepared the food?" I asked.

"The staff," said he dismissively.

"Are the staff—are they persons? Or are they...?"

He smiled, wiping his lips with the napkin. "Automatons, my dear. There are no persons in this house other than the two of us."

"How many have you?" I knew not what I would do with this information, but it seemed wise to learn all that I could.

But he only smiled again and sipped his wine. "A sufficient number," said he. "Are you enjoying the meal?"

"The pheasant is excellent," I admitted.

"Good. Very good."

"Doctor Blackthorn," I began, speaking most carefully, "you said that at some point I might have a tour."

"Yes indeed. Perhaps not quite yet, I think. You are still very weak."

I could not deny it, but I said: "I should like to know how you see the future."

"The future?"

"The two of us," said I, inwardly shuddering at the very idea of an *us.*

"We shall live here, of course. But first we must make you well."

Again the reader may question my behavior. Did I shout? Did I scream? Did I denounce him as a sickening madman and rush from the room? I did none of those things. As chilling as his words were, I knew it was preferable to bide my time rather than rouse him to rage.

"I feel ever so much better than I did." That was true.

"I am glad of it."

"And—henceforth—we shall live here?"

"Indeed."

"What shall we do here?"

"Whatever we like. There are no limits here."

"Might we have guests?"

"Perhaps."

"Might we travel?"

He looked at me for a long moment. "Possibly," said he. "In time."

The dinner went on in this fashion, my asking seemingly anodyne questions while he gave only the most evasive of answers. He knew, I am sure, what I was about, and was far too wily to give out any definite information. I would have to learn what I needed to know in some other way, I realized.

After a dessert of mixed fruit and cake—also delicious—Doctor Blackthorn looked at me through his thick glasses and asked, "My dear, are you feeling well enough for a few minutes' entertainment?"

These words struck fear into my heart, but I was determined to learn all I could about this house and my situation as a captive in it. "Of course," said I.

"Splendid." He rang the little bell next to him and in a moment, to my astonishment, a small group of identical wood-faced automata entered the room. There were three of them, all in formal wear and carrying musical instruments—violin, viola, cello. A fourth carried chairs into the room and arranged them in a far corner. When it was finished, the three musicians sat and, without any direct communication between them, began playing—playing with what I can only call mechanical precision—a waltz I recognized as being by Carl Maria Von Weber. I suddenly realized that the doctor was standing next to me.

"Shall we dance?" he asked.

And thus I entered into the strangest dance of my life. It was all I could do to keep from tearing away from the old vulgarian, whose close breath and touch were as repulsive to me as would have been the breath and touch of a diseased rat. But even stranger was the little chamber group playing for us—they used no sheet music, I noticed, and moved only as was necessary to play their instruments. They sat stiff-backed and did not look around the room, or at each other. I found myself swallowing rapidly and blinking my eyes as the unreality of the scene sank into my consciousness. I was determined neither to faint nor scream, and I did not.

After one dance I stepped away from him. "I thank you," said I, genuinely breathless, "but I think I must rest now."

"Yes," said he, sympathy oozing from his voice. "This has been wonderful, my dear. I thank you for your company and your superb dancing." He took my hand again and raised it to his fleshy, shining lips. He kissed it slowly, lingeringly. I realized that I was in danger of vomiting up my entire dinner and so shut my eyes and forced myself to breathe slowly for a moment.

"The nurse will see you to your room," said he, dropping my hand again and looking dreamily at me. "Good night, my dearest."

For a week or more events followed this basic course. I stayed in bed during the day and in the evening would be escorted to the dining room where Doctor Blackthorn and I would consume a superb dinner followed by some few minutes of dancing.

"I apologize for the quality of the musicianship," said he during one such interlude. "I am still working out some of the problems of their fingers. It is difficult to make the motions as subtle as they must be for the likes of a Mozart waltz."

"On the contrary," said I, "they play quite well. They are very professional." As we swept past them I looked at the trio. The fantastic quality of watching large mechanical toys play classical waltzes had not yet faded for me, but I made every attempt to act as if it all seemed perfectly normal. I felt that the smoother and more compliant I was with this man, the likelier my chance of eventually forging my escape.

"Professional, yes," he admitted. "But my goal is to make them truly *great* musicians. I want them to be more accomplished than any fiddler of flesh and blood."

"Are you a devotee of music, Doctor Blackthorn?"

"Not at all. I enjoy it for times like these—" he smiled at me, his grotesque face so dreadfully close to mine—"but otherwise I have little use for it."

"Why devote such time to the perfection of mechanical players, then?"

"That, my dear, is the joy of science, the joy of research and of invention. These are the *first*, do you understand? There are no automata anywhere in the world like these. Maillardet had his little drawing machine, Merlin his Silver Swan, Martinet his musical elephant—bah! Silly toys, the lot of them. My machines are a hundred times those primitive experiments."

"How did your machines become so advanced?"

"I think in different ways," said he, as we swooped and dived to the music. "I proceed from different premises. You see the results."

"They are quite astonishing," said I, flattering him, but also telling the truth.

"Yes, they have a quality," said he. "But I have many more inventions to show you. This house is filled with them—the work of my lifetime."

"I should love to see them."

And in time I did. Eventually he allowed me into other rooms in the house, remote high-ceilinged rooms on the top floor. Always he accompanied me, and at least one of his machines remained present at all times. Most of these rooms were filled with paraphernalia the likes of which I had never seen before—much of it seemingly scientific in nature, great bars and canisters and beakers and gears which I was utterly unable to comprehend. In one such he had a huge brass and mahogany contraption that emitted a bright beam of light (he called it "limelight") onto a wall opposite; in the light was an ever-changing succession of images of all kinds, people, landscapes, animals—a magic lantern, yes, but it was far more than that. In every magic lantern show I had ever seen the images themselves were still. Here, however, the images *actually moved*—whether it was some form of trick, a kind of optical illusion, I knew not, but one beheld the face of a man, say, with wondrously lifelike qualities, and the man would move—one would see his lips curl into a smile, his eyes dance this way and that, his brows move up and down. In another room was a smaller mechanism of what appeared to be black onyx on which he revolved cylinders of metal which emitted, through some process of which I also had no understanding, a kind of sound—scratchy and metallic, admittedly, difficult to comprehend, but *sound*—a voice, a voice which I quickly realized belonged to him, saying again and again, "This is a test. This is a test. This is a test." Doctor Blackthorn was standing next to me, but his lips did not move—the sound of his voice had instead been preserved at some earlier time within the cylinder he showed me and was now recalled by the magic of the onyx box.

But even these marvels paled in comparison to what he called his *thought-projector,* a device in some ways reminiscent of the magic lantern he had shown me, yet of a different nature altogether. It was a box that, like the lantern, projected light onto a wall, but in this case Doctor Blackthorn sat down behind the instrument and placed a set of what appeared to be earmuffs on his temples, earmuffs that were connected to the box device by means of a thick black wire. For a time he stared at the screen, which showed nothing but the bright "limelight"; but after a minute or two rough, imprecise images began to appear on the screen. They were multi-colored, indistinct; they moved jaggedly, erratically, appearing and disappearing in seconds.

"These are my actual thoughts," said he, "translated into light-impulses and made visible. What you see is the actual working of my mind." He looked at me. "Would you like to try it?"

I admit I recoiled at the very idea. But, in my effort to

maintain a calm and pleasing aspect to his eyes, I smiled and said, "Of course. If you promise me that it is safe."

"It is very safe," said he. "The device is merely a reader. There is no pain whatsoever, no sensation of any kind." He removed the earmuffs and stood, offering them to me. I sat and placed the earmuffs carefully upon my temples.

"Just relax your mind," said he. "Think of nothing. The device works best when the mind is in a state of repose and tranquility."

I tried to follow his directions, but for some minutes no images except the feeblest gray streaks appeared on the screen. Then, after a time, another image—hazy, but slowly growing in distinctness. It was the outline of a man, his head and shoulders, but for some moments it entirely lacked any human features—it was instead like a clay figure. Another set of moments passed and the figure resolved to a degree—it materialized eyes, a nose, a mouth, a beard—and with shock I realized my mind was forming the image of Jim Gamble! I hastened to take the earmuffs from my head, hoping Doctor Blackthorn had not realized, but he had. He literally knew what I had been thinking of—and that it had not been of him.

"That is enough for one evening," he said gruffly, putting away the equipment and turning abruptly away. "The nurse will show you back to your room." He walked briskly out, ending that evening with none of the sentimental endearments with which he had regaled me on earlier such occasions.

Later, in my room, I thought about what my brain had apparently created on that screen—and what image his own had. To have seen, if only indistinctly, the image of my Jim begin to form was strange, but also oddly familiar—it was, after all, if Doctor Blackthorn was to be believed, a projection of my own brain I saw. I mulled over the dramatic contrast between the image of Jim—an image which, I thought, would have sharpened to lifelike clarity if I had continued sitting there for a few more moments—and the jumbled and incoherent abstract patterns that were displayed when the doctor himself was at the machine. Could it be, I wondered, that I was the first person besides himself to ever try it? Was it possible that he had been not so much shocked by the particular image pouring forth from my brain, but rather that mine was so very clear as compared to his own? And might the explanation lie in the madness with which I was convinced he was afflicted? Perhaps a sane person who tried the device projected a focused, natural image; whereas someone who was as unbalanced as Doctor Blackthorn....

I was beyond my depth in such musings, but I was quite sure the doctor must have been thinking along similar lines. Perhaps he had found a justification—a rationalization—to explain away the contrast in some way other than the obvious one. He may have reasoned that women's brains were different than men's—simpler, perhaps—and that accounted for the difference. And yet, while he might make himself believe it, I would not. I found myself certain that what we each saw on that screen was a perfect reflection of our individual thoughts: my own of love and devotion to a man's memory; his of irrationality and madness.

To my surprise, after the night with the thought-projector I did not see Doctor Blackthorn for several days. Instead a variety of books was brought in by the nurse for my perusal—anodyne fiction and inspirational poetry, of no interest to me except for the base purpose of making the hours go by—and I was allowed to walk the halls for some minutes, closely monitored. Into none of the rooms was I allowed to enter.

In this interregnum I gave myself over to my thoughts. The time for resistance, I knew, was drawing near. I was stronger now than I had been since being brought here, and while I doubted my ability to overcome the doctor in an actual physical altercation, I believed that I might have a chance if I had the advantage of surprising him. Still, I was uncertain where I would go—I had been nowhere near the ground floor of the mansion since coming here, and did not know which of the several winding staircases might take me to a door through which I could escape. Again and again I had noticed that the stairs in this house were twisted and bizarre—first they looped off in one direction, then another—so that, without great familiarity with the house, or else a map of it, it would be most difficult to find any direct path to an exit. Too, I did not know to what extent the mechanicals would attempt to keep me from flight. And in all my time at Blackthorn House I never once saw or heard another human being besides my captor. He must have had deliveries made of food, scientific apparatus and other supplies; but when or where these occurred I had no idea.

And yet the notion of escaping, of going away forever from this nightmarish cavern of strange and bewildering things, began to obsess me. How maddening it was to realize that only a few miles away lay the town of my birth! I had not seen the sun in ages; all the curtains were kept permanently closed, and on the one occasion I quickly peeked past the purple curtain in my own room (the nurse was picking up a tray), I saw only a dull gray glow. The window had been soaped, or oiled, and nothing was discernable beyond it. By looking I was able to determine whether it was night or day, but that was all.

Still, it was something—a beginning. After that single incident I tried looking around the curtain again, to discover that the nurse made no move to stop me. I was free, it seemed, to look at a soaped window as long as I pleased. And yet, I reasoned, surely it was valuable to know whether it was morning or night. It provided me a starting point for my thinking.

I considered various plans, but none was suitable. The window, I discovered by attempting to lift it, was locked. In theory I could hurl a chair through the glass—that is, assuming it was not some sort of unbreakable glass invented by the doctor and unknown to the outside world—but from my previous knowledge of the house I guessed I was at least fifty feet from the ground. I needed a rope, then—a ladder—some way of climbing down. But this seemed an utter impossibility; the nurse missed nothing in her daily visits to my room. The idea that I could secret anything at all was improbable. The notion of tossing out a note occurred to me—though from where I would obtain the necessary ink, pen and paper I could not imagine—and even if I could, there was no one around the mansion for miles. I knew that all too well. How I recalled riding freely past this dismal place with my father when I was a child, no more than two or three hundred yards from where I sat imprisoned now!

Could I mount an escape from another room, then? That

was even less likely. I was never alone for an instant when I was outside my own room, and all the mechanicals had extremely fast reflexes. It seemed to me that if I were to launch an escape it would have to be from my room, but escape from my room was infeasible. I would have to wait, I knew, though such waiting was agonizing. I would have to learn what I could through constant observation of the doctor and the mechanicals. I would have to see Doctor Blackthorn had in store for me—and decide when, where, and how I might strike.

3

It took months of patient effort, but eventually I learned a great deal.

Since I was unobserved only when in my own room, and since I could hear the humming sound of the nurse whenever she came near, I resolved to study my room—my *cell*—as closely as I could, to scrutinize it in every detail whenever I was alone. At first this seemed a futile exercise that yielded me nothing, but the more I studied the more I found ideas coming to my brain. It might be possible, I speculated, to quietly strip away part of the purple window curtain—some of the hem on the inside, the part facing the wall—and fashion some manner of weapon with it, but I was unsure that the material would prove strong enough to act effectively as a garrote. More promising was the fact that, as I investigated the understructure of my bed, I found that a number of metal beams secured the frame to the head and footboard—one of which might, with patience and effort, be removed and used as a crude club. But again, it was difficult to see how this would work in practice. Even if I managed to remove one of the beams, they were not in truth very large or heavy, and I might only manage a single pitiful blow before the nurse or Doctor Blackthorn—whoever would be my intended first victim—disarmed me. Each new plan seemed to contain a fatal flaw that would doom its successful execution.

In the meantime I had spent many evenings with Doctor Blackthorn and his automatic orchestra. Once I recall asking him about an oddity I had noticed in the various rooms

"Doctor Blackthorn," said I, "how is it that there are no fireplaces in this house, and yet the rooms remain comfortable?"

"Ah," he smiled. "Yes, I have a system for that—a method of warming the walls. It's quite simple, really." That was all I would ever learn about the heating system at Blackthorn House.

On another such evening one of the musicians—it was the violinist—developed some sort of mechanical difficulty and began playing out of time from the rest. The doctor, cursing under his breath, broke from his dancing with me and marched angrily to the machine, and I watched as he appeared to reach behind the thing's head, somewhere at the base of its neck, upon which moment it completely ceased moving. The doctor then stepped to face the now motionless automaton again, reaching to its chest and, to my surprise, opening it—the formal wear, obviously custom-cut for the purpose, broke smoothly away with the panel—and I beheld the inner workings of one of Doctor Blackthorn's creations. A mass of clockwork it was—silver and gold gears of varying sizes packed within the cavity, with mysterious levers and screws apparently holding it all together. Nothing moved for a moment, as the doctor's nimble fingers made an adjustment here or there; then he reached behind the thing's head again, and in a moment the clockwork all began to emit a slight humming sound and to each individual gear circled smoothly in its place. Apparently satisfied, the doctor shut the door to the machine's chest and stepped back as the thing raised its instrument and bow again and began to play, perfectly in time now.

The doctor smiled at me. "A simple problem to fix. Now we may return to our dancing."

"Doctor," said I as our hands met again, "are such mechanisms not dangerous?"

"Not at all, my dear. You are perfectly safe with them. They are the support staff for the house, that is all."

The next day I managed to move behind the nurse while she was changing my sheets and saw that, indeed, there was what might have appeared to a casual observer no more than a sort of skin lesion or mole on her neck, just below the hairline. Over the ensuing days I also managed to see this lesion-style mark on another of them, and so I knew it was the switch for the creatures' animation. I had no idea what would happen if I tried to interfere with one of them, but at least I now had information—valuable, even priceless information.

How aware the doctor was of my amateur detective work I could not know. Whenever he was with me his eyes, as distorted through his *pince-nez*, rarely left me—it was clear that his obsession with me was complete and all-encompassing. I wondered how I might use this to my advantage. He remained a wily antagonist at all times, but I could hardly believe that he thought as clearly when my warm body was in his arms as when he was alone with his experiments and his thoughts. And yet I hesitated to become forwardly flirtatious; I knew that any change in my behavior would be received with suspicion. However his perverted mind rationalized what he had done, and was doing, he was well aware that I was a captive and should attempt escape given even the remotest chance. I was, in truth, his pet: well cared-for, well-fed, praised and pampered, but always—*always* his prisoner.

Our relationship, or what he believed was a relationship, continued to develop. He began talking regularly about "our future, our life together," and I did nothing to dissuade him from such words. I had to carefully navigate between sympathy and womanly reserve in my feigned responses, and while I believe I did the best I could, there was sometimes a look in his eyes that suggested he was not entirely taken in by my act. I realized that, paradoxically, I was being perhaps *too* agreeable, *too* pliant—that I was not displaying any of the anger and rebellion that he may have expected of me, and thus his apparent suspicion.

From that time I decided to mount small resistances—to show him a more rounded version of myself, however dramatized and unreal. To that effect I deliberately worked myself into tears one evening as I made my way with the nurse to the dining room. It was not difficult—all I had to do was visualize Jim Gamble, allow myself to hear his voice in my mind, and the tears flowed most satisfactorily. In a way I felt guilty using Jim Gamble's memory for an ulterior motive like this, but on the other hand I felt he would have understood—that he more than anyone on Earth would have wanted me to do anything necessary to escape the clutches of the fiend.

And so upon entering the dining room to join me Doctor Blackthorn immediately espied tears flowing down my cheeks. They unnerved him. "My child, my child!" he cried, moving swiftly to my side. "You are upset. Oh, this is terrible. Sit down, my dear, sit down," said he, guiding me to my usual seat. "What is it that has upset you so?"

"I cannot tell you," I sobbed.

"You can tell me anything, Annabel. Do you not know that by now?"

"It's just that I miss my other life," said I. "I miss my friends. I miss being outside under the trees in the sunshine. It is—it is like being buried alive here, Doctor Blackthorn!"

This speech greatly disturbed him, and the intensity of his reaction proved to me that he was completely convinced by my show of tears. "You mustn't feel that way," he said gently. "What we have here is the ultimate freedom, my child—freedom from the world. Here we are *truly* free."

"It does not always feel so," said I.

"Of course," said he with sympathy in his voice. "The change is a great shock to you. I cannot expect you to absorb it in such a short time."

"Are we to be here forever, Doctor Blackthorn? Am I never to see sunlight again, or grass, or the stars?"

This question made him visibly uncomfortable. "In time," he murmured hesitantly.

"I do not think you are telling me the truth."

"But of course I am!" he cried, standing suddenly. "Annabel, we shall go wherever we want! Boston—New York—Canada— all the great capitals of Europe! Anywhere at all!"

"But how, if you keep me here?"

"All in time," he said at last, moving close to me again.

"This is a promise?" I asked.

He took my hand. "Of course, my dear," said he.

I managed, entirely for his benefit, a wan smile.

Other times he showed me more of his extraordinary experiments. One night after dancing he led me and the nurse to a room filled, to my surprise, with living creatures—rats and mice in large glass cages.

"What do you do with them?" I asked, strangely happy to see some other form of life besides Doctor Blackthorn's gross and corpulent one, though caged animals have always somehow depressed me. I gazed through the glass of one such cage, a big white rat with a quivering pink nose stretching up to look curiously at me.

"Tests," said he. "Experiments. Look here." He guided me to a long metal table on which was scattered a variety of what appeared to be veterinary instruments. He pointed to a glass contraption which held in metal braces several bottles of what seemed to be blood. "I have been studying the possibilities of extending their lives through the addition of certain enrichments to their blood supply."

"You give them new blood?"

"Enriched blood, yes. You see how what is in each of these bottles looks slightly different than the other?"

"Yes." One was a bit darker, one brighter. One seemed to glow dimly.

"I try exchanging as much of their blood as I can with my new, improved supplemented blood. Then, over time, I study the results."

"And what have those results been?"

He smiled. "Look here. At your friend." He led me again to the glass cage in which sat the white-furred rat. It occurred to me that its situation and my own were not so very different. "A rat of this type can be expected to live a year, perhaps two years. Do you know how long this specimen has been alive?"

"I do not."

"Five years and two months."

"Goodness." I studied the creature carefully. "It looks just like any other rat."

"But it's not. By rights this fellow should have been in his grave three years ago. And you see, it shows no signs of age. It is healthy and inquisitive."

"Are the rest like this?" I asked, indicating all the other rodents in the cages.

"In various ways," said he. "Some have been given different blood serums in different ratios. Some remain untreated, so that I may use them to establish a baseline for research. I keep all the records scrupulously." He indicated a large stack of ledger-books.

"Doctor Blackthorn," said I as we returned to the dining room, "what is it all for? Your researches are extensive and extraordinary. Surely you have made huge advances in half a dozen fields of research—and yet the world knows nothing of any of them, does it?"

"It does not."

"Why the secretiveness? These experiments could push research forward in all the fields by decades, surely."

"They could."

"Is it not your duty to share your findings with the world?"

We had reached the dining room, where the mechanical musicians were still blindly playing. He took my hand and we slid into a slow waltz.

"I care nothing for the world," said he.

"But a man of your abilities…"

"I care nothing for it at all," he insisted. "Everything I require is in this house. I have no interest in anything outside it anymore. I am an old man, my dear. The world does not interest me. I have money. Fame and glory mean nothing to me. I merely wish to live out my days here, with my various experiments… and with you."

I felt my face grow hot. "But you said we would travel. We would see Boston and New York and Canada and the capitals of Europe."

"Ah, that." He frowned. "Surely we must, my dear. But there are so many other things to do first."

"And they are?"

"Our marriage, for a start."

I swallowed, feeling slightly queasy. "Our—marriage."

"I realize that you are not yet ready, my dear," said he. "You still think of me as an ogre, a disgusting old man who—"

"Doctor Blackthorn, I did not say—"

"But you think it. I see it in your eyes. I hear it in your voice.

First I must win you, my dear. I must *make* you love me. And I shall!"

Alone in my room I continued my studies and speculations. How I wished I might approach one of the mechanicals to see how it worked—I had no idea if one of these artificial people would resist if I reached to it, or if it would allow me to touch the mole on the back of its neck to determine if it was truly a switch. Could I turn them on and off myself, or would they viciously attack me for trying? And if I successfully switched one off, would Doctor Blackthorn know? Was there in his scientific system a way of detecting that one of his creations had been disabled?

The automata were only part of my problem. Assuming they could be defeated, there remained the question of Doctor Blackthorn himself. How could I defeat him? No matter how long and hard I examined the things in my room I could not determine a weapon, and I doubted I could overcome him physically without one. He was brilliantly intelligent and surely would not be duped by any crude diversionary tactic on my part. I knew I could not continue in this existence much longer—that I must break free somehow, or die in the attempt. What, then?

To keep him convinced of my perfect sincerity I continued making occasional shows of emotion and even direct protest. These seemed to please him, though they were entirely manipulative on my part. He appeared to enjoy appeasing me, placing his thumb on my cheek while we were on the dance floor and brushing away my tears, speaking to me in his most soothing voice when I raised mine in simulated anger. But the truth is, something was unloosed in me when I encouraged myself in these dramatic performances. The tears, which were initially the product of only the most cynical of feigned feelings, sometimes had a way of becoming real. I might think to myself, "Tonight I will plead tearfully with him for my release," and carefully work up my emotions in the minutes before I knew the nurse would arrive to escort me to dinner, but once the tears were actually flowing I had at times the sudden realization that quite real emotions were flowing as well. It was rather as if an actress on stage suddenly found herself in the exact situation in life which she had just been performing artificially for an audience. And so it was sometimes unclear to me which of my emotions were actually real. My situation, after all, was intolerably horrifying. A part of my mind was able to assess this fact dispassionately even as another part felt all the hysteria and rage any person would feel at being kidnapped and confined—and while still another chose to manipulate and exaggerate those emotions in an effort to gain favor with my abductor. It was all a boiling confusion of feeling which, over time, began to exhaust me.

At one point I remember that it became difficult for me to arise from bed. A bitter melancholia had settled over my spirit, and this one not feigned at all. I felt listless and dull—utterly without hope. I could not picture in my mind a future which did not include the doctor's repulsive face. I was doomed, I thought. I had overcome so much in my life only to be destroyed by this mad genius, this man who might have contributed so much to the world but instead was lost in his insane preoccupation with me. And who was I? Merely a girl, still in her tender teenaged years—a girl without any truly distinguishing traits. I had been told that I was quite pretty, but surely my emaciated frame and surgical scars had changed that. What else was there, then? It all seemed an endless darkness, and I myself lost in it forever.

I became unresponsive and very near catatonic. I ate little. I did not attend the nightly dinner and dances, though I could still hear, night after night, very distantly, the music of the automatic orchestra. Tears frequently ran down my face, but I did not cry—I seemed beyond tears.

Doctor Blackthorn visited me each evening—I believe it was in the evening—and clucked and fretted. He examined me—took my pulse, checked my temperature, gave me various strengthening liquids and foods. He was genuinely worried, I realized—and even in my very real despondency I knew that this gave me an advantage.

I decided finally to attempt something that would bring the matter to a climax in one way or another. To this day I do not know how real or legitimate was my action—how much a staged drama, how much a valid and true expression of feeling—but one evening as I sat dejectedly in bed pushing my dinner about on my plate I suddenly, in one smooth motion, smashed the glass that had held fruit juice against the headboard—sticky juice splashed everywhere—and, before the nurse could reach me, took the jagged edge of the glass and ran it up my left arm as hard as I could, crying *"I shall die!"*

The jagged glass sank into my flesh with a sensation of ice, and though the nurse had the glass out of my hand within seconds, the damage had been done—blood flowed freely from half-a-dozen gruesome cuts three or four inches long along my inner arm, flowing across my arm and dripping into the bedsheets. Though there was as yet no pain, my arm felt as if it had been doused in freezing water and I found myself shaking violently. The nurse moved quickly to take my arm by force and wrap it in a portion of loose bedsheet as the world tilted in my consciousness and I believe I blacked out for some minutes.

When my mind returned again Doctor Blackthorn was there, quickly and professionally cleaning the wound and applying iodine. Quickly and professionally, yes—but I could see that he had been weeping.

"Child, child," said he in a voice little more than a whisper.

"It cannot be helped," I whispered in return. "If you insist on keeping me prisoner here I must die."

"No, child, no."

"I will find another way. You cannot stop me."

He said nothing for some minutes, until he was finished binding my wounds. The bedsheets, I noticed, had been changed during my unconsciousness.

"I will leave the nurse here with you," said he.

"The nurse is not as fast as I am."

"Mm." He seemed to think. "But if you need something…"

"I need my freedom."

He stared at me for a long time. He removed his *pince-nez* and cleaned them with his handkerchief sorrowfully.

"Do you know how much I love you, child?"

"You are obsessed with me."

"That may be true."

My arm had begun to blaze with pain, but something told me to press the conversation forward. "Why?"

"What do you mean, my dear?" His voice had taken on a sad quality I had not heard before.

"Why do you feel as you do about me? I have always known it." I was entering dangerous ground but felt I must continue. "Ever since I was a girl I have known that you had some odd feeling about me. I knew it when I was hardly more than a toddler—the way you looked at me, the way you touched me. At first I thought you were just—just friendly and that was all. But as I grew older I started to sense something else. Something unhealthy."

"Child, child," he said, shaking his head.

"Do you deny it?" I demanded, trying to sit up on my elbows. "Do you deny the looks, the sighs, the sense that you wanted something more from me than what a family friend might ask? When you sent me to Sadmore you wept. There was a look on your face that seemed to hold all the sorrow in the world. I have never forgotten it. What I do not understand is *why*—why you should have had such a look on your face."

He stared silently at the wall opposite.

"Speak to me!" I demanded.

"There are things," said he finally, very hesitantly, "that you do not know about me."

"Of that I am sure. What of it?"

Still his eyes were averted. "You know so little, my dear."

"You are evading my question. I demand an answer. If you do not answer my question I pledge to you under God's watchful eye that I shall certainly kill myself, and I shall do it soon. You have left me nothing to live for. What is the answer to my question?"

"Oh, child." He looked at me. His face had the hollow, sunken-eye look of any wearer of spectacles when those spectacles are removed.

In that moment I stared at his face and saw something I had never seen before—something new—something unprecedented, ghastly—something impossible. My body suddenly tingled with shock and horror.

"Yes," said he, recognizing my understanding.

My breath came quick and short. I trembled all over.

"It cannot be," said I. "It cannot be true. It *must* not be true!"

"It is. You have seen it yourself now."

"No. *No!*"

He reached out to my face then and touched it. He touched my hair—my temples—my eyelids—my cheeks—my lips—my jaw—my neck. I could do nothing to resist. I could but stare speechlessly at him.

"It is true, Annabel," said he. "You are my daughter."

"That is impossible. It is disgraceful for you to say such a vile thing."

He looked down. "It is the truth."

"I have a father," said I. "Or I had. My own father." As I spoke these words a quick series of evanescent visions cross over my mind: Father and I in the library, reading Shakespeare or Biblical verse to each other; Father and I in the garden, talking of the flowers; Father and I out riding, the two of us taking in the landscape around us. I had buried him in my mind—the memories were too painful to confront—and suddenly he was there again, vivid and alive in my brain.

"Selwin Lee was your stepfather, child."

"You lie! You are an awful, vulgar, terrible liar!"

He looked at me again, his eyes filled with an infinity of sorrow. "Child, look at me. Subtract the eroding effects of my many years upon this Earth. Tighten my skin. Eliminate the fat. Make my eyes bright and youthful again. Now consider the shape of my forehead, my eyebrows, my nose, the curve of my lips. Do you not now see the clear resemblance?"

"Be quiet. Stop talking. I will not hear you."

"You bear some resemblance to your mother," said he. "Your cheekbones, in particular, are like hers. Your hair is much like hers was in her young days."

"You are a disgusting beast. How dare you speak of my mother and father in this manner. You repulse me."

Then he did something which I found truly shocking. He stood slowly, tiredly and, to my astonishment, pushed back his coat with his arms and took hold of his vest. He quickly unbuttoned and exposed the shirt underneath.

"Doctor Blackthorn!"

"It is only to prove a point, child."

Upon saying this he opened his shirt in the vicinity of his belly and I beheld the black hourglass shape there—the same hourglass-shaped mole I myself possessed, in nearly the same spot on my skin, and which I saw now as a veritable Mark of Cain.

The world blacked out.

I lay in bed many days, shivering and convulsing and weeping. There was no possible artifice in my emotions now—they were all too, too real. I would sink into unconsciousness and suffer horrible nightmares and then wake again to the even more abominable phantasm of reality. The awful blow had caused me to contract brain fever. My entire frame seemed alternately blazing hot and frigidly cold. I felt continually as if I were drowning, that everything was sinking away into eternal darkness. My mind could not remove his horrible visage as much as I tried to replace it with the picture of my wonderful, dear Selwin Lee, my gentle and kind father, the man who first cared for me, took me seriously, listened to my questions and answered them with genuine thought and reflection, the man who taught me—amused me—loved me! That was my father! That would always be my father! Selwin Lee of sainted memory!

I know not how long I remained incapacitated. In rare lucid moments I feared that I was quite losing my mind, literally running mad—and yet at other moments I accepted the madness, welcomed it, as the only path out of the intolerable prison of life and sanity. The nurse fed me and changed my bedclothes as she had done before, but for a time I did not see Doctor Blackthorn. No doubt he had come to the conclusion that his visage would send me swirling down father down the sinkhole of despair. Probably he was correct in this, but in truth my memories of this period are so confused that it is as if a hurricane had hit my mind and scattered everything hither and thither across a dozen miles of landscape. What I thought I knew—the solid bases of reality on which I had built my life—lay in tatters, shredded and ripped apart by facts and forces I could not comprehend.

But at some point—it may have been weeks or even months after the precipitant crisis—I became aware that he had begun reentering my room and spending time looking down at me. At such times as I saw him I would invariably utter an oath of disgust and turn my face to the wall. And yet he continued, never coming close, never trying to touch me, for which I was profoundly grateful—such a touch might have caused me to start screaming and once started, I thought, I might never stop. He would just sit some distance from me and look at me with an expression which I do not think I could ever properly describe—part loving, part salacious, part panicked, part grief-stricken—a mélange of emotions that played continuously over his bloated and sagging face.

And then—I know not exactly when or how—I became aware that at times he would speak to me. He took to visiting around twilight and seating himself in the plain chair just behind me, near my head but too far for me to reach (had I desired to, which I certainly did not) and out of the range of my vision; to see him would have required a considerable twist of my neck and body, one for which I possessed not the strength.

He spoke quietly. His voice, always deep, took on a sonorous and reflective quality in that small room, with just the two of us present. I was always awake when he came, but perhaps not always fully conscious—I know I drifted in and out of his long monologue from time to time. And monologue it was. Stretched over numerous evenings, the monstrous Doctor Blackthorn spoke to me about his life and experiences. I was too weak to resist, but I confess that the narrative thus unfolded to my ears was not without interest, and even held a certain fascination for me. While my heart continued to rebel at the idea of this villain being in any way related to myself—I had one father and only one—still my mind recognized that the possibility did in fact resolve certain issues and confusions that had always reigned in my family regarding my background and that of my mother. The idea was sickening, and yet—while keeping always in view the fact that Selwin Lee was my father, my only father, my *real* father, father of my heart and emotions, my soulmate, my proud hero—I was able at times to puzzle out how such a gruesome notion as Doctor Blackthorn being my natural or "biological" father might in fact not be untrue. The idea was bewildering and sorely difficult to contemplate, but he had been correct when he surmised in my shocked and appalled expression just before my seizure that I had actually realized that there was, never acknowledged by myself, a—the phrase horrified me to the bottom of my soul—family resemblance between us.

Over time, as I thought these miserable and perplexing thoughts, Doctor Blackthorn told me his story. His voice was ever soft and calm—he sought not to make me react with any kind of female hysteria. But he talked, and I confess that instead of demanding, however weakly, that he leave my room and never sully my sight with his face again, I listened. I listened with interest and sometimes with a terrible fascination. What he told me I have transcribed as best I could from long-ago memories of his voice in my sickroom. The tale was not told in such a strict order, and it was, as I have indicated, delivered over many sessions rather than as the single continuous narrative I have recreated below. But, with a few trifling exceptions where I have felt the need to smooth a transition or have interpolated a few words for clarity, what I have recorded is essentially what he told me over those evenings. I cannot and do not vouch for its specific truthfulness, though I did later verify many of the larger particulars of his tale. But the narrative itself seems to me of sufficient interest in terms of understanding not only Doctor Blackthorn but the source from which I myself seemingly sprang that I have included it here. The reader must make his own judgment about it.

4

NARRATIVE OF DOCTOR HUDSON BLACKTHORN

I am by birth a Bostonian, belonging to that distinguished tribe of Blackthorns who played such a quiet but crucial role in the American Revolution and later in the state governments of New York and Massachusetts. I was raised in material comfort; my own family, consisting of my father, mother, and two sisters, were not part of the main line of Blackthorn politicians and statesmen but rather a side branch which nonetheless enjoyed a certain degree of privilege and distinction. Father was a cleric, and ministered to all our more celebrated cousins in their baptisms, marriages, and funerals. Mother was gifted at womanly pursuits such as knitting and embroidery, and of course she ran the house. Both of them were mild-mannered and gentle in their approach to their children, and indeed to life generally.

I was not like other boys. Not for me were the spirited games of physical skill; not for me the rough-and-tumble of boys' play. I was not physically strong, and my interests ran to more intellectual pursuits. My first great passion was natural philosophy. The workings of the natural world, its plants and trees and grasses, were a source of endless fascination to me. Later I became preoccupied with the heavens, building for myself a telescopic lens to search for life on the moon and other planets. At a still later period I grew interested in technological inventions, reading all I could about such novelties as magic lanterns and automata and attempting to apply my knowledge in experiments to develop new, more advanced varieties of such things. I was but seven or eight years old in this period, and of my efforts it need only be said that I totally failed.

Boys mocked me for my intellectual pursuits, and occasionally I would be the butt of jokes and even of mild assaults. This had the tendency to drive me further inward, into myself and my private thoughts and ideas. I had no friends. I suppose I was a peculiar-looking boy, with my long face, strangely-colored hair (something between rust-red and orange), and tendency toward excess weight; certainly I had few social skills. And yet my teachers discovered soon enough that I was in possession of an intellect quite unlike anything they had hitherto encountered. A book a teacher would plan to spend two weeks covering I would read in a day—even in an hour—and enjoy nearly total recall of it thereafter. Mathematics were like a second language to me, a language I grasped and conquered virtually before I was even instructed in the subject. I remember once—I must have been six or seven years of age—my mother coming upon me in my bedroom writing on my slate numbers of which she had no comprehension whatever. She believed them to be childish gibberish. The numbers were, in fact, quadratic in nature; I was creating and solving problems in algebra before I knew the word itself. So too with experiments—again without instruction, or far ahead of what instruction I was receiving, I learned about chemicals and gravity and momentum and electrical forces. No one taught me these things; I was discovered them almost entirely on my own.

My intellect drew considerable attention. Once my father drove me to the Harvard University where I met with a professor who quizzed me closely on my knowledge and had me solve certain problems in geometry which he put before me. The old man found my performance so astonishing that he dismissed both my father and me as charlatans, though he was utterly unable to describe how such an astonishing trick might have been effectuated. I was ten years old at this time.

As I grew into my adolescent years I entered college—it was Harvard, in fact, my father having had numerous other experts test me in the intervening years and convincing the institution that I was neither a criminal malefactor nor an abnormally small adult of high intelligence—and I flourished there. I flourished *intellectually*; my social development was another matter. I was of course many years younger than any of the other students, being thirteen when I entered studies there, and the other pupils had little interest in me. I was a freak, and so far beyond their own not-inconsiderable mental capabilities as to excite suspicion and even fear. I lived on the campus, constantly surrounded by much older boys and their odd smells and mysterious subjects of conversation. One such subject was, of course, the female sex, which they discussed in quite shockingly gross detail. I learned that there were "good" women—some of the young men were in informal engagements with such as these—and "bad" ones, who, it seemed, resided in certain houses in Cambridge known to all and sundry and who would perform certain acts, quite unknown and incomprehensible to me, in exchange for money. These young men would laugh when they realized I had over-heard them in such talk, and occasionally they deliberately cornered me to tell me things about girls and women which I could scarcely understand, but which frightened me with their strange details regarding the female body.

So you see I was enormously sophisticated in one sense and yet completely naïve in another. Indeed, this naïveté of mine persisted as I passed the ages of fourteen and fifteen; completely engrossed in my studies, I had little time and even less inter-est in discovering that for which the other boys traipsed into Cambridge on a Saturday night. And yet as time passed I did begin to feel, as I might put it, certain stirrings within my young self, and what my compatriots talked and laughed about began to exert a certain vague, uncertain hold on me. It was nothing I could have expressed in words, yet on the rare occasion on which I saw a female—the wife or daughter of a professor visit-ing the school, perhaps—I found that my imagination became enraged with wild, incoherent visions.

At last one Saturday night I was inveigled by some of these boys to accompany them on their dark pursuits. I was reluctant; I was preoccupied with my lessons; but eventually I acquiesced, my curiosity getting the better of me. Down to town we wan-dered, the boys in a very giddy mood, to a narrow street of old brick houses which seemed quite dirty and dilapidated. At the door of one such house one of the boys knocked rapidly, and we were allowed entrance almost immediately.

I found myself in another world—a world the likes of which I had hardly imagined. My eyes must have been as big as saucers as I stumbled gracelessly into this room—its walls were papered with a pattern featuring a naked Cupid and numerous undraped nymphs, I remember—and beheld as many as seven women in various states of partial dress. These were not women of the same type that I had seen occasionally in the halls of the university. These were loud, lackadaisical creatures whose bodies draped themselves carelessly over the plush red sofas and whose hair, instead of being arranged properly above their heads, instead hung loosely over their bare shoulders. They laughed at a volume I had never before heard from members of the fairer sex. They drank alcohol openly, and one or two of them even smoked ciga-rettes—a phenomenon I not only had never seen, but which I had never even imagined possible. They were highly painted, these women, with ruby-red lipstick and rogue and whatnot, which gave them something of the appearance of children's dolls. Their clothing, what there was of it, was brightly-colored and loose-fitting. In the far corner of the room one of the women banged away at an old piano, playing jolly tunes I did not recognize.

We were greeted as conquering heroes when we entered, and I was made a particular fuss over. They rushed to me, cooed over me, touched me, took my hat playfully from my head and pushed a glass of some pungent liquid into my hand. I confess I was quite overwhelmed by all this and nearly broke away to leave the establishment entirely, but something about the wom-en's giggling and playfulness encouraged me to stay. The other boys, I noted, had quickly paired off with one or another of them and soon I was left with a partner of my own, an attractive girl with a round face and exceedingly womanly physique who moved me to an unoccupied sofa and proceeded to shower me with attentions the likes of which I had never before known.

I will refrain from offering any more detail except to say that I was eventually led upstairs by this girl, where there were small, rather dank bedrooms all along the hall, and events occurred which, I suppose, have occurred between innocent young men and women of this particular variety since time immemorial. One fact I would later find interesting was that at no time was I asked for money. It was only later, upon returning to the university, that I realized the money I had been carrying in my coat pocket had completely vanished.

What I have described is essentially a banal experience the likes of which, as I have indicated, have been known to countless thousands of others like me. But I believe my reaction to it may have been somewhat different. For, while I continued with my studies with great fervor, I found it almost impossible to remove thoughts of the experience from my head. Day and night I would reminisce, quite involuntarily, about that night, and soon I found myself intensely desirous of repeating the experience. Down to the house of ill repute I went, seeking out the same girl as before, and again I had a delightful experience. Again and again I returned to that nondescript brick house on that dilapidated street, and when one night I discovered that my round-faced friend was absent, I sampled the offerings of another girl—and found her even more delightful. She became my companion of choice for a time, and then I branched out again. I became such a repeating customer that they all came to know me by my first name and I was embraced as a valued steady patron rather than just another anonymous boy, a fact which made me feel perversely proud.

However, certain inevitable results soon ensued. The other boys began mocking me for my preoccupation with that house of women, but more importantly, I found my money supply dwindling at a shocking rate. My family had given me an allowance to last the semester, but the constant financial drain of my new hobby took much of it away within weeks and I was forced to write to my parents and ask them for more, claiming that a goodly portion of the original amount had been picked from my pocket in a street robbery. This of course led to some few remonstrations about my reckless character and how I would have to learn to be much more careful on the streets of Cambridge, but I cared not about such words. What mattered was that they had sent more money, money which I burned through at a similar rate as I had before.

I was in fact obsessed with what I was doing with my night-hours. But I must say that I felt no particular shame about it. What I was doing seemed very pleasant and natural to me, despite society's disapprobation; soon, in fact, I became reluctant to return to the university at all, preferring to remain for as long as they would have me in the house of women. I still studied, still made progress in my various researches, but my life had been changed. Even when I beheld the symbol of my immorality on my body—a symbol which was only finally erased by numerous treatments involving on a doctor's orders the repeated inhaling and devouring of the ghastly substance mercury—even then, I say, I thought nothing of what I was doing.

At this tender age, then, I had little use for society and its petty moralities. I lived as I pleased; by day I studied, researched, invented, and at night I lived the life of a godless sybarite. This was quite a fate, surely, for the proud son of a cleric!

Inevitably, however, things came crashing down. It was but a matter of time until my family, who after all were only a hundred miles or so away, heard of my actions and the reputation I was building as the most dissolute and immoral of undergraduates. When my father came to speak with me I protested—after all, was I not keeping up with my studies? Was I not well advanced beyond even my most brilliant professors' own works? I was by far the most superior student in the entire institution in natural philosophy, astronomy, anatomy, and half a dozen other fields. As long as this was true, I argued, what I did with my leisure hours was of no concern to anyone but myself.

The argument might have prevailed except for the fact that I was spending vast amounts of money at this point and found myself desperate for more. I sold most of my belongings and began borrowing from friends, whose generosity quickly evaporated when I proved a laggard in repayment. Indeed, I lost numerous friends due to my debts, and soon I was no longer the amusingly innocent young boy who had to be shown the ways of the world but a dissipated profligate whom many avoided altogether. My father, ever morally upstanding, was appalled by all he learned, calling me a wastrel and a disgrace and demanding that I return home.

This I did. It was not a happy homecoming. I was an embarrassment to the family. My father attempted to secure me various menial jobs, but these held no interest for me. All I wished to do was go on with my researches in the day and my debaucheries at night, but this was intolerable to my parents. Enraged, I began stealing items from the family home which I would then pawn in a nearby town—one which also contained a disorderly house not unlike the one I had left behind in Cambridge. When my father became aware of the thievery he ordered me out of the Blackthorn home forever. I refused to go, and when he threatened to summon the local constable, I took a heavy vase off a nearby table and used it to smash in his skull.

It is difficult to describe the frenzy in which I found myself—the turmoil of my emotions. I say this because there is no other way to justify or rationalize my actions thereafter. I was terrified of discovery, and so hid behind the door when I heard the younger of my two sisters, Adelaide, approaching. When she entered the room I used the same vase to crack open her head; she fell without a sound. I moved her body to a position next to my father's and soon my older sister Louise entered and met the same fate, sighing gently as she fell uncomplainingly to the floor. I spent several hours with the bodies lying on the rug of our sitting room until at last Mother arrived. I would like to say that this final crime was difficult for me to accomplish, but in truth it was not. By this time I was an experienced murderer and it was accomplished with no fuss or bother whatever.

Now that the family had been dispatched, the question came of how to dispose of four fresh corpses. I closed off the sitting room and pondered this problem for some time before arriving at the conclusion that hydrofluoric acid would be the best solution. I had some in a chemical supply kit I had brought with me from the university, and in a large bathtub tested it on parts of my father's body. The results were satisfactory, and so I wrote to an old friend at Harvard asking what the cost would be for a certain amount of this highly destructive substance. He told me, and after selling a few more family items I was able to pay the agreed-upon price. The acid was delivered to the house, along with various items of safety equipment, in a special reinforced carriage equipped for the transport of such dangerous substances. Once I had the necessary materials, the job was surprisingly easy, and what little was left of my poor family after concluding my operations I placed into two old trunks and dropped into the Charles River one rainy midnight, along with the remaining supplies. Those trunks have never been discovered and my story of the family suddenly deciding to visit Europe has never been questioned. It is surprising how easy it is to commit murder successfully provided one uses a certain amount of judgment and intelligence.

The question naturally arises whether I have ever felt any remorse for my actions—what society would call my misdeeds. The answer is no. My family had become an impediment to my satisfaction in life and so I took the most logical and reasonable approach to solving the problem. I was never close to any of them; though even if I had been I doubt I would have felt any differently about it. In the end most people seem to me but puppets, real enough but empty; shadows in a shadow show upon a shadow stage. I am neither for them nor against them except insofar as they assist or impede my progress. I am never willfully rude or uncaring to anyone; indeed, I have quite a good reputation in Grimsleytown and its environs as a kind and helpful old gentleman—and I am one.

My medical career came about slowly, over a long period of time. At first I was simply delighted at my good fortune—and a good fortune it was: I was suddenly in possession of a great deal of money, and whatever the small-minded local people thought about it, I availed myself of it. I purchased the latest and best laboratory equipment along with the finest instruments, and proceeded to rebuild the house as a kind of headquarters for scientific research. At the same time I ceased visiting disorderly houses and instead had the women come to my own abode; it was far more convenient and satisfying that way. Two or three would arrive at a time some nights, and we would exert ourselves into the wee hours as only the young and strong truly can. There was talk of raiding the residence, but two facts kept this from occurring. First, many people had toured my home, and saw that it was in fact a serious locality of profound searches in half a dozen scientific fields; I could show by then my numerous publications in a variety of scientific and technical journals detailing my various findings. Second, there was enough money available to quietly quash any proposed investigation into the private affairs of Hudson Blackthorn. I was young, I was a genius, and my work was doing good in the world. The rest was no one else's business.

Thus my life proceeded for some years. I took delight in my researches and discovered many important facts in the fields of natural science, medicine, and electricity as well as inventing a number of scientific apparatus—a new kind of swivel mount for telescopes earned me a great deal of money, and is still in wide use today. I was quite happy in that period. I knew many women, and not all of them of the disorderly variety; my physical requirements were met with delightful abandon.

And yet a serpent appeared in this Eden—a "League of Concerned Citizens," as they called themselves, who were determined to force me from the community because my life did not meet their strict moralistic standards. Not only was I behaving scandalously with many women, but my researches were, they said, "unholy." I could only laugh; what was unholy about discovering new facts about the world in which we lived? It was not as if I was researching how to raise the Devil! But a number of hearings and public meetings ensued, gatherings which I refused to attend. I was assured by some of those who had been present that there was a feeling abroad that I should be tarred and feathered and run out of town. Eventually actual violence came—a window broken, one of my horses shot. I called upon the local constabulary, but they were no help. Indeed I suspected that those very gentlemen might have played a role in the recent activities against me. When one day I was accosted by ruffians in the street who threatened me with "more where this came from," I began to realize that the town had turned against me and that I must needs leave it at once.

I packed my most important scientific things into a carriage one night and vanished from the town, leaving a real estate dealer to negotiate a price for the house itself with whomsoever might wish to purchase it. Over the course of my long life I have never again returned to the city of Boston.

Thereupon ensued a period of travel. Money was not an issue. I had my belongings stored and booked a ticket on a sailing ship heading to Liverpool, England—a lengthy journey of some weeks and very little comfort—but upon arrival I was able to tour all the important cities of Europe, staying always in the finest hotels. I attended Shakespeare productions in London and exhibitions in Paris of the Royal Academy of Art. I watched bullfights in Spain and spent many days traipsing over the fascinating ruins of Greece and Rome. Finally my journeys took me further, even to a steamboat on the Nile River and a caravan into the deserts of Egypt where I beheld with my own eyes the Great Sphinx of Giza. I learned of other peoples and cultures; although it was some years ago now, I still am a master of the Spanish, French and Italian languages. There were women too, many of them, in all of these countries, and I found all of them delightful in their own particular ways.

It was in all a wonderful learning experience for a young man, but after some ten years abroad I began to hunger for home. Not, understand, for the city of my birth—it was clear to me that I would never return there. I mean rather for America. I missed its beautiful landscapes, the mountains and valleys, and the particular sound of American-accented English being spoken around me. And so at last, determined to resume my researches, which had been largely suspended in this period, I booked a first-class ticket back to the United States.

There was naturally the question of where I would go and what I would do. I traveled for a time up and down the Eastern seaboard, avoiding Boston entirely, attempting to find a direction for my life. I knew I had much to offer mankind. I knew that my intellect was the equal of and perhaps the superior to anyone whom I had ever met. But without a proper university affiliation or advanced degree I was limited in my options. I therefore decided to settle in New York and complete my medical degree, which I did under an assumed name. I lived in New York City for many years, practicing as a private physician and researching as best I could, but in truth the position was a draining one. I was not only a diagnostician but a surgeon; I performed operations on hundreds of men and women in this period, a very high portion of whom survived. My skills were unsurpassed and I invented new techniques of incision and stitching which remain popular in the medical world even now.

The years passed in this way, and soon I was no longer young. I began to chafe under the pressures of urban life; I sought something quieter and more sedate that would also allow me greater time for my researches. I had made a great deal of money over the years and invested it wisely, and so I might fairly have been thought of as rich. Finally I decided to find a more bucolic setting for my talents and a quieter location to enjoy my later years.

In time I discovered the delights of Maryland, and in particular Grimsleytown, which in those days was hardly more than a one-horse sort of hamlet. It was I who decided to build it up—I constructed the hospital and the school with my own money. But most of all I spent my time having this very house built—this magnificent structure that is the final towering testimony of my life. Into it I poured all my creativity, my innovation, and my aesthetic sense to make it a mansion and fortress unlike anything else in the world. It took many years; it involved builders and contractors from all over the region; and in some ways it is still unfinished. I suppose it shall remain unfinished, but then, that is the story of human life, which never finishes. It simply stops.

Your mother was a delightful woman, attractive and intelligent. She was married at the time I met her—she had come into the hospital for a complaint regarding her stomach—but I recognized from my examination of her certain telltale signs that she had once been, as is said, "in the profession." She and her husband had very little money and I confess that I found her extremely desirable. It was for this reason that I made her a perfectly respectable offer concerning her payment for her medical visits—numerous such visits were required, as her symptoms kept changing and so her treatment plan had to be continually amended. The kind of arrangement I describe was not at all uncommon then, nor is it uncommon now. Needless to say your mother never actually paid as much as a penny for any of the medical attentions I bestowed upon her.

Eventually, of course, you arrived—perhaps the most beautiful girl baby I have ever seen. I charged nothing for the service of your delivery—and it was a complicated delivery, with a labor that went on for something like fourteen hours. You were born in my hospital in town, a big, healthy child—and I knew virtually from the moment I first saw you that you were not Mr. Lee's at all. You had not his facial structure or skin tone; and of course there was the hourglass on your belly, identical with the one I had had since my own birth. I recognized immediately that you had to be mine.

Your mother knew this too, of course, and your Mr. Lee as well. But it was in no one's interest to speak of it. I supported your family for years, Annabel, without your knowledge. Did you never wonder how your father, employed only occasionally as he was, afforded such a nice plot of land, with a fine little house and all those beautiful books? You know your mother had no money. Perhaps he told you it was a family inheritance of some kind. It was not. If you had had to rely on your stepfather's income your family would have lived in perpetual penury, I can assure you. The money that paid for it all was mine.

And so you see that I have been with you from the beginning, my beautiful child. Therein lies the secret of what you have said you noticed from early on—that look I would give you—I confess quite without intent—the look you have said you saw in my eyes. The extra attentions that I, as a mere family physician, seemed to have no reason to bestow upon a young child who was, apparently, nothing more than another patient. But you were my daughter! Perhaps it is impossible for you to understand what this can mean to a man—an unmarried man without a family. My flesh and blood! And then when your parents both died within such a short space of time, and I recognized that you would be alone in the world, I could not simply unmask myself, tell you in words that would have been a bolt from the blue, "I am your father, Annabel Lee." It seemed better—much better—to simply take on the role of a kindly family friend, supporting you affectionately and looking after your interests.

But that day, Annabel—that day that you were taken away from me, to that orphanage—that was the day my heart broke. I will never forget watching the cart traveling on over the hills, and myself standing there on the land of what had been your home, and weeping, just weeping, for my lost little girl, the daughter who, I thought then, would never know the truth— would never know *me* for who I was.

And so I confess that I monitored you, Annabel Lee. I had persons at Sadmore Place who would report on your progress to me, and I was miserable when I came to understand how unhappy you were there. When you ran away, I quickly put my own men on your trail—but you proved a cunning quarry, and they were unable to find you for a very long time. When one of my men finally thought he had located you in that terrible beach community on the Chesapeake, I knew I had to have you again in my life—I had to fetch you, bring you home, make you a part of my family as you have always been, though you have not known it. I had to bring you home, Annabel. And I rejoice that we are together at last, under the same roof, without lies or secrets anymore. It is what I have most desired for much of the latter part of my life. I feel that with your presence here my life is complete—that I have fulfilled my destiny. To have sired a daughter—that is worth more than all my experiments combined.

Indeed, you are my greatest experiment, Annabel Lee!

5

"What do you want with me?" I whispered.

I was exhausted. Though my health had been improving, I felt as if I had been listening to his soft, low, purring voice for years. The story he had narrated to me over many a long evening, sitting just out of view behind my bed, was one of unequivocal ghastliness and horror. I knew, more deeply than ever before I had known, that Doctor Hudson Blackthorn was a madman—albeit a brilliant madman. I thought about his unfortunate family—my grandparents, I realized, my grand-aunts—their lives cruelly extinguished by this callous villain. He was utterly without remorse for anything he had done. I had never before met such a person—one who made the terrors of Mother Sackett and Sadmore Place seem as nothing by comparison. And yet the way he told his story—his gentle voice and manner, his oddly emotionless recital of events—made it all seem, over those long evenings, almost normal; almost as if this could be the tale of any young man from a fairy tale or romantic poem—his troubled upbringing, his many *Wanderjahrs* in far-away countries, his eventual return to the bosom of his home-land and establishment as a respected professional man. Yes, all of it was perfectly normal, even romantic—except the murder of his family, the successful disposing of evidence, and of course his obsessive relations with so many of the world's harlots. It is a wonder that such a narrative—a narrative being told, after all, by the man who was, at least physically, *my father*—did not drive me mad. Yet it did not; when one is exposed to an endless parade of horrors one soon stops responding at all, instead simply accepting each new display with a sense of indifference.

This was how I felt about my father's abominable tale.

Doctor Blackthorn moved near my bed and looked down at me with an expression I suppose others would have thought kindly. I found it wicked.

"Want?" he asked.

"You keep me prisoner here," said I. "You must have some purpose, some ultimate goal. Do you plan to murder me, as you did your poor family?"

"Murder you? Gracious, child, that is the furthest thing from my mind. Not you, my daughter. Never you."

"And yet you murdered the others."

"That was a very long time ago, Annabel."

"But you did it."

"They were inconvenient."

"What if I become inconvenient?"

"That can never be," he replied, shaking his head. "Never."

"So you simply see us—living here? In this house?"

"It is a beautiful house, is it not?"

"And yet it is but a house. What of the travels you promised me?"

"Oh, I have a plan for that, child. I do. We will travel, in time."

I thought. "So we shall simply live here, together."

"Yes."

"I wish only my freedom."

"You will have freedom. In time."

"And until then we simply stay in this house, living together as father and daughter?"

He looked queerly at me. "Father and daughter? You misunderstand, child. We shall not live as father and daughter."

"What, then?" I asked, puzzled.

"Why, we shall live as *man and wife*."

How far into the depths of horror might I fall! "Doctor Blackthorn, you have said that I am your child!"

"And so you are." He smiled lubriciously. "What could be more perfect? You are—you are *ripe* now, Annabel. I feel closer to you than I do to anyone else on Earth. And you will feel so to me...in time."

I felt my breath coming fast. I was trembling. "That time will never come, you despicable monster. The idea is appalling. It is unnatural."

"It is only society which says so," the doctor maintained, "and I have told you what I think of the petty morals of society."

"Never," I cried, shaking my head. "Never, never, never!"

He smiled ingratiatingly. "When the time comes you will be happy to accept me as your husband."

"I promise you that will not happen."

"And I promise you that it will." To my astonishment he reached out his hands and touched my temples—almost tenderly, one might have thought. "You see, Annabel," he said gently, "I have been working on new researches. I have been considering how to create automata not of wood and metal, but of flesh."

"What on Earth are you talking about?"

"Human automata," he purred, stroking my temples softly.

"That is impossible."

"Not at all," he said. "The techniques are actually not complicated. I will explain them to you eventually, but for now..." He touched my brows softly. "...Just know that it can be done, and that the recipient of the process will live a simple and happy life ever after. That is what I have in store for you, my darling Annabel."

At last I batted his fingers away. "How? How would such a thing ever occur?"

"It will involve a surgical procedure," said he. "A procedure of a rather different type than I have performed on you hitherto."

"What procedure?"

"It has to do, Annabel—" he smiled his terrible unctuous smile again—"it has to do with the performance of certain procedures on the front-most sections of your cerebrum."

"My what?"

"Your brain, my dear. I shall operate upon your brain."

This was the ultimate terror—beyond learning of my physical father, beyond my imprisonment, beyond the nightmarish narrative of murder and concealment he had told me, beyond even his unspeakable conceit that he and I would marry—came this. An operation, said he, that was simple and quick, an operation in which the surgeon entered with his scalpel the front sections of the brain—*my own brain*—by penetrating under my eyelids (I squirmed in revulsion as he said it and involuntarily clenched shut my eyes) and cutting two sections of it apart. After that, he assured me, I would become calm and docile, gentle and cooperative, and my troubles in this life would be over.

It was then that we would travel. It was then that he would take me to the far corners of the Earth as his wife. Once I had been surgically placated, he assured me, I would be delighted with his company and indeed have no memory at all of the objections I had earlier expressed.

"It is quite a new idea of mine," said he. "I have performed the operation on two men, vagrants of no account who came here looking for work. In both cases my theory confirmed itself perfectly. Each operation was a complete success. After some time, of course, I disposed of the patients—cleanly and humanely, I assure you. But the process, which hasn't even a name yet, shall do wonders for the hopelessly deranged. It will revolutionize the practice of medicine upon such people."

"I am not deranged," I whispered in horror.

"No, my dear, but you are unhappy. My procedure will change that."

"Get out of here."

He nodded politely and stood. "As you wish, my child. I have preparations to attend to, as it happens. Preparations for our marriage—tomorrow!"

I lay staring into the darkness for many hours. At first I was unable to think coherently at all—I simply tossed and turned in my bed, strange and terrible visions of Doctor Blackthorn's loathsome face and echoes of his despicable words ringing and clashing in my mind. To calm myself I tried to think of happier times—of my father, my true father, reading with him the poetical works of Shakespeare and Poe—of sitting in the little alcove off the kitchen and watching the rain fall as I sipped my tea—and of course of the beach on the Chesapeake, Jim Gamble's sun-darkened face, our times on his little boat and cooking sea-food over the fire and holding each other in the night hours inside his makeshift hut. I say I *tried*; for in truth I could not hold any of these remembered things in my head for more than a moment. Ever and again it was the repugnant visage of Doctor Hudson Blackthorn, his deep insinuating voice and hard calloused hands—his sinister smile—that flooded over and drowned all my other thoughts.

Tomorrow! Our marriage—this immoral, illegal, grotesque farce of a union—was to happen tomorrow! I knew not how he planned to effect this ceremony, but my mind was clear enough to understand that, whatever he meant to do, it could have no possible standing with the law. But what of that? No doubt the ceremony he envisioned merely as a step to his ultimate desire, the one that would arrive on our wedding night—the unholy union of our physical bodies. The idea threatened to cause what little food was in my belly to erupt from me in a torrent, but I forced myself into a quieter emotional state and my stomach calmed as well. I had to think. The sands were running through the hourglass each hour—each minute—each second—and there was nothing I could do to stop them. I needed a plan, but I could not conceive of one. I could not escape. There was no possible weapon with which I might arm myself. And yet it could not, it *must* not be! I knew I was intelligent, strong, and resilient. I had faced down daunting challenges in my life again and again—challenges that would have felled a lesser woman. Was all that to end here—in this house—with a false ceremony followed by a monstrous interlude in his bedchamber followed by knives slashing under my eyelids into my brain and taking my personality, my *self*, away—obliterating me—perhaps forever?

I confess that I prayed. I prayed soulfully and sincerely for a very long while, all the time knowing my hypocrisy. I did not truly believe in God—I never had. God had too often been absent in my hours of direst need. And yet like a doomed soldier about to go into battle, one for whom the church had never been a familiar visiting place, I found myself praying. The wishes I attempted to transmit to the heavens were indeed sincere, and I meant them quite deeply. I prayed for a way of escape. I prayed for a weapon which could lead to my deliverance. I prayed that before the morning light shone he might suffer a speedy death. For all this and more I prayed; but I received no answer.

I may have slept a few fitful minutes in the early morning hours, but those minutes did nothing to revive my flagging energies as the dawn came. It seemed to me that all was lost, and I began to consider any available means of self-murder. The nurse was there, of course, at the foot of my bed, and any hard or sharp objects had long been taken away. I considered hanging—visions of poor Mary Mahoney darting desolately through my mind—but there was nothing from which a bedsheet noose might have been suspended.

When morning had been glowing under the curtain of my cataract-window for some time one of the automata came to the door with my breakfast. It was a sumptuous repast, I remember—eggs, bacon, buckwheat cakes, beautiful sliced fruit, bread, aromatic coffee—but I mistrusted these items, suspicious that perhaps they had been somehow drugged. I refused the meal, desiring to keep my mind clear on this day—though for what, I knew not. Indeed, it seemed as if it might be a better idea to eat the breakfast, and let any potions or poisons do with me as they would. But there was something in me, something that refused to let go of the final strands of life and sanity. It seemed impossible that my life would end this way. Still, I thought, something...there had to be *something*....

An hour or two after the breakfast was taken away the nurse returned with a gown in her arms—a classic white wedding-gown, in which any young girl might be delighted to marry. It was elegant indeed, with everything of the finest quality; laces and frills abounded upon it everywhere. There were shoes to match and, of course—I noticed with a sickening of my heart—a beautiful, diaphanous wedding veil.

The nurse had laid all the things out on my bed and I was standing before them, studying them, when my mind suddenly entertained a strange, disturbing fancy—so strange and so disturbing that even I, with my thick catalog of terrible experiences of life and death, literally began to tremble. It was a vision of something so monstrous it caused my very reason to totter on its throne. I touched the material of the dress softly, letting it play through my fingers, watching my fingers shake with the sheet enormity of the hideous thought in my mind. I attempted to obliterate the thought by focusing on the texture of the silk on my skin and the loveliness of the intricate patterns woven into it. I forced myself to wonder how such an exquisite dress had been obtained at all.

The soft, distant sound of music came to my ears then—organ music, from some faraway portion of the mansion. It was wedding music. I realized that my nuptials would soon begin.

The dress fit perfectly. I knew I looked every inch a bride, even as I felt every inch a doomed and despairing woman. There were two automata, the nurse and one other, who guided me in my exquisite finery out of my room and down the corridor, up a dark staircase and down a long hall. As usual, I could not successfully orientate myself and could only continue moving forward with the machines. Escape would have been quite impossible; I would have run without direction, no doubt in hopeless circles. I attempted to drain my mind of thought, to disconnect myself mentally from what was happening to me. I simply placed one foot in front of another. Down another staircase now, and down another that twisted and turned. The organ music grew louder and I knew we were approaching the place of Doctor Blackthorn's dreadful assignation.

At last we reached a set of high, elaborately carved oak doors—even more elaborate than those outside the dining room where I had danced with the monster numerous times. One of the automatics reached forward and opened the door—and I stepped into what was surely a scene from the fevered imaginings of Hieronymus Bosch himself.

It was a chapel—I remembered abruptly the occupation of Doctor Blackthorn's father—but what I saw was unlike any wedding ceremony I had ever seen. The room was softly lit with sconces mounted high in the walls. At the back of the chamber sat the organist before the great instrument—and it *was* a great instrument, a vast and complex organ such as might grace one of the finest churches in the world. The organist was an automaton dressed absurdly in formal clothes, exactly as one would expect a man to dress for such an occasion. Under this was the pulpit, festooned now with what seemed to be thousands of flowers all over, and along each side stood the wedding guests—automata all, some dressed as men in black and others in bright formal dresses which seemed to have been tailored to their inhuman forms. The only actual living things in sight other than myself were, incongruously, the little creatures from the doctor's science laboratory—the cages of the mice and the white rat had been lined up against the wall, as if they were being made witnesses to this unholy spectacle! The nurse turned to me and placed in my hands a bouquet of fresh carnations as I looked around at this ungodly nightmare of a room.

The music stopped abruptly, and from a side door near the pulpit Doctor Blackthorn emerged. He was dressed resplendently, in tie and tails, and his revolting smile was wide on his fat, pallid face. He moved slowly toward where I stood at the back of the hall. The only sound was that of his shoes as they touched the wooden floor of the chapel.

"My dear," said he. He reached out and touched my hands as they held the flowers. "You have come."

"I was not given a choice."

He chuckled. "Of course. And yet you see—" he gestured widely—"you see the celebration that has been planned in your honor. Is it not beautiful?"

I did not answer.

"Come, my child," said he, wrapping his arm closely in my own. "It is time that we fulfill our destiny."

As he turned to walk up the aisle toward the pulpit the music began once more—a familiar wedding piece, Bach's "Air on the G String." I walked slowly, my mind blank. I knew not what to do or what to think. This was an unreal world, something that surely could not be happening, and yet I was here, I knew that I was not dreaming. The pulpit approached. At last we stopped before it, and the music again ceased.

I wondered what was in store. I had not long to wait to find out. Suddenly, through two horn-like contraptions I only just then noticed on either side of the stage, came a strange new sound, a low susurration filled with hissing and quite low in volume. It took me a moment to realize that it was Doctor Blackthorn's voice.

Of course—he had made a sound cylinder. The effect of the mechanical reproduction of the voice only added to the weirdness of the scene—it sounded like Doctor Blackthorn and did not sound like him, and I could look at the man next to me and see his lips not moving at all even as the mechanical Doctor Blackthorn spoke.

I recall not the words, but they were standard wedding fare greeting all of us and explaining that we were gathered together in the sight of God to witness the marriage of this man and this woman. I was distant from the scene then, mentally floating somewhere else even as I felt the warmth of his arm in mine. The recorded voice went on for some minutes—I did not listen—until at last I heard Doctor Blackthorn's voice—his own living voice—say the words, "I do."

At that moment I was snapped back to reality. The mechanical voice then asked if I, Annabel Lee, took this man in holy matrimony and promised to love, honor, and obey him until Death us do part.

I offered no response. The voice on the cylinder whispered, "The ring," and Doctor Blackthorn brought from his pocket a gold ring with numerous small, brilliant diamonds mounted upon it. He took my hand and slipped the ring upon my marriage finger. I did not resist.

"You may kiss the bride," said the whispering voice.

He smiled and leaned toward me. He lifted the veil from my face. His flabby, grotesque lips sought my own. Bach suddenly soared up into connubial joyousness on the organ. And I, Reader, I, Annabel Lee, at that very moment—I fainted!

Upon waking I found myself in a narrow antechamber that seemed not to be a great distance from the chapel—the organ music, now serenely romantic, was quite audible as it echoed and re-echoed throughout the mansion. I was lying on a simple daybed, one designed perhaps for the use of a maid—assuming this house had ever employed human maids—but now seemingly unoccupied. The bed had no sheets or blankets, the walls no decorations.

I sat up. I was still wearing my wedding gown; only my shoes, sitting tidily next to the bed, had been removed. I left them there. I noticed a corridor that led out of the antechamber and decided to investigate where it led. Any momentary hope that I might find my way out of the house entirely was immediately dashed as I found myself entering a bedroom, capacious and beautifully appointed, with a huge four-poster bed covered in white at its center. Handsome oak chairs and tables were scattered around the room, covering the elegant rugs on the floor—rugs that appeared to be Oriental in origin. There seemed to be windows, but they were covered with purple velvet curtains. Two sconces at the far end of the room provided a gentle illumination to the scene.

I stood there dumbly for a moment as from the far end of the room, through the single door there, appeared Doctor Blackthorn.

He was dressed differently than before. The formal wear had been discarded for an elegant blue robe, also velvet, with a blue sash at the waist, along with dark leather slippers. His *pince-nez* were nowhere in sight. He stood in the far doorway looking at me with a happy expression which nonetheless betrayed something less certain—and it suddenly came to my awareness that he was feeling shy! Hudson Blackthorn, the mastermind behind my abduction, the murderer of my lover, and inventor of countless scientific wonders, a man who had known me since the day of my birth and who was intimately familiar with my body due to the many surgeries he had performed upon it—this man was timid, and hesitant! He might have attacked me at will at any time in the months I had been his helpless prisoner, but now my presence made him anxious!

"My dear," said he in a quiet, husky voice.

I looked at him silently.

"Are you feeling better?" he asked, stepping toward me. "You became overexcited, I think. I had the nurse put you in the old dayroom. It has been several hours."

He was closer now. My heart heaved. I found my breath

shallow and skittish.

"Do you need anything, my child?" said he, coming closer. "I can certainly see to it that you get water, or perhaps something to eat?"

I could not speak. I shook my head.

He smiled. "Very well." He was close to me now. Only inches separated us. The music had grown very soft and quiet, gentle romantic chords wafting through the air into this chamber of horror.

"It is time, my dear," he said softly, taking my hands. "It is time for the moment I have wished for—dreamed of—been possessed by for so many years. It is time for us to finally bond, bond as man and wife, bond forever."

I stared at him. I felt that my eyes were wide.

"Come," said he, turning slightly and leading me toward the bed. "It is time for the two of us to enter Paradise."

I stumbled slightly as I followed him. My body shook violently. So many thoughts and images and memories seemed to rush across my mind, all of them at once, a wild flood of them from my childhood and my time at the orphanage and on the Chesapeake and the faces and voices of all those I had known, known and loved and lost. And I recalled the vision I had had when first I had been brought here: I was the *Angel of Death*—everyone I touched sunk forevermore to their graves— my father, my mother, my sister, poor Mary Mahoney, my dear darling Jim Gamble, all dead, dead, and I the unwitting avatar of their executions!

Turning me around, he began removing my dress. He was smooth in his movements, with hardly a hesitation at all. I wondered if he had practiced this. The idea was grotesque. But soon the lavish garment had been pulled from my shoulders, the underthings gently removed, and I stood there naked as he placed his hideous hands once more on my shoulders and turned me around to face him.

"So beautiful," he whispered, his eyes holding a strange liquid expression.

He turned slightly away. He kicked off the slippers and then opened the robe. At that point he seemed to hesitate. For a long time he appeared not to move at all, his head angled downward. At last I perceived that one of his terrible hands was moving at the front of the robe and I knew—I knew from long experience on the night streets of Baltimore—I *knew* what was happening. I knew why he would not face me. His sick mind and perverted spirit were completely prepared, but his body had betrayed him!

We stood there for many minutes, I simply staring at his back and shoulder, he hiding his face and moving his hand ever more frantically beneath the robe.

It was at this moment that everything coalesced in my mind, all the ghastly thoughts and visions I had had before suddenly arriving again in my field of vision. My life passed before me in a tumbling parade of images, mostly disgusting and horrible—the things that had been done to me—the uninvited touchings—the paid encounters in filthy alleyways—even a young boy in a barn once, it seemed a thousand years ago, demanding that I humiliate myself, bare my body to him in exchange for a thing as simple as food. My silly body! My skin, my muscles, my thighs, my breasts, my face! What was it about them that seemed to drive men mad? Sometimes that madness was benign and wonderful—no one had ever been more wonderful to me than dear Jim Gamble—but more often it was violent, abusive, exploitative, painful. And now here was the ultimate degradation, beyond which it seemed to me no woman could ever recover. A prisoner—a forced marriage—my own father!

In this moment I suddenly came to feel a great calm.

I inhaled deeply and reached my hand out to touch Doctor Blackthorn's shoulder.

"Let me," I whispered.

He glanced back at me with a panicked expression on his face, but when he saw my gentle smile and soft eyes he seemed to relax. Without waiting for permission I reached my hand under his robe and did what I knew was likely to please any man. After a moment he turned to face me fully, his eyes growing unfocused with pleasure. The robe dropped from his shoulders.

"Annabel," he whispered. "I had not—not expected…"

I leaned forward then and kissed him, kissed him fully as

a woman. He groaned in ecstasy—and as he did so I pulled my lips softly away from his own and, in one smooth, simple motion, went down on my knees before him. His hands touched my hair—the music flowed softly—his breath grew shallow and fast—

I will not reveal what I did next except to remind the reader of a fact which I have mentioned previously in this narrative.

I have very strong teeth.

His scream was louder than I had ever imagined possible. High-pitched, yet with peculiar guttural growls mixed in, it filled the room and, I thought, the entire mansion with its howling agony. The sound seemed to blend somehow with the music still pouring forth from the chapel into one indescribable auditory nightmare, the sound of Hell itself unleashed. His fists rained blows down upon my head but I hardly felt them as my jaws held fast. He frantically tried to pull away, but in this he unwittingly hastened my mission and in no more than a moment he began to fall backward onto the beautifully patterned rug, blood gushing from between his legs onto my face and body and all over his belly and legs, a river of blood, a gushing stream, and he collapsed while still I kneeled there, unmoving.

After a moment and without thought I stood and turned. The nurse had entered the room but it offered no resistance as I marched boldly to it, reached behind its head, pressing the button which rendered it still; once I had feared such interference might set off some sort of alarm to the doctor, but that no longer mattered, and nothing happened. I then spat out the object in my mouth onto the elegant rug. The music still flowed on as I looked back at Doctor Blackthorn, whose screams continued unabated. He was moving now to pull away sheets from the bed, no doubt to attempt to stanch the flow of blood. With sudden grim determination I looked around the room and then stepped through the far door, from whence he had entered earlier. There I found a small bathroom. Rifling the drawers in the bureau there I found nothing of use, but then I discovered a drawer that was locked. I proceeded to pull the bureau forward until it toppled, allowing me to access the locked drawer simply by bashing in the wood of the cabinet with a stool. In the locked drawer I discovered, as I had suspected, a man's shaving kit. I ripped the razor from its handsome sheath and turned back again to move toward Doctor Blackthorn.

He had successfully pulled some sheeting from the bed and was holding it to his groin. His scream had quieted to a loud groan and his eyes looked at me in helpless panic. I stared down at him with an utter lack of pity. In an instant I had straddled his large body and begun slashing the razor back and forth, back and forth ever and again, until all the screaming had reduced to a nauseating gurgling and there was nothing left of his neck at all but rivers of red gore. And yet I still was not done. The man was still alive. I stood again, stepped back into the small bathroom again, and this time espied a large mirror mounted on one wall. With the same stool I had used to access the bureau drawer I smashed the mirror to pieces and picked up the single shard that seemed most in size and shape to resemble a dagger along with a lengthy piece of the now broken steel frame. I took these back into the bedroom and tore a strip of bedding to use as a makeshift handle. This accomplished, I straddled the chest of the doctor a final time as I plunged my dagger into his throat repeatedly, as deeply as I could. His blood soaked my arms and hands but something in me could not stop—kept stabbing and hacking, first with the glass, then with the jagged strip of steel— until at last the monster's head rolled completely away from his body.

I stood and quite emotionlessly surveyed the scene. The music continued on, gently romantic; and when I looked to the doorway I realized that several more automata had arrived in the doorway but seemed not to know what to do. They were turning this way and that, bumping into the walls and into each other. It seems that the sight of what had happened completely unnerved them, and they were bewildered and confused as a result. I switched each of them off in turn. But the musician automaton in the chapel played on.

The bedroom was a scene from the *Inferno* of Dante—a wedding chamber spattered and streaked in blood, with the groom in pieces at the foot of the bed. As I studied the scene I had an odd sensation—not disgust, not horror (those would come later)—but rather a strange idea that I was forgetting something. I knew not the source of this feeling. After a moment I brushed it off and, leaning to the blood-drenched bed, picked up my mirror-dagger and wiped it clean on the bedsheets. I knew not why I did this. But in a moment it was quite clear again. I held it up to my face and beheld myself. Blood, blood everywhere, blood lacing my hair, scarlet gore dripping from my cheeks, blood in thick ropes dangling from my mouth—and my body, red-streaked, his blood and my own intermingled on my naked flesh.

I bent over then and vomited violently.

At this point my memory blurs. I know that I followed the corridor past the bathroom and eventually found the kitchen of the house, where there was an ample supply of water. I used a saucepan to pour great shovelfuls over my head and body, cleansing myself as best I could. I took a long time doing this, I believe. Then I made my way back to the bedchamber and slipped on the dress again—it had received only a few spatters of blood—and began to search the house, this dreadful place in which I had been imprisoned for so long. I left markers of cloth from a bedsheet during my search so that I might find my way back should I become disorientated. The corridors, I understood, were deliberately constructed to confuse the unwary—sudden twists and turns combined with staircases that sometimes led nowhere would have left even the hardiest explorer in a state of perplexity. And yet in a while—I know not how long, perhaps an hour or two—I had a rudimentary sense of the design of at least one part of the house. I found my room again, and there changed from the dress into a more functional gray dress. I looked around the room carefully, knowing I would never return to it, and packed a few clothing items in a bag along with a handful of toilet items and a few other miscellaneous things. This bag I carried out of the room, retracing my steps back to the chapel, where still the music went on.

It was not difficult to find my way to the front door by this point. It was heavily locked, doubly and triply bolted, and it took me a few minutes to figure out the intricate interlocking system, but I am not unintelligent and found my way clear after not terribly long. The door was unlocked—I turned the brass handle, and pulled—

The world at twilight awaited me! The air was fresh, the breeze deliciously cool on my face. The vista before me was one of many weeping willows and, in cracks between their lush branches, visions of the hills and of Grimsleytown far beyond. I placed my bag next to me and stood there for a long time, listening to the crickets beginning their night songs. I was free!

But I was not yet finished—I knew that. Turning quickly, determined to make a fast conclusion of my mission, I again left cloth markers as I made my way back to the kitchen and found the supply of lamp oil. Presently I located a supply of kitchen matches. Taking a large container of the oil with me, I began pouring it over the floors of as many rooms as I felt I could safely visit. I poured it over the furniture as well—over anything I could.

One of the last rooms I visited was the chapel, where the last automaton played on for no one but the little animals in their cages. *The little animals*—and suddenly, on impulse, I gathered up the cages and carried them through the now simple-to-navigate corridors and took them outside. I quickly opened each cage door and encouraged the small things to find their own freedom. What chance they had I knew not—I did not know what had been done to them, perhaps they could survive outside, perhaps not—but I could at least give them the chance.

The final cage was the one which contained the pink-nosed, inquiring mouse Doctor Blackthorn had showed me once. I opened the door to his cage and said softly, "Be well, my friend." The mouse looked at me, apparently confused for a moment—then it wisely took the opportunity offered and scampered down the path, losing itself among the shadows and the deepening darkness.

My time was finished now. I stepped once more into the house and, starting with the room farthest from the door, began lighting matches and dropping them into the spilled oil. Flames jumped up immediately each time, in room after room. I moved quickly. The musician kept on playing even as I lit the *auto-da-fé* all around it and watched it become engulfed in flames. Even then it played on, the music growing faster and faster.

I glanced into the wedding chamber a final time, feeling no emotion at all at the sight of the several stilled machine-people and the bloody decapitated corpse that lay motionless beyond them. I again had the odd sensation of having forgotten something, but there was nothing I needed here—nothing at all. My few needs would be satisfied by what was in my bag at the doorway of the house. I had taken a few items from the kitchen to eat, as well.

At last I moved to the front door, flames rapidly rising behind me. The organ had grown frenzied now, random notes and discords breaking through jumbled phrases of Mozart and Bach. I stepped beyond the threshold and out into the front garden. I picked up my bag and, espying a fallen branch near the pathway, laced it through the knot at the top of my bundle. I placed the stick, now with the tied bundle at the end of it, over my shoulder, remembering having traveled in exactly the same way when escaping the orphanage so long ago. My back felt warm with the heat of the rapidly-rising flames. The darkness of the night was complete now and the bright shadows of the many fires behind me illuminated the path ahead flickeringly. I heard violent whooshing sounds and glass shattering. At some point the organ fell silent at last—silent forever. I did not look back. I simply walked, as I had done so many times before in my life. I placed one foot in front of the other as I moved forward into a destiny I could not imagine.

BOOK FIVE.

The Sounding Sea

1

And so came yet another period of wandering. I spent time walking the roads of Maryland and Virginia, with no goal in mind—I found myself at a loss in my life, with an infinity of options before me, yet the situation was such that I might as well have had no options at all. I gravitated toward cities, riding public conveyances when I could, and soon enough found myself again in Baltimore, where I had lived not so long ago (and yet it felt like centuries!) as a young boy. Now I had recovered my female self and so had no anxiety about meeting those I had known before: they would not recognize me in my womanly dress, with my by now shoulder-length hair. But I never again met anyone from that period.

Early on, within a few days of my leaving the holocaust at Blackthorn House, I had discovered an odd fact—that I had unknowingly continued to wear the wedding ring Doctor Blackthorn had given me during his unholy ceremony. Sitting in a café in some town or other, sipping a coffee, I realized that it had remained on my finger, though I had been entirely unaware of it. Immediately I pulled it off, determined to throw it in a sewer somewhere; but as I sat there looking at it I wondered. I had almost no money and had already determined that I might very well have to return to some version of the life I had once led—the life my mother had once led—when I became aware of this glittering ring in my possession. The notion of profiting from Doctor Blackthorn in any way frankly disgusted me, and for a while I rejected the idea outright; but the more I thought about it, the more I realized that such a gesture—the gesture, that is, of hurling the hated thing into the street or an ashcan—would be an entirely sentimental one. I *had* the ring; it had been given to me; it was my own property. What reason was there, then, to dispose of it, thus leaving myself with no financial support whatsoever? True, it felt uncomfortable—dirty, even—to take money for it, but in the end a woman must look after herself, and this was the only method I had for doing so.

I walked to the nearest pawnbroker and sold the ring. With the proceeds I would be able (despite the fact that I was sure the proprietor had robbed me) to live for several months without fear of penury. My moral qualms quickly faded in the presence of decent meals, reasonable rooms, and a modest new dress and pair of shoes. This surely was the least that Doctor Blackthorn owed me.

"But what," I can hear my reader asking, "was the mental state of a woman who had been a prisoner for many months, forced into a sham marriage with her own father, and who eventually murdered him in the most violent and unspeakable way?" The truth is that I thought little of the doctor in my initial wanderings. That entire horrid experience, from waking to the realization that I was imprisoned through his ultimate gruesome defeat many months later, hovered somewhere near my thoughts but never entirely within them. Perhaps it was simply too much to bear—few, I thought, could even imagine the horrors I had experienced—but in time I did begin to reflect, especially when I arrived in Baltimore, a town that was already memory-laden for me. I had seen coverage in the press of the final catastrophe at Blackthorn House—big artists' impressions of the conflagration, vivid descriptions of the flames and destruction, sorrowful paragraphs—even memorial verses—on the sad passing of the esteemed doctor. The belief of the police was that something in one of the laboratories must have caught fire and caused the disaster. Everything, the articles said, had been destroyed—a lifetime's work obliterated in what was surely a tragedy of the most pathetic sort. No mention was made of the fact that the doctor's body had been decapitated, and if the police investigated the case as a murder, as they surely must have done, no word appeared in the newspapers, and the matter seemed to quickly vanish from the public's attention.

I was not a suspect, for the simple reason that my presence at Blackthorn House had been entirely unknown to anyone. There was literally not a single person other than the doctor who had been aware of my being there at all, and no one saw me leave it in the gathering dark of that dramatic night. I had walked away free—freer even than I had known at the time.

One might imagine that I would be haunted ever and again by terrible dreams of that experience, but truthfully, I hardly dreamed at all in that period and I slept the best I had in many months. If I had any mental images in my night slumbers it was mainly flitting, evanescent ones of dear Jim Gamble and the life we had once lived on the shore of the Chesapeake Bay—the only time, other than a few years in my early childhood, that I had ever been happy. O for those long-lost days, I thought. O Jim! My Jim!

There was a public house not far from my lodgings called The Two Foxes—an odd name since, while there was one large fox depicted in metalwork on one side of the establishment's front door, its mate had apparently vanished some years earlier. One could see, in fact, by looking closely at the corresponding section of the other side of the door, a faint discoloring in the shape of the other fox, and this gave the place a somewhat melancholy aspect—a fox in eternal pursuit of its ghost-fox companion, whose presence would never again brighten their mutual door. The neighborhood in which The Two Foxes was located was not a pleasant one, and in fact it reminded me very much, though they were in a different part of town, of the streets I had roamed upon my first sojourn in the city. Still, my rooming house was nearby, and whatever grime and overcrowding was present was nothing compared to the horror of my months of confinement at Doctor Blackthorn's. Simply to walk freely under a free sky was itself a delight.

I stepped into The Two Foxes one afternoon quite by accident. It was not my habit to patronize drinking establishments, for in fact I rarely partook of alcohol; but the afternoon had turned suddenly cold and wet and I was without my umbrella.

The establishment, as I saw it through the front windows, looked not entirely disreputable, and as it was not crowded, it seemed a reasonable choice to pass a half-hour while waiting for the weather to clear. I saw another lone woman sitting at a table and so I knew ladies did not have to be accompanied in order to be served.

I stepped into The Two Foxes—and once again my life changed.

I did not know it at the time, certainly. But in retrospect I see that my opening that door and taking the steps into that room changed many things in my life—most in ways I could never have imagined as I simply walked in, an unknown young woman looking for respite from the downpour outside.

I sat down at a small round table near the back—I was still uneasy at the idea of being seen, though I knew no one could possibly recognize me—and what if they did? I was an indepen-dent woman with her own money; I owed no one anything. The barkeep, a big bearish man of gruff but not unfriendly mien, took my order for a glass of wine and then turned his attention to a figure in the shadows who was sitting somewhere behind me. The barkeep's tone grew harsh as he said, "I've told you, you must have cash to keep drinking here. I cannot sell you liquor on credit. I would go bankrupt if I started such a practice. If you have no money, I can only suggest that you leave here now."

I glanced back—and my heart virtually leapt from my chest in surprise. The man sitting in the shadows, hunched over a mess of papers before him, bore an uncanny resemblance to—no, he *was* the famous poet and writer, Edgar Allan Poe! I had seen his image in newspapers and once had beheld his daguerreotype reproduction in a small frame in a shop that sold such images of well-known individuals. It *was* Poe; the man who wrote *Tamerlane and Other Poems*, all those strange and beautiful verses my father and I had read with such delight when I was but a girl; the author of "The Lake" and "Spirits of the Dead" and "Irene"—so many unforgettable works, so much language that had fired in me as a child the love of literature and poetry.

But how the great genius had fallen! Indeed, I know not how I realized it was Poe at all, he looked so very different from the images I had seen of him. His clothes, black and torn, were those of a beggar, but they were not what I primarily noticed. It was his face that held my shocked attention. The images I had seen of Poe displayed a handsome, gracious-looking man, well put out, with strong features, gracefully kept hair, very masculine mustaches, and two of the deepest, darkest, most soulful eyes I had ever seen. The man at the table—it was as if the healthy, virile man of the images had been drained by some terrible force, like something out of one of his own dread-inducing stories, to become but a sallow husk of his former self. He was thin—even emaciated—and his cheeks were sunken in a pallor of obvious illness. His hair was in disarray; his mustaches had clearly not been attended in some time. But most of all it was his *eyes*—they had receded into his skull, or so it appeared; they seemed to have shrunk, become pale and vague, with a pathetic lost look to them. He seemed dejected and utterly without hope as he looked up at the barkeep, shook his head, and began to gather the papers before him.

Completely without thinking, I said to the proprietor, "I will pay for the gentleman's refreshment."

The bearlike man looked at me, surprised. "Are you sure, ma'am?" He leaned closer to me and added quietly, "It does no good to supply a drunkard like this one. Only makes him sicker. I'd rather have him out."

I stood, feeling my eyes glow with anger. "I will pay for the gentleman," I said again. "Please supply him with anything he desires." With that I took a coin from my dress and handed it to him.

He frowned, but was not about to reject the coin. "As you say, ma'am," said he, and moved heavily off.

Mr. Poe and I were now only a few feet apart. I looked down at him piteously.

"Thank you," he whispered in a husky voice. "I am not in the habit of accepting drinks from ladies, but…"

"Think nothing of it, sir."

He seemed to smile, though the effort only made him look sicker. "Would you like to join me at this table?"

"Indeed I would. Thank you, sir." I sat. For a long moment

we said nothing. The papers scattered everywhere were all covered with writing—his own, I surmised.

I studied my table companion. Seeing him at closer range, I could make out the man he had once been—that man was clearly visible even through the ravages of whatever illness he was obviously suffering.

"Excuse me, sir," said I, "but are you not the celebrated Mr. Edgar Allan Poe?"

His eyes studied me, blinking rapidly. "I have that misfortune," said he.

"Oh, sir," said I, suddenly emotional, "your works—the beauty of your thoughts and your poetry—you cannot know what it has meant to me in my life. I grew up with your *Tamerlane and Other Poems.*"

He frowned at that. We were silent as the barkeep delivered a whiskey to the table. I sipped at my wine. "You have me at a disadvantage, my young friend," he said at last.

"Of course—I'm sorry." I introduced myself.

"I am delighted to make your acquaintance," said he. "Pardon me for not standing when you arrived, but I feared that if I stood, I might fall."

"Oh, Mr. Poe," said I. "Surely things are not as bad as all that."

"They are quite bad," said he, gesturing at the papers before him. "Nothing comes. Look." He gathered some of the papers and pushed them across the table to me. I felt unworthy to touch them, but saw in their incoherent mix some lines of poetry, some sentences of what appeared to perhaps be an essay of some sort, and another page which bore what was surely the beginnings of a short story, something narrated by a man in a lighthouse.

"I can finish none of it," he said in his quiet voice. "As an author I am utterly ruined."

"That can never be," said I, with the utmost sincerity, "for a man of your genius."

He drank half the whiskey in a single swallow. "My genius, if indeed I ever had any at all, is quite dead—as dead as I myself nearly am."

"Mr. Poe," I said quietly, "it breaks my heart to hear you talk this way."

Something about those words seemed to cause him to rally. He sat up, straightening his spine, and toyed with his cravat, straightening it as best he could. Poe was a smaller man than I had imagined—but then don't we always imagine the artistic titans of the world to be ten feet tall? He smiled then, clearly making an effort at a true smile and not the sad simulacrum I had noted before on his lips. It was not particularly convincing, but the fact that he tried touched me. His poetry came back to me—all those beautiful women he wrote about, all the paeans to their souls and spirits—and I realized that he was seeing me now not as simply an unknown stranger who took pity on him enough to buy him whiskey, but as a woman. I knew I was far from ugly, even as I was much thinner and paler than once I had been; still, in the morning the mirror showed me a very pleasant feminine countenance, despite all that had been done to me.

"I apologize, miss," he said. "It is nothing for you to concern yourself with. You are clearly a fine and caring person, and I appreciate these attentions very much." He seemed to sag slightly then. "I fear it is too late for me, however."

I leaned close to him. "Why do you say that, Mr. Poe?"

"My dear wife is gone," he said quietly, "and my talent has fled me. I have no work. There is nothing left for me but—this." He took the glass in his hand and emptied it.

"Your wife?"

"Virginia," said he.

"She is—she has passed on, sir?"

He looked at the table and nodded slowly.

"I am so terribly sorry, Mr. Poe. Surely there is no pain like the pain of losing one's spouse and soulmate."

He looked at me. "Yes," said he. "Spouse and soulmate... exactly."

I knew something about losing one's soulmate, but I had no desire to refocus the conversation to myself. My heart swelled with awe and sympathy as I sat across a small table in an obscure inn conversing with the greatest poet of the modern age. I knew this was a moment I would never in my life forget.

He began to talk then. His voice was soft and low, not

prepossessing but filled somehow with what I can only term *presence*. It was easy to see why he had at one time packed lecture halls all over the eastern United States with his speeches and recitals. His voice was like a musical instrument—a lute, perhaps—a musical instrument that was battered and broken and yet was, when the occasion demanded, still capable of producing glorious sound. He talked mostly of his recent past. I learned of the catastrophe of Virginia Poe's passing, the years of poverty and the impossibility of ever providing his consumptive wife with enough warmth in the winter. She had been a long time dying, and Poe had kept watch every day, every hour, as the single human being who had meant the most to him wasted away to a scrap, a shadow, and finally to nothing at all. He talked of other women whom he had known as well—his mother, his stepmother, a dear friend, all women who had died, each leaving another part of his soul bereft. Virginia had been the final blow, and the worst.

"I shall not recover," said he, whisperingly. "I cannot recover."

The rain had long ceased, but we continued sitting there in sad companionship as the skies darkened with the approaching night. I knew that alcohol had loosened Mr. Poe's tongue considerably, and I wondered if it was somehow inappropriate for me to sit there listening to the intimate details of his life, but I was too fascinated—too fascinated and too *anguished*—to stop him. He seemed to need to talk. And in between his autobiographical reminiscences, all jumbled and out of sequence as they were, he would stop occasionally, seem to recall to himself that I was there, and offer to entertain me by reciting a poem. He spoke "Dreams" to me ("Oh! That my young life were a lasting dream!"), and "Evening Star," and "The Lake"—all verses my father and I had read to each other, bedazzled by the poet's imagery and rhythms. Despite his condition he spoke beautifully, his voice filled with feeling and passion, his poet's heart shining through every line.

I learned a great deal about Mr. Poe in those hours, but very little of what I learned was happy. His life had been mostly a miserable one, he stated, though in talking about his mother he shared a few intimate reminiscences which occasionally brightened his countenance for a moment. "She perished when I was but three years old," he lamented, "and yet I recall her as a shining light to my soul." He discussed his Army career, which I had not known occurred at all and which greatly surprised me—he seemed the last man who would flourish in the discipline of the military, but he had some pleasant memories of that time in his life—"A time long ago," he sighed, "and very nearly forgotten." I said little as he spoke. Occasionally I would try to help him back onto a topic if his words seemed to wander, but for the most part I simply listened, entranced. After I had purchased several whiskeys for him I suggested that he eat something—the suggestion was met with indifference, but he did not actually refuse; and so I purchased from the proprietor several examples of the only foodstuff available for sale in his establishment, hardboiled eggs. Cracking one for my friend, I was able to encourage him to swallow a few bites, but his focus was entirely on the alcohol.

Hours passed. It occurred to me only gradually that The Two Foxes was an establishment which did not close for the night at all. I knew not the legality of this, but then Baltimore—especially such a seedy section of town as we were now situated in—was not, as I knew all too well from my earlier experiences, a city in which the rule of law obtained with any particular vigor. I was far beyond wondering what anyone might think of a young woman who sat up with a man in a drinking establishment throughout the darkest hours of the night. And so I stayed there as the darkness settled over the city and as the traffic outside quieted. I heard rain spatter the roof occasionally. Now and again a customer would open the door and find his way to a table, but there were no more than a handful of such persons over several hours. The gruff proprietor looked at our party occasionally, seemingly trying to decide whether to remove us—or at least Mr. Poe—bodily, but in the end the fact that I kept paying for drinks kept us there.

At length Mr. Poe's monologue grew more personal. He began discussing his various relationships with women—women he had loved, women he had lost—in a voice that, in

the near-darkness of The Two Foxes (only a few oil lamps provided a dim illumination to the scene), came to seem ephem-
eral, almost disembodied. No doubt part of this change was
the enormous amount of alcohol he was consuming. From time
to time I attempted to slow his drinking, insisting that he sip
water in between swallows of whiskey. I fear that my efforts
were only very minimally effective. Sitting there in the quiet
semi-darkness I began to feel—almost as if I were in a verse by
Mr. Poe himself—as if we were nothing now but spirits, ghosts,
two humans who had known more than their share of pain and
suffering and who now were leaving the world, floating free,
transcending time and space together to go to some brighter,
happier land.

"Miss," said he at last, after some hours, "you have told me
nothing of your own story."

"My story?" I shifted uncomfortably. "I have no story, Mr.
Poe, none at all."

"That cannot be true." He clenched his eyes shut and opened
them again several times, as if to get a clearer look at me. "Your
face is—is *suffused* with sorrow."

I looked at him. "I was not aware of that."

"Oh, yes." He nodded wearily. "You are a fellow sufferer.
You cannot hide it."

I smiled wanly. "I have tried to."

"But a fellow member of the Society of Sufferers always
knows."

I could but chuckle grimly at this unhappy assertion. "I
believe that you are correct, Mr. Poe. But I have no wish to inflict
my little problems on you."

"If they were little," said he, "you would not be in this disreputable place at three o'clock in the morning, listening to a
drunken man's ravings."

"Mr. Poe—"

"And your expression would not be so utterly, miserably
haunted—like someone who has been through the tortures of
the damned."

The look in his eyes then—the soulfulness that I had recalled
from the images I had seen of his face returned and I felt as if

he were examining me with some sort of special spyglass that could see beyond my skin and into my very soul. And yet the sensation was not an intrusive one. Here was a man, I thought, who understood all, sympathized with all, *felt* all. I cannot explain it, but somehow as I sat with the great poet I sensed that I was safe—that I might say anything at all and I would be heard without judgment of any kind.

"Ah, Mr. Poe," said I, my voice a trembling whisper, "how I wish I could tell you that you are wrong. But I am speaking to the creator of the great investigator C. Auguste Dupin. Clearly you see all."

He smiled. "Not all. Dupin was not a magician or a metaphysician. He needed facts, which he gleaned from observation—and from listening."

Thus it was that, with some further coaxing, I began to unburden my mind to Mr. Edgar Allan Poe. I talked for a long time and I fear I hardly know what I said, although the reader of this chronicle surely knows the basic facts I would have imparted to him. He studied me closely as I spoke, even as his head sometimes seemed less than completely steady on his thin frame. And I, too—I had consumed several glasses of wine over the hours, and I was not accustomed to the bodily effects of alcohol—I felt light-headed and just slightly dizzy.

I know I told him about my early life in Grimsleytown—about my parents—about their untimely deaths, and that of my unborn sister—I know I spoke of Sadmore Place (I do not recall if I discussed poor Mary Mahoney). I remember speaking of my wanderings and, of course, of dear Jim Gamble, and I know I spoke of our relationship there in the little hut on the Chesapeake without shame. And I must have spoken of Doctor Blackthorn, for I recall Mr. Poe being particularly engaged at times and asking me questions, one of which I can conjure from my memory quite easily: "Automata, you say?"

"Yes," I whispered. "The most amazing creations." I described to him some of the things they could do, including nursing services and the playing of musical instruments.

"I have had experiences with such frauds," said he. "The Mechanical Turk—"

"This was no fraud, Mr. Poe. I saw their inner workings, like the machinery of a clock. He showed me how they functioned."

"Mm. Fascinating. Please go on."

And I did—for many hours. Occasionally I cried, and once the proprietor came over to our table—not out of any concern for me, but rather to ascertain whether Poe himself had caused my emotional overflow; if he had, I suspected, the man would use this as a pretext for banishing the poet from the premises. But I purchased another drink for Mr. Poe, and another egg, and the man went away again. I revealed all to Mr. Poe, or nearly all— the specifics of how I escaped Doctor Blackthorn I withheld (I simply could not speak them), along with the fact that the doc- tor was in truth my own father—this not because I feared Poe's reaction, but rather from a deep and abiding shame.

At last I saw that dawn had begun to break across the skies. A cold sunshine slowly spilled over our table. Mr. Poe and I had not spoken for some time, instead sitting in companionable—if despairing—silence. I felt as close to him as I had ever felt to another human being, even if I was mildly intoxicated by this point and Poe was nearly in a stupor.

I knew it was nearly time to go, and I rustled in the bag I had been carrying with me in order to find a bit of money I might leave the poet so that he would not be kicked out into the street as soon as I left. As I searched, I came across a sheet of paper that brought my breath up short.

Poe, still somewhat aware of his surroundings, looked up suddenly. "What is it?"

"Oh, Mr. Poe." I brought out the sheet of paper on which the news of the death of my dear Jim was printed. I had no actual memory of taking it from the house, but I knew that the paper had remained in my room after the terrible moment Doctor Blackthorn had shown it to me. I had read it many times, seek- ing in its cold and awful words some comfort or understanding but finding none. Now here was the same paper in my hands. "It is the newspaper announcement of Jim Gamble's passing. That terrible man—Doctor Blackthorn—he gave it to me."

His hand, noticeably shaking, reached to the hated thing. I gave it to him. Again his eyes seemed bleary and unfocused;

he tried to read the words several times, but scowled in apparent frustration. However, he kept studying the paper—in fact he looked at it very closely, holding it no more than an inch from his eyes, slowly turning it over several times.

"This..." he began to say, but then exhaustion and inebriation seemed to overtake him. His head slumped and he dropped the paper onto the table.

"Mr. Poe?" I said. "Did you mean to say something?"

"The—paper," said he, his voice a husky whisper.

"Yes?"

"You say—you say it is a newspaper?"

"Yes, Mr. Poe."

He tried to look at me. His eyes were a bloody red in the early morning light. "What—what newspaper?" he asked.

"I—I don't know. What particular newspaper? I don't know, Mr. Poe."

He grasped the paper firmly again and looked at it, closing one eye and holding the paper close to the other. "This—no...."

"What did you say, Mr. Poe?"

"This—this paper—is not a newspaper."

I looked from his sad visage to the paper he held in his hand. "I do not follow your meaning, Mr. Poe."

"Not a newspaper," said he, shaking his head. "The paper—wrong."

"Wrong?"

"Too heavy," he said, his voice seeming to sink away into near-silence. "Too heavy. Not...not a newspaper..."

With those words, Mr. Edgar Allan Poe fell into unconsciousness.

Though I felt some guilt at doing so, I confess that I left Mr. Poe slumbering there at the table. I gave the proprietor another coin and asked him to swear that he would treat the poet kindly, and he said that he would—"I have some sympathy for those with the affliction," said he. "I barely escaped it, myself. I let him stay there at that corner table many nights, as long as he can pay for his drinks."

"You have my coin. That will cover many drinks."

"Yes, ma'am, it will."

"You swear that you will not abuse my friend?"

"I will let him sleep. He's bothering no one back there."

I looked back at the dark shape collapsed over the table. "He needs medical attention," said I, more to myself than to the proprietor.

"That I can't help with, ma'am."

I looked at the big man again. "Do you think he will still be here later?"

"No telling, ma'am. He comes and goes as he pleases. But your money should last him awhile."

I looked at Poe again, my heart filled with sorrow. "I shall return," said I. "I shall return this afternoon."

"As you wish, ma'am."

"Please give him that message when he wakes, if you would be so kind."

I could see that I was wearing his patience thin. He frowned. "I'll try to remember, ma'am."

I nodded and stepped out into the morning street. Business was beginning to pick up on all sides; many people were on the sidewalks now, many carriages in the road. The skies were clear and the autumn air invigorating. It cleared my head quickly of the dizziness I had experienced from the drink. My bag in hand, I wandered without destination for a while. From time to time I pulled the paper about Jim Gamble from my pocket and studied it. It looked like an ordinary newspaper clipping to me, but Mr. Poe had claimed, oddly, that it was *not* from a newspaper. I tried to think of where else Doctor Blackthorn might have procured such a cutting. A magazine, perhaps? A pamphlet? But who would have published such news—the news of an obscure fisherman's death—in a magazine or pamphlet? The more I thought of it, the less sense it seemed to make. I knew I had to face the possibility that Poe had simply been mistaken, that his alcohol-besotted vision had seen things that were not there. He was the creator of C. Auguste Dupin, yes—surely; but M. Dupin never drank as did Mr. Poe.

I stopped in the middle of the walkway, sighing. I wondered why I kept this terrible document at all; for a moment

I considered simply throwing it into the street. It contained words that left me without hope, my spirit deadened, my soul shattered. Why must I read them ever and again?

The business I found myself standing before was a printer's shop, a somewhat cracked and warped sign over the door of which read *Miller's Printing Service*. I looked vaguely through the window at the counter in front and the various machines for the creation of moveable type behind it, the names of which I knew not. No one seemed to be in the shop until the door suddenly opened and a little gray man wearing a dirty white garment of some sort—like an apron, but not a kitchen apron—stepped out with a broom in his hands. He commenced to sweeping the front stoop, hardly glancing at me. Round wire eyeglasses were perched atop his nose.

At once an idea seized me. "Excuse me, sir," said I.

"Hm?" Again he did not look at me.

"Sir, this..." I brought the paper from my pocket again. "This paper..."

He glanced up. His eyes were pale and colorless behind his lenses. "Yes? What about it?" His voice was dry and reedy; the man, I realized, was quite old—at least fifty.

"I—I wondered if you could tell me about it."

"Tell you about it?"

"The—its provenance, sir."

"Provenance?"

"Yes." I struggled to find the words and suddenly felt myself a fool for standing there. "I wondered—can you tell me the source of this? How it was printed? Is it from a newspaper?"

He scowled, seemingly prepared to tell me to go away—but he leaned the broom against the door and his manner softened a little. "Let me see what you mean," said he.

I handed him the paper and he stood in the doorway studying it for a moment.

"What do you want to know, now?"

"Is it—sir, is it from a newspaper, or is it a broadside, or—or what is it, sir?"

"Hm." He looked again, turning it over in his hands as Poe had done. "Well, it's not a newspaper, I can tell you that."

I felt my heart beating. "How—how can you tell, sir?"

He looked at me carefully then and, perhaps finding something sympathetic in my countenance, gestured to me and said, "Step into the shop, young lady, if you will. I'll show you."

I followed him in. The shop was smaller inside than it had appeared and the machines behind the counter seemed to loom over us like unholy monsters in the semi-dark.

"Now, you see here," he said, stepping behind the counter and pulling up a single sheet of newsprint, "this is the Baltimore *Sun*. Penny paper. Put your fingers on this paper if you will, miss." I did. "See how that feels? That's news print. It's lightweight, thin, inexpensive. Has a brittle quality—do you feel that?"

"I do, yes."

"See here." He pulled more papers from under the counter. "Here's a page from the *Gazette*, and here's one from the *Patriot*. They all use the same kind of paper, you see?"

I touched each in turn. "I understand, sir. But this..." I placed the news article about Jim's death on the counter. "Could it be from another newspaper? One not so well known, perhaps?"

He picked up the document again and studied it skeptically. "I know every newspaper of any importance from Boston to Richmond, miss. This isn't from any of them. Newspapers just don't use this grade of product."

"Who would, then?"

"It's near the weight of a broadside," said he. "Just a moment." He turned and found a stack of blank sheets, felt one with his fingers, then felt Jim's article again. "Yes, here we are." He placed a blank sheet on the counter before me and I touched it. "Standard broadside weight. That's what you've got there, miss."

I stared at the obituary notice and at the blank sheet, a sudden feeling of hopelessness overcoming me. "Sir..."

"Miller is my name, miss."

"Mr. Miller. Of course." I tried to smile. "I don't—what does it *mean*, Mr. Miller? I don't understand—if this didn't come from a newspaper, then where *did* it come from?"

For the first time he seemed to study the words themselves

on the paper, and the advertisement on the back. After a moment he looked at me. "I don't mean to intrude, miss," said he, "but I take it this person was someone important to you."

"He was the most important person in the world to me."

He looked down. "I'm sorry, miss. The best I can guess…" He took the paper again and held it to the light. "The best I can guess is that this is a custom job of work. Any one of a half-dozen shops within a mile of here could have done it up." He tilted his head this way and that, studying the paper. "It's a fine job. Well-printed, right to the advertisement on the reverse."

"But not a newspaper."

"Not a newspaper, miss."

"And you don't believe that it's part of a magazine, or a pamphlet?"

"Not such as I'm familiar with, miss. I think someone came into a shop like this and ordered it done. Though why they would have included the advertisement on the other side is beyond me. Was the late gentleman connected to this company in some way?"

I stared into the middle distance for a time, no thoughts in my brain at all.

"No," I said finally. "He was not."

"Well, I hope I've been helpful to you, miss."

I looked at him. "You have been extremely helpful, sir." I folded the paper and replaced it in my pocket. "You have been most helpful indeed." I reached for a coin, but he stopped me with a gesture of his hand.

"You don't owe me anything, miss," said he. Then he eyed me speculatively. "I hope you find whatever it is you're looking for."

"I hope so as well, Mr. Miller. Indeed I hope so."

I found my way along the street to a simple little restaurant and ordered tea, which I drank without tasting. What did it mean? Had Doctor Blackthorn created this document by hiring a printing shop to produce it, with the specific intention of deceiving me? And if so—my breath came short at the very idea, an idea so outlandish, so impossible, that I hardly dared even formulate it in my mind—if so…

Was it possible that my dear Jim Gamble was *alive*?

I spent the next hours wandering from printing shop to print-ing shop, asking the same questions about the document in my hands and receiving much the same answers. No one knew of a newspaper printed on such thick bond paper; it would be much too expensive, I was told. Penny papers, it was explained, must use the humblest possible materials lest the cost of print-ing become impractical. Each shop owner gave me the address of the next nearest shop and so I went from one to the next, asking—asking!

At last, in mid-afternoon, I found the answer. A fine-looking printing establishment on the north end of Light Street beck-oned me with its bright décor and clean, clear windows; inside, the man behind the counter—I was so rude as to never to think to ask his name—immediately identified the death notice as having been printed in his shop some months before.

"I remember the chap," said this man, whose very appear-ance has vanished from my mind but whose words are etched as if in stone upon my brain. "An elderly man, quite heavy, with a deep voice. He was quite particular about his needs on this document. I found it curious at the time, but I didn't ask ques-tions. I had no reason to. He wasn't a very polite gentleman, quite demanding really, so I made sure to print his document on my priciest stock." He smiled then, revealing that he was missing one of his front teeth.

I asked more questions regarding the elderly customer's appearance and was left in no doubt that it had been Doctor Hudson Blackthorn.

In an ecstasy of excitement I rushed out of the shop with-out so much as an expression of gratitude to the proprietor. I ran madly down Light Street, jostling passersby, stumbling and nearly falling but never slowing. I was laughing and weeping simultaneously—tears of thrilled emotion. The death notice was not real! It was a forgery! And that meant—not that my Jim was necessarily alive, but at least that there was a *possibility* he was alive. I hardly even wondered at the moment how I would go about attempting to find him, if indeed he was living and could be found; I simply ran like a crazed young girl, heedless of traffic, not knowing my destination, until at last I found myself, somewhat to my surprise, in front of The Two Foxes once more. The sun had passed behind a cloud and the street was slowly growing dark as I collected myself quickly and, still somewhat breathless, stepped again into that establishment.

The proprietor saw me immediately and made a gesture with his head—Mr. Poe was still there, all these hours later, at the same table. I rushed to him. He was conscious and alert, with pen and paper in front of him, though his eyes looked pained and his skin was even more sallow than it had been before. It was obvious that he was a sick man, but I simply collapsed onto the chair upon which I had sat before and began babbling at him—"Mr. Poe! Mr. Poe, you were correct! The death notice was not from a newspaper at all! Mr. Poe, I found the printer himself! He remembered the man—Doctor Blackthorn—he remembered him ordering this to be printed for him! The document is a fake, Mr. Poe! It means—" I hesitated to say it aloud—"it means that my Jim might be alive somewhere!"

He took a long time to respond, as if his mind had been far away. He was clearly exhausted. "That is wonderful," he said at last, in a voice hardly above a whisper.

I looked at him. "Are you feeling poorly, Mr. Poe?"

"I? Poorly?" He seemed to consider the question. "No. I am not feeling poorly. I am not feeling anything at all. I am in the midst of writing."

I saw the papers before him. Indeed he had his pen and ink bottle and fresh writing was upon the pages on the table.

"But that's wonderful, Mr. Poe!" The proprietor came and I ordered drinks and eggs. In the time it took me to do so, however, Poe drooped perceptibly.

"Yes," said he. "Writing—a poem."

"Oh sir, that news brings me such joy."

He smiled tremblingly. "I must rest now," said he as our order arrived. "I have been working for hours here." He cleared his throat weakly. "Would you like to read it? It is not finished."

My heart swelled. "It would be an honor."

He pushed the papers toward me nonchalantly as he turned

his attention to his drink. His florid handwriting had inscribed at the top of one page the words "Annabel Lee," a name not known to me (the reader will recall that this memoir is published pseudonymously), but as I began reading I realized that it was myself of whom he had written—myself as imaginatively recreated from his own remarkable imagination. Indeed I was unrecognizable to any but myself. He had completely reconceived the man in the verse—instead of the horrid Doctor Blackthorn he had transmuted him, like lead into gold, into one of his typically sensitive, brooding young heroes, a man, it seemed to me, not unlike himself. Reading the poem was like looking at a reflection of myself in a flawed glass—this was my life and experience, yes, but completely changed, made into someone and something else. It was most melancholy and most beautiful.

The poem was not complete. Some lines were unfinished and had blanks or question marks in their place, while some of the lines did not yet properly scan, but the basic elements of the poem were all there—the two young lovers, the world's disapproval, her decline and death—yes, I had told him of that too, my own death—and the lover's unceasing sorrow. The poem *was* me; and it was *not* me.

"It is for you," he whispered, his head dropping slowly. "When I finish—dedicate—to you."

He fell to sleep. My excitement at the news of the forgery of the death notice was now replaced with my fascinated thrill at the idea that my story had somehow inspired the greatest poet of the age to fresh creation. I looked again at the papers and realized that the poem continued; there was on another page the Roman numeral "II." The second part of the verse narrative was only a few lines long so far, and at this late date I cannot conjure its exact words in my mind (how I wish that I could!), but I remember quite vividly their general import: the young lover decides that he cannot live without the late Annabel Lee, and so he breaks into the sepulcher and carries her body away to his room. The imagery of this was more vivid than life itself—the despondent young man, the moonlight falling over his shoulders as he carries his beloved along the beach, the terribly waxen look of her pale face, the sound of the crashing sea—and the revelation in the last line that he has a plan to bring her *back to life....*

But the poem stopped there. I wanted to wake the author, beg him to continue—the work seemed ineffably wonderful, even as it had been so utterly changed as to hardly have anything to do with my own life. Yet my story had clearly inspired it! And, just as his wife Virginia had become the lost Lenore of "The Raven," I had become "the beautiful Annabel Lee"! Never had I served as a literary model, and the feeling was indescribably exciting. I read over the rough pages several times, wondering what choices he might make for the words and lines not yet filled in. I particularly noticed a blank near the end of that first part, which read:

"And so, all _____, I lie down by the side
Of my darling—my darling—my life and my bride..."

It was obvious that the author sought an internal rhyme for "side" and "bride" but had not yet conjured it. Yet as I studied the page a phrase I thought apposite jumped quickly to my mind: *"night-tide,"* poor doomed Mary Mahoney's expression for her bouts with unhappiness and melancholia. "All night-tide" did not scan, but an insertion of "the" at the start of the phrase solved the problem, it seemed to me, perfectly.

I reached for Mr. Poe's shoulder, intending to wake him with this impertinent inspiration of mine, but I hesitated. Instead I dipped his pen into the ink bottle and wrote, in very tiny, thoroughly modest letters, *"the night-tide?"* above the relevant line.

It was outrageous temerity on my part, of course—absolute impudence! How dare I, a mere teenaged vagabond girl, seek to collaborate with the great Poe? Yet this feeling was overcome by my desire to help the man, the man I now considered a dear friend. Perhaps he would finish the poem more quickly now, and earn a few dollars with it. He could always reject the suggestion, I reasoned, simply by lining it out. And yet I fretted so about defacing Mr. Poe's precious manuscript that I nearly lined out the addendum myself.

In the end, however, I let it stand, because as I looked at the great poet with his head fallen on the table my excitement darkened to worry. He clearly needed a doctor—something had to be done for him. Forgetting my versifying ambitions for the present, I stood with resolution and told the proprietor that I would be back shortly with someone who could offer assistance to Mr. Poe, and walked out into the street again.

It took me a little over an hour to find a doctor who was willing to drop what he was doing and come to The Two Foxes, but at last I did. I led the man quickly through the dimming streets and through the now-familiar door—only to discover that the table where we had spent our time together was no longer occupied! The papers, the inkwell, the pen, and the man—all were gone!

When I asked him, the proprietor merely shrugged. "He comes and goes as he pleases, ma'am. He stumbled out of here about fifteen minutes ago."

"Do you know where he might have gone?" I asked.

He shook his head and moved to turn away. "He's not my brother," said he, "and I'm not his keeper."

I returned to my room—my new room, in which I now had no interest. I sat for a long time in the deepening dark, simply thinking. I felt sorrow about Poe but, I thought, he was obviously a habitué of the Two Foxes, and so I should be able to find him again if I merely checked in now and again. My real attentions were devoted to Jim Gamble. How could I begin to find him? I wondered. How did one find a man who might well be dead? Where did one start?

After an unhappy night spent tossing and turning in my bed I arose the next morning and made my way to the police station, asking the first man there that very question. I was told that the most logical thing to do would be to check the local hospitals, which I did—with no results. In my hours searching I also stopped by The Two Foxes not once but twice—also with no results.

A matron at one hospital took interest in my story and, after asking for further details, suggested that I visit the nearby sanitariums. This I did as well—in fact, I searched sanitariums for two days. In the end, however, there was no result, just as I failed to find Poe again at The Two Foxes.

It occurred to me that if Jim were living, and in a hospital or sanitarium, he might be located well outside Baltimore—there were surely such establishments closer to the Chesapeake Bay community where we had lived. I returned to the sympathetic matron at the hospital and received in return a list of all such establishments within a hundred-mile radius. Thus armed, I purchased pen, ink, paper, and envelopes, and set to in my room on a furious letter-writing campaign to every such possible location, pleading with anyone reading the letter to please reply to me if they knew the whereabouts of James Gamble, with a description provided.

I sent the letters in a big stack one morning at the post office, and found myself suddenly with no further avenues to explore. I would simply have to wait for replies.

I checked The Two Foxes ever and again, but Mr. Poe did not reappear. I suspected that the bearlike proprietor had a hand in Mr. Poe's disappearance from the establishment, but it would have done me no good to confront the man. I kept looking in, but with no success.

One afternoon, however, about a week after I had sent my communications to all the sanitariums in the region, I received an answer—one of several, but this one was the key to my heart and happiness—the key to my soul—the letter that opened the possibility of joy into my aching heart again!

2

The Chesapeake Regional Hospital and Asylum was an imposing gray brick building located only some twenty miles east of where I had once lived with my dear Jim. Specifically designated for "paupers," its grim edifice reminded me in some ways of Sadmore Place—why must all such institutions appear so intimidating and hopeless?—but the grounds were actually rather pleasant, with well-kept grass and serene walkways. I found my way there through a variety of modes of travel one bright, cool morning in September, my heart crashing ever-harder in my chest as I approached the front door. The letter I had received the day before was from a Mrs. Radcliffe, who identified herself as an administrator at the establishment, and she told me that they indeed were currently housing the gentleman of whom I had inquired, and that I would be quite welcome to visit him if I chose. "He was profoundly injured," read the woman's letter, "but is now tranquil."

Profoundly injured...tranquil... My mind raced around and around trying to understand the meaning of those words in the hours it took me to reach the asylum. I imagined terrible things—had his body been shattered, his brain destroyed? Was he mentally sound? Again and again I thought of those final awful moments, the sound of Doctor Blackthorn's weapon, Jim collapsing and telling me to run, and my sense that my life was over, that Doctor Blackthorn had murdered my very life as surely as if the pistol had been aimed at my own breast. Horrible memories! I found tears trickling down my face continually as I traveled, tears of hope and terror, of misery and resignation. And yet, I reasoned—and yet, whatever his condition, whatever had happened to him, *Jim was alive*. This fact in itself caused my heart to soar again and yet again. Alive! He was alive!

I was led into a dark and almost totally unfurnished establishment with unadorned walls and only a few plain desks and chairs around. After I identified myself, the young secretary smiled and said yes, Mrs. Radcliffe had mentioned that I might come and that if I waited a moment he would fetch her. She arrived presently, a brisk, slender woman of the middle age dressed in simple gray professional attire. She remembered my letter instantly and greeted me with all the warmth I had feared I would never find in such a place as this; she put me immediately at my ease.

"We have had Mr. Gamble for some time," said she. "He was grievously injured."

"Yes, I know," said I. I proceeded to explain briefly that I had been present at the moment of his catastrophe.

"Ah, I understand. Yes. Well, please know, madam, that while the doctors did a fine job with his physical injuries, there are often other, hidden injuries in cases like this."

"Hidden injuries?"

"I refer to the mind. The trauma of the physical injury and the long recovery period have, I fear, turned his mind."

"Turned it?"

She looked down pensively, then up again. "He is quite sanguine," said she. "He is of no danger to anyone."

"Why would he be a danger?"

"His type of melancholia can sometimes manifest in violent tendencies. Thankfully, that is not the case with Mr. Gamble."

"Violent...?" I felt I could speak no longer with Jim so close. "Please, where is he? May I see him? I beg you."

She smiled softly. "Of course you may. Come."

Mrs. Radcliffe led me down a long dim corridor. I registered nothing of it, as I could think only of the fact that I was about to see Jim—my Jim! Whatever his health, he was alive and I was within moments of seeing him again!

We stopped at a colorless metal door and Mrs. Radcliffe produced a ring of keys.

"You must not expect too much of him," said she. "He may

not recognize you. Even if he does, he is unlikely to display any real reaction to you. That is the nature of his condition."

"Please, Mrs. Radcliffe," I whispered breathlessly, "please, please just open the door!"

She nodded, inserted a key into the lock and turned it. The door pulled outward. I peered into a semi-dark space which at first appeared to be unoccupied. I espied a bed in the corner, and there was some pale light glowing dully through a small barred window in the far wall. It took my eyes a moment to adjust sufficiently to see that, sitting in a chair near the window, facing toward it, was a man. His dark shape was slumped over, yet his head faced upward, toward the light.

"Jim?" I whispered. "Jim...is it you?"

After glancing at Mrs. Radcliffe to ensure that it was all right, I moved slowly to the dim figure at the far end of the room.

"Jim? Jim, darling? I've come to see you, my dear."

The figure offered no reaction. I stood looking at the profile of the man and for a moment did not believe that this was Jim Gamble at all. My heart sank as I stared at the unfamiliar countenance and I was about to turn to speak to Mrs. Radcliffe of my disappointment when the light in the window grew a bit brighter—the sun came out from behind a cloud—and I realized that this was indeed my life, my love, the man I had sought so fervently. He looked terribly different—much older, his eyes recessed in his head—but what had truly confounded me was that his beard had been shaved off. He looked like another person entirely, but—he was not! It *was* my Jim!

I knelt beside him and, unable to control myself, took his hand and kissed it countless times, my tears dropping onto his skin. I heard myself whispering his name—"Jim, Jim, Jim, Jim, Jim"—and the feeling of his hand in mine was thrillingly familiar. I touched his arm—it was covered in a cheap wool shirt—and looked at his face, changed now but still the same, the same dear face.

"Jim, can you speak to me? Can you speak?"

From behind me, Mrs. Radcliffe said quietly, "He does not speak. We have never heard him speak in this institution."

"Never?"

"Not one word. There is nothing wrong with his vocal apparatus, according to our doctors. It is simply his melancholia. As I told you, it has turned his mind."

I gazed at him, at his beloved eyes and nose and lips and cheeks. He had shown no awareness that I was there at all—he simply continued to stare at the light coming through the window. His anguish had somehow transformed his face—in the light he looked to me like one of the saints from the Bible, all knowledge of the world and time in his hollow and weary features.

"Oh Jim," I said through tears, stroking his arm, "Jim, it's—it's Annabel. It's your Andy, Jim. Please look at me. Please speak to me. Just a word, just—one word..."

I was weeping uncontrollably now, and Mrs. Radcliffe moved to touch my shoulder consolingly. "If you would come to my office," said she, "we can discuss Mr. Gamble's condition privately."

"I—I cannot leave him!" I cried.

"You can return in a few minutes," said she. "We have a very liberal visitation policy. He will still be here, and you may spend time with him. Please come."

I squeezed his hand in mine and stood at last, attempting to collect myself but being largely unsuccessful. I felt lost. I believed that to leave the room now would be a terrible betrayal of my Jim, even as I realized that such thoughts were completely irrational. I gazed down at him with the deepest longing in my heart—I wanted to turn back time, I wanted him to be the man he had been and I the girl, I wanted those paradisiacal hours together again. I wanted to be happy again.

"I will return soon, Jim dear," I whispered, touching the hair at his temple. In a moment Mrs. Radcliffe guided me out of the room and locked the door behind us.

"Please," said I, "must you do that? You said yourself that he is harmless."

She smiled sympathetically. "It is for his own good. He is safer this way."

I was led down a corridor and around a corner until I found

myself in a small, boxlike office with only the plainest of furniture and no decorations at all. She sat behind her simple desk and I in a straight-backed wooden chair.

"Please understand, Miss Lee," said Mrs. Radcliffe, "that we are doing all that can be done for your friend. These cases of deep melancholia are sometimes untreatable. But in time, some of the afflicted do improve. Your Mr. Gamble may be among them; we do not yet know."

"What treatment does he receive?"

"Rest," said Mrs. Radcliffe. "Rest and a serene environment. Safety. Reasonable comfort. It is all we can do."

"But you have seen no improvement?"

"Physically he is greatly improved. He was severely wounded, as you know. The bullet entered his chest just above his heart and he lost a great deal of blood. My understanding is that he was saved by some of his friends on the beach who discovered him and transported him to a doctor."

"God bless them," I whispered, thinking of the various colorful personages we had known on the beach, the fires and meals we had shared with them.

"He was in physical convalescence for two months," said she, consulting a chart that she took from a stack on her desk. "He nearly died in the early days of it. His body was badly broken, and he contracted pneumonia."

"My Lord."

"Yes." She looked at me. "But he has an iron constitution, and he was strong enough to survive. It was only later that we realized melancholia had set in, a disease of the mind every bit as dangerous as pneumonia is to the body. We attempted to communicate with him, but had no success. It was only through his friends that we knew who he was at all." She seemed to consider. "It is a difficult case."

"And his prognosis is uncertain, you say."

"Physically he will become stronger. He will never be as he was; he will likely always have limited mobility on the side of his body which suffered the injury. He may have some pain for a long time. But he will be at least close to whole again—in body. As for the mind..." She sighed. "We can keep him here. He is an indigent in need of care and the state provides in such cases. But as for his mental soundness…only time will tell the answer to that question."

I sat there staring at the floor, my emotions an impossible mix of joy at the fact of his living and despair at the truth of his condition.

"How often may I see him?" I asked at last.

"Every day, if you like. The visits may do him good."

"I will visit him every day. For as long as I am allowed."

She smiled sadly. "Regular visiting hours are from one o'clock to four each afternoon."

And so I began my vigil at Jim's side. I found a room in the town, less than a mile away; but I spent little of my time there. During most of my waking hours I was at the Chesapeake Regional Hospital and Asylum, waiting outside until visiting hours began and then rushing to see my Jim and staying with him until the staff insisted that I go. Often I simply sat with him in his room, touching his hand and saying soft nothings to him in what I hoped was a soothing voice; other times, pleasant days, he was allowed outside and we walked together—first with an attendant, later with just the two of us—all over the grounds. Jim, moving slowly, used a cane. I would take his arm at such times as we traversed the gentle landscape and for a moment or two it was almost possible to believe that we had succeeded in reversing time and that we were as we had been in that other, long-lost era. But when I looked at his face in the sunlight I would know this fantasy to be false. His eyes had a sorrowful and haunted look in them I had never before seen, and in general the lines of his face and the movements of his body—how he stood, how he walked—indicated a man decades older than I knew him to be. At such moments of realization I would feel a total sense of hopelessness and defeat.

But I continued to visit every day, and Mrs. Radcliffe came to trust me sufficiently that after a month or two she ceased strictly imposing the visiting hour rules in my case; I was allowed a good deal more freedom than other visitors. I was no longer supervised at all during my visits with Jim; the metal door remained open and at times a nurse would pass by, but no one spent their time observing us and there was no hint of any censorious feeling regarding my many long hours alone with him.

What did we do with all this time? What does anyone do with the time spent with a mute convalescent? I held his hand, brushed his hair, tidied his clothing; but mostly I talked. After the initial days in which I had simply tried to be pleasant I found myself telling him, in a soft and gentle voice, all about what had happened to me since we had been violently parted. I knew not how much penetrated into his understanding, so I omitted many of the more horrific aspects of the story. I did not confess to him that I had become a murderess. That would come in time, I thought; when he was better, when his mind and soul had improved, when he had gained back the great moral strength I knew that he possessed, then there would be time for the ultimate accounting.

It was difficult to know whether my visits were making any difference with him. For months he remained unchanged; his eyes sad and unfocused, his lips silent. And yet something within me was convinced that he was making some sort of progress, even if I could not see it. I *sensed* rather than saw that he was slowly becoming more engaged—was beginning to recognize me; if not as Andy, his old lover, then at least as a frequent visitor who was, I hope, kind to him. At one point even Mrs. Radcliffe acknowledged it, saying that Mr. Gamble seemed livelier when I visited.

This went on for some three months. I know that during this time I must have walked back and forth to and from the hospital—must have eaten—must have slept; but in truth I remember nothing whatever of such activities. My entire life centered on Jim Gamble and our life together. And in an odd way it *was* a life, if only the life of a silent patient together with his devoted if amateur nurse. Throughout the entire process I forced myself to be sympathetic, to be strong and steady, to be supportive at all times. I confess that on occasion I became highly frustrated, and it was not unknown for me to have to turn away from Jim for a few moments to allow my tears to flow. But I do not believe he was much aware of such failings on my part—at least I hope that he was not. I know, and can attest to any God in Whom the reader may happen to believe, that I did my best.

And one day, something happened. We were sitting on a wooden bench together in bright spring sunshine, the air cool. He had on a heavy burlap shirt and loose trousers, while I wore a plain dress with my shoulders covered in a wool wrap. The breeze lightly touched our faces. I was looking out across the lawn at an old oak tree there. I had no particular thoughts in my mind.

But then I seemed to hear a voice—or something like a voice. For a moment I knew not its source, as I had grown so accustomed to Jim's silence that it did not even occur to me that the sound came from him. But in a moment I realized, and I stared at him wide-eyed.

"Jim?" said I quietly, not wishing to startle him. Loud noises could cause him, I had seen, to become agitated. "Jim, dear, did you say something?" I tried to hide the excitement in my voice.

Jim looked at me. What I mean to say is, he *looked at me*. Until that moment his eyes had invariably held same vague, watery expression in them; I knew it could have been my imagination that he had ever recognized me at all. But at this moment, and for the first time since I had arrived at the hospital some months before, Jim Gamble looked at me! His eyes were clear and comprehending, and his lips began to move—to quiver.

"Jim? Jim dear?" I leaned close to him. "What is it, my love? What do you wish to say to me?"

The lips trembled. His entire face seemed to quiver with the effort. I could feel my heart pounding as I leaned my ear close and tried to hear a word, any word from his beloved lips.

And at last I did. It came slowly—haltingly—and at first I could not understand. But he tried again and yet again until at last I could make out the sounds, the sounds that came in a low, broken voice from Jim Gamble, my Jim.

"Boy…girl," said he.

After that blessed day Jim's progress was rapid. At first, of course, Mrs. Radcliffe was skeptical of my account, and for some days Jim spoke only to me and only in private; but his vocabulary increased at a fast pace, and finally he was able to greet Mrs. Radcliffe one fine day with the weak, slowly spoken, but clearly audible words, "Good afternoon." Virtually from that moment Jim was treated as a patient rapidly improving instead of one with no real hope of recovery. He received more attention from the staff, more practice with forming words and increased physical exercise. Jim himself seemed, in his way, enthusiastic, and ever more steadily did I see the old look in his eyes, the love-look he had always reserved for me given over to me again. He was a very sick man, but he was a *man—my* man; and my heart was giddy, as if butterflies fluttered around within it, each day when I came to see him.

Naturally there were setbacks, days on which he did less well than others; the effort to learn to speak and interact with others again was clearly exhausting, and at times he could not quite rise to the challenge. But these failures were short-lived. My Jim's tremendous will and spirit told, and soon we were able to have short conversations. His words were halting and uncertain but they were *words*. His body too took on more strength and vigor, though once I was present in the room when the nurse came to change his shirt and I was shocked and horrified to see what had happened to him. The region above his heart looked rather as if someone had affixed some sort of spider-shaped sculpture to it, red-gray in color; it splayed out from a central point in brutal webs in all directions from the wound. The skin was scarred and puckered and appeared altogether unhealthy. I wanted to touch him—to hold him; but there were limits even to this liberal institution, and I had to keep my feelings—and body—to myself. Yet I was heartsick at what had happened. I realized that we were now bound together not only in spirit and soul but now too—in scar. Both our bodies had been gruesomely abused, and we both clearly showed the signs—the evidence of violent trespass of our very skins.

A month of progress seemed to pass in an instant, and Jim was hardly the person at the end of that month than he had been at the beginning. He had become himself again—a slower, quieter, more tentative version of himself, but a recognizable one and one I knew I loved with my whole heart and soul. It was a miracle, sitting with him again in his room or on a bench outside or in the sitting room provided for family visits. His brain seemed to gain speed and flexibility with each passing day—he had suffered no brain damage, Miss Radcliffe told me confidently. Soon we were having conversations that, while slow-paced, were not otherwise unlike those we might have had together while sitting on the beach in the twilight. His memories came back—he knew what I was talking about when I mentioned this little thing from the past or that one—and in a short while he was bringing forth his own memories too.

It became apparent that Jim was well on the road to recovery, and at one point Miss Radcliffe along with one of the medical men, Doctor Ewing, spoke with me in a private meeting about their patient's future. "We have subjected him to numerous mental tests," the doctor said—he was a young man with mutton chops and an affable manner—"and I must say he has done remarkably well. I think he is very nearly completely recovered. That is due to some extent to our efforts, but very much more to your own."

"He is my life," said I.

"Yes." The doctor looked down at his papers for a moment, seemingly embarrassed by such a bold proclamation from a woman.

"But how is he physically?" I asked.

"That is a somewhat more troublesome area," the doctor admitted. "He will certainly be able to function in the outer world, but from what I understand he was an intensely physical man before."

"He was. He is a fisherman."

"Yes." The doctor appeared pensive. "That way of life may not be possible for him—not now, at least, and perhaps not for quite some time, if ever. His heart is weakened, you see, and his muscles on that side of his body severely damaged."

"What does that mean for—his future?" I asked.

"He may need to take light work," said the doctor. "And that after some time. Even once he is released, he will need an extensive convalescence. Has he any financial resources at all?"

"He does not," said I. "But it does not matter. I do."

"But you are not a member of his family, isn't that correct?"

"That is incorrect. I am his only family."

"But legally..."

"I will take care of him, doctor," said I, rising. "I will take care of all his needs and I will do so for the rest of my life."

For a time it seemed as if Jim's progress would only continue to increase, surprising and even dazzling the staff of the institution. Soon our walks became quite lengthy, though he invariably had to use a cane. His eyes brightened; he laughed the laugh I remembered from times that seemed to belong to another century; he spoke intimately with me, though we were not yet to the point of declaring exactly what our feelings were for each other in this new, changed world. I was of course quite certain, for my part; but I was wary of moving too fast, of frightening him. He had been through so much, and part of him was still a fragile butterfly with a broken wing. Butterflies could not, I knew, survive such an injury—could my Jim?

At last it became apparent that my love had slipped backwards into a slough of despondency again. He became less energetic, grew listless on our walks; his eyes would not meet my own with anything like the earlier focus and frequency. He was still mentally much improved—he still talked with me and we read Emerson and Shakespeare together—but something was clearly preying on his newly recovered mind. I talked to Miss Radcliffe and Doctor Ewing; they had observed the same phenomenon, but knew not the cause.

At last, one cold evening as I was about to leave for the night, Jim said, to my surprise: "May I speak to you, Andy?"

It always thrilled my heart to hear him call me by the old nickname. "Of course, dear," said I, pulling my wrap over my shoulders. "Have we not been speaking all along?"

"I mean something different this time. Would you please sit?" He gestured to the other straight backed chair in the room. I sat down in it, directly across from him. Our knees nearly touched.

"Yes, Jim?"

His face in the rapidly dimming light looked pained. His expression was difficult to interpret—part anger, part sorrow. He looked this way and that, but never into my eyes. I sat unmoving, looking at my Jim in his burlap hospital costume, wishing I could take him in my arms as we had once done so long ago, take him in my arms and rock him tenderly through the darkness of his long night.

"Andy," said he at last, his voice low, "I am enormously grateful for everything you have done for me. I wish to thank you."

"There is no need," said I, in an equally soft voice. "I did what I have done not just for you, but for myself. For us."

He scowled and looked at the gray slippers on his feet.

"I am not the man I was," said he at last, with a tightness in his voice.

"You shall be."

"No." He shook his head. I noticed how rapidly the room's light was failing. "Andy, you have seen me. You have seen how damaged I am."

"We are both damaged, Jim." I had told him of my own scars, mental and physical.

"Yes, but…but…Andy, what is the future? What do you see as the future for us?"

"I see you leaving this hospital," said I. "I see the two of us together."

"Where?"

"It matters not a whit where."

"But it does, Andy." He cleared his throat and ran his hands through his hair. "It matters—to a man. A man is…"

"A man is what, Jim?"

"A man—is expected to provide. A man is expected to…to *be* a man."

"You are the finest man I have ever known, Jim Gamble."

"Andy…" He fell silent.

"Jim," said I at last, "what is it? I have talked with your doctors. They assure me that other than some limited mobility you may suffer in the area where you were wounded, you are otherwise all but fully recovered. There is no other damage."

"The damage is within myself," he said, his voice suddenly filled with misery. "I no longer have the strength of confidence. I cannot visualize going out into the world and caring for you."

"I will care for you. In time we will care for each other."

"Andy..."

"I love you, Jim," I said then, my voice throbbing with emotion. I leaned forward and took his hands in mine. His were cold and I tried to warm them. "I love you more than I love life. There is no world for me without you; there is no life. I love you so much, Jim. You cannot know how much." I felt tears trickling down my cheeks.

But he pulled back his hands then. "I am weak now. I cannot shift for myself."

"You will in time."

"But..." He looked up and I realized that his own cheeks glistened. "You deserve better than—than what I have to offer, which is nothing."

"Oh Jim, how can you say that? With all the memories we share? How can you say that you offer me nothing?"

"I say it because it is true." His voice became stronger. "Andy, you must leave me."

"For tonight?"

"For all time."

"I must refuse."

"You cannot refuse. Andy, for the love of God, you deserve a real man—a real future—not a man shipwrecked in body and soul. I can offer nothing to you—nothing to any woman."

"That is not true, Jim."

He scowled and shifted his gaze to the ceiling. The light was almost completely drained from the room now, but neither of us moved to light a lamp. "I have decided, Andy. I do not wish you to return here. I thank you from the bottom of my heart for all you have done for me. Now—you must go out into the world and find the man you deserve. You are young, brilliant, and beautiful. A crippled fisherman is no man for you."

We sat in the deepening dark. I watched Jim's face fading toward blackness.

"Is this truly what you feel, Jim?"

"It is truly what I feel."

"And there is nothing I can say that will change your mind?"

"Nothing," said he. "I will always think kindly on you, Annabel—Andy. I will always think of you as the woman who saved my life. But now you must save your own."

We sat in silence. My breath was shallow. My head hurt.

"Jim…" I began.

"No more, Andy!" he cried. "Please just go. In later years you will thank me for releasing you. You will have a wonderful life, a dazzling life. You will do anything you wish to do. You are an extraordinary girl. I above all know that. Go live the life you have it in you to live."

After a long moment I stood. I said nothing for a time.

"Go, Andy. Go and please do not come back."

Silently I turned from the dark figure in the chair and made my way to the door. When I looked again I could see only the vaguest outline of him, a slightly darker form against a dark wall—a dark room—a dark world.

"I will go, Jim," said I.

"Thank you."

"I—I will go, but please, before I do, I have one question. Just one question for you."

There was a long silence, and then he said quietly, "Very well. State it."

I looked into the dimness, toward my dear Jim Gamble whom I could now hardly see.

"Will you marry me?" I asked.

EPILOGUE

Thus it was that I became Mrs. James Gamble, and entered into a new life—a joyous life. It was not without its pains and sorrows, of course. But the day Jim and I married in a plain little chapel near the hospital, attended only by Mrs. Radcliffe, Doctor Ewing, and the friendly old local minister, I knew that one chapter of my days on Earth had ended and another begun. The ceremony was as simple and wholesome and right as the nightmarish one at Blackthorn House had been bizarre and unnatural. But in truth I do not think I gave a single thought to those terrible events on that day—my wedding day. My only thought was that here, at last, was my life made complete, and when we accepted each other in sickness and in health until death us do part and kissed for the first time as man and wife, I became—somehow, in some way I will never be able to fully express—a new person. Mrs. Radcliffe and Doctor Ewing beamed with pleasure and congratulated us profusely as we made our slow way out of the church, Jim leaning partly on his cane and partly on me. He would have to lean on me for a long time to come—and his was a weight I welcomed always, and cherished.

It was his last day at the hospital. We purchased a small house outside Baltimore City, sufficiently distant from the urban center itself that we had an acre of our own land and yet quite near the sea—near enough that in time Jim would keep a skiff there and fish for our dinners many afternoons. That would not be for some time, however—at first his mobility was indeed quite limited, and he often suffered pains in his shoulders that I suspect distressed him much more than he liked to let on. And yet he had many good days too, days in which we simply basked in the sun and did light work around the property together, laughing and carrying on like children. At nights we read to each other, of course—Emerson's essays or the poetry of Keats or Shelley or long novels by Jane Austen or Walter Scott, each of us taking turns by the glow of the oil lamps. As for the more intimate aspects of marriage, I was delighted to discover that, however limited his movements in some respects, his condition had done nothing to dampen the enthusiasm and passionate productivity of his activities in this area. He was still quite able to generate in my body the most astonishing sensations, ever and again, to the point that some nights I would find myself collapsing nearly to unconsciousness in wild deliriums of plea-sure. I can only hope that I was able to return that pleasure to him in equal degree—I certainly tried!

I realized early—though I did not tell Jim for some time—that I would never bring forth a child into the world. Among the effects of Doctor Blackthorn's various violations of my body was the fact that my womanly cycles went permanently silent, and thus I was barren. And yet it was not a source of any great sorrow between the two of us; we had each other, and neither of us had ever pined for children. I feared that a female specimen as damaged as I—damaged in mind, body, and soul—would make a poor mother anyway, as indeed my own mother had displayed little skill in this task. The fact that we were destined to be only two merely brought us together even more closely—more lovingly—more joyfully.

And so we lived. I suffered occasional nightmares which often featured distorted and horrifying visions of Doctor Blackthorn, and occasionally Mother Sackett as well, or else a floridly dressed, corpulent corpse rising from its death in a greasy Baltimore alley. Sometimes I saw my mother, eyes wild in her final madness, plunging a kitchen knife into the flesh between my collarbone and neck, a searing pain engulfing me. Jim too had terrible dreams, ones that would cause him to rise up suddenly in the middle of the night and cry out—he was being shot by Doctor Blackthorn, I knew, ever and again. We had many quiet, comforting talks in the darkness about our night-dreams, warmly entwined in each other's arms. Over time I told my husband everything of what I knew about what had happened to me and who Doctor Blackthorn really was. He said that such knowledge only deepened his love for me.

Occasionally we took trips. Once we rode as far as the Chesapeake beach where Jim and I had first met; but we discovered that more factories had been constructed since our time, and the "bohemian" society we had known was quite gone. Even Mrs. Prouty, my landlady upon my initial arrival there, had passed away, and it was a stranger who greeted us at what had been her front door. Several times we visited the outskirts of Grimsleytown to see my parents' graves; we even paid for new, permanent granite markers to replace the cheap wooden ones there. When we passed through the area I tried not to notice the strangeness of the skyline—strange because the familiar looming silhouette of Blackthorn House was no longer there. We did not ride near the spot, of course. I had no interest in it anymore.

Jim grew stronger, more manly and independent, and we kept our little property well, deriving an income from our animals as well as from Jim's ever-improving abilities as a fisherman. One source of sorrow came, however, on an awful October day when we had traveled into the city together for supplies and I purchased a copy of the Baltimore *Sun* for perusal on the ride home. As the cart made its leisurely way toward our home, Jim at the reins, I espied on an inner page this horrible news:

DEATH OF EDGAR A. POE—We regret to learn that Edgar A. Poe, Esq., the distinguished American poet, scholar and critic, died in this city yesterday morning, after an illness of four or five days. This announcement, coming so sudden and unexpected, will cause poignant regret among all who admire genius, and have sympathies for the frailties too often attending it. Mr. Poe, we believe, was a native of this state, though reared by a foster father in Richmond, Va., where he lately spent some time on a visit. He was in the 40th year of his age.

"Oh no," I heard myself crying, "Oh no, no, no, no, no, no."

"What is it, Andy?"

I showed him the dreadful words.

"That's terrible," he said. "I know how much he meant to

you. I myself love him as a poet, but you…"

"He was my friend," said I, through tears. "Jim, it was he who showed me the way to you. If it had not been for Mr. Poe…" Imagining what might have happened had I never chanced across the great author was so disturbing that I could not speak. Instead I wept, so miserably and unreservedly that Jim drew up the horses and simply held me in his arms for a long, long time. That night we read the sad and beautiful verse of Mr. Poe aloud to each other for many melancholy hours.

It was around the time I reached the age of twenty-three that I had a sudden revelation—one that altered my entire under-standing of myself. I had begun a flower garden a year or two before, and was this year enjoying, among others, an extremely handsome patch of red roses. One evening whilst Jim was tend-ing another part of the property I was doing some clipping around the bushes when, as can happen to any rose gardener, one of my fingers caught on a thorn and I felt my skin tear. It was nothing of any importance—a shallow wound indeed, wor-thy under normal circumstances of no more than a moment's attention with a handkerchief or cloth. But as I looked down at the tear in the dimming light I abruptly saw something that sent a cold chill down my spine. *My blood glowed.*

I tried to pass it off as mere idle fancy or a trick of the light, but I had seen it—seen it clearly—as indeed I saw it again as I pressed the finger to produce yet more blood. It was a mere drop that oozed forth—but it glowed. The effect was subtle but unmistakable. I stood there for a long time, aghast. It was the first time my body had shed blood since the nightmarish events of several years before. In a kaleidoscopic rush my mind careened back to my little white friend, the rat—the creature's glowing blood—how Doctor Blackthorn had explained the experiment to me—and then, great God in Heaven!—it veered to a memory it never visited, the unspeakable scene in the bed-room, Doctor Blackthorn's dismembered body—the blood—and the nagging feeling I had had of having somehow forgotten or neglected something. It came to me now, like a fist to my face—in that horrible moment as I prepared to leave, staring vacantly at the charnel house scene in that bedroom, Doctor Blackthorn's blood had glowed!

What did it mean? Apparently the doctor had given himself the same treatment received by the white rat—but just as apparently it had done him no earthly good when I cut his head from his body. But my own blood—the life-extension treatment—it was inside me!

I thought for a while, resolving to tell Jim nothing. It would only worry him, and at least as of that time, I felt quite well. Would the treatment have any effect on me? Would it make any difference? I had the sudden, overwhelming sense of my body being alien to myself. Things ran in my veins of which I had no knowledge and to whose presence I had never consented. I had thought I had triumphed over Doctor Blackthorn, but he had left me this dreadful discovery!

We lived—Jim and I. The years passed. His body became very strong, though never as limber and flexible as it had once been, and with his strength came his self-confidence again. He became the Jim I had known—though that is not quite right. He was never that Jim again—never so innocent, never so optimistic. He became a *different* Jim, quieter, wiser, and more thoughtful. Reader, he was a wonderful man—changed, but yet also the same.

As was I, of course. Our times together were no less joyous than they had ever been, but they were tempered now with the experience of reality—the experience of the closeness of Death to us always. In many ways we had been children when we lived so shamelessly on the beach together. Now we were adults, and whatever was dampened in terms of youthful verve was made up for in depth and maturity. We loved each other—that is all.

For long periods I would forget about the condition of my blood. It made no practical difference, I thought; it seemed not to affect my health in any way. Years would pass in which I hardly thought of it. And yet—there came an evening when I was watching Jim smoke his pipe on the porch, noticing for the first time that he was growing older. We were in our thirties then, and Jim's skin had wrinkles now, and his wonderful hair and beard had achieved some few streaks of gray. These facts in themselves were nothing, but my awareness of them made me think of my own image I saw in the looking-glass each day.

"Jim," said I, looking up from my knitting, "do you think I am beginning to look old?"

He glanced at me, surprised. I was not vain about my appearance and I am sure he was taken aback by the unprecedented question. "Why no, Andy," said he at last, very sincerely, "you don't look any older at all. In fact, I think you look exactly the same as you did on our wedding day."

I never told him. I never told him as he grew into his forties and then fifties and became inescapably an older man. I loved him just as I always had; I loved every one of his gray hairs, every slight sag of the skin around his jaw. To me he would always be simply my Jim. But I—I became a woman of whom friends would exclaim, "Mrs. Gamble seems never to age a day—upon my life, she has been married for twenty years and she still looks for all the world like a girl of eighteen!" Jim recognized this and it only made him prouder of me—the looks we would receive in town when people who knew us gaped at me. More than once we came across some old acquaintance of Jim's who would express delight at meeting me and say that he never knew old Jim had a daughter.

It did not affect our relationship, since we rarely traveled to town or saw anyone besides each other. There were times when Jim would look at me somewhat quizzically, as if he himself could not quite understand how I, a woman in her forties, could look quite as I did. But he accepted me for who I was, just as he always had, and we farmed and fished and played and read and did all the things we had always done. It was the best of marriages—the best of lives.

My Jim died in his fifty-seventh year after a brief illness. A fever overcame him. He did not feel any tremendous pain, and as he lay in bed near the end—the doctor having told me grimly there was nothing more to be done—he looked at me with the glowing eyes of the very ill and said whisperingly, "I only regret having to leave you behind, Andy…how will you get along?"

"I don't know, Jim," I said.

"I've loved you," said he. "I've loved you as much as any man has ever loved a woman."

"I know that, Jim."

"I am sorry to leave," he whispered. "But I have no choice."

"I know that too."

His chest rose and fell in heavy shudders. He took my hand. Twilight came through the windows.

"Have the animals been fed?" he whispered.

"Yes, Jim."

"Wood laid in?"

"Yes, Jim."

He looked at me, the glow of fever in his eyes.

"Goodbye, Andy...farewell, my boy-girl."

My throat caught. Tears flowed down my face. I wanted to cry out—to scream—but he was passing at that moment and I knew I had to hold myself for him.

"Thank you for our life together, Jim," I whispered. "Be at peace. It's all right. Rest, my darling. Rest now."

He looked at me a moment, nodding his head slightly. The light faded slowly from his eyes and he died, with the same extraordinary courage and grace with which he had lived.

For years afterward I approached life with an utter desolation of soul. I went through my daily routines devoid of any emotion but sorrow. I did nothing but work, and that joylessly. I went for long walks in nature but no tree or twittering bird did anything to lift my spirits. Instead of reading at night, as Jim and I had done for so many years, I simply sat and stared out at the darkness. I considered self-murder.

In my forties I decided to travel. The farm had done well and I had a goodly sum in the bank. Hiring workers to take care of it in my absence, I boarded a steam ship to Europe and visited London, Paris; I walked the ancient ruins of Rome and Greece. It occurred to me that I had accidentally recreated the approximate route my physical father told me that he had taken on his youthful trip, and sometimes I wondered if I was standing where he had stood, seeing what he had seen.

For, although I despised his memory, it was impossible not to think of Doctor Blackthorn whenever I espied myself in a looking-glass and saw that Annabel Lee, a woman forty-five years of age, forty-seven, fifty, continued to look eighteen. At social affairs in Europe I was invariably asked to dance by men twenty or twenty-five years of age; mere girls socialized with me, talking fluffily of clothes and trinkets. I moved from one place to another, increasingly uncertain of how I should act—of who indeed I *was*. I considered visiting a doctor, but the idea terrified me—the only thing more frightening than not knowing about my blood would be, I thought, knowing about it.

Eventually I returned to the United States. The Civil War was over by then, the North victorious but the President dead from a bullet fired, incredibly, by a son of the great Junius Brutus Booth. The country—at least the Northern section—was returning to some sort of normality. As my farm continued to earn money I continued to travel, rushing from one place to another, an old woman in a young woman's body. Ever and again I considered throwing myself off a high bridge or lying down on the tracks of the new locomotives that were now streaking the landscape with steel and smoke. And yet I did not. What, I wondered, if my attempt failed—what if I left myself a helpless cripple, crippled for who knew how long? And who *did* know? No one—I was a new experiment on Earth, Doctor Blackthorn's greatest triumph.

I moved hither and thither. Every few years I found another place, staying in lovely houses in the far mountains of Maine and in furnished rooms in Providence; alienated from everyone, my experience unlike that of any other human being who had ever lived, I thought myself a monster—a freak.

And yet, as time moved on, I eventually came to a quietus about my situation. I was alive, after all, however old I was. Life surely is a gift—or so we are told. Over the years I became more accustomed to mine, and finally began trying to make myself productive in it. I returned to the farm for a time, passing myself off as the granddaughter of Annabel Gamble, and I went to school to become a teacher. I moved from school to school, staying no more than a few years anywhere, changing my name as it suited me. I sold the farm at a huge profit and became a very wealthy, very old woman—who looked eighteen years old.

Nothing ever really assuaged my pain at losing Jim, even as I would realize with shock that he had been gone fifty years— sixty—eighty! There was never truly any man for me but my Jim, and yet I was alive—I was a woman—I had feelings and needs—and eventually I found myself in a relationship with another man. It was a good relationship, as I recall—but the terrible fact is that I do not recall it at all clearly now. His name was William Benson, and he worked as a clerk in a general store; he was good to me; I felt a tenderness toward him; but, though we were together over a decade (he died in a fall), the entire marriage has obliterated itself from my mind. The same can be said of the many relationships since. They occurred—they were, for the most part, caring and true men—but after some time I discovered that a sameness would set in with such relationships— meeting, courtship, the love-making, the hand-holding, the first kiss; it was always different but yet it was always the same.

I have learned many things. I have several college degrees in a variety of subject areas, though some date so far back in time as to be essentially useless now. I have continued to travel, and indeed to some very distant and exotic locales, but little of what I have seen holds any real pleasure for me today.

The world has changed, of course—changed to the point of unrecognizability. The great technological innovations of the late nineteenth century arrived one after another to my surprised eyes—automobiles, telephones, recorded music, moving pictures. And yet of course not all of these were entirely new to me—some of them had been previewed many decades before in the Blackthorn House by my physical father, a man I am now convinced must have been one of the great scientific geniuses of human history, on a par with Newton or Galileo or Leonardo da Vinci. But unlike those great men, Doctor Hudson Blackthorn was obsessed and ultimately immolated by moral degeneracy of the vilest kind. He might have changed the world; instead he changed only me.

"But how is it," I can hear the reader asking, "that in the many years you say you have lived you have never suffered an accident?" To this query I can only reply—some people have luck that way. One man might suffer the torments of the damned through disease and injury all his born days; another, standing directly next to him, might skate through life with nothing more than a small tear on his skin from a rose thorn. I belong to the second category. I know not why.

And so I find myself here, in a time of terrible weapons and wars, in cities that dwarf what I thought of as a crowded urban space nearly two hundred years ago. For, Reader, I continue to live—I continue to exist. I work as a teacher still—I have tried other professions, as I am qualified for a number of them, but something about working with the young is amenable to me. I am popular enough in my current position, though I am considered somewhat old-fashioned. I am capable of wearing modern clothing and talking in modern ways; I have through long experience become quite flexible in that sense. Yet this is not really my world. I know that to the marrow of my bones. My world was another place entirely, one I shall not see again.

Over the year I have occasionally visited the old haunts, but such trips only fill me with melancholy and loneliness now. The house were Jim and I lived for so many year—years which now seem like mere hours in my memory—no longer stands, the entire property replaced by paved streets and condominiums. Grimsleytown itself is gone, the name changed and the entire area a suburb of housing tracts and shopping malls. All that still exists there from my time—my original time, my proper time— is the old graveyard where my parents reside, overgrown and mostly abandoned now. The names on their memorial stones are all but unreadable today, the stones themselves weathered and chipped and green with mossy age.

In my role as teacher I have often shared the works of Edgar Allan Poe with my students. I have watched his reputation rise over the decades until it has equaled that of the giants of world literature, something that makes me very happy. "Annabel Lee," the poem, has become a staple of all the verse anthologies, and I often share it with young people, even showing them my now-rare 1850 edition of Poe's collected works, published by J. S. Redfield, which Jim and I purchased as a memorial to my great friend when it was brand-new in the shops. I have never learned what happened to the remainder of the poem—the section I read with my own eyes as Poe sat there in The Two Foxes, the section in which the young hero takes Annabel's body from the sepulcher and crosses the beach in moonlight with it to his room. It seems obvious Poe never finished the poem. Did he discard the beginning of that second section then, instead electing to publish the first part as the whole? Or was this the decision of some editor somewhere? Was the section simply lost in the chaos and confusion of Poe's last days? In any event, I think of the poem of "Annabel Lee" something like a ruined sculpture—the Venus de Milo, say—incomplete, but still startlingly beautiful. And I can never fail to smile when I read the line about "the night-tide," my silent contribution to that great work as well as my private memorial to poor Mary Mahoney, my doomed young friend of so long ago.

At the beginning of this chronicle I wrote that I had a particular reason for writing the story of my life now—a reason that I would reveal at the end. The time has now come for that revelation. The reason, simply, is this—I have decided to visit a doctor.

I do not feel ill. But looking at myself in recent months, I have noted to my surprise that I no longer seem to look eighteen years old. I still look young, certainly (and my surgical scars faded away many decades ago), but the slight lines around my eyes and an almost imperceptible coarsening of my skin would lead the casual observer to guess my age at closer to, say, twenty-five or even thirty. Is the effect of Doctor Blackthorn's blood treatment weakening? Or was it always finite in its effects? Will I now begin to age more rapidly?

What is happening to me?

Now that there is a written record of all I have thought and done over these many years I wish to reveal myself to the world—I, Annabel Lee, the oldest human in history, victim of a sadistic and immoral genius who was also my father. Soon I will step out of my little ocean-side cottage, where indeed I am always in the comforting presence of what Poe termed "the sounding sea," and I will find a doctor to whom I will complain of tiredness and apathy. I will convince the doctor that I must have, as this world calls it, a *blood test*. Either the doctor or a technician will bring out a syringe—I have seen this done—while tying off my upper arm. A long needle will be inserted to my vein—my blood will seep slowly into a transparent glass tube—

And something will happen. What it might be I know not. But I will make some kind of medical history, and that history may help others in some way. Who knows the truth of what flows inside me? Who knows what secrets of life and death a mere glass tube full of my blood may unlock? But I want to be of use to someone—I want my life to have meant something other than loneliness and pain, unceasing, unending...a loneliness such as no other person on Earth has ever known....

Except of course that is not all my life has been. I have enjoyed the heights of ecstasy as well as plumbed the depths of pain. I have in my mind so many memories—of times and people and places gone forever—of being a little girl sitting with her true father, Selwin Lee, in a little library, reading poetry with him; of my mother and fallen sister; of Mary, my sole friend at Sadmore Place (the location of which, I discovered years ago, is now covered by a portion of Interstate highway); of so very many later men, husbands and lovers, above all the first, the noble and high-spirited Jim Gamble, my love, my life—for *all* my life.

But my life is about to change again—and this time the life of the world will change with me. I can only pray that the change will be for the better.

Yes—"pray." My relationship with God remains as uncertain and fraught with doubt as it has been since I was a girl. I have experienced many religious ceremonies and traditions all over the world, and have managed to find faith at times that has lasted me even unto decades—but in the end no faith has proved permanent, while at the same time such faith has never completely been obliterated from my soul either. The best I can say for my spiritual journey is that I fervently believe in a God whose existence I utterly reject. That seems to be enough for me; perhaps it is enough for Him, as well.

My chronicle is finished now. This morning I made an

appointment with a nearby doctor; in a moment I shall put down this pen, stand, pull on a light sweater, and prepare to walk to that doctor's office.

It is raining outside, just as it always is in my memories of childhood, and this fills me with some sort of unidentifiable emotion—nostalgia it may be, or love. But love for whom, or what?

As for what will happen to me next—that no one knows, except God.

Perhaps....

About the Author

Christopher Conlon is the author of the novel *Savaging the Dark*, acclaimed by *Booklist* (starred review) as one of the Top Ten Horror Novels of its year and by *Paste Magazine* both as one of the 21 Best Horror Books of the 21st Century and one of the 50 Best Horror Novels of All Time. His Bram Stoker Award-winning Richard Matheson tribute anthology *He Is Legend* has appeared in editions from Gauntlet Press, Tor, and the Science Fiction Book Club, as well as in several translated editions around the world. Two of his earlier novels, *Midnight on Mourn Street* and *A Matrix of Angels*, were Stoker Award finalists. He has written numerous collections of stories and poems and two full-length stage plays.

Curious about other Crossroad Press books?
Stop by our site:
http://store.crossroadpress.com
We offer quality writing
in digital, audio, and print formats.

Enter the code FIRSTBOOK
to get 20% off your first order from our store!
Stop by today!